BLUE SHIFT

A Discovery Beyond Imagination
A Future Beyond Horror

Book I of a Trilogy

BLUE
SHIFT

A Discovery Beyond Imagination
A Future Beyond Horror

Book I of a Trilogy

Howard Johnson

WINEPRESS WP PUBLISHING

Printed in the United States of America

Packaged by WinePress Publishing, PO Box 428, Enumclaw, WA 98022. The views expressed or implied in this work do not necessarily reflect those of WinePress Publishing. The author(s) is ultimately responsible for the design, content, and editorial accuracy of this work.

ISBN 1-57921-377-4
Library of Congress Catalog Card Number: 2001088455

To my wife, Barbara, whose love,
tolerance and invaluable help
made this book possible.

There are a number of pages of information at the back of the book, which maybe of interest to readers. These include a glossary of native language words and scientific terms as well as information about some of the astronomical facilities.

In the text, the first time a word in the glossary is used and not defined, it will be in italics.

1

A legendary pro football running back, idolized Mohawk athlete and acclaimed role model for youths of all cultures turned his many talents away from the gridiron to pursue his earlier dream of being an astronomer.

*A*ngus Thomas and Pat Yamaguchi sat down in front of the desk of Dr. Ann Rivers, senior member of their working group of nine astronomers and physicists at the University of Arizona. This meeting was regarding a new procedure Dr. Thomas had developed.

Dr. Rivers, a thin, smallish, hawk-nosed woman of fifty-five with frizzy salt and pepper hair, greeted them warmly. "Welcome, gentlemen. Let's get right down to business." The two nodded their heads in agreement. "Angus, we've put together a set of trials for your new procedure, and I've asked Pat to help you with testing, improving and standardizing it." She handed Angus a fresh tan file folder containing a few papers. "Here's a list of nearby stars for test subjects and a tentative schedule of time on the telescope at Kitt Peak. You'll have to confirm the schedule. Do you have any questions?"

Angus looked at Pat and back at Dr. Rivers. "Not from me until I look through the stuff in that envelope. I know we'll have questions then."

Pat nodded in agreement. "I have none at the moment either."

Dr. Rivers, her slightly rumpled suit hanging on a gaunt, angular frame, stood up in an obvious signal of dismissal. "Then let's see how well your procedure works."

Pat Yamaguchi was the newest member of the group. A small, thin man with a big heart, Pat became Angus' closest friend when they were in grad school together. His father, who taught high school chemistry in Fresno, was a multi-generation American of Japanese decent and his mother was mostly English. They lived their entire lives in the central California city where Pat and his two sisters grew up. When he walked out of Dr. Rivers' office beside the burly Mohawk, Pat looked almost tiny.

*   *   *

Angus Thomas, whose name in Kenienkeha, the Mohawk language, is Anias Atonwa, was thirty-one when he received his doctorate in astrophysics from the University of Arizona. The famous Mohawk had come a long way from his days as a star high school soccer player on the St. Regis Reservation in New York. Recruited by Penn State University as a place kicker, he starred in that role as a sophomore. During a mid-season game, his team behind by four points and bogged down on the opponent's thirty-five, the burly place kicker trotted onto the field to try for three points. When the high snap bounced off the holder's outstretched hands, Angus snatched it from in front of an onrushing lineman, tucked it instinctively in the crook of his arm and headed down the field. Running around, through and over would-be tacklers and aided by blocks from his startled teammates, he scored the winning touchdown. In that famous moment a great running back emerged. This powerful and talented ex-place kicker was soon ripping through opponents and setting records.

By the time he graduated, Angus had added his name to the college record books, become a scholastic All-American and was a top pick in the NFL draft. He graduated with honors from the science school in physics with a minor in astronomy, his first love. He toyed with the idea of staying in school and getting a master's degree, but the lure of the multimillion-dollar pro contract soon changed his mind. By his second season he hit his stride as a premier running back and his fame grew rapidly.

In November 1995, near the end of his seventh season in the pros, he sustained a career-ending knee injury. After several surgeries had rebuilt his knee, Angus could walk quite normally, but there was no chance of his return to the gridiron. While everyone expected the popular athlete to become a coach or sports commentator, Angus had other ideas. With his considerable income wisely invested, he could go almost anywhere and do almost anything he wanted. When he decided to pursue his earlier dream of becoming an astronomer, he enrolled at the University of Arizona in Tucson. It amazed everyone except his immediate family. He chose Arizona because of the excellent program and their nearby observatories. After earning his doctorate, he stayed in Tucson as a faculty member and researcher concentrating on searching for planets around nearby stars.

At first, Angus' colleagues had great difficulty taking a football legend as a serious researcher. When he developed a significant new and far more accurate method of comparative spectral analysis of light from the stars, the attitude of most of his colleagues changed drastically. They realized he was serious about his new career and was a valuable member of his group at the university.

*   *   *

Early in June of 2000, more than six weeks after the meeting with Dr. Rivers that initiated the current project, Angus stalked in like a man on a mission and dropped a printout of the *spectrum* recorded for *Barnard's Star* on Pat's desk. He leaned over with a look of puzzlement on his face, pointed to the print and remarked, "Take a look at this. These two faint *spectral absorption lines* don't belong there at all, but they certainly look real. That's gotta be an error in the equipment. If it's not an error, then it's something weird. We would run into a problem on the last test reading of the whole series."

"Lemme see." Pat examined the print carefully, trying to match it visually with the standard he pulled from his desk. "They look real enough, like a faint image of strong lines superimposed on . . . you sure this isn't a double reading? Another star on top of Barnard's?"

"They show up on both the *plot* and this print. I don't see how a double reading could give us those lines; they align perfectly. They just don't belong."

"Let's look over some earlier images and see what we can find," Pat said as he swiveled his chair to retrieve the earlier images from the computer behind him.

Angus came around to Pat's side and leaned over his shoulder to look at the screen as Pat displayed earlier images of *spectra* from Barnard's star. They could find none with the errant lines. Angus stood up, a blank, questioning look painted his face. "Somehow I must have messed up, made a mistake when I took that reading. I'll have to take another shot as soon as practical."

"Since we finished our scheduled use of the telescope, it'll take a while to get back in," Pat commented, frowning up at Angus. He was not hopeful. "The schedule at Kitt Peak has been tough since they shut down the old Mt. Hopkins MMT for an update. It may take a month to get a date for another spectral analysis."

"Got no choice. I'll go see about a time right now." Angus hurried back to his desk to arrange to do another spectrum. A few minutes later he phoned Pat. "We're in luck. I got a spot three weeks from tonight. Let's pray for a clear night."

*   *   *

"Look at these danged lines! They're even more distinct than before," Angus exclaimed to Pat when he walked in holding the new spectrum print from his redo. He plopped the print down in front of Pat and quickly sat in the chair at the side of the desk. "What the devil could be generating them? I still can't find a match anywhere."

Pat picked up the print, looked at it closely, scowling, then placed it back on the desk. He paused thoughtfully and leaned back in his chair, hands clasped behind his head. "You can't tie them into any known lines? Can't recognize their pattern? Of course, that's nearly impossible with only two lines. That's really weird."

Angus leaned forward, pursing his lips and shaking his head in frustration. "One thing I know for certain, they don't belong where they are."

Pat looked perplexed. He picked up his coffee mug and fondled it for a moment, seeming to examine it closely while thinking. "If you're as baffled as I am, why not take the whole thing to Ann. She's done lots of work on matching spectra. Or show it to the guys at our next group meeting. More, older and, hopefully, wiser heads should at least be able to point you in a direction. I'm completely out of ideas."

*   *   *

At Dr. Rivers' suggestion, Angus brought this new information before their group of nine scientists at the university. He and Pat explained the circumstances thoroughly during an open, casual discussion.

After the group had examined the spectra, group leader Dr. Rivers looked as puzzled as Angus and Pat had been. "You're correct! Those two lines are definitely out of place where they are. Could it be a ghost image? You know, a photographic anomaly, lines reflected from inside the instrument?"

Dave Hopkins, the jokester in the group and quite jealous of Angus, leaned back in his chair and grinned with sarcastic derision. "Yeh! You must have a ghost in that marvelous program of yours, a ghost instead of a virus. It's making new lines for you to confound the rest of us. Can't the famous football kid come up with an answer?"

Angus looked directly at Dave, cool and emotionless, ignoring his sarcastic jabs. "You'll notice, all the plots also indicate those same features. Both plots and spectra were made without benefit of my program, so it can't be the cause."

Bernie Frank's clenched teeth and closed fists showed how ticked he was at Dave. "That'll teach you to wise off. Why don't you get off it, Dave? This could be something new and different." Transformed by his words and with a laugh and a wink at Angus, he suggested, "Since it's Barnard's spectrum, let's call it Barnard's Ghost. I can see it now, with headlines, 'Football star discovers ghost in the heavens.'"

"How about a headline at the checkout counter, 'Ghost discovered in sky by running back.' They could include one of your football pictures," Jack Kershaw joked.

The kidding continued for several minutes, mostly good-natured, but at Angus' expense. Not one to put up with much nonsense, Dr. Rivers stood up to corral her group and get things back on track. "All right, you've had your fun. How about some serious suggestions. Are any of you capable of serious thought or are you all vying for clown of the month? Now, does anyone have any ideas?"

"Am I the only one?" Bernie asked as he looked around at the group and saw all blank faces. He turned to Angus, quite serious by the look on his face. "As you explained, it's obvious the lines do not belong where they are. There are no known absorption lines at precisely those positions. They are quite faint, so I'm suggesting they are very strong lines, shifted from another part of the spectrum. Could you have focused on another object near Barnard's, perhaps a faint *galaxy* or *supernova* with very strong absorption lines? You could be dealing with a *red shift*. Unfortunately, with only two lines, it will be almost impossible to match."

"If there was anything close by, it was either masked by the light of Barnard's Star or so faint it couldn't be resolved. Pat and I both checked carefully at several resolutions. A distant, bright object, almost directly behind Barnard's could be hidden, yet still contribute light to the spectrum. We found no known object Barnard's is occluding at this time. Background light from Tucson or elsewhere nearby has been ruled out as a possible source. That leaves us nowhere. We thought you might be able to help."

Dr. Rivers looked around the group, questioning with her eyes. "It looks as if no one has a thought other than Bernie. I would check other astronomers to see if they have any recent spectra you could use for confirmation. Keep me informed of any progress. Now, let's get on with the next item on the agenda."

Angus was thoroughly dejected when he and Pat left after the meeting. "So much for the idea of help from the experts. They're as stumped as we are. This stupid thing is driving me nuts. I guess the next step is to do what Dr. Rivers suggested."

"I guess so. We can start first thing in the morning. It's late and Beanie's waiting for me, so I'm buggin' outta here right now. See you in the A.M."

"I'm going to get on the 'net for a while and see what I can find. Tell Beanie I said 'Hi.'"

After several hours of searching, Angus found no available recent spectra of Barnard's Star. The next day they searched for similar data from other research groups. None had a duplication of the strange lines, but none of the data was very recent. Angus began to think this might be something new and unknown. When the third spectral analysis showed the same faint, unidentifiable lines, Angus began looking for ways to get confirmation from other sources.

*   *   *

With first light of the new 6.5 meter MMT telescope on Mt. Hopkins a year away, Angus needed another giant telescope to better search for the source of the lines. When Pat brought this up at a group session, he made a proposal that would soon change Angus' life completely.

"With the Mt. Hopkins MMT in process of being replaced, our viewing capacity here in Arizona is considerably diminished. Why don't we help Angus get time on the new 8 meter *Gemini* in Hawaii? It's past first light and will soon be turned over to astronomers. Its near-infrared capability is outstanding and it suits Angus' research quite well. I think it's a great opportunity. Maybe there he can discover the cause for those crazy lines."

After Pat's suggestion and with his group behind him, Angus applied for and was granted research time on the giant new Gemini North telescope on Mauna Kea on the big island of Hawaii.

When the time came to leave, Pat was helping pack the instruments for the trip and harassing him about the change. "Here you go, deserting me and heading for a tropical paradise. I can just see you now with all those Hawaiian beauties dressed in . . . what do they call those long, form-fitting Hawaiian dresses, *moo-moos* or something like that? You'll be dancing on moonlit beaches, sipping Mai Tais, wearing *Aloha* shirts and . . ."

Angus momentarily stopped stuffing padding around the last instrument. "I suppose you expect me to feel sorry for you."

"No, but you could take me along . . . at least for a while."

Angus began stuffing again. "And just how do you think your little Chiricahua sweetie would like that?" He threw a handful of the packing material at Pat. "She'd do an Apache war dance on your body if you even mentioned it. I'm on her side, remember? We injuns have to stick together."

"Alas! True love has its drawbacks," Pat said, speaking dramatically with a flamboyant wave of his hand and finally gazing skyward in parody. After standing frozen in the last pose for a moment, he returned to help Angus lift the packing crate on end.

Angus leaned on the now upright, but still open crate and brought Pat back to reality. "Come on, pal. Beanie's about the best thing that ever happened to you and you know it. You'd be lost without her."

"How right you are. Seriously, I'm really excited for you," Pat said as he finished nailing the lid on the crate. "A new opportunity, a new challenge and maybe the chance to make a great discovery, that's what it's all about, isn't it?"

"Yes, it is and quite exciting," Angus replied as he rested against the crate, legs crossed casually and staring thoughtfully into space. "I've been dreaming about discovering something really new. It would be a completely different excitement than when I played football, but just as heady. Maybe I can discover something important."

Pat grabbed the dolly and brought it up to the case. "I hate to bring you down to earth, pal, but we've got to get this crate on the truck and you off to the airport."

The two friends talked about the separate paths their lives were taking as they rolled the heavy crate to the waiting truck.

Man has been wondering about and reaching for the stars for thousands of years. For this continuing quest we demand bigger telescopes, faster computers and more commitment.

Mililani Namahoe nimbly dodged fresh rain puddles as she walked purposefully from the parking lot into the Gemini Operations Center in Hilo's University Park. Lani, as everyone called her, a recent astronomy graduate of the University of Hawaii, worked full time for the Gemini Project. When Lani walked in, Jenny, the receptionist motioned for her to stop.

Jenny brightened the room with her friendly smile as Lani approached her desk. "Have I got news for you! I have your first permanent assignment. No more shuffling all over the place. This should be a good one."

As Jenny began thumbing through a stack of brown envelopes under the counter, Lani beamed and leaned over to watch. "OK! Who's the lucky one?"

"It's the new guy, the one coming from Arizona next month. You heard about him, didn't you?"

Not knowing whether to feel pleased or not, Lani frowned at the news. "No, I didn't. I was hoping to work with someone I knew. I'll just have to wait and find out what kind of man he is."

Jenny continued fumbling with the stack of envelopes. "He's that famous football player, Angus Thomas."

Lani looked puzzled. "Never heard of him, but then I'm no fan of football." She was definitely unimpressed.

Jenny frowned, her face showing disapproval of Lani's lack of interest in the famous jock. She finally found the right envelope and handed it to Lani. "It's the information about your new assignment. Take it to Director Carroll's office. He's expecting you and will give you the whole rundown on Dr. Thomas and his project."

She took the envelope, started to open it, paused and then furrowed her brow and looked knowingly at Jenny. "He's probably some Neanderthal in a white coat with an ego as big as Mauna Kea."

Jenny leaned forward and said earnestly and almost in a whisper, "Not so! I hear good things about him. He was a star player. Held all kinds of records in college and the pros. More important, he had a reputation for being a really good guy both on and off the field. I didn't realize he was an astronomer until I heard he was coming here." Jenny sat back and crossed her arms on her chest. "That's quite a switch, football to astronomy. I understand from at least one of our people familiar with his work that he is quite well respected professionally."

Lani took an aloof, almost haughty stance to demonstrate indifference to the fame of her soon to be boss. "At least he has some redeeming traits. To me that's far more important than his celebrity. Still, I'll wait and make my own judgement about Dr. Thomas." Lani looked directly at Jenny as she emphasized the last phrase, then turned and headed for John Carroll's office.

*   *   *

Her session with Dr. Carroll confirmed Jenny's comments and provided specific information about her new permanent assignment. Afterward, Lani headed for her workstation to tackle her new responsibilities with an aura of excitement. Her first task was to go through the list of Angus' requests she received in the envelope. The list included a number of items: several maps of the area, a list of references to be made available, a specific computer configuration for his network workstation, arrangements for his equipment to be transported to the observatory when it arrived in Hilo, a preferred layout for his office and a number of minor items. She was also asked to find him a nearby, comfortable apartment with a guest room suitable to be used as a home office. That terse request left much room for question, but she would try to find what she imagined would be suitable.

One request intrigued her. It was for detailed information about the local people, their history, their customs and a dictionary or thesaurus with any native words or language still in general usage in the area. This was certainly an unusual request for a *haole* to make. She used her computer to access the university library for that information. It was the first thing she did before organizing his other requests and then filling them.

* * *

Monday, September 11, Lani was introduced to Angus in his new office. She was quite surprised at this burly, amber skinned man with black hair and dark eyes much like her own. His smile radiated his friendly nature. His warm handshake and cheery greeting quickly began disarming her apprehension about working with her new boss.

"I really want to thank you for the information you sent," Angus remarked. "It gave me a good understanding of my new home."

He stood for just a moment, drinking in the vision of this rather tall, beautiful young Hawaiian who would be his assistant. He wondered, *Working with her will certainly be different from working with Pat. She could be a model, but an astronomer? I hope she works out as great as she looks.* Finally tearing his eyes away, he walked about to familiarize himself with the layout and furnishings. Admiring the plants Lani had so carefully placed, he asked the name of each as he looked at them.

"I'm really impressed with how you set up my office. If you're that good at the technical stuff, we'll get along just fine," he commented as he fingered through the small pile of documents on his desk.

Despite the friendly introduction, Lani remained somewhat aloof. She knew first impressions are not always accurate and that working closely with a person will eventually bring out the true nature of both. Slow to relax her guard with men, she would wait a while before passing judgement on her new boss.

* * *

By late afternoon it became obvious to Angus that his new assistant had brains and was an excellent worker, in addition to being drop-dead gorgeous. He looked admiringly at his now neat, orderly office. "We've had a very productive day. All that new material I brought in has been organized and put where it belongs. I never thought we'd have it done before that four o'clock meeting. I have to commend you. You're very efficient and easy to work with."

Lani sent him a controlled, mildly appreciative look. "Thank you. It did go rather well."

"I'm sometimes a bit careless, but with what you did before I came and what we did today, things are really shipshape."

"Let's hope we can keep it that way." Lani's words and manner sent a veiled message that she fully intended for him to do his part.

Angus noticed but ignored the hidden challenge and sat down for a momentary rest. "We have about fifteen minutes before our meeting. I'd like to learn a bit more about you. I know you graduated from the University of Hawaii and are hoping to achieve an advanced degree, but that's about all. I'm certainly not prying, just interested."

"Where would you like me to start? What would you like to know?" Lani was immediately on guard as she wondered, *Oh my, is this a come on?*

"I'm particularly interested in your culture. It's so different from my own Mohawk culture, yet I read of some similarities in the things you sent me. It's obvious you are native Hawaiian, but are you from nearby or one of the other islands?"

Still cautious but so far less apprehensive after working with him all day, she decided to relax her guard. Her look softened noticeably as she got up, turned her chair to face Angus and settled back into it. "I'm a local native, you might say, with lots of family nearby. I grew up just a bit south of Hilo in Kalapana. Do you know about Kalapana?"

"I remember reading about it in the information you sent me. It's the city destroyed by a huge lava flow from the active volcano isn't it? You would have been quite young then. Were you involved?"

"If you call watching your family home being devoured by the cruel black lava *involved,* I certainly was," Lani replied, a pained, almost teary expression flowing over her face.

Angus winced as he responded, "I didn't mean to bring up painful memories. I didn't know you lost your home. That must have been devastating. You don't need to talk about it if you don't want to."

Reacting to the obvious compassion in his voice, Lani relaxed a bit more. "No, I don't mind. It's been eleven years and my whole family has rebuilt their lives since then. Kalapana was the home of my family for many generations. I was eleven when I watched our home being burned and swallowed by the lava that buried almost the entire town. I will never forget that horrendous experience. The tears streaming down my father's face as he watched his home slowly being destroyed made an indelible impression I still see in my mind. I had never seen my father in tears before. He just stood there quietly watching as the house crumbled into ashes that were gradually swallowed by the slowly moving lava. He was born in that old house."

Angus shuddered, watching her understandably pained expressions. "What a horrible experience. I can hardly imagine."

"It happened over such a large area. Replacement of the lush green forest landscape by the stark black lava flow was the worst kind of complete devastation. It left absolutely no hope for rebuilding. Kalapana was utterly destroyed, permanently entombed by miles of black stone desert and will remain so, probably forever. The profusion of tropical plants, the birds, the flowers and even the incredible fragrances all vanished. There were palms, banyans and plumeria everywhere. Orchids and ginger grew wild, and the ginger smelled so lovely when in bloom like it is here in Hilo right now. It was a lot like Hilo but a bit wilder and less populated.

"The main highway joining the southeast section of the island with Hilo and the northern coast was buried, isolating this part of the island. It changed what had been a rather short drive through lush country into a tortuous journey of many miles around the volcano. In between two fresh green areas lay total destruction and miles of cruel black wasteland with molten rock flowing just a few feet below the hardened surface. The lava still flows to the ocean where it steadily adds to the island as it boils into the surf. The eastern part of the Big Island was cut in half changing forever the lives of thousands.

"Like many others, my father lost his business as well as his home. Our family went from comfortable affluence to a hand-to-mouth existence. I remember staying with relatives near Hilo for several months before the lava reached our house. Knowing the oncoming lava would destroy anything in its path, my parents moved into storage everything they could take. My dad removed many of the fixtures he would later use in our new house. He moved all his construction equipment and machinery from Kalapana to a rented location several miles north of the cooled lava flow on Route 130. He was even able to break down his storage buildings and haul them away as well. Taking a loan on his equipment, he acquired a suitable piece of land and was back in business within less than a year.

"After more than six months that seemed like forever, we moved into a small new house my dad built on a corner of the new construction company location. It was rather stark compared to the lush greenery around our old home. I remember watching my dad reassemble his storage buildings and build an equipment shed. He set up his office in an old portable office building on our new land. We used much of the furniture from our old house, mainly some older pieces that had been in the family for many years. My folks did what they could to provide us a home that would have at least some of the flavor of our old house. We shed some tears when we moved in among the reminders of the home we lost."

Angus could feel the pain of loss in Lani's voice. "How is your family doing now?"

She smiled thinking about her family. "They're doing fine. Since my sister, brother and I grew up and moved away, the little house suits my parents well. My dad's business is flourishing and both parents enjoy good health. I worked part time here at Gemini while in college and became full time after I graduated. You're my first permanent assignment."

Angus thought sadly of their loss, showing it in his voice and on his face. "What an intriguing story. You must have a close, strong family. You speak of them with such . . . care. I think that's the right word. You seem to have survived and adapted quite well."

"We're real survivors and found strength we never knew we had. We got right back to the business of living. Life moves on. I don't suppose the pain will ever go completely away."

"I always find the twists and turns of people's lives fascinating. I'm looking forward to our working together."

Lani leaned back, crossed her legs and slipped her hand up under her hair. "What about you? You now know my life history. I've been told you are rather well known as a sports figure."

"That was in another life," he said, clasping his hands and leaning his elbows on the desk.

"I'm not a football fan and your name was unknown to me until Jenny told me about my new assignment. Sorry about that."

"No need to be sorry. It's refreshing to be seen as just another astronomer. I rather like that." He glanced at the clock. "I'll have to fill you in later. Right now, we need to leave for that staff meeting."

As they walked to the meeting, Lani thought, *No come on this time. Maybe he'll be OK. That would certainly be refreshing.*

*   *   *

In November, five months after Angus' last spectral analysis of Barnard's Star, his first observations were made. He was anxious to see what this giant, state-of-the-art telescope would show him. He was startled at the clarity of the strange spectral lines in the first analysis. They were more evident and there were more of them. There was no doubt this was something quite unusual.

While examining several recent images, Angus asked Lani to confirm his observation of another unusual item. Pointing to one of the stars in one image and then to the same one in another he asked, "See that object? Tell me what you think."

Standing and leaning over the desk, Lani examined the photos carefully. "That star seems to be slightly elongated in this photo, but perfectly round in the other. All the other stars in the first one look perfectly round. It couldn't be a photo distortion or all stars would have the same shape."

"Very good! That image is fuzzy, but it reminds me of a similar photo that led to a major discovery some years back. Do you know the discovery I mean?"

Lani dropped into the chair at the right end of Angus' desk and grinned, pleased she knew the answer. "You're referring to the photo of the planet Pluto that lead to the discovery of Pluto's moon, Charon, right? Could that be a planet orbiting the star? It would have to be a large one, wouldn't it?"

Angus leaned back and changed into lecture mode. "Right discovery, wrong conclusion. In the 1960s, one group claimed to have found two planets, bigger than Jupiter, orbiting Barnard's Star. They used an apparent wobble in its motion as the evidence for their conclusion. Later observations with the Hubble space telescope could find no indication of any large planet near the star, although they did not rule out smaller ones."

Lani sat thoughtfully for a moment. "The only other conclusion is that it is another object, possibly a galaxy, but probably a star. Since it couldn't be much smaller than Barnard's and still be a star, it must be farther away. If it were a near-earth body, a comet or asteroid, it would have moved during the exposure and left a streak on the image."

Angus leaned forward again. "The lady gets an 'A.' Check the archives for some other images of that same area, several months apart and back as far as you can. Then we'll try to find out more about that *lump* on the star."

The "Aha!" experience of finding something truly new is one of the greatest joys of being a scientist.

It took Lani a few weeks to obtain the prints from the photo archives. When finally she had several of them ready, she spread them out on the table in Angus' office to view and compare. They sat down, side by side at the small table.

"Look at this!" Angus exclaimed, pointing to the image on a photo from a year ago. "There, see that slight distortion? It looks almost like a faint smear. Something is definitely there."

"I can just barely see it," Lani remarked. Bringing the two prints as close together as possible, she stared at them and then exclaimed. "Only in this photo, it's on the north side of the star and much fainter. We know what it can't be, but what is it?"

"It has to be a very faint star or even a galaxy. The change in position is solely because Barnard's Star has moved. It can't be visual evidence of a new object near Barnard's Star. I wonder why no one has seen this object before?" Angus shuffled through the older photos. "I don't see any evidence of that object on the photos from before that one taken a year ago. We would never have noticed that faint smear if we hadn't been looking for it. Now we have two mysteries: this object and the strange spectral lines I showed you before. Maybe it's a supernova in a distant galaxy. That would explain its relatively sudden appearance."

Lani turned and looked at Angus. "Wouldn't the spectrum tell us that? Wouldn't it have a red shift?"

"If it's far enough away, it should. A supernova has a definite spectral pattern. Maybe that's why we couldn't identify it."

Lani's eyes widened in realization as she stared intently at Angus with excitement. "It seems like those two mysteries are really only one."

"A good, probable conclusion. OK, Miss Namahoe, what is the next logical step? Where do we go from here?"

"I'd suggest we run some more spectra. We can block out the star and try to get a spectrum on the object itself. That would make it much easier to analyze."

"Excellent! I'm impressed. It will take some time, but we are in position to get those readings right now and for several more months. I'll check the schedule and see when we can get to it."

Again Angus checked through several newly found records of earlier spectra taken of Barnard's Star before the strange spectral lines first appeared. Not one showed any of the strange lines.

*   *   *

It was Thursday, December 21, and in the relatively short few weeks since the last viewing, Barnard's fuzzy image had elongated noticeably. Whatever it was, the object was definitely brighter relative to the star. Using the technique Lani suggested to block most of the light from Barnard's Star, Angus obtained several spectra of the distortion alone. Finally, he and Lani sat down to look at the spectrum directly on the computer display.

They gazed at the screen as Angus panned across the spectrum using a split screen. "Whatever that object is, it is definitely the source of those strange lines. I find no obvious match between the new object on the top and the supernova reference spectrum on the bottom. Of course, with this broad spectrum it would take forever to find a match visually unless we were close. I'll run that computer comparison again with this latest data. Those line patterns must match somewhere."

Lani sat back. "Surely your program will find us a match," she commented as Angus set his program in motion.

They watched the display as the computer ground away and after fifteen minutes it displayed the terse words, "No match."

Disappointed with the results, Angus ground his teeth and grumbled in frustration, "I can't believe it."

Lani looked intently at Angus, trying to cheer him. "If it's a distant supernova couldn't it have a rather large red shift?"

Angus restarted the program, moving the search criteria far into the red. "OK! Let's see what comes from your idea."

They were dumbfounded when again the computer proclaimed there was no match.

"This is crazy! Spectral lines have to match somewhere. What are we doing wrong?" Angus remarked, his face skewed in a quizzical expression.

Again and again, his program ran with negative results. "That's impossible! What kind of weird object is that anyway? The lines must match some part of the spectrum. That's the third time I've set up the computer and it just grinds away and then reports no match." Lani could see him becoming more and more frustrated.

Suddenly, her face brightened with realization. "Look outside the box. That's what my father used to say whenever we were stumped by a problem. Most people box their minds into a limited view of a problem and must break outside the box to find the solution. I'm sure you experienced the old 'join all the dots with just four straight lines' problem at sometime in your life, haven't you?"

Angus chuckled to himself, remembering well that very puzzle posed to him at some time in the distant past. "I know what your father meant. I was positively elated when I solved that puzzle by drawing the lines outside those imaginary limits. How do we apply that here? I'll have to rethink how to go about solving this mystery. Why don't you help me get out of the box? I'm so close to the problem, it may be difficult for me to escape my tunnel vision. You could provide a less biased view."

Lani was ecstatic being asked to help with a real research project. "I'd love to. Most of what I've been doing is what I call 'paper clip' work: searching the files for needed records, getting photos ready for comparison studies and converting older paper documents into computer data. You know what I mean—necessary, but not really creative research. Challenges are what really turn on my mind."

Angus was encouraged by her enthusiasm. "Let's see what you can come up with."

Lani thought carefully and with that sudden insight that often leads to unexpected discovery, finally said out loud, "Blue! I wonder if we could find a match toward the blue end of the spectrum. We've been looking at the infrared where Gemini works best. Maybe we could find a match farther up the spectrum toward the blue or even ultraviolet. We could have an object that's got a *blue shift*."

Using the same starlight blocking method as before, Angus obtained several more wide range spectra in the blue area of visible light. Again, he and Lani watched intently as the computer ground away at its task, testing match after match as it was moved farther and farther up the comparison spectrum. After what seemed like hours, it began divulging the results.

"Look at this!" He almost shouted to Lani. "We've found a match. If it's correct, the light from that object has an *incredible* blue shift." After a quick, rough calculation, Angus sat back dumbfounded and nearly speechless. "Unless my calculations are off, that object is a wild star, moving toward us at almost ninety percent of the speed of light."

They looked at each other silently for several seconds in amazed disbelief. Angus opened his mouth to speak, but nothing came out. Finally he forced a hoarse whisper. "That's absolutely impossible. Nothing that big can move that fast."

The startled look on Lani's face gave way to concern. "Maybe we made a mistake. Let's do it over."

Testing another set of data produced the same results. "Of all the unexpected surprises research at the fringes of knowledge provides, this has got to be one of the biggest," Angus remarked, his face registering incredulity. "I know no one has ever reported such an object before. We'll have to get someone to check and recheck both old and new data with confirming calculations. I know! I'll call Pat right away."

Within a few minutes Pat was on the phone. "How are things in Hula land? Met any Hawaiian beauties?"

Angus wouldn't mention Lani at this time. "Hundreds! All over the place, but I've got something really important to send you. Are you ready for this?"

"Yeah! So what cooks, pal?"

Angus' voice was shaking with excitement. "I've found an object moving in our direction at nearly the speed of light. I believe it's a star."

"Come on! You're kidding of course."

"Never been more serious in my life."

"Really? You're not pulling my leg? That's impossible!" Pat was caught between believing and being certain Angus was joking. His emotions were wavering quickly and wildly.

Angus was beginning again to be frustrated. Pat should know he wasn't kidding. "No, I really mean it. That sucker's coming directly at us at more than ninety percent of the speed of light and I want to set up a secure method of communicating with you so you can check out my findings."

Pat finally got with the program. "You're really serious, aren't you? Is it those crazy lines that got you to Hawaii?"

"Right on, partner! That is them. We knew they had to be shifted from somewhere, but we've only been looking in the red. Never dreamed they could have a *blue shift*. Now I need confirmation. Can you do it?"

"How are we going to transfer data? E-mail?"

"Encrypted e-mail would work. There are encryption programs available that even the feds can't crack. We can use one of those. I'll have my assistant find us the best method. She's quite good at things like this."

"She? You have a female assistant? What's she like? I'll bet she's a doll."

Angus watched Lani's expression as he answered. "Nah! She's an old hag, about three hundred pounds, warts, scraggly hair and missing teeth."

Lani almost fell off her chair trying to keep from laughing out loud.

Pat was extremely dubious. "I'll bet!" After a pause he got back to business. "As far as the e-mail is concerned, I know you have my personal address, so let's use that. Use you-know-who's name as the initial password until we get the encryption in place. If what you say is true, you will want to keep this under wraps. Sometimes even the phones have ears, so lets keep it light. Use e-mail to send the details."

"Right you are. I'll be sending within a day or two. Tell you-know-who I said 'Hello.' I wanted to hear your reaction to the news, so that's why I called. We can do the rest by e-mail."

"Tell that fat old hag to keep you on the ball, OK?"

As soon as Angus cradled the phone, Lani reacted. "What was he asking? That was quite a complimentary description. I take it your friend Pat kids a lot?"

"We worked together long enough to become good friends. Used to harass each other unmercifully. He's a friend I can count on."

"If you don't mind my asking, who's *you-know-who*?"

Angus laughed. "That's Beanie. Pat's lady friend. She's another Native American, a Chiricahua from Arizona. I won't try to pronounce her Chiricahua name. Her language is as far from Mohawk as Hawaiian."

"How did she get the name, *Beanie*?"

"I think it came from her childhood when she used to wear one of those little beanie caps. The kids started calling her 'Beanie' and it stuck."

Lani put on her serious face. "You want this kept under wraps until you have confirmation?"

"You bet! I don't want to let this out until I know we're accurate. I know of the premature announcements of other findings that were later refuted by additional work. That did great damage to the credibility of those responsible. It could even be a career ending fiasco under certain circumstances. We must make certain this is valid. I hope you can handle that."

Lani would still not abandon caution. "As long as you play the game fairly, I'm with you. No one will hear a word of this from me without your knowledge and OK."

Angus became emphatic. "If our preliminary work is not flawed, we may have a monster discovery on our hands. Let's hope we handle it properly."

"What about someone else releasing knowledge of the discovery before you? Couldn't that happen, and wouldn't that be a disastrous blow?"

"That's a chance every researcher takes with every discovery. By sharing with Pat, I secure the date of discovery. It's sort of a who-found-it-first situation. We'll most likely be OK. People have been looking intently at Barnard's Star for many years. It's doubtful there are many looking now, if any. I was only shooting Barnard's as the last test in a series of tests to prove and refine the comparison program I developed. That's when those crazy lines appeared."

"Is there anyone here you could use for confirmation?"

"I really need someone elsewhere in the world with different instruments and seeing conditions. Pat may soon be able to use the new 6.5 meter MMT on Mt. Hopkins. I think that's scheduled for first light in the near future."

Lani leaned forward to emphasize her words. "I'm a bit nervous being the only one here at Gemini, other than you, who knows about this."

"I'll go talk to John Carroll to get his opinion. Maybe that will help ease your mind. One more thing. We now need to take a *parallax* reading on that star, just in case it's near enough to measure."

Lani stood up and walked over to the large wall calendar. "You know, don't you, the first parallax readings could be taken in just a few days. You have the time scheduled for a different purpose, but this would be the time to do it. Then comes Christmas and the real millennium end. Lots of people will be gone over the holidays."

"I almost forgot about that. We barely have time to set up for a parallax image. Maybe I'll wait until things quiet down before talking to John. That will be two or three weeks at most."

Lani began gathering the paper strewn around the table and Angus' desk. "Makes sense to me. I can handle three weeks OK. Now, the day's almost over and I've this mess and my own desk to pick up."

Angus started picking up papers. "I guess I'd better help. I still remember that first day and what you told me, no *ordered* me to do about keeping the place neat. How have I been doing?"

Lani had completely forgotten her first tense days three months ago before Angus earned her professional respect. Since then, they developed a comfortable working relationship. She was a bit embarrassed by what she had said, but he would never know it. "I never knew that even registered on you. It worked though, didn't it? I must say, you've been helpful keeping your office clean and orderly. Was I really that obvious?"

Angus laughed. "Yes you were, very stiff, very cautious and quite obvious."

2

The latest decade, the twentieth century and the second millennium ended on December 31 of the year 2000.

An early celebration of the New Year/Century/Millennium was held the afternoon of Sunday, December 31 in the reception area of the Gemini offices. A relaxed, casual affair, it was a small party since many of the scientists and technicians had headed home for the holidays. Only the most necessary staff remained, along with those who either lived nearby or couldn't go home for other reasons. Lani and Angus stopped at the party before heading for Lani's home for dinner and a festive evening with her family. As one of those who couldn't leave his research to make the journey home for the holidays, Angus was invited by Lani to share a traditional Hawaiian New Year celebration with the Namahoe family. Angus was eager to meet these people who were Native Americans, like him, but of another sort. Since his recent arrival on the island, he had been so busy there was little chance to meet local people other than those at Gemini. As usual, Angus was eager to make some new friends.

Dr. Richard Rumley, an astronomer from the United Kingdom, joined the growing group at Gemini North as a specialist in deep space research. Smug, self-centered and egotistical, he remained apart, earning little friendship among the group. Loud mouthed, balding, bug-eyed and with a large potbelly, he nonetheless imagined himself to be irresistible to women. He pursued any attractive female he met, soon establishing his reputation as a womanizer. With that callous indifference of blind ego typical of the sexual predator, he ignored even the most direct negative responses to his advances. When he first set eyes on Lani, he decided this gorgeous Hawaiian would be his next conquest.

One ugly incident marred the day. Soon after the party started, Dick Rumley approached Lani. "Hi, beautiful. How'd you like to spend the evening with the greatest lover in the Islands?"

Lani put him down cleverly. "Infantile remarks like that are unbecoming to a true professional." Then she walked around the small group away from Rumley.

Dick was not going to let things alone. Though no alcoholic drinks were being served, it was obvious he had been drinking. Soon, he barged through the group chatting with Lani and Angus and started in again. "What's the matter, Miss Snooty? You too good to talk to a British astronomer?"

At this point, Angus, always the peacemaker, decided to act quietly. "Please let the lady alone. She obviously doesn't care for your crude remarks. Maybe you should go and sober up."

Dick rejected Angus' quiet suggestion. "Just who do you think you are? You her latest swinging partner?" He then gave Angus a slight push away. Big mistake!

In response to the push, Angus whirled around, grabbed Dick's right arm, twisted it behind his back and pinned his left arm to his side in a tight bear-like grip. He held Dick firmly from behind, nearly lifting him off the floor.

"I believe you owe the lady an apology," Angus growled in Dick's ear as he held him. Although the two men were about the same height, Angus was much stronger than Dick expected and though he struggled, he couldn't break free.

There was a tense moment as Dick refused to respond and struggled to get free. "We're going to stay here until you apologize to the lady."

Realizing Angus meant what he said and was probably capable of doing so, Dick finally gritted his teeth and apologized to Lani.

"Apology noted." Angus then excused himself, lifted Dick up bodily without losing his grip and carried him out the front door where he unceremoniously dumped him on the lawn.

Angus stood over the sprawling troublemaker. "Don't come back! If you do, I'll just have to remove you again."

No blows were struck and the only thing injured was Dick's pride. Sure that Angus meant what he said, Dick lay there on the grass for a few moments, then got up and left. He would not come back.

Angus straightened his rumpled shirt and came inside. One of the senior staff came over and complimented him on his handling of what could have been a nasty situation. "You did well not to lose your temper. A number of people here were quite happy to see that one put in his place. He is a definite troublemaker and may not be here for long for that reason. This incident may just be the final one to force his removal."

Lani was somewhat embarrassed when some of the ladies came over to tell her how handily Angus had dealt with the situation.

One shook her head a bit angrily. "That Dick Rumley is really a bad one."

An older, female astronomer reached out and placed her hand on Lani's forearm. "Dick Rumley's had that coming for a long time. I think your Dr. Thomas acted with a great deal of restraint. Many men would have just struck him on the spot."

"Or ducked off and avoided the whole thing," another added as the party returned to peace and the sounds of friendly conversations.

Thankful the incident ended as it had, Lani smiled with admiration and respect as she walked up to her boss. "You controlled that bad situation quite well, keeping the scene as low key as possible."

Angus stood casually, striving to minimize the effect of the fracas. "Drunks can be so obnoxious. Moving them out and shutting them up is about all you can do. I'm glad he chose not to push the issue."

Lani was most appreciative. "I especially admire your avoidance of explosive, shouting, adolescent reactions. You just quickly, coolly and definitely took control of a difficult circumstance not of your own making. I'm impressed."

Angus was quite modest about his actions, remaining relaxed and matter-of-fact. "I guess that comes from handling similar situations with football players who've had a bit too much to drink. The main thing is to make the scene as small and controlled as possible. Sometimes they still get out of hand. Let's get back to pleasant company."

Lani's face brightened when Angus changed the subject. "I'm so glad I thought to invite you to spend the celebration with my family. They're always asking about the people at work, and I know they want to meet my new boss. I couldn't see you spending the holiday alone."

They walked over to join the main group at the refreshment table. "Well, I appreciate the invitation. You're about the only one I've worked with for more than a few minutes since I arrived. I've been so busy I've had little time to make friends or do anything social. This is the biggest social event, in fact, the only social event I've attended since arriving."

Lani spoke no more about the episode. She did not tell Angus about the many past incidents with Dick Rumley.

Leaving the party, they put Angus' bicycle in the trunk of Lani's car. "That's my sole means of transportation since my arrival," he explained as they headed for his nearby apartment to drop it off. "I use it both as transportation and for exercise. I found some great places for serious exercise riding up the nearby Mauna Kea roads. I have a compulsion for staying in condition, a holdover from my football days. My rebuilt knee bothers me at times, but not seriously."

Eyebrows raised, Lani's face registered surprise. "You had your knee rebuilt?"

"From the injury that ended my football career."

"It must have been a serious injury."

"Serious enough. I couldn't walk on it for many months. Rehab was the most painful and tedious part. I just hope it holds up for a few more years."

"Is there much chance it will cause problems in the future?"

"The doctors said it should last for many years if I behave myself. I can't jog or run. That's why the bicycle. Low impact exercise is OK. Here we are. This will take just a sec." He locked his bike in the rack outside his apartment, went inside and retrieved his suitcase.

He returned and sat down, smiling just a bit smugly as he adjusted his seat belt. He was thinking of the coming event and the little surprise he had with him. "I'm really looking forward to meeting your family and friends. Why don't you give me a rundown on them so I won't feel completely ignorant when we get there?"

"You're grinning like the cat that swallowed Tweety. What's up?"

Angus faked it as he changed expression. "Nothing, just anticipating your party."

She didn't buy it but made no other remark. During the forty or so minutes it took them to drive south on Highway 130 to her home, Lani named the members of her family and some of the friends that would probably be there. It turned out to be a rather large group.

Finally Angus held up his hands. "Whoa there! All those Hawaiian names are confusing this haole. Let's concentrate on getting the main characters straight. I can sort out the rest during the party."

Lani laughed and replied, "OK! Only I don't know if you should rightly be called *haole*. That word is normally used for white mainlanders. Being Native American, you are different. Let's find a good Hawaiian name to call you, one that better suits your character and ancestry."

Angus laughed suddenly. "How about Sitting Duck? That's what I'm going to feel like out here with all these natives." They both laughed for a long time, passing back and forth ridiculous names for Angus, laughing at each new suggestion. They were still laughing when they pulled into the Namahoe Construction Company lot and parked a short distance from the house.

*   *   *

Near the parking lot and to the rear of the house, the Namahoes prepared for a full-blown Hawaiian Luau. The family decorated the entire yard with flowers, colored paper and strings of lights with different colored mantles. They carefully placed furniture for the meal: low tables with matting on the ground for seating, several serving tables covered with colored paper and palm leaves for the food and another table for Hawaiian beverages with plastic cups, glasses and several large insulated jugs. In a sandy area slightly away from the tables was a pit where a pig was cooking in the traditional Hawaiian manner.

Through this entire scene moved the Namahoe family, putting the final touches to the preparation. Several men were attending to the *kalua pig* cooking in the sand pit. The pig had been cooking since early morning. The colorful Hawaiian attire of all of them added to the decorative scene.

Angus chuckled to himself as he thought that except for the difference in the trees and clothes, this could have been a family holiday gathering back on the Mohawk reservation. Knowing something of what would transpire during the evening from the information about native customs Lani sent him, Angus had packed a little surprise of his own in his suitcase.

As he took the suitcase from the trunk of Lani's car, he laughed out loud thinking about it. "What's so funny?" Lani questioned.

Angus grinned broadly with a twinkle in his eye. "You'll see. I've a little surprise for you later in the evening."

"You're just full of surprises aren't you?"

A group of small, brightly clothed children ran to the car shouting "Lani, Lani, Lani's here!"

It was clear they adored her as they hugged and kissed her in greeting. The little girls giggled as Lani introduced them to Angus. He knew he would really have a hard time remembering their names. Though Lani had mentioned them during the trip, he had concentrated on trying to get the adults straight and that was hard enough.

Angus squatted down to near their eye level. "You girls are so pretty in your bright outfits. Let's see, two of you belong to Lani's brother Pilau and one to her sister Leinaala. Right?"

The little girls giggled shyly with huge toothy smiles, nodding their heads emphatically.

Angus turned to the small boys, clinging to Lani. "And you guys must be Leinaala's boys. Will you all tell me your names?"

An explosion of Hawaiian names and giggles left Angus without a clue. He stood up and shrugged his shoulders at Lani who was laughing at the scene. "I couldn't make anything out of that. You'll have to fill me in later."

As they walked toward the house, a rather handsome couple came forward to greet them. Angus knew they were Lani's parents. Her father, Alika, or "Ali" as everyone called him, was a large, rugged, outdoor type. Obviously Hawaiian, he had curly dark hair liberally sprinkled with grey. The lines on his face spoke of a lifetime of smiles and hearty laughs. Lani's mother, Charlene, was a slightly heavier, older version of Lani. A very lovely woman, she had soft, dark, friendly eyes and fine dark hair. They both looked younger than their fifty or so years.

Ali stuck out a work-roughened hand to Angus. "Welcome to the Namahoe reservation. My daughter has already told me I should call you Angus."

"Thank you. I really appreciate the invitation. I see your daughter has told you of my ancestry." As he and Ali shook hands Angus thought, *I'm going to like these friendly people.*

"This is Lani's mother, Charlene."

"So nice to meet you. I understand you are new to our islands."

"Yes, I moved here in September. This is certainly a beautiful place, a bit wetter than Tucson."

They chuckled at his understatement. As they entered the house, Charlene turned her pleasant smile on Angus. "You could almost pass for Hawaiian. Are you sure you're not a distant relative?"

"Only if you're a Mohawk," he replied, laughing.

Charlene showed him the room he would be using. "Put your things in here. If you need to freshen up a bit, the bathroom is just across the hall." She turned to leave, then turned back for a parting comment. "Oh, and when you're all set, come outside. We'll put you to work. There's still plenty to do."

Angus shook his head and grinned, thinking how much Charlene was like his mother. *That's just about what Serena would have said in the same situation*, he thought as he opened his suitcase to change from his work clothes.

The room was rather small with a couch that made into a bed, an easy chair, a small desk with a lamp and an upright desk chair. It was obvious this was Charlene's domain, neat and functional. One wall of the room held a large closet with folding doors and a built-in bookcase with many books, a few decorative items and lots of photos of the family. Angus looked over the pictures noting the ones of Lani at their old home in Kalapana. There was just one photo of the destruction caused by the lava as it crept inexorably down the street in front of their home. He wondered what it was like facing such an irresistible force knowing it was to destroy your entire community. *You definitely know who is not in charge*, he thought as he viewed the photo and considered the circumstances that brought him to Hawaii.

He hung two shirts and slacks in the closet along with his surprise for later, keeping it in its bag away from prying eyes. His slacks and bright red Hawaiian shirt fit right in. Topping off his outfit was a ridiculous, tattered straw hat. Angus headed outside to see how he could help with the preparations. Lani had changed quickly into a *muumuu* and preceded him outside by several minutes.

As he came out the door, Lani spotted him, howled with laughter and shouted, "Now you look like a real Hawaiian . . . tourist."

Angus laughed as he thought, *The hat was the crowning touch.*

Lani walked up and gave him a head to toe once over. "You are definitely not one of those pompous scientists, are you?" She was still laughing. "I'll bet you enjoy being ridiculous at times. Now just get yourself over there and help with the kalua pig." Turning toward the men by the fire she called, "Pilau! Pilau! Here's another hand for the pig." She turned back to Angus. "That's my brother Pilau. He'll show you what to do."

Ali and Pilau introduced him to several other male relatives who were going to assist in wrestling the hot pig out of the pit and onto a bed of palm branches. After instructions from Ali, they removed the pig from the pit and placed it on the palm leaves where it would later be carved.

*   *   *

As the afternoon passed, more relatives and friends arrived and were introduced to Angus. By early evening there were nearly sixty people of all sizes, shapes and ages gathered in small groups. Laughter and lighthearted banter filled the air. *It's definitely shaping up to be a day to remember*, thought Angus.

It was nearly seven o'clock when Ali stood up and walked over to the cleared area in front of the tables. The atmosphere of noisy, animated conversation quickly changed to one of quiet anticipation as all eyes focused on Ali.

"Aloha! Welcome to the Namahoe Luau. We hope you all have a terrific evening with family and friends. I know you are all hungry, so let's have our prayer before we eat. Charlene."

After Charlene's prayer, they exploded into animated conversation as they took plates and went down the tables selecting their meals.

Angus turned to Lani. "These are definitely my kind of people. I feel more at home here than I have anywhere since leaving St. Regis. It's a very good feeling."

With laughing, small-girl enthusiasm she grabbed Angus' hand and led him into the food line. "I'm glad I brought you. You certainly fit in. Now, let's head for the food. This gang will treat you like a guest for about five minutes. After that you're just one of the family."

When the feasting began winding down, the pleasant sounds of Hawaiian music introduced the entertainment. Several men in Hawaiian costume, including Lani's brother, began dancing by the fire that now burned brightly in the pit where the pig had been cooked. The brightly colored costumes—tanned, sweat drenched skin over taut muscles—twirling, fire tipped batons—all glistening in the flickering firelight, were quite impressive.

Angus watched intently. "They are really good! The twirling burning batons and that dance, they're positively spectacular."

He turned to Lani, but to his surprise, she had slipped away shortly after the dance started. As the dance ended, Pilau stepped into the firelight and took on his role as emcee for the evening. He tried to tell a few jokes but was hooted and harassed by the whole group who showed little mercy.

They began to shout rhythmically, "Bring on the girls! Bring on the girls!"

Finally, the crowd grew quiet as soft music began playing and Pilau announced, "Presenting the beautiful Namahoe hula girls."

Lani, her sister, her mother and several others came into the firelight and began a sinuous hula around the fire. Angus was mesmerized. The hula girls in their native Hawaiian outfits, long legs flashing through slit skirts, danced fantastically and were very beautiful. Angus thought Lani was absolutely gorgeous.

After the hula dancers finished, Charlene sang the Hawaiian wedding song to Ali who walked into the firelight to join her.

During the song, Lani returned to her seat on the mat beside Angus. "Isn't she fabulous?"

"I can hardly believe how well she sings. This is one warm, beautiful experience." Angus was spellbound for the moment.

When Charlene finished, she and Ali walked out of the firelight to a standing ovation. At this moment, Angus thought it was about time for his surprise.

When Pilau returned to his spot as emcee, Angus leaned over and whispered in Lani's ear, "Stay right here. I'll be back in a minute." He left her side to get some things he needed.

Earlier, before the meal, Angus had taken Pilau aside and asked him to help with his surprise. Pilau thought his idea would be great entertainment and proved a willing coconspirator, planning with Angus just how to pull it off. Pilau received a tape from Angus and assured him it would be played over the sound system when he was ready for it. Chuckling to himself as he hand signaled Pilau, Angus headed for the house to change into his outfit.

When Angus was ready, Pilau stood up. "And now, at great expense, we bring you from the wilds of New York State, the *Ali'i Nui* of the Mohawk nation, Chief Star Gazer."

"Ah-hee-a ha-eee!" a Mohawk war chant split the air as Angus charged around the fire to the sounds of drums and tribal celebration chants. Decked out in his full Mohawk dancing regalia, feathered headdress, loincloth and moccasins, he put on a spectacular show.

His muscular bronze arms and legs flashed amidst the leather and feathers. No one in the audience had ever seen such a dance.

Lani pointed out to Leinaala the hand motions Angus used. "Look at his hands! How expressive! Their movements are so different from our hula, but quite expressive in their own way. I'll have to get him to tell us their meaning."

Leinaala nodded her head in agreement. "How spectacular!"

After the almost stunned silence at the end of the dance, she and Lani joined everyone in a standing ovation. His dancing was so different, yet in the same vein as their own Hawaiian dancing. Angus was a big hit with everyone.

He is truly extraordinary, an unusually decent man and a hunk as well. Lani thought and then smiled at herself remembering how cautious she had been when they first met.

The Namahoe children flocked around him as he took off his headdress and headed for his seat next to Lani.

"Angus! Angus!" they said in chorus as they reached to touch his feathered headdress. There was no doubt about his enjoyment as he teased back and forth with the children. They all wanted to know more about this stranger who so quickly seemed to be one of them.

Pilau stood up suddenly, his eyes wide with enthusiasm. "I propose we make Angus an honorary Hawaiian right here on the spot."

With happy shouts they all agreed.

Angus immediately stood up with a huge, bright smile and glanced around. "As Chief Star Gazer, I pronounce you all honorary Mohawks."

Two different cultures had found one another much alike in many ways. The formal entertainment over, Lani walked Angus slowly through the now scattered group of people stopping to talk with them and introducing Angus to those he hadn't met. The party evolved into several constantly changing knots of people. They played games, danced on the sand and taught Angus several Hawaiian songs until just before midnight and the big change over.

As the evening went on, Lani and Angus discovered their eyes meeting more and more often. When separated by friends or family, they were a little anxious until they were back together. As midnight approached, most of the couples were dancing in the sand to slow music. The rugged Mohawk warrior and the tall, beautiful hula dancer made a striking pair as they danced barefoot on the sand. Pilau counted down the seconds to midnight. They would celebrate a New Year, a New Century and a New Millennium.

At the magic hour, Angus gathered Lani into his arms for the traditional New Year kiss. That kiss turned out to be anything but traditional. Fireworks were set off in the parking lot by the young people. These were nothing compared to the fireworks within the handsome couple. Embracing while standing in the sand under the starry sky, they were oblivious to the absolute pandemonium going on around them. They could have been alone on a mountaintop, so engrossed were they in each other

As their lips finally parted, Lani looked almost startled as she leaned back to look directly into Angus' eyes. "Wow!"

Angus was absolutely speechless.

For two people who are normally very much in control, that explosive moment had kindled an uncontrollable fire. A major change had suddenly come into their lives and neither one had any idea where it would lead. They were both breathless with excitement for the moment, neither being able to move nor turn away their gaze. It was a moment, frozen in time, a vivid memory for the rest of their lives. When their locked eyes finally did break away, there was an awkward moment.

Lani's sister, who had been standing waiting nearby grinning like a Cheshire cat, finally broke the spell. "Are you two going to stand there moonstruck forever?"

The sudden emotional happening had not gone unnoticed by several of Lani's family who nodded to each other knowingly. Pilau grinned broadly. "What do we have here, a budding romance?"

"Oh, Pilau!" was all that Lani could manage in reply.

Slightly embarrassed and hardly knowing what to do or say, the two merely walked slowly out of the firelight and away from the party in complete silence. Off by themselves in the dark, they stood locked in an embrace and devouring each other's lips. Hands, lips and eyes spoke untold volumes in the dark silence. It was a long time before any words were spoken.

A stunned Angus finally managed to regain his voice. "Lady, you've turned me into absolute jelly. Let's sit down somewhere before I pass out."

Lani led Angus over to a bench beside a palm tree where they sat for a long time, holding hands and talking. Once the silence was broken, words came in torrents. Lani began to gain some semblance of control. "This was definitely not included in my plans for the evening."

"Mine either. Where do you suppose we're headed?" With Angus' words, a loving verbal fencing match began.

"I don't know. What do you think?"

Angus, too, began to regain thoughtful control. "I think we may be headed in an interesting direction."

"I've never experienced such a sudden, intense attraction. It makes me giddy."

"It's been a heady experience. You really decked this old running back."

Lani leaned her head on his shoulder. "This was a very special moment. I don't know about you, but I've never been so overwhelmed in my life." She backed up, almost cautious, paused, looked intently at Angus and began trying to lighten the tone of their conversation. "Who were those two crazies anyway?"

Angus leaned back, his mind racing. *Where is she headed now?* He glanced up in the sky for a moment then back at her. "I'm not sure just who those crazies were or are, but I really like them. It was a special time for me, too. I just can't believe how suddenly it all happened. That simple New Year's kiss turned into a whole symphony of wonderful feelings."

Lani let loose again, stood up and twirled around, her hands held high. "Wonderful! Wonderful! Yes, wonderful feelings. I can't help but feel all this is quite real. It feels like a beginning to me. I hope you feel the same," she murmured lovingly as she again took his hands in hers.

Angus stood up and took Lani back into his arms. "Oh, I do! I certainly do! I feel as if I've known you forever already."

They were in that incredible, delicious, giddy, totally unconquerable state of new love excitement. It would be a long time before either would be able to talk sensibly.

*   *   *

Things were very different as they walked hand-in-hand back to the dwindling party. "Are you two serious?" Charlene asked in that concerned mother's fashion.

"Serious about what?" Lani asked, trying to control her face which seemed to want to break into a broad smile all on its own.

"Well, just what do you think? We all noticed that little romantic interlude at midnight. How long has this been going on?" Charlene asked in a tender way and with a pleasant smile on her own face that mirrored Lani's. She was not prying, just interested, as any mother might be in her daughter.

"Honestly, Mom, up until this moment we've been strictly professional. I don't remember if we've even shaken hands before. Whatever took us over was real." Lani had regained most of her composure by this time.

The look on Angus' face demonstrated his new attachment to Lani. "We may not have been serious last year, but we definitely are now. I'm not sure yet just what happened, but it's definitely on the spectacular side."

Ali joined them in time to hear the conversation. "What a way to celebrate the big change. A brand new romance."

Earlier, Ali remarked to Charlene just how well Angus adapted to their family. "The Namahoes' active, outgoing manner can intimidate some people. Angus fits right in."

Charlene mirrored his feelings. "I really like this man. He seems so much like one of our family. The children certainly like him. It seems strange; he's from a place and culture so far away, yet he fit right in almost immediately."

Ali was one who could size up a person quickly and accurately. He was certain Angus was a good man. *Maybe Lani has finally found someone,* he thought.

The two couples stood there chatting uninterrupted in the dwindling firelight for some time. During this time, the family stayed away, not wanting to intrude and almost not knowing just what to make of things.

Finally, Lani's sister could hold herself back no longer. Taking her husband's hand and encouraging the others, Leinaala strode up, grabbed Angus by the arm and announced, "Time to initiate this one into the family rituals. Circle around the fire and sit," she ordered, smiling.

Eighteen adults remained gathered in a circle around the embers of the fire. The young children had been put to bed and many friends had parted for home. Of the eighteen, in addition to Angus, were six close friends and eleven members of the Namahoe family. When they were seated around the fire, Leinaala stood directly behind Angus, her arms crossed and in a solemn manner spoke several long phrases in Hawaiian. Angus had absolutely no idea what was going on but would participate in innocent trust with just a little apprehension. Lani sat quietly at his side with arms crossed and the same somber look on her face as Leinaala. Not all of them were so serious and Angus took comfort in that. He had no clue as to what Leinaala was saying.

Finally, Leinaala spoke solemnly in English. "We now pronounce your new Hawaiian name, Koloa Ho'omoe! From this day forward you will be called Koloa Ho'omoe at all Namahoe family gatherings. Please rise, Koloa Ho'omoe." There was some muffled snickering among the group, so Angus knew something was up.

"Now, Koloa Ho'omoe, would you like to know what your name means in English?" Leinaala continued.

"Yes!" replied Angus, now knowing he was going to be the goat in a good-natured plot.

"Sitting Duck!" she answered, as she broke out in laughter.

As the entire group exploded uproariously, they gathered around Angus, hugging him and slapping him on the back. Obviously, Lani had shared some of the conversation of the trip with her sister. When he looked at her sternly, Lani gazed skyward in that innocent, *who, me?* look. Angus had been had. He thoroughly enjoyed it. He was truly among good friends.

Pilau walked over and slapped Angus on the back. "How do you like your new Hawaiian name?"

Angus laughed just a bit sheepishly. "I have just been had and had good, and I actually enjoyed it. I have never been made to feel more at home than I have tonight." Looking at Ali, he added, "You've a wonderful family. You must be quite proud of them."

"I certainly am. They are a real joy to me."

After things settled down, they all sat around the fire, singing and telling stories about each other until the sun came up. Angus told them something of his family back in St. Regis, remarking about the similarities between the Namahoes and his own extended family. All the while, he and Lani kept locking eyes over and over. No matter how hard they tried to be casual, that moonstruck look would appear whenever their eyes met. As the sun appeared, they all finally said their good-byes and drifted away. Only Angus, Lani and her parents would remain at the house. Everyone else headed home, gathering still-sleeping children as they left.

A night without sleep takes its toll no matter how enjoyable and exciting. It was past ten in the morning and Angus thought about just staying up but was persuaded by Charlene to at least take a nap. After crawling into the converted sofa she had prepared for him, Angus lay thinking of the night's happenings. Lani was all he could think of until he finally fell asleep. He slept soundly and dreamlessly.

NEW YEAR'S DAY, 2001—THE FIRST DAY OF A NEW MILLENNIUM

Angus awoke with that instant jolt that attends awakening in a strange place. It was dark outside and dead silent. He glanced at his watch and found it was nearly seven. He had slept much longer than he thought he would. He slipped into his clothes, stopped at the bathroom and headed for the living room. Finding no one there, he said, "Hello? Anybody around?" There was no answer. Stepping outside he saw only the scattered remnants of the party and most of that had been cleared away. Little more than the hanging lights remained and they were shining brightly. There was no one around. He turned at the sound of the door behind him to see Ali standing in the doorway rubbing his sleepy eyes.

Ali grabbed a chair on the porch and sat down. "What year is this? I don't know how many days I slept. You seen the women?"

Angus parked himself on the porch steps. "No. I just woke up. I have no idea where they are."

"That was some party. As you can see, our bunch knows how to have fun. The only problem is the price you pay the next day. It'll take me a week to get my clock readjusted and catch up on my sleep. We surely did have a great time though, don't you think?"

"Yes, it was a terrific party. Anything I can do to help clean up?"

Ali moved down next to Angus on the porch steps. "No need. We're used to picking up as we go along, so there's not such a big mess the next day. That spreads out the work."

Angus remembered seeing things being picked up and moved about during the night, but his thoughts were fully occupied. He even recalled seeing Pilau raking the sand around the fire at some time during the festivities. "You folks do know how to make a person feel at home. That's impressive to someone so far from their own home and family."

"Well you certainly fit in here. We really enjoyed having you and we thoroughly enjoyed that dance. You'll have to tell me about its meaning."

The two got up, went inside and sat down at the kitchen table where Angus explained the Mohawk celebration dance over some Kona coffee that Ali had started as soon as he awoke. It was obvious they hit it off quite well. Angus had a fleeting recall of Serena's stories about his own father as they talked. He must have been a man much like Ali. There was a sense of interconnection, almost kinship between the two.

Charlene and Lani walked in after parking the car. Charlene held a heavy bag of groceries as she stepped into the kitchen. "You boys finally decide to get up? I wondered if we'd see you before tomorrow morning."

"Where have you been?" Ali asked Charlene as he kissed her in greeting, took the grocery bag from her and placed them on the table.

"We ran over to return some things to Pilau. You know, his sound system and beverage jugs. Then we stopped at the market to pick up some fruit. We've been gone less than an hour."

"Why didn't you wake me?" Ali asked knowing the answer.

"We thought the two of you needed your beauty sleep," Lani joked.

Charlene sat down at the table next to Ali. "Since when do I wake you after a party? You're on your own for that. You two seemed to have managed quite well."

Ali smiled broadly at his wife. "How about a little breakfast? You haven't eaten, have you?" To their nodded no he replied, jokingly, "Pork sandwiches OK? I know we could work up some leftovers from last evening."

Everyone groaned!

Charlene opened the bag of fruit on the table and out tumbled a pineapple, several papayas, mangos, oranges and apples. "Here's what we went to get, some fruit for dinner. The time for breakfast is long gone."

All of them sat down and joined in preparing the fruit, placing large colorful sections all together in a huge bowl. While preparing and then eating the sweet, juicy fruit and drinking coffee, a long, animated, verbal exchange ensued. Tomorrow it would be back to the old grind and they savored this pleasant visit. Getting to know this new man in Lani's life, and letting him get to know them in return, was a distinct pleasure to Lani's parents.

3

The best plans of the best people can be scuttled by an act of God, by innocent interference by a friend or by skullduggery by a scheming antagonist.

They rose early Tuesday morning for the trip back to Hilo. It was only an hour trip and Lani planned to drop Angus at his apartment before she went to her own, just over a mile away. She lived in the same small apartment near the university that she lived in while a student.

On the way, they had an extended discussion about their new relationship and how to treat it at Gemini. Lani thought it would be a good idea to "cool it" for the present. "We will have to behave professionally at all times. Do you think you can handle that?"

"I can if you can. Just watch those beautiful eyes. They can say far more than words."

Lani laughed and grabbed Angus' arm. "Did I just get a compliment? I can't believe we're planning this great deception."

"We'll also have to be careful about that touching thing," Angus replied. "No hands, remember?" Lani drew back in a mock pout, releasing her grip on his arm quickly. They both laughed. "Keep both hands on the wheel," he added with a chuckle.

"Why don't we make a game of it? Let's see how professionally we can treat each other. We just might have a lot of fun with it. You know, fooling everyone, but in a good way."

"That may be the way to do it," Angus replied, smiling. Turning serious he added, "Sooner or later we'll have to let people know about us. I don't want to be sneaking around, hiding these sensational feelings forever."

*   *   *

After Lani dropped him at his apartment, Angus went inside, changed his clothes and then hopped on his bike for his habitual daily ride up the mountain. He would return and shower before going to work. He peddled especially hard this time, thinking about all that had happened since the middle of last week. He began thinking again about his recent findings. *What could that object be? Were the results he found in error? Was anyone else working on the same thing?* Sometimes, looking for answers merely generates more questions. Concentrating on his thoughts, Angus didn't notice the small car pull out of a side street behind him when he passed. Negotiating a turn on the narrow, deserted road, deep in thought, he caught a brief glimpse of a grey fender to his left just before it hit him. The last he remembered was the sound of his bicycle crunching under the wheel and the pain of branches breaking against his body.

Angus awoke in considerable pain, jouncing along in the back of an emergency vehicle. He looked up into the round face of a paramedic attending to him. "Take it easy man. You've had a nasty accident," the paramedic warned, realizing Angus was now conscious. "I don't believe you're in serious danger, but we'll know better soon as we get you into the trauma center. Just don't move!"

Confused at first, Angus soon remembered where he had been and what happened. The picture of the front of the grey car etched in his mind, he knew this had been no accident. Strapped firmly to a board, his neck immobilized, Angus realized he was in a great deal of pain. *I wonder just how badly I'm hurt?* he thought. Knowing not to move when injured had been deeply ingrained in him while he was playing football, so he lay very still.

The round-faced paramedic leaned over him. "We're about there! You can thank your lucky stars for two kids who happened to see your bicycle in those bushes by the road. They told us they stopped to look at the bike and heard your moans coming from far back in the bushes. One happened to have a cell phone and called 911 immediately. Otherwise, you'd still be back there for who knows how long."

Angus gritted his teeth at the intense pain. "What's the time? What time is it?"

The round-faced man raised up and looked at his watch. "Nine-thirty. Don't talk unless you have to."

Angus quickly backtracked in his mind to when the accident had happened. He realized he lay injured in the bushes for more than forty minutes. *Why would anyone do such a thing?* he wondered. *Whom could it have been? Kids out for mischief? A crazy who hated bicyclists?* He knew there were some of both around. Suddenly he thought of Lani. She would have expected him at Gemini just about now. How could he get in touch with her? "I've got to call someone!" he said to the paramedic.

"First thing is to make sure there's nothing too seriously wrong. Soon as that's done, they'll contact whomever you want. You may even be able to do that yourself if you're not too bad. Your head seems to be clearing. I can tell that since you're at least making sense, but we've no idea yet just how long you were out. You were lucky to be wearing a helmet. Lots of guys won't, and we have many head injuries in bike accidents, some are really serious."

Angus remembered being kidded a few times about wearing that helmet. The years of football taught him its value and he never rode without it. The ambulance pulled up to the emergency entrance of the trauma center of the University Hospital where Angus was quickly wheeled into an emergency room. Now, fully awake, he watched the nurses scurry about, cleaning his wounds and checking his legs. His head and neck were still restrained and would remain so until x-rays were checked. One nurse with a clipboard sat down and began asking questions for the document she was preparing: name, address, allergies, medical history—droning on and on. Angus started when she asked whom he should notify. For a moment he thought about having them notify Director John Carroll or the personnel office. "Lani Namahoe at the Gemini Research Center," he replied, giving his office number. Lani would be there wondering why he was late.

*   *   *

It was almost noon when a worried Lani watched Angus being wheeled into the room he would occupy for the next few days. She walked in with Dr. Lane, the attending physician.

The doctor reported his situation. "Despite numerous cuts and bruises, two broken ribs and a mild concussion, you are in much better shape than you have any right to be. You're going to be very sore for several days, and I want you to lie quiet because of the concussion. By the way, number thirty-five, I was a great fan of yours. Thought you were one of the very best ever. You'll be happy to know I checked out that knee and it seems to have come through unscathed. That bush you landed in probably saved your knee and maybe even your life, though it did cut you up a bit."

Angus smiled through the pain. "Thanks, doc, and thanks for checking the knee. It's nice to know I still have some fans who remember."

Lani made no pretenses. "I, too, want to thank you, doctor. I just found this man and I certainly don't want to lose him!"

"Don't worry. He'll be good as new in a few weeks. He's a tough one. Just remember, no tight hugs or squeezes for at least a month. Those broken ribs will take a while to heal. Take it easy on him." With that the doctor left to continue his rounds.

"Well, Miss Professional, right off you let the cat out of the bag. So much for the big secret," Angus said, grinning as broadly as possible through the repairs to his face.

Lani flashed a knowing look. Relieved knowing her man was going to be OK, she seemed almost to bounce as she spoke. "Not a chance! I was talking to the doctor before they brought you back and found out he was a truly great fan of yours. When I told him about your work at Gemini, he could hardly believe it. He had so many good things to say about you, I was sure he could be trusted. I explained enough about us to ask him not to tell anyone. He was pleased and asked if we might come to visit him and his wife sometime. He wants you to see his recreation room with your picture covering one entire wall. I told him we'd love to come."

"There you go! Messing with my life already."

"*Our* life!" Lani chastened. "I'm messing with *our* life."

"Oh! I do stand corrected." He laughed and then winced in pain. "Forgot about those ribs. I'll have to remember not to laugh until they're healed."

RECOVERY

Lani stayed to keep him company. She leaned against the empty second bed. "Angus, I told them at Gemini all about the accident, and you were to have no visitors the first day, other than your assistant, that is. I'll be back tomorrow with some of your papers to go through. You can lie there and answer my questions. That way we will keep our project on track while you recover from the accident."

Shortly after three, the police were at the hospital, investigating the accident. Officer Loomis was polite, but insistent. "I want to know all you can remember of the accident. This is the second hit-and-run we've investigated in just two months and we like to catch those responsible. Tell me everything you can remember, no matter how insignificant."

Angus gave him as many details as he could remember about the accident and the car. "It happened so quickly, I have no idea what make it was."

"Did you get the license?"

"No, I never saw it. I'm certain it was grey and that it was a small car, not new. I'm absolutely sure it was not accidental. Whoever hit me did it on purpose." There was something else specific and familiar about the car that he couldn't quite put his finger on.

"Your crushed bike is now at the police lab. The technicians will search it for evidence: paint chips, vinyl scraps, tire imprints, anything that might tie the accident to a suspect. So far, they had nothing. For the present, all we can do is search for a small, grey, older car with possible minor damage to the right front fender, and that's very little to go on. If you think of even the slightest new fact, please call immediately. Homicide may want to talk to you as well. If this was deliberate as you suggest, the case may be turned over to them."

*   *   *

Two days in the hospital seemed like forever to Angus and by the time he was discharged on Thursday, he was chaffing at the bit. Orders to take it easy were especially hard to take. Angus did not like restrictions and vented his wrath to Lani. "Can you believe it? No bike riding for the next two weeks. No strenuous exercise for at least a month. I can go to work, but I can't walk that far for a full week. I haven't been so restricted since my knee surgery."

"Look at the brighter side. Director Carroll asked me to arrange to get you to and from work for a while. The hospital provided a regimen for treating all your cuts, so I've got several good reasons to be with you."

Still feeling a bit angry at being restricted, Angus continued to grumble. "I must get back to my project right away. Did you pick up the clothes I asked you to get from my apartment?"

"Right there in that bag," Lani said pointing to the small canvas athletic bag on the floor. "If you continue to be so grouchy, I'll make you laugh, and you know how your broken ribs will hurt, so lighten up. Incidentally, I have never seen such a sterile apartment. How can you stand to live there?"

"You got it for me. I only sleep and change clothes there anyway."

"It's for certain I didn't decorate it. I'll see about changing that soon." She picked up the small bag of clothes and dumped it on the bed. "If you're about ready to go, I'll step out while you change."

Angus opened the door when he finished dressing. "I'm ready; all we have to do is stop by the desk, so let's get going. I've got to get back to work."

Lani was dismayed. "You are nuts! You should stay away from work until next week to rest. There's only one more full workday left. Let me drive you to my parents' home, so you can recuperate in peace and quiet and we can watch over you. Then come into work well rested on Monday."

Angus would have no part of that plan. "I've just too much work to do. I have to go in."

Nearly everyone at Gemini told him he was crazy to be back so soon. "Take some time off to rest and recover! You're not worth a thing the way you are now," Director Carroll said.

By noon Angus was done in. He hurt from head to toe and grimaced with every step.

"OK! OK! You all were right," An exasperated, frustrated, pain-wracked Angus finally admitted to Lani, "*No*, I shouldn't have come back so soon. *No*, I'm not getting anything done, and *yes*, I will take a few days off and come back next Wednesday."

Angus hobbled down to the parking lot entrance where Lani was to pick him up. Just as he arrived at the gate, he had a momentary flash of memory of the accident. The sound of a car leaving the lot was unmistakable. It was the same sound he had heard just before the accident. He looked over just in time to see the bug-eyed face of Dick Rumley through the right side driver's window. He was driving his small, grey, British sedan on his way out for lunch. Angus noticed Dick's car was bright and shiny, at least the right side looked almost like new. It was definitely not the faded grey of the car that had struck him. As Lani drove over to get him, he wondered, *how many of that particular make and model are on the island? Certainly not many.*

Over Lani's objections, Angus insisted on immediately telling the police what he had just remembered. They stopped at a phone booth and Angus called, giving his name and asking for officer Loomis. After a wait of several minutes another man came to the phone. "This is Lieutenant Peter Hiakawa of homicide. Your case has been turned over to me to be treated as an attempted homicide. That's my department. Can I help you?"

"I just remembered something that may help. I remembered the characteristic sound of the car that struck me. It was a Rover, a British car. I'm quite sure of that." Angus did not tell him that Dick Rumley had just such a car.

"Thanks for the information. That should help. I'll let you know as soon as we have any news."

They started out again as soon as Angus hung up. In obvious discomfort all the way to the Namahoe home, he didn't have much to say, not even about his phone conversation with the police. Lani tried to comfort and cheer him up without much success. "I'm really sorry I'm being such a bear, Lani," he finally said. "I'm just so miserable. Maybe I'll feel better once we stop traveling and bouncing these bones about. I really do appreciate all you've done for this grumpy invalid. I don't know how I would have gotten along without you."

"Well there, Sitting Duck, I plan for you to never find out how to get along without me. How do you like that?" Lani said emphatically. "If I've much to say about it, you're going to have to put up with me for a very long time."

"I rather like the idea," Angus said through clenched teeth as they pulled up at Ali and Charlene's.

It was just before two and Ali was away on a job. Charlene put a comfortable easy chair on the porch where she motioned for Angus to sit. Lani filled her in on his needs.

He sighed as he sank into the chair. "I never thought it would feel so good just to sit back and be quiet. I've been rather a bear to your lovely daughter in return for the terrific care she's given me. I'm truly sorry."

Lani laughed. "He's right on that count. He has been a bear. Don't worry! I'll have him eating out of my hand in no time."

Angus laughed and then grimaced. "Don't make me laugh," he pleaded. "Whenever I laugh, it feels as if my broken ribs are going to break me in two."

"Sorry, hon! I'll probably be even happier than you are to have you all healed and back to normal."

Angus struggled to find a comfortable position. "I never told you about the phone call to the police. Now I can tell you both. When I called, I talked to a Lt. Hiakawa who explained the case has been turned over to homicide. While I was waiting for you to pick me up, Dick Rumley drove out past me in his little grey Rover. The sound it made was exactly like the sound of the car that struck me. Only Dick's car was a bright shiny grey, not the dull faded color of the one that hit me. I told Lt. Hiakawa the make of the car."

Lani looked startled. "Dick Rumley's car *is* dull, faded grey. I've seen him park it many times, and I've never seen it a bit shiny."

Boom! It immediately hit Angus. "I'll bet it's shiny since he just got it painted. At least the right side, the one that hit me, is newly painted. Could that idiot have tried to run me down?"

Lani stood up in anger. "I'll bet it was Rumley. He must have wanted to get back at you for the incident at the party. I can't believe anyone would do such a thing, let alone a professional and a scholar."

Angus grimaced at a sudden pain in his ribs. "I don't know, I really did a number on him at the party. He may have had it coming, but who knows what happens in a mind like that. From my experience, I'd say it wouldn't surprise me. No, not at all."

"What's this all about?" chimed in Charlene, questioning. "I must be missing something. Just what happened at that party?"

Lani related the entire scene for her mother and also some of her earlier encounters with Rumley. "Why that sleazy . . . why didn't you tell me about this before?" Angus asked.

"I didn't think it warranted attention. Really, I didn't think it serious enough, and I thought I had handled it. Believe me. I wasn't keeping it from you. It just was of no consequence. Now, it may be an entirely different matter, and I thought you should be told."

Angus sighed, "You were right. There was no reason. In fact, maybe it was a good thing I didn't know. I'm not sure just how differently I would have reacted given that knowledge before our little run in."

They sat on the porch with Angus until time for dinner. It would be late since Ali was quite far from home on a job and wouldn't be back till after seven. Angus was just as happy not to have to get up for a while.

Finally Ali arrived home, stepped onto the porch and looked closely at Angus. "It's nice to see you back here, but I certainly don't like the circumstances. I trust you don't make a habit of running into cars with your bicycle. I hope you feel better than you look."

Angus squirmed in his seat trying to find a comfortable position to talk to Ali. "Except for ribs that kill me when I laugh and a face that hurts when I smile, I'm fine. I owe it all to the marvelous care of your daughter and your wife. Of course, the people at the trauma center had a small hand in it too."

Over dinner Ali was brought up-to-date on the accident and related items. "It boggles my mind to think there are people on this earth who are so stupid as to do such a thing," Ali said after hearing the story and their suspicions. "How does a man like that ever get to hold the position he holds? I doubt a person like that can really do good science."

*   *   *

During his recovery, Lani stayed at her folks' to help care for Angus, driving the forty miles back and forth to work. She worked hard on Angus' project to make sure all would be in order when he came back. Early on Tuesday afternoon, she left to get some new information on the project to help bring him up to speed for his return. Shortly after she left the Op Center, the police arrived to arrest Dick Rumley.

Angus stayed until Wednesday morning. Rested and feeling much better, he headed back to Hilo with Lani. Angus knew something was amiss the moment he walked in and Jenny motioned to him.

"There's a man from the British Consulate waiting for you in your office. What's going on?"

Angus spread his hands, fingers extended in the universal don't know sign: "I have no idea." When he entered, he found a short, rather round English gentleman waiting for him.

"I'm Weldon Conrad from the British Consular Service," he said, standing. "You are Angus Thomas, I presume?"

Angus extended his hand, his face wrinkled with puzzlement. "That's right. What's this all about?"

"It's all about one of your colleagues here, a Richard Rumley. Do you know him?"

Now Angus was really curious. "Only very slightly. I met him just one time."

"And when would that have been?"

By this time they both were seated. "Sunday before last, New Years Eve. What's going on here? I don't know whether I should answer your questions, at least until I know more what it's about. Why are you asking me anyway? I barely know the man."

Conrad settled back in his chair, hands interlocked in his lap. "It seems Dr. Rumley has been arrested and charged with leaving the scene of an accident and may even be charged with attempted vehicular homicide. You are the person he is alleged to have struck and I will have to ask you some questions. As a British subject, he is entitled to certain protections under the law. It is my job to investigate on his behalf and provide that protection."

Angus was dumbfounded. He stared silently at Conrad for a moment before regaining his composure. "Let's get this over with quickly, please. I've a job to get back to and I've already lost four days."

Conrad leaned forward, his round face quite serious. "Unfortunately, your job has a great deal to do with the problem. It seems your police, with a warrant, searched Dr. Rumley's place and found some very interesting papers. These papers included recent copies of your work here as well as some from your work in Arizona. They are being held as evidence against Dr. Rumley."

Angus stood up straight, shaking, his fists clenched; his face wore the mask of anger. "Are you telling me that sleazy scoundrel was stealing my research work? How in the devil was he managing that? I kept those papers under lock and key at all times. Also, no one can access my computer files except . . . the only ones to have access to them were a few in my research group and . . . my assistant, Lani."

Momentarily panicked at the thought of Lani as suspect, Angus was visibly shaken. This was not possible he decided. If it were Lani, a big part of his world would collapse. A thousand conflicting emotions were suddenly battling over his heart and soul.

Conrad's words brought him out of panic. "I know this is a shock to you, old boy. Believe me, we want to get to the truth as much as your police do. If this man is the villain you seem to think he is, we will want him punished to the full extent of the law. However, we must still see to it that his rights are protected. In the meantime, he will be detained until the matter of the papers is investigated. Incidentally, while the bulk of the papers was yours, there were some found from several other projects underway here at Gemini. They were from projects like yours, which he had no legitimate reason to have in his possession."

Angus was still dazed and somewhat confused. "I'll be glad to help if I can."

"Frankly, sir, and off the record I might add, I think the scoundrel is just that, a real scoundrel. I hope he gets his due. I am still bound to protect him regardless of my opinion. That's about it for now." Conrad rose and left as he finished his last statement. Angus was still noticeably shaken as Conrad went out the door.

Passing the departing Conrad, Lani walked purposefully toward Angus' office, a pleasant smile on her face. She apparently knew nothing yet of what Conrad had told him. As soon as she stepped into his office and closed the door the phone rang. Jenny's pleasant voice announced, "There's a Lieutenant Peter Hiakawa from the Hilo Police asking for you. He says it's very important and he needs to see you right away."

"Send him back," Angus said, sighing then turning to Lani. "Another interruption. It's that homicide guy, Peter Hiakawa. I wonder what he wants."

When Lani opened the door, a stocky man in a conservative pastel shirt and gray slacks was about halfway through the outer office. She motioned him toward the door. An obvious mix of Hawaiian and Japanese ancestry, he appeared to be about forty.

As soon as he stepped into the office he looked at Angus and announced, "I'm Lieutenant Peter Hiakawa. I talked to you on the phone about your accident."

"Yes, so our receptionist told me. This is my assistant, Miss Lani Namahoe," Angus replied. "I'd like her to stay and hear what you have to say if that's all right."

"I'm pleased to meet you, and you certainly are welcome to stay." Hiakawa replied, smiling.

"Do you mind if we all sit?" Angus said, grimacing. "I'm still hurting some from the accident."

"Not at all," Hiakawa replied, "In fact, that's a good idea. What I'm about to tell you may be quite a shock, and, incidentally, at least for the time being, do not let anyone else know anything of this. We have arrested Richard Rumley and charged him with leaving the scene of an accident. We did some investigating after you told us about the sound of the car and found his was the only one of any model of that particular make on the entire island. He had it shipped over from England when he came. When we examined his car, we found it had just been repainted. Checking around, we found the shop that did the work, and look what they gave us." With that he took several photos out of a brown envelope. One was a photo of an obviously faded gray fender with fresh scratches and a few dents. The other showed the same fender, repainted and looking like new.

"It seems this particular shop, which is clear over in Kailua on the other side of the mountain, takes before and after pictures of every job they do. With this evidence, we were able to get a search warrant for his apartment to look for corroboration. While searching his apartment, we found, lying in plain sight on his desk, a stack of data, photos and some type of graphs, all with your name clearly marked. There was also a schedule of your activities for more than three weeks. He had gone to a great deal of trouble to determine just where you would be and at what time. At first, we thought it was part of a plan to run you down, then we discovered he was plotting your every move to know just when you would not be in your office.

"There's more. You see this little baby?" he said as he took a small, black object from his pocket and placed it on the desk. "This is a very hi-tech surveillance camera. We found it right up there in your air-conditioning outlet," he said pointing to the ceiling. "This little baby takes a picture every ten seconds and it was aimed so that it saw your computer screen and part of your desktop right where those papers of yours are setting. All the pictures taken are in color and saved on a single, large memory chip in the camera. It only needs to be unloaded about once a week by popping the old chip out and inserting a new one. The lithium-ion battery can be changed at the same time. The whole process can easily be done in two or three minutes at the outside. We've been checking your air-conditioning people and the fluorescent bulb service you are using and we think we'll soon have the courier."

Lani's face had that raised-eyebrows look of incredulity. "How did you find this out so quickly? You've only been at it for a few days."

For a moment, Hiakawa seemed uncustomarily a man full of his own cleverness. "Good police work and the tip from Angus about the car that struck him put us on the right track. Blind good luck in almost unbelievable amounts did the rest. Finding those papers on his desk while searching with a warrant for corroboration of the so-called accident was the biggest break. We wouldn't have obtained the warrant except for those photos of his car, and that was pure good fortune. I've seen these types of investigations take many months. Once we saw those photos on his desk, we knew there were cameras somewhere. With the director's permission, we conducted a thorough search on Saturday and discovered three of those cameras in as many research offices. With your office locked in your absence, the courier could not get in to recover the latest photos. We've staked the other two offices with no activity so far. We'll keep your office locked and act as if you are still gone for the rest of the week. We don't believe the courier has been spooked yet and we really want to catch him in the act. That would give us a much stronger case against Rumley than what we have at present."

Angus told him about Conrad and what he knew. It was obvious he had yet to get all the information that Hiakawa possessed.

"He's a decent guy just doing his job," said Hiakawa of Conrad. "I will pass this latest information onto him. If there's to be an information leak, it won't be through him. By the way Miss Namahoe, there were a few questioning fingers aimed in your direction at first, but you've now been placed above suspicion. I didn't know you had a cousin on the force. Joey's been a good policeman for more than twelve years here in Hilo. When your name came up, Joey almost went through the roof. He straightened us up in a big hurry. When we confirmed his information for ourselves, we knew you were not involved."

Joey and his wife had been at the Namahoe New Year's party. Angus was elated that one wrenching problem had been laid to rest. He wondered if he would ever share those momentary fears with Lani.

Officer Hiakawa reminded them to keep all this confidential. "By the way, I don't think Rumley actually planned to kill you until shortly before he tried. Everything else he did was very carefully planned. That act was poorly conceived and very carelessly executed. It was more like a spur-of-the-moment, opportunistic action. He might have gotten away with whatever he was planning without being caught if he hadn't tried to run you down. We really have no idea what he planned to do with what he was taking."

Angus was quite sure he knew exactly what Rumley was planning. "We'll certainly keep this under our hats. Please keep us posted on new developments."

As soon as Hiakawa was gone he turned to Lani. "I've got to talk to Conrad about Rumley and find out how he got to be where he is. There has to be more to this than the spying at Gemini. Do you suppose Rumley received his research reputation on the basis of other thefts from other astronomers?"

Lani's eyes narrowed in wonderment. "It is entirely possible." Her look of curiosity turned to wide-eyed realization of the need for action. "I hate to change the subject, but we've work to do in spite of all this activity. Now, let's get to it."

WHAT'S HAPPENING?

About a week after their meeting at Gemini, Angus called Weldon Conrad in Honolulu. He was interested in talking to him about Dick Rumley and what he thought about his past work. Weldon seemed fascinated by Angus' questions, which drew him out on every point. "No, Rumley has never been caught at this in the past."

"Has anyone accused him of stealing their data?"

"Yes, there had been a few accusations of inappropriate information published by Rumley, but they all remain unsubstantiated."

"What about the courier? Has he been caught?"

"Yes, the courier has been apprehended. A local petty criminal, he was questioned and released. Posing as a pest control inspector, he gained access to some of the offices to install and maintain the surveillance cameras. Rumley recruited and trained him, provided his uniform, equipment and cover under the guise of outside security surveillance for Gemini. The courier admitted to being suspicious, but the pay was good, so he asked no questions."

"Were there any others involved?"

He avoided answering Angus directly. "There are ongoing investigations in both Hawaii and in England. Thus, I cannot share that information. I will keep you informed of any new information that might be in your interest and that I am permitted to pass on."

Angus was certain Conrad was not just a consular official, but an investigator of some sort as well. His avoidance confirmed Angus' suspicions, at least in his mind. He was now certain Rumley had reached his present position on at least partially stolen information. Who were his cohorts? That worried Angus. He suspected the elaborate scheme to spy on the scientists at Gemini could not have been concocted and operated by Rumley on his own.

He then contacted officer Hiakawa and asked for the most recent information on the charges against Rumley. Hiakawa was very evasive. He asked Angus if he was planning a suit against Rumley. The "no" answer seemed to open up Hiakawa a bit. "The only charge to be pressed is leaving the scene of a personal injury accident. Rumley claimed it was an accident and that he had no idea who he struck. He says he swerved to miss another car just as he was passing you."

Angus was terribly frustrated and replied vehemently, "There was no other car on that road! It was completely deserted."

"We know that, but it would be impossible to prove. He says he was so frightened he drove around for some time before heading back to help. By the time he returned to the scene, Emergency Medical Services was already there. It was just the usual bull we get when we catch a hit-and-run driver. I've heard that same story many times."

"What about the other thing, those copies of my work, the cameras and all that?" Angus asked. "What's happening there?"

"The only thing I can say about that now is it's under investigation. I'm sure you understand. I'll gladly give you any information I can as soon as it's released. I can't promise you'll hear it from me before the news gets it though. They sometimes get releases before I do."

Angus sighed, resigned to the inevitable reality. "I understand. I just hope there's no one else picking up where Rumley left off."

"At this point, I don't think there is. I can tell you as yet we've found no evidence of any accomplice. We're reasonably sure he was working alone, at least here in Hawaii. There's another bit of information I can divulge. We are getting increasing pressure from the British to have him released to them. They want to take him back to England for some reason. Since we have been assured he will be returned here for trial on the hit-and-run, we'll probably release him to them when we're through with our questioning. That could be within the week."

"What going to be done about the cameras and my papers he copied? Isn't that criminal?"

"I just can't let you in on what's happening on that as yet. It's a much more complex situation than the hit-and-run. We have contacted the other observatories here, advising them of possible intrusions and looking for evidence of mischief. It's an ongoing investigation, and all I can tell you is what is already public knowledge. I'll gladly let you know what I can, when I can." When Hiakawa added, "I understand you already know about the courier," Angus knew he and Conrad were sharing information.

Angus had to accept Hiakawa's position, but still, he didn't like it. He really wanted to know just what Rumley had found out. Why had Dick been watching his work so much more than others? The thought he might have seen the confirmation of the speed of the *ghost* bothered Angus. If not, there was probably little chance of problems. If he had seen it and passed this information to others, who knows how it would be used.

THE GHOST

To get back into the swing of things, Angus decided to review all the significant information obtained so far on the ghost. He was feeling much better than when he left on Friday, but his ribs still ached and he definitely did not want to laugh. The healing cuts on his face made him a sorry sight, and it still hurt to smile.

With Lani's help, he located and studied many images of Barnard's star from several locations taken during the last few years. By plotting the movement of Barnard's star against those much farther away, he was able to locate precisely where the image of the ghost was located. Two of the three most recent images showed just the slightest hint of an object. Obviously, the middle image was made while the ghost was occluded by Barnard's Star. Even that was unusual. If he hadn't known where to look, he would not have noticed the barely discernible, fuzzy smear on the first image from Arizona. One confirming image was enough. The object was real.

With its unprecedented speed in the direction of earth it may only have come close enough to be seen by the largest telescopes in recent months. It would be several weeks at least or maybe even months until Barnard's Star moved far enough away from in front of the ghost so it could be resolved individually. Until then, it could not be accurately positioned. Questions like distance, size and trajectory would be answered in time. Normally patient, Angus would remain anxious until he discovered these answers.

*   *   *

The scientists at the Op Center knew Angus was looking for evidence of planets around nearby stars. They also knew he was currently concentrating on Barnard's Star and found some evidence that spurred his current effort at Gemini. Nearly all were so engrossed in their own research in other areas, they hadn't time to consider his work which went on relatively unnoted. They could read about any significant discovery when Angus published. Previous to the Rumley incident, Angus had little to worry about his discoveries leaking out early. Unfortunately, this brought an entirely new factor into focus for his concerns. Had Rumley learned everything Angus knew about the ghost? Had he passed the information on to others? Was he working alone or were there other scientists involved? How much did the others at the Op Center know now that Rumley had been arrested? These questions gnawed at him almost constantly.

Lani noticed him staring off into space and waved her hand in front of his eyes. "Hello! What's on your mind? The usually steady Dr. Thomas seems to be daydreaming frequently lately."

"I was just wondering what the people here really know or think they know about what's going on. I'm concerned at how it might affect our research effort. Nothing seems to have come out, but what about the future? The cloak and dagger aspect has been kept under wraps by the police, but I'm sure it will eventually be found out. I doubt Rumley's one to keep his yap shut."

"From rumors I've heard, everyone thinks Dick Rumley went off the deep end after his scuffle with you. They're sure he ran you down in retaliation for what you did to him at the party, nothing else."

"You know, I think that's probably why he did it. Especially after what Hiakawa told us about it being poorly planned and all. For whatever reason, retaliation seemed to fit with his overall plan, so he did it at the very first opportunity. From what I know now of his twisted mind, he is quite capable of murder."

"Dick's probably surprised you're still alive. From what Hiakawa said, if it wasn't for your good physical condition and those bushes, you'd be dead. I shudder even to think about it."

Creases crinkled around his eyes and mouth as Angus smiled at her. "Me too! Look at all the excitement I would have missed."

"We'd best get back to work. I don't think I can handle all this hilarity," Lani cracked in reply.

"OK! For starters, I want some new images taken in the blue end of the spectrum. We also need to estimate its distance from us. I can get a rough idea from the change in brightness between that very first image made in Arizona and our first parallax image six months later."

Using the faint fuzzy smear on the first image from Kitt Peak and the first parallax image from December, Angus made some rough calculations and came up with an estimate for the distance to the ghost. "It's far too distant to measure accurately," he explained to Lani. "It will be June before a more accurate distance calculation can be made using the second parallax image. With no measurable change of position between the earliest and latest data, we can assume it to be at least three hundred light years from us."

At this time, Angus published his first preliminary results with little fanfare. The more startling aspects of the ghost were left out since he wanted to wait for further confirmation before doing so. He would report only that he had found evidence of an unusual object in the vicinity of Barnard's Star. The astronomical community had been there before and would wait for more information. It suited Angus just fine. The Dick Rumley incident caused too much notoriety and interference in his work already. Angus didn't need more attention until he was more certain about the ghost.

*   *   *

During the next few months Angus and Lani worked feverishly on the ghost. The spectrum, speed and location were all confirmed with more and more accuracy. In four months, its position had not changed. There was no doubt about it. The ghost was hurtling toward the solar system at nearly ninety percent of the speed of light. It could pass within a dozen light years of the sun. In astronomical terms, it would be very close indeed. Exactly how close could not yet be determined. In late April a preliminary second parallax image was made. Calculations confirmed the earlier estimate and gave the distance to the apparent position to be about three hundred light years. This was at the limit of accuracy for parallax measurement and would be refined in June and after each six-month period.

On May 2, after he confirmed the distance, Angus turned to Lani and said, "Do you realize, right at this moment it's actually about thirty light years away from us? That wild star will pass right by us in just thirty years!"

"I realized it was much closer than it appeared, but I never thought about just how near it was," she replied. "How close will it pass by?"

"Right now, I'd say within about four light years. That's really close. It'll take a few more readings every six months to know precisely how close."

"I hope that's as close as it comes. It's scary thinking about what could happen if it passed by any closer." Lani knew something of the cataclysm that would happen if an object as big as a star passed too close to the solar system.

"If it passes through or even near the Oort cloud, the gravitational disruption could send many comets rushing toward the sun. The chances of one hitting the earth would be vastly increased. Remember when comet Shoemaker-Levy struck Jupiter? Imagine thousands of those objects coursing through the solar system," Angus replied with a worried look. "Let's hope it passes us too far away to do any damage," he added. "There are so many unknowns with an object moving so fast."

"That's a terrifying scenario, but isn't it still just guesswork?"

"Mostly. Don't worry. It will probably pass by without incident."

"I hope you're right," Lani remarked, not losing her concerned stare.

"It certainly will be a sight, a bright, bluish white star moving quickly across the sky. It should change from blue to red as it passes. Do you realize, to the eye it will be moving faster than any of the planets? While at its nearest to us, we should even be able to notice it moving against the background of stars."

They both went back to work; a little apprehension continued gripping them with an uneasy feeling. They would feel much better when the ghost's path was more accurately known.

4

Real horror is to discover a truly, unavoidable, irresistible menace, fatal to life on the entire planet and threatening total destruction on an unprecedented scale. Whom can you tell?

THURSDAY, MAY 10, 2001

By May, Lani and Angus could see the ghost was clearly visible on images taken by Gemini at the highest possible resolution. In the infrared it was a hazy blur with a slight halo. Images made in the blue showed a tiny point of light amidst a circular haze fading out away from the star. It was really quite beautiful. By now a more accurate plot of the ghost's path could be made. The two viewed the computer screen as it ground out the first results of the months of careful measurements. They were silent as they concentrated on the screen. When the latest projected position, speed and path finally were revealed and determined, Angus stood up suddenly and looked at Lani. He couldn't speak. A look of surprised horror contorted his face.

"Oh no! It can't be!" Angus finally said in a loud hissing whisper. He was visibly shaken.

Lani stood up and grabbed his arm. A sense of panic overcame them. "What's wrong? You're scaring me!"

Shaking, Angus put his arms around her. The two of them stood there clutching each other in silence. In a mixture of fear, anger and disbelief, Angus stated carefully, "In just thirty years that wild star is likely to pass right through the solar system. Do you know that could destroy all life on earth? Maybe even pull the earth apart?"

The realization would take some time to sink in. After what seemed like an endless silence interrupted only by their troubled breathing, Lani finally said, "You can't be right. I don't believe it. Dear God! Let us be wrong."

Angus stiffened and stepped away. "How can we possibly let others know? Or should we?"

Slowly the explosion of horror was passing away. "We'd better think this through carefully or who knows what the result could be," Angus replied, his voice charged with tension. "Certainly we have to check those calculations again. We must be absolutely sure before we let anyone know."

They spent several hectic hours, checking and rechecking everything. They were emotionally drained as they slumped in the chairs in Angus' office, their adrenaline levels slowly returning to normal. Angus started to speak, paused, then spoke calmly. "Follow me here. Since the light we are using to measure it has taken three hundred years to reach us, the star has actually traveled two hundred and seventy light-years toward us in that period. This means the ghost is approximately thirty light-years away at this precise moment. Our widest range of probabilities of its path tells us it will certainly pass within a few light years of the sun. The worst-case scenario has it passing right through the solar system at about a ten-degree angle to the plane of the *ecliptic*, inside the orbit of Jupiter. In any event, the consequences will most likely be cataclysmic. Am I missing anything?"

"I don't think so. None that I can think of. At least that's more encouraging than your first reaction. Just how accurate are those measurements?" Lani asked. "Isn't three hundred light years right at the limits of our instruments for parallax calculations?"

Angus agreed sadly. "You're right there. The margin of error is at least ten. It will take months, maybe even years, to determine the exact time and path of the passage. A great deal of data from the telescope must be fed into the computers for simulations. We'll also need to learn the gravitational interactions between the star and the sun and the combined effects on the planets. It's a daunting task even thinking about it. We'll need some help with those simulations."

Lani shook her head, looking dismayed. "The worst thing is the total futility of any human effort to divert such an impending disaster. It's déjà vu, the volcano all over again on a huge scale. I remember how I felt watching the lava destroy our home many years ago with forces far beyond any human efforts to stop them. Only this isn't just Kalapana, it's the entire earth. If it passes too close there can be no escape."

*   *   *

It was nine o'clock Thursday night when they finished reviewing all information. Before leaving, they downloaded the day's data to removable media so no one could find it. Lani placed the disks in her purse. As a further precaution, Angus wiped the hard drive, inserting ones in all unused characters in data sectors of the hard drive.

"Thank God we didn't back up any of this new data to the network," Angus said as he finished erasing his data drive and placing the paper and photo records in his briefcase. "We don't want anyone to see this information until it's been thoroughly checked out and confirmed. I'd hate to wave that red flag and then find we made some silly mistake somewhere."

Angus stared off into space thinking for a moment, then looked back at Lani. "I'll have to contact Pat and get him started on confirmation." Angus paused, obviously thinking carefully. "Maybe we should delay that until we've slept on it for a few days. Monday will be soon enough. After all, we've got thirty years."

They sat down and talked about what could happen while the world waited until the ghost arrived. Lani turned to Angus with that surprised look of sudden inspiration. "Let's take off tomorrow. We can go to my parents' tonight and stay for a long weekend to think over what we should do."

"Great idea!"

"I'll call my mom to let her know we are coming tonight. We should be there before midnight."

Lani tried to sound normal, but Charlene caught the worried sound in her voice anyway.

"What's wrong? You don't sound like your usual self."

Lani glossed over it quite skillfully. "It's probably because of some new concern about Angus' research papers stolen by Dr. Rumley."

"It's a good time to come. Your dad will be here all day."

"Splendid! We're leaving right now. See you in about an hour."

Angus left a note at the desk explaining they would be gone all day Friday. They stopped at his apartment to pick up what he needed and headed for Lani's. As Lani unlocked her door, Neva Roberts and her boyfriend passed them on the way to their apartment.

"Well, what do we have here," Neva said disdainfully as she walked by, "a romantic tryst with Miss Goody-two-shoes?"

Lani rolled her eyes back as she opened the door. They entered without a single word in reply. "That's the local nosy busybody," Lani explained when they were inside. "She makes it her business to know everything she can about everyone. What she doesn't find out, she invents. Wonder what she'll invent about this?" She threw her hands up. "So who cares?"

As Angus sat thoughtfully on the couch, Lani gathered some clothes and packed them into a small suitcase. She paused to pick up a framed photo of the Namahoe family in front of their home in Kalapana before the eruption. Tears filled her eyes as she placed the picture back on her dresser thinking, *We escaped that natural calamity. This one will be quite different.*

"Memories, memories," she murmured to Angus in explanation as she wiped the tears from her face. He placed a comforting arm around her. "I can just feel that same hopelessness I felt watching that lava move slowly down our street. We knew it was only a matter of time until our beautiful home would be destroyed. Not only was there no way to stop it, but the destruction would be permanent. Even the land would be destroyed and buried under that cruel, black rock."

They paused for a moment, clinging to each other without speaking. Lani finally broke the silence. "Only this time it's infinitely worse. Is there even the slightest chance we won't all die?"

As they headed for the exit, Angus had a real hangdog expression, as though the words had very little meaning. "I don't know. Short of a real miracle on a huge scale it doesn't look good. We'll have to wait for more accurate data and a lot of computer work before predicting what the outcome will be. There's always a chance of a mistake in the work done so far. We shouldn't give up hope yet."

They walked wordlessly from the apartment, got in the car and quietly drove south. They were both deep in thought while moving along the highway, only occasionally making a concerned comment.

As they neared the end of the trip Lani straightened up, stealing quick glances at Angus as she spoke. "How are we going to tell my parents? Should we wait until our minds are clearer about what to do? I don't want to just blurt it out, but they'll know something's up right away. My mom can read me like a book and you know I'm not good about hiding feelings to those close to me."

Angus half turned in response. "In the short time I've known your folks, they impressed me with their character. They'll surely be able to help us decide what to do. I think we should sit down with them as soon as we can and tell them the whole story. I certainly don't see them as panicking or blabbing to others. I trust their confidence as much as anyone."

Lani leaned back and looked steadily at the road. "You're probably right. They certainly were bulwarks for our family when the lava came. I just hate to think of telling anyone such horrible information." She glanced his way again. "Can you imagine? Some people are going to go right off the deep end. What havoc do you suppose the news will create when the general population learns about it?"

Angus looked forward at the roadway. "I don't even want to think about that. It certainly won't be pleasant."

*   *   *

It was nearly eleven as they pulled into the parking lot and Lani said, "Let's get a night's rest and sit down with them as soon as we can in the morning. If we tell them now, we'll be up all night. Let's try to be nonchalant and cheerful. That may disarm them so we can get some sleep."

"Let's give it a try anyway," Angus replied, forcing a smile. "I don't know whether I'll be able to sleep in any event. My mind's been racing since we got the bad news and it doesn't want to slow down now."

"Here we go!" said Lani as they walked up to the door.

Charlene prepared coffee and a snack upon their arrival. After putting their traveling things away, they sat down at the kitchen table for a visit.

As soon as the usual amenities were finished, Charlene crossed her arms on the table and looked at Lani. "What's this new problem over that jerk, Rumley? I thought he had been whisked off to England."

"It's really nothing Mom," Lani answered quickly, acting as casual as she could.

Angus leaned his arm over the back of his chair. "I've just been checking on that situation and found out he may have passed some of our research to some other people. It's no big deal," Angus added, using the truth to hide what loomed in his mind. He avoided looking at Lani.

There was a slight awkward silence as Ali glanced from one of them to the other. "How are you two getting along? Any new news?"

Charlene spoke up, "Now, Ali, don't press them. They'll tell us when they're ready."

Lani knew immediately what they had been thinking. They were expecting some news about the two lovers. They apparently thought this visit would bring an announcement. Relieved at first, she looked at Angus who was staring straight down at the table in front of him. Then it hit her. *They're expecting a joyous announcement and we're bringing a message of danger and despair. What a cruel twist.* Lani forced back the tears about to well up in her eyes and smiled at her mother as convincingly as she could.

"No, Mom, there are no new announcements about us quite yet. We just wanted to get away for a while to talk things over."

Ali glanced at Lani; concern mapped his face. "Not having any problems are you? Disagreements? Arguments?"

Angus looked softly at Lani. "No, none at all. We're getting on just fine. I love your daughter more each day." He reached over and grasped her hand, then looked back at Ali. "I'm sure the announcement you're expecting will be coming soon."

Lani looked at her father, then back at Angus. "As a matter of fact, it's almost painful how many things we see eye to eye on. We've even learned to disagree with a smile."

Charlene nodded her head and smiled. "Well, that's good. We both decided you two are a good match. We just made an assumption. We certainly were not pushing."

Pleasant conversation and even a few laughs relieved the tension in their minds for the moment. When they finally went off to bed, it was after one. Angus slipped into the now familiar daybed in Charlene's room and tried to go to sleep. After a half hour he gave up any attempt to sleep, put his clothes back on and headed outside for a walk.

As he stepped onto the porch, Lani's voice came out of the darkness, startling him. "Where are you going? My mind kept me awake, so I came out to sit on the porch to relax."

He stopped and turned, one foot on the porch, the other a step down. "I couldn't sleep either. I thought a walk might help. Care to join me?"

With a quick, "Of course!" Lani stood up and was at his side. They walked for about an hour, trying to figure out the best way to tell Charlene and Ali.

When they returned, Lani followed Angus to his room and snuggled up to him on the couch. "I don't want to be alone just now. This thing is terribly disturbing."

Her warmth, her nearness, even the smell of her was overpowering. In spite of the other tension, maybe even heightened by it, strong sensations coursed through his body. He fought those urges, saying to himself, *Get thee behind me Satan—and push,* a comment he sometimes repeated in jest to bring himself back from strong temptations. *Wait! Calm down.* An inner voice urged him. He listened.

They drifted off into a fitful sleep still cuddled on the couch. For a while they awakened frequently to comfort each other. Finally, they went soundly to sleep, dead to the world until late the next morning.

*   *   *

Angus awoke first, looked up and saw four eyes staring at them from the open doorway. Charlene and Ali stood side by side, eyeing them silently. Lani stirred slightly. "Look who's at the door, sleepy," Angus said softly, waking her. Lani turned, then sat bolt upright on seeing her parents.

"Look at the two of you! You fell asleep with your clothes on. Even your shoes," Ali said laughing and relieving the potential tension. "We heard you on the porch and then when you came back. There are no secrets in this little house."

Charlene turned to walk out, then leaned her head back and asked. "How about some breakfast? It's after nine already."

Angus and Lani freshened up before joining Charlene and Ali in the kitchen. They knew there was another big day ahead of them. It would not be easy sharing the frightening news.

They had a pleasant breakfast, with Ali and Charlene doing most of the talking. As they were finishing breakfast Charlene finally stopped and looked them straight in the eyes. "All right. What's bothering you two? You've hardly said a word or eaten a thing. Something's wrong, I know. I don't want to press you, but you know you can talk to us."

Tears welled up in Lani's eyes as she looked back and forth at her parents. "Oh, Mom. That's why we came up here, to talk to you about . . . I mean . . . we need to share something with you, so you can help us find the best way to handle it."

Angus looked thoughtfully at Lani. "Yes, we do need your help. It's quite serious."

"I just knew there was something wrong last night when you got here," Ali said, concern lining his face. "Your mom and I talked about it when we went to bed. We knew something was not right."

Lani drew her chair up between her mom and dad. She took a deep breath and blew it out noisily, puffing her cheeks and then she hugged them both. "I hardly know where to begin. I'll start and Angus can fill in what I miss. You know the project I told you Angus has been working on with Barnard's Star? Well, it's about that. Angus has discovered what may pose a really terrible menace to the entire world. It's a star that's hurtling directly at us at an incredible speed, a star that's much like the sun. It will pass near and maybe even through the solar system in just thirty years. Angus won't be able to plot the precise path or time for at least another year, but it will definitely cause a major disruption, probably ending life on earth as we know it."

Angus looked from Lani to the others and back. "We wanted to ask you to help us decide how and when to let the rest of the world know. We finished the results that gave us this conclusion just yesterday afternoon."

"Are you sure?" Charlene asked. "A lot could happen in thirty years. Maybe when it gets closer you'll find your star is going to miss us."

Angus shook his head. "We checked and rechecked the data at least half a dozen times. Unless we've missed something substantial, there is little chance that star will pass without harming us seriously. I prayed we were wrong and made a mistake, but the more we checked the more certain it became that the world is in for a real cataclysm." The serious look on his face emphasized his words.

Charlene uttered a big sigh and leaned back in her chair. Her face showed growing confusion as she considered the situation. She looked at Ali. "We'll try to help come up with some answers, but I really think we could all use some spiritual support. It's the first thing that came to mind. Would it be all right with you both if I called and asked Pastor Malikalohe to come over? I believe our pastor could really help us."

Angus looked quickly at Lani. He really didn't want the information to go any farther right now. "Are you sure he can be trusted not to tell anyone? He may feel it his duty to spread the information to others. I don't think we should lose control of this just yet."

Lani almost laughed. "Don't worry! If ever there was a person who could be trusted to keep a confidence it's our pastor. Incidentally it's Pastor *Ruth* Malikalohe, a wonderful woman, not a man. I've known her all my life. She was there for all of us when the lava came. Even when it finally destroyed her church she remained a strong spiritual support for everyone."

Ali added, "She will definitely be a help to us. We could use a spiritual input to help our decision making, especially in this case. She's a tiny woman with a huge heart and really knows how to counsel those in need. Like the rest of you, I am quite troubled about this, and I say we call her."

Angus now felt much more confident. "You've convinced me. With what you're saying there's no way I could object. I'd rather like to meet this little lady. Another caring view certainly couldn't hurt."

Ruth Malikalohe was indeed a tiny woman. Several inches less than five feet with a rather pleasant round face and well rounded body with tiny waist, hands and feet, she was always right in the thick of things. A childless widow, she gave herself fully to her church, her only family. Busy as she was, she somehow managed to find time to help and comfort many people in the community. She was respected and well liked by those whose lives she touched.

Charlene phoned Pastor Ruth. "Can you come here, Ruth? We need your help with a serious problem. Plan to stay until evening if at all possible."

"Charlene, that doesn't sound like you. You sound upset. What's wrong? Are you all right?"

"You know me too well and no, I'm not all right. It's not personal, but it is a major problem and we really need you."

Ruth thought for a moment and replied, "I can cancel my plans for the rest of the day. I'll be there within the hour."

*   *   *

Pastor Ruth arrived before noon, about an hour after Charlene's call. She hugged and greeted everyone and then stopped in front of Angus and looked square into his eyes. "So you're that marvelous man I've been hearing so much about lately. An astronomer is it? Well, we both deal with heaven then, don't we?"

Angus winced at her words. Seeing the pain in his eyes, she reached up and gave him a hug to which he responded and grinned. He liked this little woman right away and decided she was a bit larger than the tiny person he watched walk in the door. Noticing the sense of peace she brought into the group, he now felt comfortable sharing his information with her.

Angus carefully explained the situation to Pastor Ruth as well as he could. The concern shone on her expressive face as she asked, "You're absolutely sure this terrible thing is going to happen?"

"We are at least ninety percent certain something devastating will happen, yes," Angus answered. "I can't say absolutely for sure, just probably. There are a number of possible scenarios, all of them bad. We don't have enough information as yet to work out a worst-case or best-case scenario. That will take many months, even years to compile. In the meantime, we are worried by what the revelation of this menace might do to the populace. That scares me almost as much as the star."

Pastor Ruth thought for some time, then sat back and looked at each of them. "I think you may be surprised at how well they take it, at least initially. Thirty years seems like a long time to most. Oh, there will be some who will 'go off the deep end' as you say. After the initial announcement, it will take some time before the reality sinks in. A great many will just simply refuse to believe it. You'll probably be vilified in the press and denounced by politicians. Harbingers of bad news are universally disliked no matter what. If I were you, I'd be kind of hard to find until things quiet down. I have no idea how your colleagues will handle the revelation. Most of all, you must be absolutely certain of your facts before telling anyone."

Angus agreed wholeheartedly with her last statement and then explained another problem. "We don't know if there are others who have discovered or soon will discover the ghost and its potential danger. Sooner or later someone's bound to find it. We did just as it became visible to our telescope. There are other eyes in the skies out there every day looking for anything new and different. Some are bigger and better equipped than Gemini at finding the ghost. Another discoverer may not be so concerned with the information and just turn it loose on the public without forethought of the damage it may bring."

"I hear what you are saying," she replied. "Do you have any contacts who might let you know of an impending release of information by any of the other telescopes with the capability to find this star? If you don't, think about how to go about doing it, making the necessary contacts, I mean. If I were you, I'd still delay releasing the information until the last possible minute. You're looking at a thirty-year time table, aren't you?"

Lani spoke up, explaining, "Yes, that's true, but there is a loose cannon out there somewhere named Dick Rumley. We are not sure what he knows or has deduced and we have no idea where he is or what he is planning to do." Lani then explained the situation of Rumley's spying and what it might mean.

They sat and talked all afternoon. What would happen to the children? What would the churches do? How would those fanatical sects in Africa and the near east respond? What about government reactions? Would governments try to hide the information to protect their citizens? If they did, would they succeed? What would happen as the time grew near? A Pandora's box of evils might be loosed on the earth in addition to the very real threat of the ghost star.

Preparing to leave, Pastor Ruth stood up and faced them. "We covered many aspects and many possibilities this afternoon. I suggest you sleep on it until tomorrow. I certainly don't envy you your decision. That's as tough a one as I've ever run across. I'll say one thing though. With the good Lord's help, you'll solve it in the best way. I just know you will. I've a feeling God's got something in store for you that will solve your problem. I pray my feeling is right. For now, I'd like you to join hands and pray with me."

The small group stood up and joined hands in a circle while Pastor Ruth offered her prayer. They closed with the Lord's prayer before breaking the circle. Each expressed hopes for the future as they walked together out into the yard and said their good-byes.

"God bless you. I'll surely be praying for your guidance and for all of us." With those words, Pastor Ruth turned and walked to her car.

"What do you think of our Pastor Ruth now?" Charlene said to Angus as they headed back into the house.

"She's definitely someone special. I'm glad she came. She was a big help."

"I remember how many folks she helped over their losses in Kalapana," Ali said. "She was there with nearly everyone, comforting them even as their homes were being destroyed. You'd never know she lost both her own home and church to the lava."

They all went into the kitchen while Lani and Charlene prepared a leafy salad with chicken for supper. Ali and Angus scurried around the table, setting silver and pouring coffee.

Angus showed a thin mouthed, thoughtful face when he finally took a seat at the table. "We covered a lot of ground today, but we made no decisions. That's probably good. Why don't we quit for to-day and start in tomorrow to make those decisions we have to make? I'm beat. This day drained me emotionally."

Three voices groaned and three heads nodded in agreement. They switched to more mundane subjects as they sat and talked until bed-time.

*   *   *

Angus awoke early the next morning. The sky was just brightening in the east from the sun still below the horizon. As he stepped outside into the morning, few puffy pinkish clouds seemed to hang just above the treetops in the hazy, pale-blue sky. *God! I hope it's not the end of all this*, he muttered to himself as he surveyed the beauty of a new day's beginning. He sat in one of the porch chairs, staring at the sky and running through the events of the last few days. He kept reliving the experience of discovering the latest condemning data in vain hope of changing the results. How many times he experienced the same process before, after dropping and breaking something or taking a wrong step into an opposing tackle's hands when he was running the football. He remembered so many times thinking, *If I'd only turned this way instead of that*, repeating the very human effort of trying desperately to think the past into another path.

A soft touch on his shoulder took him out of his reverie. "I'd like to show you something," whispered Charlene as she handed him a thick photo album. "These pictures help recall lots of special memories of places we will never again see."

Moving a chair right next to him, Charlene sat down and opened the album. She explained each significant picture, identifying people and pointing out buildings and places now gone forever. There were many pictures of the extended Namahoe family and their homes. Angus remembered many of them from the New Year's Eve party.

"See these? They are several groups of pictures of our relatives' families. There's at least one picture of lava in the process of destroying each home. Our extended family suffered the loss of five homes to *Pele's* anger. Only two homes of the Namahoe relatives were outside her path of destruction. There's Pastor Ruth standing with our three children in front of the small church. There's one showing the church in flames as the lava slowly swept over it. See this?" Charlene turned the page and pointed to a picture of an iron cross standing at an angle sticking out of the now cooled lava. "That's all that remained of the church. It's the steel support for the wooden cross that stood atop the steeple. Significant, don't you think? That steel cross is the only thing to survive. You can still find it out in the lava field if you know where to look. It usually has a few flower leis on it, placed there by people who make the long trek across the lava, almost like a pilgrimage."

There were several photos of Lani with her white cat in their home.

"Lani named him Meowii when she was about three," Charlene explained, pointing to the fourteen-year-old Lani holding her cat. "That's about a week before the lava reached us. By then, we were rather certain our home was going to be destroyed. Meowii disappeared about the time the lava reached the house, and we never saw her again. The vet thinks she hid in the house in fear and then perished in the fire. We all missed the little one, but Lani was heartbroken. She still cries when she sees that picture."

The last page held four pictures of the lava demolishing their home, from the first attack on the side porch to the final grinding under of the last remains. The picture he had seen on the bookcase was part of this set.

Angus moved his chair back and faced Charlene. "It must have been devastating watching so much of your life being slowly obliterated. I think I understand why you're showing me this now. It is so much like what we are now facing, on a much larger scale."

"I thought it might help. Understanding the feelings of utter helplessness everyone experienced in Kalapana may be critical in the decisions you have asked us to join you in making. I want you to have some understanding of where we are coming from."

"I think I understand. I can certainly identify with your feelings of helplessness. Once you knew the end was inevitable, the waiting must have been horrible."

"Lani was absolutely devastated by the experience. She was only fourteen then and it took a long time for her recovery. She seems to have dealt with that quite well, however. Now, I wonder how this new challenge will affect her. I worry much more about you, our children, grandchildren and all the younger generations than I do about Ali and me. We will be well past eighty when the end comes if your calculations are at all accurate. The end of it all is what frightens me. It seems so final."

"That's certainly the word for it, *final*. I've always been an optimist, but no matter how I look at it, I see little chance for optimism under the circumstances. I haven't been able to run accurate calculations on the gravitational effects of the star's passing as yet and won't be able to for several months at least. It's moving so swiftly, at nearly relativistic speed, we don't really know everything about how gravity acts at those speeds. It's possible the actual effects could be bizarre."

Charlene turned to face Angus, a hopeful light in her eyes. "Are you saying it may not destroy our planet? If there's the slightest chance, at least we have some hope."

Angus leaned forward in his chair. "There's always a slight chance. The best I can offer is the possibility. It will take a lot of computer time to run the calculations to predict the paths of the sun and planets as the ghost goes through. It may be a year or even two before we know for sure. In the meantime, how do you deal with a general populace that may go ballistic? That's the problem we face right now. As a matter of fact, that's the only problem we can actually deal with. The star is going to do what it will no matter what we do. Just like the volcano did to Kalapana. There's absolutely nothing we can do about that."

A sleepy-eyed Ali walked out on the porch. "What's going on out here?"

Charlene turned to face him. "We're just reviewing the problems at hand. Angus says there may be just the slightest chance for survival, something about relativistic speed and gravity. It's a little over my head. As long as there's the slightest chance, I'm not about to give up."

Ali leaned against the post holding the porch roof and looked at Charlene. "Remember Joey Namakura? He's the one who lives at what is now the end of Lakelani street near the ocean. He knew his house was going to be swallowed by the lava flow and moved everything moveable over to his brother's. Well, the lava came right up to his yard and stopped just fifty feet away from the house. He now has the last house on Lakelani. The street dead ends in a wall of frozen lava right in front of his house. Joey knew his house was a goner, but there it stands and there he still lives. His wife now grows plants in cracks in the lava wall at the edge of his shortened yard."

Charlene turned to Angus. "That's right. The experts all said the flow would bury all of Lakelani, clear down to the ocean. They had no explanation when it stopped where it did. Even now, the lava is still flowing under the frozen surface right down and into the sea, southeast of his house. I don't believe I'll give up on mother earth just yet."

Angus looked up at Ali. "I don't know. Perhaps we shouldn't pass judgement on the future until we are certain. Unfortunately, that still doesn't solve our dilemma. How do we release the information we do have without causing a panic reaction? Can you imagine how the tabloids might treat it? Or, for that matter, how any of the media might treat it?"

"Treat what?" came from inside the house. Lani was finally awake.

"The news about Angus' wild star when it comes out," answered Ali loud enough so Lani could hear from inside. "What's going on in there?"

Lani came to the door. "I'm fixing breakfast and it's about ready. Come on in."

The atmosphere seemed a little less grim as they sat around the table. There were even some smiles and small talk.

"Maybe it's just that the shock is beginning to wear off," remarked Lani. "How about a walk across the lava, Mr. Astronomer? That will give us some exercise and there are some things I'd like to show you. If we leave right after breakfast, we should be back before noon, maybe earlier."

"OK! I'm game," Angus replied.

*   *   *

After breakfast, Lani took Angus to the small open shed behind the house where several bicycles were stored. She selected one for him and then retrieved her own. Together, they rode the bikes five miles to the cooled lava flow on Route 130. Angus had seen only pictures of lava before. This was his first on-the-scene experience.

As they approached the end of the road, Angus stopped and stood with his bike. "It's weird seeing the highway, painted centerline and all, disappear under the lava. I didn't realize it would be so shiny. It seems almost fluid with those round edges where it meets the road. It slopes right up to the horizon. I can imagine it slowly covering everything like a giant flow of stiff molasses. Actually being here provides an entirely different perspective than the pictures."

They walked their bikes over by a small tree away from the road and parked them. Climbing up onto the lava over rounded shafts that looked like large, black loaves of twisted bread, they walked up the gradually sloping flow for about a hundred feet.

Angus stopped and looked around. "We must be ten to fifteen feet above the roadway right here."

"It's at least twenty feet thick a little farther from the edge, and there is hot lava still flowing beneath the frozen surface," Lani said as they picked their way, hand-in-hand, carefully over the lava.

Again, Angus stopped to look around and talk with Lani. "It looks almost as though it is made of huge, black ropes some giant laid haphazardly from west to east and then partially melted together. It's so different. We climb up and down, sometimes only half a foot or so, other times we must climb up or down six feet or more. It's almost like being on a wavy sea. When on top, you can see far in the distance. When down in a depression, you can only see a few feet."

Lani pointed far off to the east where they could see a white plume rising. "That is steam created as the red-hot lava pours into the ocean after passing beneath our feet."

Angus wondered for just a moment if the ghost's gravitational distortions of earth could cause it to crack open and spill lava out all over the planet when the star got close. He did not trouble Lani with this thought.

They walked silently for nearly an hour and a half across the hot, black desert, stopping occasionally to look around and talk a bit. At one point they stopped to take a drink from one of the two water bottles Lani had placed in each of the small packs they wore. Angus walked in a small circle looking at the lava. "There are no markings, but it's plain to see we're following a path many others used before. The lava is shiny and smooth away from the path. The path is where it's been worn dull and covered with small, broken pieces. It's easy to follow."

As soon as they began moving they passed a couple with two teenagers walking in the other direction. Hellos and smiles were shared as they passed and went on.

Lani pointed ahead. "There it is, up ahead."

Angus quickly spotted what looked like a small piece of brightly colored cloth attached to a thin pole. About ten minutes later, they were there. The remains of the church cross were badly bent, thin, rusty and looked extremely fragile. Half a dozen brightly colored leis were hung carefully at the center. Several colored pieces of paper formed into origami objects lay at the base of the cross.

"I overheard Mom talking about the cross with you this morning. You know, that picture she showed you is nearly ten years old. I can hardly believe it's been so long." Lani removed the two leis in the worst condition and replaced them with two fresh ones from her pack.

She carefully placed the ones she removed back in her pack. Lani walked silently in a circle around the cross, inspecting the lava as she passed. Twice she stopped to pick up items and place them in her pack. "We try to keep the place clean. Most of the people who come here know about the church. There must be at least one or two visits each week from caring people who replace the older leis. We have no idea who brings the origami figures, but they are always replaced when they get worn. There was a Japanese family who lived near here and we're assuming it's that family."

Angus listened carefully. He couldn't hear a sound except the wind and what he surmised was the far away sound of the ocean breaking against the lava. There were no bird or insect calls, only the wind. "It's so quiet here. A light breeze can get quite loud."

"Yes, it is quiet and peaceful here, almost other-worldly. I've been coming to this cross since I was fifteen. I did it the first time with my sister and brother. After that first time, we came out at least one Sunday each month to freshen the leis. Since we all moved away from home, we've done it a lot less often, maybe twice a year. I come here once in a while by myself to meditate and pray about problems. That's why I wanted us to come out here this morning. We could use a little thoughtful quiet."

They stood side by side gazing at the cross for at least ten minutes in complete silence. They were two minds and hearts as one. Tormented by the knowledge they carried, searching for both peace and answers. They would not come to this sacred place again for a long time.

*   *   *

It was nearly noon when they came back from the lava field. On the way, Angus and Lani discussed what they were facing. They were now ready to sit down with Ali and Charlene and make some firm decisions.

While finishing lunch, Angus said suddenly, "I've just thought of something. I was wondering just how to tell my mother and decided to bring her out here to do it. I want her to meet you all anyway, and she's never been to Hawaii. In fact, the only traveling she did was going to my games when I was playing ball. While I was at Arizona, I always flew home to visit her. I'll bet she hasn't been out of New York in four, maybe five years."

"That's a great idea, Angus," Charlene replied. "We'd all be thrilled to meet her."

Lani stood up and started clearing the table. "What have you told her about us? She does know about us, doesn't she?"

Angus was caught completely off guard. "Ah . . . well . . . I wanted to tell her in person."

Lani glared. "Angus Thomas, I could smack you. I suppose you told her I'm just a coworker?"

"Well, actually, I never mentioned you. I wanted you to be a surprise for her."

"Ooooh!" Lani's face grew rather hostile. "What about the accident? When you told her about the accident, how did you keep my name out of that?"

"I . . . I . . . never told her about the accident. I thought she might worry. You know how mothers are." Angus was trying to defend himself but was not doing well.

"If your mother is anything at all like you, she's not a worrywart. What about the stolen papers, the New Year's Eve party? Have you told her anything?"

"I called her New Year's Eve and told her I was going to a party." Angus tried desperately to regain at least a little lost ground. "I didn't want to tell her about the stolen papers since that is still open."

"I can't believe I'm hearing what I'm hearing. Your mother must be an extremely tolerant person. Did you keep secrets from her when you were hurt playing ball?" Lani remained on the attack.

"Now wait just a minute!" Angus was beginning to regain confidence. "Things have been happening so fast since New Year's, I've hardly had time to breathe, what with Rumley, the papers, the ghost and me going goo goo over a terrific Hawaiian lady. I just haven't had time to call and talk to her since early New Year's Eve."

Lani softened a bit at his explanation. "I'm sorry, hon. I guess things have been flying thick and fast for you. I'd love to meet your mother. Why don't you call her right now?"

Angus thought for a moment. *It's evening back in New York, probably a good time to call.* "That's a great idea!" he said, heading for the telephone.

After a few minutes, he heard her friendly voice. His, "Hi Mom!" was answered with the usual words of greeting from Serena.

"It's about time I heard from you. I was beginning to think you had fallen off the edge of the earth."

"I'm sorry. It's just that things have been happening so fast lately. Anyway, I want you to come out for a visit, as soon as you can."

Serena's motherly instincts came instantly to attention. "Is something wrong? You sound worried."

"Mom, you know I'm no worrier. I just want to see you and talk with you in person, and I can't take time away from my project right now to come back there. Besides, I'd really like you to see this beautiful island, and I know you can use a vacation."

"I don't know about that. I'll have to give it some thought. It's getting near to our busy season here you know."

"Come on, Mom!" Angus chided. "I know your people can handle things just fine while you're gone. With Kat and Peter in charge, you know everything will be in capable hands. Could you leave by Wednesday?"

"That's only a few days from now," she exclaimed defensively. Noting the sense of urgency in Angus' voice she continued, "I might be able to get ready by then. Why don't you let me think it over? Call me tomorrow about this time and I'll let you know for sure."

"I'll make all the arrangements. I can have the trip arranged for you by the time I call tomorrow." Angus knew her *maybe* would turn into a *yes* overnight. She was always a little cautious about such things.

They carried on the usual mother and son dialogue for about fifteen minutes. Angus never hinted at anything about Lani, her family or his work. Those items were best left until she arrived.

After he hung up the phone, Lani became very sarcastic. "I wonder if we'll get to see her when she comes? Or do you suppose Dr. Thomas will keep us all a secret?"

Charlene jumped all over her daughter. "Oh Lani, don't be so nasty. I'm sure Angus would like everything to be just so when you meet his mother. I think it will be a splendid surprise for her."

Lani grinned. "I just couldn't resist one more dig. I so rarely get the chance to get him on the defensive; I was just carried away. You know I'm just teasing, don't you, hon?"

"I hope so," he replied with a grin, ducking from Lani's mock attack in response. "I'd like to make a few more calls to arrange for her trip. Then we can get down to the business at hand. I think we've come to a consensus about keeping secret the information about the ghost, at least for the immediate future."

There was general agreement among them, so Angus got on the phone. He first contacted his old friend Warren Tusla, the charter pilot. He had flown Angus and some of his teammates during his football days. Angus knew him to be one of the best.

"You still flying?" he asked when he finally heard the familiar voice.

"You betcha!" came back through the phone. "That can't be ol' thirty-five on the line can it? That really you, Angus? I'd reco'nize that voice anywheres."

"I thought you'd have retired by now or died. How old are you anyway, ninety?"

"Almost, but not quite. Still spry enough to slap ya 'round. Where ja wanna fly to anyhow, the moon?"

Angus explained what he needed. He knew it was impractical for Warren to bring Serena all the way to Hawaii. He also knew Warren would know the best way to get her there. He agreed to call Angus back as soon as he devised a plan.

"Were you kidding? About his age I mean," Charlene asked.

"In a way, both yes and no. He's got to be past seventy by now. We used to call him Ancient One back in the early nineties when he flew us around. He's among the best. He lied about his age and enlisted in the Navy Air Corps when he was only sixteen. He flew Corsairs in the Pacific and ended up in Japan at the war's end. After twenty years in the Navy flying all kinds of aircraft, he retired at thirty-seven and started a charter service with several of his Navy buddies. I have no idea how he got into the pro sports taxi service, but by the time I first met him, all he did was fly pro athletes around."

"Sounds like an interesting character," Ali added

"You can't believe the yarns he used to tell us about weird flights and weirder passengers. He could keep us in stitches for a whole flight while the other pilot was flying. He's quite a character. Still, I'd trust his flying as much as anyone's. If he had any doubts about his ability, he'd ground himself. He'd pull his own ticket before the FAA would. That's one reason he's still around. He double and triple checks everything. In all those years, his service kept a spotless record. I have no idea how many planes he has now, but you can be certain they are all in topnotch condition, as are his pilots."

"That's quite a testimonial," Lani replied. Just then the phone rang. Warren already had a plan.

"Call as soon as ya git that OK'd with yer mom," Warren concluded. "I'll take care of my end. Ya can do the Delta flight thing yerself."

Angus put the phone back in its holder and sat down with the others. "That's done. She should be here Wednesday. Warren will pick her up at Watertown, New York. That's just a short trip south by auto. It's the airport nearest to St. Regis able to accommodate his jet. From there he'll fly her directly to Delta's Cincinnati hub where she'll catch a flight for her trip here. We'll pick her up at the airport in Kailua in the late afternoon."

He spent some time talking about his mother and how she raised him alone after his father was killed. He shared stories of his growing up in St. Regis among his Mohawk relatives, especially Kat and Peter and their family. These were the pleasant memories of a happy childhood in a close and loving family. By the time he finished, they all knew a great deal more about this man from a culture so different and yet like their own in many ways.

Charlene smiled pleasantly at Angus. "Your mother sounds like a marvelous lady. I'm more anxious than ever to meet her. Where will she stay? Do you suppose you could bring her here for the weekend?"

Angus glanced at Lani. He knew what was coming. "I'll put her in my spare bedroom."

Lani bristled and glared at Angus. "Not until I get over there to do a little redecorating." She turned to her mother. "You should see his place. It's as sterile as an apartment can be. Looks as if it were decorated by an accountant."

Angus shrugged his shoulders defensively. "I never passed myself off as an interior decorator. Up until now, I've just used it as a place to hang my hat and sleep when I'm not working. You found the place for me, remember?"

Lani took charge with a vengeance. "We're going shopping for decent furniture and some decorations as soon as we're back in Hilo. I hope you've got room on your credit card because I'm going to spend a lot of your money. We'll have to move quickly in order to have things ready when your mom arrives."

"How do you know I can afford all this luxury? I'm just a struggling scientist."

"Six or seven years as a pro football star? Charter flights at the drop of a hat? I may not be a sports fan, but I know they didn't pay you peanuts. I've learned quite a bit about you since we've become chummy. I doubt you're hurting for money in spite of your modest lifestyle."

"Now I see it. You're after my money." He ducked at the ensuing onslaught.

As Lani doubled up her fists and tried to beat Angus on the chest he grabbed her arms with his hands to defend himself. They were both laughing so hard they fell back together on the couch where Angus had been sitting. "If I thought for even an instant you meant those words, I'd throw you out of the house," she muttered in mock anger, still struggling to get free of his grasp.

Ali chuckled, watching his daughter struggle. "Would you two cut it out? You're going to break the couch. Besides, we've some really serious business to attend to."

"To answer the question you asked before I was so rudely interrupted by your daughter, yes. I'm sure she would love to come here for the weekend."

NOT DECIDING IS A DECISION

Given enough time, extreme emotional pain, even terror can become matter-of-fact.

*   *   *

The atmosphere in the small living room quickly changed from
joviality to one of serious considerations. They launched into a discussion of what to do with what they knew.

Angus stood up. "I think it best to hold off releasing any information until the last possible moment, even at the risk of having someone else make the first announcement. That will give us time to obtain
more accurate data and formulate an effective, comprehensive, overall plan."

They discussed the pros and cons and finally came to a consensus to do just that, for the moment at least.

When that was settled, Lani leaned back in her chair. "We will
search through all available resources to see if any others are looking
at Barnard's Star. If we find nothing, it will be unlikely that the ghost
has been noticed by anyone else."

Angus agreed. "Barnard's Star has been studied so thoroughly in
the past, it's most likely ours is the only study being done right now.
There will be questions asked about the progress of our work, but if
we can enlist the help of John Carroll, Gemini Op Center Director,
we should have few problems. The only open question is about the
security of our data. We'll have to deal with that as best we can without drawing attention."

Angus continued. "It's a good thing the Rumley data thefts have
been kept quiet so far. I wonder how long we'll be blessed with official silence on that? It's been more than five months since he was
found out, and I haven't heard a peep from anyone. Somebody is
doing an excellent job of keeping it a secret. John Carroll knows something of this because Hiakawa had to get his permission for the search
which found those cameras. My bet is he doesn't know as much as we
do, certainly no more."

"I'd surely like to know what else the investigations into
Rumley's activities have turned up," Lani remarked. "With the

police investigation here and the British working on Rumley over there, they must know a lot more by now."

"I talked to Hiakawa a few weeks back. He still refuses to let me in on anything new they have discovered. I can understand their caution, the secrecy and all, but I would really like to know a lot more than I do. He says that no news is good news. As long as they keep the lid on tight, we have nothing to fear about our data getting in the wrong hands. That's the one big unknown and it worries me to think what might be happening to that information. Suppose a snooping reporter had someone on the inside, passing him information? Just a hint of the data in those stolen records could be the food for a media feeding frenzy."

Ali looked intently at Angus. "I thought you weren't a worrywart. Not to put down your work, but would anyone outside your tiny group of astronomers even care about that data, at least the bulk of it? If I remember, from what you explained, you didn't have the information you shared with us about the danger until after the cameras were removed."

Angus looked at Ali, remembering. "That's true. There was nothing there related to any possible danger. We found out about that later on. To discover that information, the work we did after the incident would have to be duplicated. There are few places on earth able to do so and most of those are right here. Anyone doing such research would have a hard time keeping it secret from anyone conducting a systematic search."

"We do that frequently as it is," Lani replied. "We're always looking for others who might confirm our discoveries. I remember doing just such a search through the university computer a week or so ago. The results were negative."

Ali smiled at his daughter. "You see? Nothing to worry about yet. You'd better keep checking though, just in case."

Lani nodded yes and scowled ever so slightly at her father. "I'll do my usual checks about once every two or three weeks. Doing them more often might draw attention. Those searches are logged on the computer and many people have access to those logs."

Angus stood up and began pacing slowly. "There's one more thing. Hiakawa is one sharp cop. When I last asked him for information, he wanted to know why I was so persistent. Was there anything I wasn't telling? 'Are you sure you've told me everything, everything at all relating to your work?' were his very words. It rather startled me. I told him yes, of course, but I'm not so sure he believed me. I'll bet he asks that again."

After agreeing on their course of action, they continued talking for the rest of the afternoon. The conversation moved completely away from their earlier subject. Plans for Serena's arrival and visit were discussed. Ali and Angus traded stories frequently punctuated with the laughter of all four of them. Charlene told a few about Lani growing up, which also brought laughter.

After a particularly loud bout of laughter, Ali said, "Isn't it amazing? We've moved from unimaginable terror to funny stories in such a short time. How quickly we adjust to all manner of conditions."

Lani agreed with her father. "It's just human nature, like what happens at a funeral. One minute the tears are streaming down your face, the next you are sharing funny stories about the departed loved one or friend. It's certainly not disrespect for the dead, just celebration of his or her life, a celebration of one life for the living."

They decided it was just the way life worked. Ali discussed his view of human nature. "Joy is the norm punctuated by moments of fear, remorse and regret. It's always been so in human events. Except for those unhappy gloom and doom characters, that is."

About midway in the afternoon, Charlene called her other two children and made plans for a family dinner that evening. She related the results of her call. "We're all going to Leinaala and Ron's house for dinner. Ali thought we should go to a restaurant, but Leinaala insisted we come there. Lani and I are going over early to help her. You boys will just have to do without us."

When the women left, Ali invited Angus for a tour of his company property. "It won't take long. It's not very big. In fact you can see the whole thing from the porch. After the tour we can sit down over a drink and get better acquainted."

5

It is May 16 of 2001. The new millennium is just a few months old, and a concerned mother heads out on a trip to visit her son a third of the way around the world.

It was Saturday, May 12, when Serena Thomas received the call from Angus. She would have to hustle to prepare to leave Wednesday for her visit. She was concerned after he called because he seemed a bit anxious and wouldn't tell her what it was all about. His assurance he was quite well and not in any kind of trouble but just wanted to see her still left that kernel of doubt. The next few days were spent preparing Kat and Peter to handle the inn and wrapping up loose ends.

Early Wednesday morning she left her modest home on the St. Regis Indian Reservation just east of Massena, New York. Her close friend and second cousin, Kat, was taking her to catch a plane. While they drove along the St. Lawrence before heading south for the Watertown airport, Serena turned to Kat. "I don't really know what to think. I'm between being elated at visiting Angus and wondering why he seemed so anxious. He told me there was nothing wrong and that he just wanted to see me, but there was something strained about the tone of his voice."

Kat glanced quickly at Serena and then back at the road. "You've never been a worrier, so don't start now. He probably wants to surprise you with something."

"I'm not worried, but something unusual is going on. You don't bring a boy up being both a mother and father to him without feeling what's unspoken behind his words or at least sensing it. The best way I could describe it is anxiety. I sensed anxiety, and you know Angus has never been afraid of anything in his life. There's something bothering him. I just know there is."

Kat scoffed, "Your imagination is going in the wrong direction. He's off in a different part of the world, far from family and friends and in a new job. That's a big life change, even for a man with Angus' experience. He's only been there a few months, and you told me this was an important career move."

"You're probably right. I guess I'll just have to wait till I get there."

In an attempt at levity, Kat suggested, "I've heard Hawaii is a romantic land of beautiful women. Maybe he's met some—as they say in Hawaiian—*wahine* and decided she's to be the woman in his life. If so, he'd be scared to death of what you might think. That's quite normal. As close as you two have been, that might trigger a great deal of real anxiety in your son no matter how fearless he is. As well as I know Angus, I'd be willing to bet the prospect of introducing his lady to his mom would be the one thing to strike terror in his heart."

"That's a wild, off-the-wall guess, but wouldn't that be something if so." Serena leaned back in the seat and thought quietly about her son.

With the sixth sense of a close friend, Kat knew Serena wanted to be alone with her thoughts, so she drove silently along the highway for many miles.

The quiet drone of the engine, the soft whine of the tires on the road and the rustle of the wind around the car were all that could be heard. These gentle sounds did not disturb Serena's thoughts as her mind drifted through memories of her past. She smiled inwardly thinking how proud she was of Angus and of the results of her efforts at raising him without a father. Her eyes grew wet as she remembered Angus' father lost in Viet Nam. His decorations and insurance were small compensation for a young Mohawk widow with a tiny infant to care for. She closed her eyes and recalled the support of a family and of the greater family of the Mohawk nation. Their support gave her the strength to do much more than survive during those painful times.

*   *   *

At the time her husband was killed, Serena was working in one of the local fishing camps that catered to visiting fishermen from near and far. Several months later, with the money she received from his insurance, she negotiated the purchase of the camp where she had been working. The camp included a rather nice motel with boats, docks and equipment for visiting fishermen. The motel had eight large kitchenette apartments, twenty smaller rooms, which could accommodate four people, and a nice little dining room. In spite of the demands of the camp, Serena was a full-time mother to Angus.

As her camp grew, Serena took her best friend and cousin, Catherine Chum, into the business. Catherine, called Kat from her Mohawk name Kateri, had a little girl named Jessica who was just a few months younger than Angus. Kat's husband, Peter, was an excellent fisherman and became one of the camp's best and most popular guides. While Kat was pregnant, Serena sent her to hotel management training school for six months. The life growing within her showed just a bit more each time she came home from school. Two months after finishing school, Kat gave birth to her first son, who was named Michael.

Peter built a playground for the children on the grounds of the camp, just outside the office. With the first expansion building project, they added two small sleeping rooms next to the expanded office. The second room was converted into a nursery/playroom with a door to the outside playground. Peter's talented hands installed large windows viewing the playground in each of the rooms and the nursery, so they could watch the children. Peter, or "Uncle Ker" as Angus called him from his Mohawk name, was a father to Angus as he grew up.

Serena brought his real father into reality by telling stories about his life and going through the photos she had saved. She wanted Angus to know his father as she did. Bringing him to life for Angus gave Serena some peace, but the fierce sense of loss and loneliness sometimes overcame her.

Serena smiled as she thought of the small house on the nearby reservation where she moved shortly after being married, where she raised Angus and where she still lived. Though living at the camp would have been more convenient, living in that little house helped keep that close sense of community she felt with her Mohawk neighbors. Angus grew up in the same place as his father. Serena could see more and more of his father in him the older he became. Shorter than most of his friends of the same age, he was stocky and muscular. Soccer was his favorite sport and by the time he was in high school, Angus was an outstanding soccer player. A brilliant student as well as a natural athlete, he excelled at every sport he tried and graduated at the top of his class. He kept growing long after his classmates had stopped. By the time he graduated, he was two hundred and twenty pounds of muscle and sinew on a six-foot frame.

                            *   *   *

Early in 1993, Kat and Peter Chum's daughter, Jessica, announced she was going to marry James Murdoch, a close friend of Angus and Michael from college. It was rather a shock to all friends and family. Serena had always assumed Angus and Jesse would end up together as close as they had been since childhood. Jessica met Jim while visiting Angus and Michael at Penn State. This introduction soon blossomed into romance, albeit a long distance one since Jessica was in school several hundred miles from Penn State. Jim claimed to have Native American ancestry, although it was Algonquin and not Mohawk. They joked about Algonquins being enemies of the Mohawks and often teased back and forth over this.

When he came home for a visit, Serena asked Angus about his interest in Jessica. A bit surprised, he laughed and answered, "Mom, we are like brother and sister. No man ever thinks about his sister romantically. Michael and I are both happy as clams for Jesse because we know Jim to be a really great friend. He'll make Jesse a fabulous husband."

His mother looked at him with a slight smile of concern. "Hmm! I feel a bit foolish for assuming what I did about you and Jesse. Maybe I don't know you as well as I thought I did." Her look brightened. "I'll have to get used to a new Angus since you've become so famous."

"Come on Mom! One little erroneous assumption can't erase a lifetime of experience. You can usually read me like a cheap novel and you know it," Angus chided.

As they walked through the inn, she wondered to herself, *Would the fame, wealth and popularity of a successful professional football career change him for the worse? Certainly not!*

She was silent as they headed for the stairs, remembering how Angus handled the popularity in high school and college. He kept his feet firmly on the ground and grew into a warm and friendly man. She suddenly began to wonder about other women in his life and laughed at herself for having these new thoughts about her son, thinking, *He probably just never met the right woman.*

Angus looked at his mom, a question defining his face. "What's so funny? You walk along in dead silence as though I'm not even here and then laugh out loud. Am I missing something?"

"I'm sorry! I was just laughing at myself for being a nosy mother. Because of my assumption, I never asked about the women in your life. Now, I can't recall you ever talking about a single one. Can that be true? I can't help being curious."

"I dated a few girls in college, but never really clicked with any of them. I had my hands too full with classes and football. Unfortunately, my professional life drew lots of women for all the wrong reasons. There is little chance to meet any that weren't filled with Angus Thomas the football player. They couldn't see who I actually was. I sometimes wish I would run into someone who never heard of me," he answered almost sadly.

"I never even dreamed of that kind of situation. See how untrue a picture an assumption can create? I can almost understand. Kat has been trying to match me up with a man for the last twenty years. She means well, but I've had absolutely no interest, even with a few quite decent gentlemen she found for me. Does that make you wonder about me?"

"You, Mom? Kat's been trying to fix you up?"

"You don't think I might be interested if the right man came along? With you a successful football professional and the younger people handling most of the work at the inn and camp, maybe the right man would do wonders for my life. I'm not that far over the hill as yet, young man."

"I didn't mean that. You're a very classy lady, but . . . you're my mom." Angus said almost in anguish as they reached the rooms they were using for the wedding.

Serena laughed. "I may be your Mom, but I'm still a woman, and maybe now is the time for me to consider a change in my life." She went quickly into her room to dress leaving him standing in the hall a bit stunned.

As she closed the door and headed for the shower, she remembered several men who had been attracted to her and seemed good prospects for marriage. Somehow, she just couldn't see that as part of her life at the time. "Maybe later," she told inquisitive friends.

As she dressed for Jessica's wedding, Serena looked at the youthful, attractive woman in her mid-forties peering back at her from the mirror. *Not bad for a hard-working hotel owner,* she thought. When she was ready, she called Angus and asked him to walk down with her.

As they headed toward the stairs, Angus looked at his mother in a new light. Besides being intelligent and accomplished, she was a striking woman who would attract many admiring glances with her long, jet black hair and dark eyes. *It will take quite a man to be her partner,* he thought with a smile.

6

A trip is what happens when one moves from one place to another.
It can be a pain, a bore or a joy, depending on the traveler.

Kat's words, "Here we are," snapped Serena's mind back to the immediate reality.

"Are we there already? I can't believe the trip to Watertown went so quickly."

Kat turned off the road and into the small parking lot by the terminal. "You've been so deep in thought, you were in another world for the whole trip. I was almost afraid to bring you out of it, but your plane is waiting and you'd better get stepping."

They parked the car and walked together into the small terminal, pulling Serena's suitcase along. As they walked up to the desk, a grizzled character appearing to be at least seventy walked up to them.

"You Serena Thomas?"

"Yes."

"I'm Warren Tusla, yer pilot. Ya ready to git?"

Warren noticed Serena and Kat exchanging worried glances. "Now ladies, I may not be a purty picture, and I've got quite a few miles on the old bod, but I'm still one o' the best jet jockeys around, and yer son Angus knows it. I used ta fly him and some of his teammates around back when he was playin' football. He called and asked fer me ta take special care of his mom. If that baby out there could make it, I'd fly ya clear ta Hawaii m'self, but it only fuels fer flights under a thousand miles. Yu'll only have my sterlin' company as far as Cincinnati."

Serena laughed. "If Angus says you're OK then you are definitely OK. I will admit I was a bit worried at first. Sorry about that."

"No need! I'd probably be a mite skeered m'self. Now let's get hoppin'. We got a jet ta ketch in Cinci."

Kat gave Serena a good-bye hug before she walked up the stairs and stepped into the neat interior of the small jet.

Serena turned and waved good-bye to Kat just before she stepped into the low-ceilinged cabin of the small jet. Warren followed closely behind and pointed to the large armchair-like seats in the plush cabin. "Grab one a them seats. They're all purty comfy. I fly some bigwigs around an' those birds like the best. There's magazines an' some books there in the rack an' some maps in that drawer, in case ya wanna see where ya are. Right there's the bar. There's everythin' there from pop and fruit juices ta the hard stuff. Coffee's on the end an' should be hot. Jest made it. I got some chores ta do, so make yerself ta home. I'll be back fer take off in a jiffy."

"Thank you! This is very posh. I think I will try a cup of your coffee."

"Help yerself," Warren said as he stepped out the door.

As she poured a cup of coffee and sat down she felt a little fear creep in. She had never flown in a small plane before, only the big commercial jets. *What's the matter with me?* she thought, *Mohawks aren't supposed to fear heights.* She laughed at herself as she thumbed through the magazines. After picking several to read during the flight, she sat down to await departure.

Ten minutes later Warren stepped into the cabin and closed the door. "Get yer seatbelt fastened and we'll be off. Ya want a slow gentle climb so's you'll hardly know yer goin' up or would ya like a sky-rocket ride? It's up ta you."

"What exactly is a skyrocket ride?"

"That's when I take off normal like, then, when we get enough power goin', I roll this baby back and go near straight up to cruisin' altitude. Yer boy Angus and his buddies always liked the thrill." Warren obviously enjoyed it himself.

"Is it dangerous?"

"Nah! I wouldn't do anythin' chancey. It's safe as bein' home in an easy chair only a lot more fun. Kinda like ridin' a big roller coaster straight up inta the sky."

Remembering the thrill she had felt riding a coaster many years ago she paused for just a moment. "Go for it! Let'r rip! I could use a little excitement, and it's been a long time since I've taken a thrill ride."

"Good fer you!" He turned to enter the pilot's seat. "If'n it gits too skeery fer ya, jest holler and I'll lower the nose. Wouldn't wanna have ol' thirty-five's mom mad at me."

After running the preflight checklist and firing up the jet engines, Warren checked with the tower for permission to take off. He taxied to the end of the runway, tested the engines at full power and waited for the final OK. When it was given, he released the brakes and started slowly down the runway. Serena felt herself pushed back in the seat as the plane accelerated to take off speed. She felt it lift smoothly from the runway and then heard the slight thud as the wheels retracted. For a few moments they climbed slowly.

"Here we go!" Warren said finally.

The plane was soon pointed nearly straight up and Serena felt herself being pressed firmly back in the seat. She looked out the window to see New York receding rapidly behind her. The horizon was an almost vertical line between green and blue. Surprised and thrilled, her heart pounding in her chest; she was excited, not frightened.

On the ground, Kat watched as the plane taxied out on the runway, turned and accelerated down the concrete, lifted into the air, flew off in a gentle climb, then suddenly turned its nose steeply toward the sky and finally disappeared from sight. She stood watching the now empty sky, wondering if there were any grounds to Serena's fears. She hadn't admitted it to Serena, but she sensed the tension and was a little worried herself. Serena had promised to call and let her know what she found out, so the answer would just have to wait.

When the jet finally leveled off at cruising altitude, Serena noticed the bright blue horizon returned to horizontal.

"That was certainly a thrill. I really enjoyed it."

"Yup! Yer Angus' mom fer real. I kinda thought ya might like that. Now you jest set back an relax. We'll be in Cinci in less than an hour."

Serena glanced through a magazine for a while, then turned to gaze out the window. Warren pointed out several sights as they flew over.

Finally they headed down into the Cincinnati airport landing pattern.

"We got a landin' spot an'll soon be there. Yu'll have a tidy trip from where they park us, so there'll be a limo waitin' ta take ya ta the Delta terminal."

"My, such service."

"Nothin' too good fer Angus' mom. Ol' thirty-five wants ya taken keer of special. I'm seein' ta that."

As soon as the jet landed and parked after taxiing for what seemed like forever, a black limousine pulled alongside.

"There's yer ride, jest like I told ya."

As they stepped out of the plane Warren said, "Ya tell that boy o' yours I said 'Hi.' Haven't seen him in a long time and I miss bussin' him around. He's a good 'un, a regular Joe. I'll bet ye're proud of 'im."

"I certainly am." Serena rather liked this crusty old character. After he handed her suitcase to the limo driver and turned to say good-bye, Serena gave him a big hug.

"Thanks for an enjoyable trip and for good company," she said smiling. "I'll tell Angus he did good."

The limo driver placed her bag in the trunk, turned and opened the door for her. He was a tall, young, handsome black man with a broad, friendly grin.

"I'm Jason, your chauffeur," he said politely.

She paused before turning to enter the limo. "Thank you, I'm Serena. How long have you been doing this? Driving limos, I mean. You look so young."

"Almost a year now." Jason held the door for her. "Don't worry. I've had thorough training to get my license."

After he moved into the driver's seat, Serena said, "I wasn't worried, just curious. Is this a good job?"

"Great job for me at least." They started moving toward the gate. "I'm a college student, and this job helps pay for my education."

"What are you going to do when you graduate?"

"I'm taking premed. If all goes well and I'm accepted into medical school, I hope to be a surgeon some day. It's a real challenge, but things look good so far. I'll graduate in a year and a half."

"That's a splendid profession. I wish you luck in your plans. I know it isn't easy to get into med school, so stick to it."

They pulled up to the Delta terminal and stepped out of the limo.

"Thanks for the encouragement," Jason said as he took her bag out of the trunk, pulled out the handle and extended the wheels. "Do you want some help with your bag?"

"No, I can easily handle it from here. It's not very big."

"Have a good trip," he said as she turned and headed for the terminal.

"And good luck on your schooling."

Serena knew she had plenty of time as she headed for the Delta counter. After getting her ticket and checking her bag, she headed for the security check through, placing her large purse on the belt of the X-ray unit. Everything OK, she walked to the boarding gate and took a seat near the window where she watched the planes moving in and out until boarding time.

"Serena Thomas! Come to the check-in counter," the PA system blared. Serena went up to the counter and identified herself.

"We've your seat assignment and a special package for you," replied the pleasant voice of the tall, fiftyish man behind the counter as he handed her the package. "I couldn't help noticing the name *Angus Thomas* on the package. Would that be the famous running back?"

"Yes, he's my son. He arranged for me to go all the way to Hawaii to see him."

The man smiled and nodded approvingly. "I'm a great fan of his. I saw him in action many times here in Cinci. He was one of the best."

She smiled pleasantly, took the boarding pass from his hand and picked up the package. "Thank you. I'm quite proud of him."

"Well you should be. We'll announce boarding shortly. You may go on board at any time after the announcement. The flight attendant will show you to your seat."

Before she could open the small package, the boarding announcement came over the PA. She picked up her purse and the package and headed for the gate. She could wait to open the package until after she was seated.

The flight attendant in the cabin greeted her as she entered the plane. "Welcome to Delta Flight 763. You are Mrs. Thomas, correct?"

Serena smiled in affirmation.

"Come this way." She ushered Serena to her seat and took her coat. "Can I get you anything, coffee or maybe some juice?"

"Some orange juice would be nice."

When the flight attendant moved off to fill her request, Serena made herself comfortable and then opened the small package. She found a book about Hawaii, some photo postcards, a map of the Big Island and a sticky note in Angus' handwriting attached to a photo showing the observatories atop Mauna Kea. He had circled one with a felt marker.

The note read: "Hi Mom. I'm so glad you're coming. I arranged a seat for you on the left side of the plane. As you come in to land, you may be able to see the observatories depending on the wind and the flight path. The one circled on the picture is Gemini. The book is for your enjoyment on the flight. I thought you might want to read about the place you're visiting. I'll be waiting at the airport when you land."

Serena smiled at the thoughtfulness of her son. *He didn't turn out so bad*, she thought to herself proudly. She glanced through the book until they were ready for takeoff noting the Hawaii in the title referred to the Big Island where she was headed. She placed it in the seat pocket and planned to read it carefully later on during the flight.

The Delta flight took her first to Salt Lake, then on to San Francisco where she changed to another plane for the flight to Hawaii. It was a pleasant if uneventful trip to the coast. Several of the flight crew stopped by to chat, saying nice things about Angus and wondering what he was doing now. They were surprised when she explained he had become an astronomer.

One male attendant remarked, "It doesn't surprise me at all. I knew he was a class act after I watched one of his interviews on TV. I remember thinking he was not only a great running back, but had a keen mind to boot. Wasn't he a scholastic All-American at Penn State?"

Smiling, Serena confirmed his question. It was rewarding hearing these comments about Angus from total strangers. Even now, out of the limelight for several years, he was still well remembered.

*   *   *

Sometime after the flight headed over the ocean toward Hawaii, a tall, friendly uniformed man stopped to see her.

"So you're Angus Thomas' mom. I'm your pilot, Captain Johnson. Just call me Hojo. Enjoying your trip?"

"I certainly am. Everyone has been so helpful and cheerful. They all seem to know who I am. At least who's mom I am."

"Yes, the word gets around among the crews. You don't mind, do you, everyone talking to you I mean?" He seemed concerned.

"Certainly not! I like talking to friendly people. Besides, what mother wouldn't want to hear such nice things said about her own boy?"

Captain Johnson sighed. "That's good. We try hard to please our passengers and not bother them. I met your son once at Texas Stadium when he was playing against the Cowboys. I had taken my two older boys to the game and they wanted to meet him. I've a friend, a sports reporter, who said he would try to get us in to meet Angus. Sure enough, after a wait, your son came over and shook hands with Rusty and Dan. He stood and talked to us for at least twenty minutes. The boys were in seventh heaven. I was seriously impressed that he took time to visit with us. The jerseys Angus gave them are their most prized possessions to this day. They hang on the wall of their rooms at home."

"That's certainly a heart-warming story for a mother to hear about her son. I can tell you're proud of your boys too. You surely must enjoy them a great deal. Thanks for sharing."

"Yep. I'm quite proud of them and of their little brother, Mike, too."

Captain Johnson excused himself and moved off. Serena had a warm feeling and thought to herself, *Most people are decent and friendly. It's those few stinkers who can make life so miserable for so many around them and all out of proportion to their numbers.*

Arrival in Hawaii

As the instructions for landing at Kailua were announced, Serena took the photo of the observatories and looked out the window. She could see the mountain clearly, but they were too far away to see the observatories. Noticing what looked like tiny white dots near the summit, she supposed they were the observatories but couldn't be sure. As they descended toward landing, she noted the stark, brownish, rock-strewn terrain stretching out beneath the plane. This was not the verdant, lush land she expected.

As the plane taxied toward the gate, Serena noticed a lot more greenery than she saw during the landing. *That's more like it,* she thought as she gazed at the terminal. When she left the walkway, she spotted Angus and Lani waiting hand-in-hand among the crowd. *She certainly is beautiful,* she thought, seeing Lani standing beside her son holding several leis in her hand. *Kat must have been right.*

Angus grabbed Serena in his arms, picked her off the ground in a hug and kissed her several times while Lani stood by smiling. As soon as he put her down, he turned and introduced the two. "This is Lani Namahoe, Mom. She's become an important lady in my life."

The two women locked eyes in silence for a long moment, trying to search into each other's souls.

Lani finally broke the silence. "I'm so happy to meet you at last. I've heard so many marvelous things about you from Angus." As she finished, she placed the leis around Serena's neck with the traditional Hawaiian greeting kiss.

"Well, I'm certainly glad to meet you, but that stinker hasn't told me a thing about you. Thanks to my cousin Kat, I rather expected to meet someone. I take it you are more than just casual friends?" She looked at Angus disdainfully.

"Mom, I wanted to surprise you. That's why I wanted you to come out for a visit, to meet Lani. She's already beaten me up for not telling you about us, so don't you start in."

Serena smiled at her son. "Well, good for her! I'm beginning to like your lady already." She laughed, turning to Lani. "He can be a handful. I hope you know what you're getting into. Looks to me like you just might be able to keep him in line though."

"Come on now," Angus pleaded as they turned to walk to the luggage carousel. "Don't gang up on me already. I don't stand a chance against you two together."

Serena knew immediately she liked this Hawaiian lady. She was seldom wrong on her first assessments of people. As they walked through the terminal, picked up her bag and headed for the car, chatting, she could see the two were in love. She knew her son had never before been as taken with any woman.

"How did all this happen? Where'd you meet? How long has this been going on? What are your plans?"

"Wait a minute, Mom. Not all at once," Angus interrupted with a laugh as he opened the car door. "We can tell you the whole story during the trip to Hilo. It'll take about two hours to get there, so we'll have lots of time to talk. You are the two most important people in my life, and I'm sure the trip will help you get to know each other."

Serena grinned, exuding excitement. "I'm just so . . . I can't believe it. I'm acting just like an impatient child. It's not every day you get to meet a new woman in your only son's life. I'm allowed to be excited. I'll have to call Kat as soon as I can to tell her she was right."

Angus turned and looked at his mom. "What was Kat right about?"

"About you wanting me to meet your new wahine. During the drive to Watertown she bet me that was why you invited me out here. She was right on that for sure."

Angus and Lani looked at each other in pained, silent communication, their thoughts in lockstep over the painful part of the reason for her trip. During the drive, they shared much, laughed often and even shed a few tears while becoming acquainted. By the time they rolled up to Angus' apartment, the two women were becoming good friends. Serena learned they were to visit Lani's parents over the coming weekend. By the time they reached Hilo, she decided her son had been lucky to find such a gracious and lovely woman.

As they entered the newly decorated apartment, Serena looked around. "It's very nice, Son, I can see you had someone decorate it for you." She looked at Lani with a knowing smile. "If he had done it himself, it would look like a cheap motel room. Angus has many good points, but decorating a place to live in is certainly not one of them."

Lani laughed. "That's exactly how it looked three days ago. There are still a few items coming, including the drapes which won't be installed until next Monday."

Angus beamed at Lani. "All this is the courtesy of 'Lani Namahoe Decorating.' She found everything and put it all together since last Sunday. I think she's amazing."

After a short tour, Serena said, "You two relax for a while. I'd like to unpack, freshen up and get out of these travel clothes into something more comfortable. I didn't bring much in the way of clothes. I thought I'd look for some new things more suited to the locale after I arrived. Lani, do you suppose you could tell me where I might find a good place to shop?"

"Better yet, I'd love to take you shopping. There are several places quite nearby where we can get you into some Hawaiian fashions. We can do it tomorrow afternoon, if my cruel boss will grant me a little time off, that is."

As soon as Serena closed the door to her room, Lani cornered Angus. "Your mom's a sharp lady. She'll soon figure out something else is up. When do we tell her?"

"I'd like to wait till we relax for the weekend. That will provide lots of time to talk about it after we tell her."

"You may be right. That's only a few days."

"We can sit down right here before we leave to visit your folks and tell her about the ghost. Then we'll be able to talk about it while we drive. The relaxed atmosphere of the weekend at your folks' will be helpful."

"That makes sense. I just don't know how many times I can handle the trauma of telling this to someone new. It's like reliving that first painful realization over and over."

*   *   *

All day Thursday, Angus worked on preparations for making the six-month repeat of precise measurement of the location and path of the ghost. With the earth at the farthest orbital position from the original measurements, new observations would provide the most accurate parallax determination of the position and distance to the ghost. He planned to take measurements and images at several different wavelengths from the infrared into the near ultraviolet. This would maximize the usefulness of the data and provide an excellent base for later measurements. He hoped these measurements would provide a more accurate prediction of the path of the wild star. He prayed this path would be far enough from the sun that there would be no gravitational disruption of the planets. The accuracy of his previous measurements projected a path for the star to pass as far as three light years from the center of the solar system. It still troubled him that the center of that range of probabilities placed the most likely path inside Jupiter's orbit.

To be certain to take measurements at the best time, Angus reserved his place on the telescope work schedule some time ago, hoping for clear skies and good seeing. While Angus prepared for the six-month observations, Lani was organizing and digitizing significant photos and spectrograph printouts.

Lani suddenly realized they worked right through the lunch hour. "Look at the time. I've got to get out of here to pick up your mom for shopping. How about dinner at that little Thai restaurant you like so much, say about 7:30?"

"Sounds OK to me. I don't know if Hilo is prepared for the two of you on a shopping spree. Just don't spend all my money."

"Should we stop by to pick you up here or at your apartment?"

"I'll meet you there at the restaurant. I could use the exercise a bike ride would give me. Then I'll have a big appetite for that great food."

"Suit yourself. Just watch out for those little grey cars."

By the end of the day, he finished setting up his computer to direct the aiming of the telescope and make the measurements and photos. He also made the necessary changes in his own spectrograph program to make a complete series of recordings of the ghost's spectrum throughout the widest possible range. Among other things, this would be crucial in determining the exact speed of the star. The determined speed would, in turn, be used in the more accurate calculation of its path. When everything was buttoned up, he left for his dinner date.

*   *   *

Friday morning about ten, Officer Hiakawa called as Angus was putting the finishing touches on his preparations. "I've several bits of information you should have," he said as soon as Angus answered. "First of all, Conrad informed me Dick Rumley is to be returned to our custody next week. I still can't tell you much about that. Things have changed little since our last conversation. Conrad did tell me he is bringing me a complete dossier on Rumley from their records, and I should find it quite interesting. I have no idea what it means, but I will let you know if anything comes up I can share with you."

"Thanks, I appreciate that." Then he chuckled. "He's been gone so long, I had almost forgotten about him."

Hiakawa sounded doubtful. "I'll bet. You know you'll be spending some time in court when we finally get him there. Think you can handle your anger OK?"

"Yes, fortunately, I do. Actually, I don't feel any anger toward him at all. He's such a pathetic character, I feel rather sorry for him. I've met a few evil people during my life and have found them to be thoroughly unhappy, miserable wretches stumbling through life with one eye cast over their shoulder. Even those with money and fame walk in constant fear of being stabbed in the back."

"You are certainly right on the money. I see a lot of those kinds of people in my line of work, a whole lot more than any decent person does. Very few people share your insight. Most just want to get even. They forget that's our job."

"You're right. Those animal instincts are quite strong. Sometimes the injured become even worse in their efforts at retaliation."

"I'll share one more bit of information with you. Please tell me anything that comes to mind as a result. I just received a rather curious visit from a Lieutenant Coffey and his aide from Pearl Harbor. He's a Naval Intelligence officer. I'm guessing he's attached to the Navy's radio frequency monitoring operation. That's a hush-hush operation that listens in on all kinds of transmissions all over the world. It's definitely a low profile, high secrecy group that we're not supposed to know exists. I have no confirmed knowledge, just rumors. Still, I'm quite sure that's where he's from. Anyway, Coffey asked me for any and all information I had about you and your work. He was not a friendly kind of person, all business and no smiles, you know the kind."

"Yes, I do. Did he say why he wanted the information?"

"No, he just handed me an official document. I couldn't argue with that. They took our complete file on you and Rumley saying it would be returned in a week or two. When I objected, asking what I was to do with our investigation without the records, he replied simply: 'Wait!' He said almost nothing else, acting as if what we wanted didn't matter at all. His aide searched through our files while we stood there watching. As soon as they had all they wanted, they left without another word. He never said I couldn't let you know. I'm sure you'll receive a visit soon, so be prepared. He could walk in your door at any time. Those boys frequently treat local cops like dirt. It's my first contact ever with the type and it wasn't a pleasant experience. I wonder if they do that deliberately to intimidate or if it's just the nature of the beast."

Angus was quite curious. "I wonder what it's all about? I'm drawing a complete blank on that one. Why on earth would Naval Intelligence be interested at all in my work?"

"I haven't a clue. Unless there's something important you haven't explained that has national defense ramifications. Those boys just don't get involved unless it's serious and bears on national defense. Are you sure you're not involved in anything in that arena? If so, they will probably work you over hard. They definitely play hardball."

"Honestly, there is nothing, no answer I know about that even remotely fits your question. I wonder if Rumley cooked up some story that triggered all this? That would take some stretch, even for the likes of him. I truly have no idea what it's all about." Angus remained at a total loss for an answer.

After he finished his conversation and hung up the phone, he sat for a moment staring into space wondering what this new development was about. Suddenly, he realized they could soon be at Gemini asking for his records. Angus jumped to his feet and headed for his computer.

At first he thought to erase all of his records, but that would only make it appear he was hiding something. *It would be better to change the records and leave intact the form of the data*, he thought as he sat down to work. Since the only startling thing about his information was the speed and path of the ghost, Angus decided to change that information. After some thought, he decided the simplest way would be to merely move the decimal point two places to the left in one component of the speed calculations and results. A common mathematical slip, this would show a speed of 0.9 percent of the speed of light or about 1,700 miles per second. While still a phenomenal speed for any stellar object, it would place its passing at about thirty thousand years in the future and a long way from the sun. It would take an expert, studying the spectra in detail, to discover the deception. Any time he needed to know a correct number, he could simply move the decimal point back to the correct position.

When Lani came in, he quickly explained what was going on and asked her to remove from the files all photos showing the ghost. They would conceal them somewhere as soon as possible. There were a number of data files in the computer which showed the incriminating spectral comparisons and results in great detail. These could not easily be altered and most certainly not be destroyed. By the time Lani had removed the photos and wrapped them in a package it was nearly noon. They would use their lunch hour to decide what else to do. With luck, Naval Intelligence would not show up in their absence before the spectral comparisons could be removed from the computer. They were too large to be stored on the available removable media, so another solution would have to be found.

They drove to a computer store where Angus selected an advanced laptop computer. It was powerful enough to run the calculations they would need while remaining isolated from his desktop system and the network. It had an advanced, large-capacity floppy drive which would allow them to download the spectral comparisons to removable media. The salesman helped them find software and cables to transfer data from their desktop to the laptop. They picked up a carrying case with room for a number of files in addition to pockets for the accessories.

Angus placed the package of photos in the file section of the case and turned to the salesman. "May I have a plain box for this?"

Lani looked at Angus and laughed when the man went to get a box. "That's clever. We can carry it around and no one will suspect what's inside."

"Exactly."

As soon as the man returned and placed the computer in the box, they left.

"This secret agent stuff is kinda fun," Lani said as they headed for her car. "It's too bad that it's so deadly serious."

"I don't know as I'd call it fun, but it is challenging. I only hope we can get those files transferred before Uncle shows up. I'd hate to be caught in the act."

"Do you have any idea what this Naval Intelligence guy is after?"

"Not a single clue. I've gone over everything I could think of and could find nothing they might even be remotely interested in. It's a complete mystery to me."

"I suspect Dick Rumley as the root cause. I still don't see what he could possibly have told them to cause such an uproar. Why do you suppose Hiakawa warned you? I, also, wonder why they didn't show up at Gemini at the same time. It seems to me they left a gaping loophole by not doing so."

"Maybe they had Hiakawa call to spook me and see what I'd do. I wonder if they are following us right now and know we picked up that laptop? I'm not used to all this intrigue. Maybe they're the ones who Dick Rumley is working for. They could have been responsible for the cameras and surveillance, but why on earth would they do so? What would they be looking for? It boggles the mind of this Injun."

"It is confusing. It's hard to know what to think. When we get back, drop me at the door. Then park my car and come up the back way. If your office door is closed or if I'm standing in it, you'll know someone is in your office and not to come in with the laptop."

"Good idea. If I get the signal, I can put the box right behind Karen's desk near the door. Then we may be able to pick it up on our way out. Sounds like a plan."

As Lani walked through the outer office toward Angus' office, she noticed everything seemed normal. She opened his office door fully expecting to find people waiting, but the office was empty. She looked intensely around the room for any signs of change since they left and found none. She gazed suspiciously at the place where the camera had been hidden. *Was another one there*, she wondered? She sat down at Angus' computer and waited. She turned as she heard Angus talking to someone outside the office door. When she saw it was Jack Mercer asking Angus about his new schedule for using the telescope, she heaved a sigh of relief. *So far, so good.* Given a little more time, they would have everything secured as planned. The tension during the time until all was in order would be great.

As soon as Angus shut the door, he took the laptop out and set it up next to his workstation.

"I've never seen you so nervous," Lani remarked as Angus struggled to get the cables connected and the power plugged in. "You're all thumbs. Would you like some help?"

"If you'll make the connection to the workstation, I can finish with this." They hurriedly attached all the necessary cables. "Now, let's turn everything on and see how quickly we can download those files."

It took more than two hours to complete the transfer of files and programs to the new laptop. They were both on pins and needles during the entire process. When it was complete and the data files were backed up on the new removable media, they finally relaxed.

"That's done. Now all I have to do is wipe the workstation disk clean of anything that references the actual speed of the ghost," Angus sighed. "That will only take about a half hour or so. If we can get the laptop out of here before they show up, we'll be home free. Then maybe we can relax a bit."

"Yes, that would be nice. Do you realize how tense we have been ever since we found out about the path of that star? It's been one crisis after another. I hope we can return to some sense of normalcy soon. We've a great deal of rather intense work to do in the next few months."

*   *   *

They finished the day uneventfully, loaded the laptop in Lani's car and headed to Angus' apartment to pick up Serena. As planned, they sat down in Angus' living room and told her the devastating news. Angus explained what they knew about the ghost and the possible dangers it threatened to the entire earth. They explained the entire situation and how they were trying to find the best way to make public the horrible news. Serena was thoughtfully quiet as she digested the terrifying information.

She looked back and forth between the two of them. Her eyes filled with tears. "How sad for lovers to have to face such a terrible thing and to be faced with such awesome responsibility. What a monstrous load to bear in secret. You have shared it haven't you?"

"With my parents and with our pastor," Lani said softly. "That's all. They were very comforting, but we're all in the same boat."

Serena was speechless, her eyes wet and glassy with overwhelming emotion. She stood up and motioned for them to stand with her. She put her arms around them both and the three stood there hugging in silence. When they slowly parted, Serena sat down and gazed into space for a long time as Lani and Angus sat silently, each in deeply troubled thought.

Finally, her voice returned, husky with emotion. "We've got to get in touch with Chelton. If anyone could help find the best way to deal with this, it would be Chelton."

Serena turned to Lani to explain. "Chelton Chum is my cousin Kat's youngest. He's a truly remarkable person, a sort of combination minister, emotional healer and mystic with some unusual talents. He came into this world with a twisted body and a very different view of life. The Mohawks called him *Otsista Okaara*, or 'Star Eyes' in English, for the way he looked at you when he spoke. When he was thirteen, his legs were operated on and straightened so he could walk without crutches and ride his bicycle. He struggled through high school, gaining steam and finishing well enough to get into college where he majored in psychology. By the time he was twenty-four he was an ordained minister working with the disabled in Albany, New York. The Governor of New York found out about his work and appointed him to the State Board of Mental Health. Before long he was using his powers of persuasion to advance the cause of mental health and of the disabled in the state. From there he went to UNICEF where he has become a real force for the children of the world. I can't even remember all the humanitarian awards he has been given."

"He has an almost mystical way with people," Angus added. "I've seen him take over when an organization was being destroyed by internal strife and turn the angry mob back into a friendly, cooperative group. He actually did that with the State Board of Mental Health in New York. Those politicians were at each other's throats when he joined them. Within about three weeks they had become a focused, productive organization. He's a marvel."

"Sounds like a truly exceptional person," Lani said as Serena and Angus finished their comments.

Serena's face brightened. "Why don't we get in touch with him and find out if he would be able to come here? Considering the situation and the few that know about this, it seems best to bring him here if at all possible."

Angus stood up and stretched. "It's far too late to reach him now. I can call his apartment tomorrow. If he's not in, I'll leave a message on his answering machine. Now then, we'd better get started for your folks'. We can continue our conversation on the way."

During the drive they discussed the details of the discovery and their concerns facing them. By the time they arrived at Lani's folks', their emotions were calmed considerably.

As they pulled into the parking lot next to the Namahoes', they noticed several cars including those belonging to Pilau and Leinaala already there. "What's this? Is the tribe gathering for another party?" asked Angus.

They stepped out of the car and headed for the house. As she stepped on the porch, Lani sensed something was wrong. It was too quiet. "They must all be here to welcome Serena."

Her sister, Leinaala, met Lani at the door with tears streaming down her face. "Oh, Lani, it's Daddy. He fell off of a building he was working on." She threw her arms around Lani, held her tightly for a moment, then leaned her head back and looked directly at Lani while still holding her. There was a look of near panic on her face. "They rushed him by helicopter to the trauma center in Hilo less than half an hour ago. We have no idea how badly he's been hurt, but he fell about twenty feet into a stack of roofing material. We were waiting for you and for someone to watch the children while we're gone. Pilau's trying to find someone right now."

Serena immediately volunteered, "I'll take care of the children for you. You just head out as soon as you can."

"Oh, thank you!" Lani said, "You're such a dear. Are you sure you'll be all right? There are five of them, and they can be a chore."

Angus turned to Lani reassuringly. "Mom's handled a whole tribe of little Mohawks at times. I'm sure your gang couldn't be any more of a challenge than they were."

Turning to her sister, Lani asked, "Did you call Pastor Ruth? She'll want to know."

"Mom called her some time ago. She'll be at the hospital as soon as she can make it."

After hurried introductions and a few instructions for Serena, they all headed for Hilo in the cars of Lani and Pilau. Angus' cell phone would be their link until they arrived at the trauma center. It would prove to be a long and quiet ride. During the trip they checked by phone to find out his condition but learned very little. Angus even tried to talk to Dr. Lane, who took care of him a few months earlier, but he was not on duty. By the time they arrived, it was a little past eight, just three hours after Angus, Lani and Serena left Hilo. They were ushered into the waiting room and seated together.

The attendant looked at Charlene and pointed to the phone on the table. "That phone is a direct line to the emergency room where your husband is being treated. He is still unconscious, but don't worry. He will stay on full support until he is stabilized and the extent of his injuries can be determined. If there are any serious or dangerous changes in his condition, you will be called immediately from the emergency room."

Seven somber faces sat watching the phone.

A half hour after they sat down the phone rang. Charlene snatched it up immediately. "Charlene Namahoe."

"Are you the patient's wife?"

"Yes."

"I'm John Ho, one of the trauma nurses. Your husband is now conscious, Mrs. Namahoe. He's a little groggy, but quite coherent. He came around just a few moments ago, so I thought I'd call you with the good news. He's still strapped tightly to keep him immobilized until we can x-ray his spine thoroughly. Since he's conscious, we'll be able to run some tests to determine if there is any nerve damage. Falls like his usually break some bones and the spine is always of concern, but the only thing we know is broken, so far, is his right collarbone. We'll know a lot more when we complete the scan of his spine and X rays of his hip joints and pelvis. We know he can move his fingers, and right now they're testing to see if he can feel his toes. If so, that rules out the worst possibilities. So far, the news is good."

"When can I see him?"

"Not until they've finished with the scans and X rays. Actually, that's good news. If he were in critical danger, they would let you be with him, just in case. I'll let you come back just as soon as I can, so stay by that phone."

A thin hint of relief fought for control of Charlene's face as she hung up and relayed the information to the family. All agreed, under the circumstances, it probably was good news. At least he was out of mortal danger.

With this information Angus ferreted out a phone and called Serena. She was glad to hear Ali's condition was better than expected. "How are you getting along with the children?" he asked.

"I'm having a great time. They're teaching me Hawaiian, and I'm teaching them Mohawk. I have no idea who's winning, but we're all having fun in spite of the worries about their grandfather. He must be quite a man. The children certainly do treasure him and will be pleased to get the good news."

"I'll keep you posted on any important changes. I'm afraid it's going to be a long night."

"Why don't you let me call you? I have the number, and I know they'll page you. It will soon be time to put the children to bed, and the phone ringing might awaken them. I'll call at eleven. You should know more by then, and I could wake the children if it's necessary."

"That'll work! I can notify the desk I will be expecting a call at eleven. I'll be right there, waiting."

Pastor Ruth arrived to join the family and was given the latest information on Ali's condition while Angus was on the phone. Angus shared his conversation with the group when he returned. They began talking about the children and their grandfather. This led to discussions of their families and of families in general as the clock ticked on. Ruth led them in a prayer for Ali's recovery.

*   *   *

Shortly after ten, the phone rang. John Ho was again talking to Charlene. "We've moved him from the trauma room to a patient room, and we'd like to meet the family in a conference room nearby. After we've talked, you may go in to see him for a short visit. An aide will soon be down to take you to the conference room. Just wait where you are, please."

Charlene immediately relayed the message. Soon a gaunt, elderly man in a maroon jacket appeared and directed them to follow him. They rode the elevator up several floors to a small, nicely decorated room with half a dozen comfortable looking chairs and two couches. There was a small, round, table with four upright chairs at one end of the room. Shortly after they entered, a doctor came to give them the news.

"He's resting fairly comfortably now. We gave him a pain killer, so he's quite groggy." Sizing up the group, he directed his next comments to Charlene. "Your husband is either lucky or unlucky depending on how you look at it. He was unlucky to have received his injuries but lucky they were not a lot worse. He broke his right collarbone and several bones in his right hand and wrist. He probably used them in an attempt to protect himself as he landed. He also has three compression fractures in his lower spine, and the bottom of his right lung is partially collapsed. He has a number of bruises on both legs, his right side and right arm. We had to use eleven staples to close the laceration in his upper right arm, but it was a clean cut. It will look worse than it is for some time. Internal organs all seem to be OK, at least nothing major there in spite of the jolt they took. It's possible something could show up later, so we'll watch him for a few days to make sure. Apparently, he received no head injury. That is a real blessing because head injuries are the most common serious injury in falls of this type."

"That's great news," Charlene replied, looking much relieved. "Thank you so much. We had expected much worse. How long will he be here, and when can we see him?"

"He'll be here at least four days until we're sure there's nothing else wrong. He's going to be in a great deal of pain at first, but he'll need to keep moving about. He should take it easy for at least two weeks, except for walking to speed his recovery. We'll provide a regimen for him before he leaves, so you will know what needs to be done. You may go in now, Mrs. Namahoe, but the rest of you should only visit two at a time along with her. He won't be very aware and probably won't remember any of you being here. We'll be keeping him doped up until tomorrow and, of course, he'll be kept immobilized until we're certain about his spine and internal organs."

As Charlene entered the room, she noticed Ali was on what looked like an operating table rather than a bed. She could see the straps holding him in position in the formed padding beneath his legs, neck and head. There was a wide strap across his forehead to keep his head from moving. The nurse in the room explained that though the straps were not tight, they still held his neck and spine in a fixed position. As soon as all tests and x-rays were finished and read, they would remove the straps unless they found a problem in his spine. Charlene leaned over and saw his eyes were open as she kissed him.

"That you, honey?" Ali whispered as she bent close. "I sure am glad to see you."

"Don't try to talk now, and don't worry. The doctor gave us great news about you. The whole gang's out in the waiting room and they're all anxious to see you. I'll be right here beside you the rest of the night, so just relax and go to sleep."

"They've been pinching and tickling me all over ever since I woke up. What's that all about?"

"They're just making sure everything works after that nasty fall. Your back seems to be OK. They were testing your sense of feeling. So far, all the tests have turned up good results. Now you quit talking and go to sleep. I'll be right here."

Ali drifted in and out of sleep during the visits of Angus, Ruth and the rest of the family. It was apparent he was dazed, since he kept asking the same questions over and over. While Angus and Lani were there, John Ho came in and began removing the straps.

"We'll be moving him into a regular bed now. We received an OK to do so from the radiologist, who said his spine was sound except for the compression fractures and they posed no serious threat. He's going to be sore for a while but should recover fully. If you'll go back to the little waiting room again, we'll call you in about a half hour when he's ready."

As the three joined the others, Charlene announced, "I'm staying here with Ali. Why don't the rest of you head back? There's nothing more you can do, and he'll probably sleep until morning anyway."

Leinaala looked at her mother. "I'll stay to keep you company, Mom. Ron can pick up the kids and take them home."

Lani took her sister's arm. "Why don't you all head back. I don't have any kids to take care of, so I can stay here with Mom. Angus lives less than ten minutes away. He can go home and sleep when he wants to. You've all got enough to do with your kids and the trip back."

Charlene added, "That's all right. No one needs to stay. I'll be just fine here."

"Nonsense!" Lani said firmly. "I'm the one to stay, like I said, and I live near here anyway."

While the discussion continued, Angus received the call from his mom. "Ali's going to be OK. Nothing serious, just painful, so it's really good news." He reported.

"At least the reports are encouraging. I can stay right here. No need to run up to get me tonight. You stay put for now. We can work things out tomorrow."

After some discussion, Angus finally agreed, "Tomorrow will be soon enough to make plans. I'll see you then."

"It looks like Leinaala and I are both staying," Lani said to Angus as he rejoined the group. "If things get too tiring, we can run over to my place for a nap. We might even take turns. Ron says he can handle the kids, and tomorrow's Saturday anyway. So it's all decided. Everyone else will go as soon as they've said good-bye to Dad."

Charlene turned to Ruth. "Thanks so much for coming. You've been a great comfort, but why don't you head for home now so you can get some sleep. It looks like Ali's going to be OK after he heals. At least we know it's not life threatening."

"I'll be glad to stay if you need me."

"Don't worry, Ruth, we'll be all right now. I'll call you if things change."

"I'll just step in and say good-bye before I leave."

7

By 11:30, all but the three women staying said their good-byes and headed back home. Charlene took her vigil in a chair by Ali's bed and the two girls settled themselves in the small waiting room. Angus took Lani's car and headed for his apartment.

As soon as he opened the door, he froze. Something was not right. Nearly everything appeared to have been moved slightly. The magazines on the table were not the way he had left them. He always kept them in a neat stack precisely placed in the center of the end of the table. They were now stacked in a haphazard pile on the corner. The cushions on the couch had been moved and the door to his bedroom, which he always left open, was closed. He opened the door to his bedroom, turned on the light and stopped in the doorway. Everything from his desk and dresser was piled on the floor as if each drawer were taken out and dumped in turn. The mattress had been removed from the bed and was leaning against the window. All the new pictures Lani had so carefully hung were lying on the desk, upside down with their backs ripped open. Whoever had done it had been very thorough and methodical, piling everything almost neatly on the floor. Angus spun around, grabbed the phone and called Hiakawa's emergency beeper.

The phone soon announced Hiakawa's returning call. "Why the devil are you calling me this late on a Friday night?"

"My room's been ransacked sometime after 5:30 this evening. I thought maybe you'd like to know about it."

"Don't touch a thing. We'll be there in a few minutes. And yes, I'm glad you called me," he added quickly before hanging up.

Within ten minutes, there were two uniforms at his door. One of them was Joey Namahoe.

"Small world isn't it, Angus? This is my partner, Sam. When I heard your name on the radio, I said we'd take the call. We were close anyhow. Did you look to see if they're still here?"

"As a matter of fact, I didn't look in my office, guest room or bathroom. I called Hiakawa as soon as I saw my bedroom, and he said not to touch anything."

Both officers drew their guns and motioned Angus away from the three still-closed doors. One by one they paused by the door and quickly entered each room in turn prepared for action. They found only a pile of drawer contents in each room, exactly as in the first bedroom. Whoever did the search was gone. Noticing the women's things in the pile on the guest room floor, Joey looked quizzically at Angus.

"Those belong to my mother," Angus said quickly in explanation. "She's at the Namahoes' right now."

Joey laughed. "Just for a moment, I wondered about you. Women's clothing in the guest room? My first thought was you'd better have a good story for Lani."

"Speaking of Lani, right now she and Leinaala are at the trauma center with Charlene and Ali. You couldn't know. Ali took a nasty fall and was taken by helicopter to the trauma center. I just came from there myself. He was lucky to have survived the fall. Looks as if he's going to be OK though."

"No!" Joey gasped. "You say he's going to be OK? How'd it happen?"

"We don't know exactly. He apparently fell off the roof at a job site and into some construction materials on the ground. He suffered a few broken bones, bruises and a nasty cut on his arm. Nothing life threatening, though, and the doctor says he will recover completely."

"Well, that's good. Ali's a great guy. He's helped me out many times over the years. I'll have to get over to see him."

As Angus finished relating Ali's accident details and the doctor's report on his condition, Hiakawa walked in with another plain-clothes officer, fingerprint expert Max "The Dustman" Ryalls.

He turned to Joey. "Is everything clear and undisturbed?"

"By the book. No one here except Angus, and nothing's been moved. I did notice, whoever did it was quite neat about dumping the drawers on the floor." He turned to Angus. "Typically things are strewn everywhere, not piled neatly as they are here. Whoever did this was neat, thorough and didn't find what they were looking for."

"How do you know that Sherlock?" Hiakawa inquired of Joey.

"Elementary! Since everything has been dumped, they didn't find it or they would have stopped. There would be some drawers intact or some pictures not torn open. Since we found nothing undisturbed, voila! They didn't find it. How'm I doing?"

Hiakawa grinned at the young officer. "OK, Joey, you're probably right, unless they were not looking for a single object. Let's see what the dustman finds."

After about a half hour of brushing, Max stopped and looked at Hiakawa. "Gloves! They must have worn gloves because there are no fresh prints. I found several smudged prints that were disturbed by something like a cloth or gloved hand being pressed or drawn over an older print. We're not going to get an identity from any prints here. Whoever did this was professional and probably governmental."

Hiakawa looked puzzled. "Why do you think that? I mean, why do you think they could be governmental?"

"It stands to reason. I've never seen a criminal search scene where things were not thrown about willy-nilly. I've been involved with many police searches of similar scenes which weren't very neat. I've never viewed a search scene where the items were piled so carefully. I have heard that governmental searches are all very neat and methodical, so there you are."

Angus and Hiakawa exchanged knowing looks as they said almost in unison, "Navy!"

Angus continued to look at Hiakawa. "I wonder if this is Coffey's work."

Then he thought about the Op Center. It was a clear night and there would be a number of people at work, so he grabbed the phone and called. The night watchman, Kerry Anaaka, answered the phone.

After the first exchange of greetings and Angus' question, Kerry explained, "Yes, we had a great deal of excitement. Two men and a woman arrived at about eight with papers authorizing a search of your work area. They were disturbed when I insisted on getting an OK from Director Carroll first. He told me not to let them in until he called somebody in Washington to check the name on the papers they held. About ten minutes later he called back and said it was OK to let them in. They took three boxes of documents and your computer. They even wanted to take the network server, but Director Carroll had arrived before they got to that point, and he was very angry. He threatened to call everyone up to and including the president unless they left the server in place. One of them, the woman, seemed to know a lot about computers. After examining the server, she suggested they would only need to take the removable duplicate hard drive to have what they wanted. Director Carroll made them wait until Jack Mercer could get there to remove the mirror drive and replace it with another one. It was very tense while they were here. They didn't seem to be the kind to mess with. Are you in some kind of trouble?"

"Were they from the Navy?" Angus asked.

"No. The papers say 'United States Office of Strategic Intelligence.' I have the copy they gave me right here. What the devil's going on anyway? Director Carroll didn't seem to have any idea what it was about. I'm sure he'll be contacting you soon."

Angus glanced immediately at his answering machine. The blinking red light told him there were five messages waiting.

"I'm sure of that. I just walked in the door a few minutes ago, and I'm as much at a loss to know what's going on as John is. Thanks for the run-down."

As soon as he finished the call, he quickly relayed the new information to Hiakawa. "I didn't think this should be broadcast until you knew about it. On second thought, it'll probably be all over the Op Center by now, so it won't be any secret."

"You're right. It's definitely out in the open. The OSI you said? I wonder why they're in the act. Naval Intelligence is one thing. They're right here in Hawaii, but OSI? They're straight out of Washington. What on earth have you done to bring the OSI after you?"

Angus threw up his hands and then scratched his head in bewilderment. "I'm completely baffled by the whole scene. I only wish I had some clue. I suppose they'll be visiting me eventually. I'm curious, but not looking forward to that meeting with joyful anticipation. Let's see what's on my answering machine."

The first two and the last two calls were hang-ups with no message. The middle one was an obviously disturbed John Carroll asking Angus to call as soon as he got the message and at any hour.

Hiakawa started toward the door. "We have everything we need here, so we'll head out and let you do what you need to do. Call me with any new developments. I'd surely like to know where this is headed."

Joey was the last to leave, repeating his concern about Ali. "Tell the old *kane* I said hello and that I'll be in to see him."

Angus wasn't looking forward to his conversation with Director Carroll but decided he might as well get it over with. John answered the phone on the first ring and immediately recognized Angus' voice.

"What's going on?" John punctuated his question with uncharacteristic expletives, then continued, "I've called everyone I think might know anything about this and have drawn nothing but blanks. Fill me in, will you? Are you in some kind of trouble?"

"Honestly, John, I haven't the slightest idea what this is all about. The only thing I can imagine is that it has something to do with Dick Rumley. You know all about that situation. I've been informed he's about to be returned to the Hilo police, but why would they want my astronomical research data. I can't believe it holds any interest for the OSI. Honestly, I'm as much in the dark about this as you."

"Angus, if it weren't for your excellent past record, I'd be considering asking you to leave Gemini. We can't afford these disruptions. If there's anything at all I should know about, please tell me. I know your word is good. If there's a problem, maybe I can help."

By now suspicious of his phone line, Angus didn't want to even hint at anything. "I'm sure you remember that little place where you and I had lunch the day I first arrived. There's an adjoining bar that'll be open until at least one in the morning. Meet me there as soon as you can. I've got Lani's car and can be there in about fifteen minutes."

He hung up immediately without waiting for an answer, hoping John would understand. Actually, it was only a short distance away. Angus sneaked out the back way in the dark and walked there. If they were listening on the phone, maybe they would be busy concentrating on Lani's car and not see him leave. When he left, he didn't turn off any lights.

                          *   *   *

Angus walked through an alley to the next street and down to the
end of the block before chancing the sidewalk. He tried to appear
casual as he strode purposefully toward the bar turning several corners on the way and glancing back each time. No one seemed to be
following. When he got to the bar, it was crowded and noisy. Selecting a booth all the way in the back where it was private, he sat down,
ordered a drink and told the waitress he was expecting a white-haired
gentleman. In about ten minutes, John was shown back to where
Angus was sitting.

John was obviously upset as he sat down across from Angus. "What
the blazes have you gotten yourself into? When I called a friend in
Washington about those people and their demands, he told me to
give them complete cooperation. Even when I cooperated fully they
were not pleasant. From your quick hang-up, I gathered you didn't
want to say anything more over the phone."

"Actually, John, I told you all I know about this. Apparently, the
people who came to Gemini are the same ones who searched my
apartment. When I came home and found things dumped on the floor,
I called Pete Hiakawa of the Hilo police. There were two uniforms,
Hiakawa and one of his forensic guys there in short order. They were
quite sure the search was conducted by government types. It was
then I found the message you left on my machine and called you
right away."

"As I said over the phone, you can safely tell me anything. I have
a great deal of respect for your integrity, both professional and personal. I just must know what's going on at Gemini."

Angus was quite sure of John's excellent judgement but still was
reluctant to tell him about the ghost. So far, he had some control
over the dangerous information because of the few people who knew.
If he told John, he would probably lose that control. Still, what could
that possibly have to do with the OSI interest? Finally, he decided
to tell him.

"There is something I haven't told you, but it's purely astronomical and couldn't possibly have anything to do with OSI's interest. I'm
merely waiting until all the data are in and checked before releasing
the information to anyone. Besides, I didn't obtain the information

until after Dick Rumley was found out and his surveillance equipment was removed."

"You still think Rumley's at the bottom of all this?"

"He must be. I can see no other possible cause. The question is, what has he told those people? I can't imagine what he could have said to precipitate such an uproar."

"I'm sure you're leveling with me, but what is this you haven't told me?"

Angus decided to bite the bullet and tell John the whole story. A well respected and well thought-of man in the local and astronomical communities, John sat there thoughtfully as Angus related all he hadn't previously told him about the ghost. When Angus completed his story, John sat in quiet shock for a long time before speaking.

"I knew you were on to something exciting from what you told me before. I never dreamed it could be anything like this. In spite of the ethics problem, I agree the information shouldn't get to the public until the star's ultimate path is known. With thirty years to annihilation a possibility, we'd better be absolutely certain you're right before letting this cat out of the bag. Wow! How do you find the best way to make the information public when you do know? Those are certainly knotty questions.

"Angus, I think you've done all the right things so far. I couldn't agree with you more. I certainly don't like your news, but you can count on me to keep it confidential, at least until your confirming data comes in. From what you've told me, I can see no reason for OSI's interest either. You may be right about Rumley. The question is, how do we handle the information you have, and how do we keep OSI from messing up our whole operation. It will be hard for you to conduct the necessary research with them breathing down your back. We must be extremely cautious until we find out why they are so interested and what they are looking for."

Angus found himself quite relieved after sharing the ghost's drastic promise with John. He knew John would be a trusted member of the growing group of those sharing his terrible secret. As they talked, Angus told him about Lani and her father's accident.

"I can't say as I've noticed anything between you and Lani. You are both behaving quite professionally on the job. I hear a little of the office gossip, but nothing's come my way about the two of you as yet."

"We've both been sensitive about that, so I'm glad it's not out in the open. Apparently, we've kept everything on such a professional level here that no one has suspected anything else. We're both quite careful of what we say and how we act."

John looked sympathetically at Angus as a germ of an idea grew in his mind. "You've had quite a few traumatic experiences here in recent months haven't you? There was the bike accident, the ghost and now the OSI. How would you like to move your operation to Gemini South in Chile?"

A frown of incredulity contorted Angus' face. "Chile? You want me to move to Chile?"

"At least until we can get the situation here under control and have an idea how best to release the information about the ghost. Gemini South is getting past first light right now, and you could run your measurements from there as well as from here. Your work could be incorporated into our checkout operations. Cerro Pachon's a great deal more spartan than Hawaii, but I doubt that OSI would bother you there. We could even send you as part of our initial setup crew. We need a liaison person anyway, and Lani could fill that niche nicely. I believe we can handle it all quite well with a minimum of fuss."

"I don't know about Lani. With her dad in the hospital, I couldn't ask her to leave now."

"She wouldn't have to go for several weeks. You wouldn't need her until those next readings are due anyway. By the way, just when are those readings due?"

"That's it. We scheduled the time on the telescope for June 11 and 12, six months after our first measurements were taken. There's no way we can possibly be ready for that in Chile. That's only three weeks from now."

"So much for that plan. We can still ship you and your stuff off to Chile, but we'll have to do your measurements here. When did you set up your schedule with Jack?"

"Just last Wednesday. Why?"

"Lani is a qualified observer isn't she?"

"I see what you're getting at. Unfortunately, she doesn't know the operation of the new spectrograph program I've written." Angus thought for a while. "You know what? I could use my laptop to set it up for her. All she'd have to do is load the program. I bet it'll fly."

"Good! I can have Jack change the telescope reservation records from your name to Lani's and no one will be the wiser. I think we're getting somewhere. Once we have the fiber optic link in operation, we'll have a secure channel for communications when we link the two telescopes electronically. I'll get in touch with Jack tomorrow. I'd like to have everything in place before Monday. Somehow, I think OSI is going to catch up with you by then."

"If they're watching my apartment, as I'm sure they are, why didn't they come up and get me after Hiakawa left?" Angus answered his own question. "They probably want to confront me in my office. I'll bet they're there when I show up Monday."

"I doubt OSI knows about Lani, you and she, I mean. As far as they are concerned, she's probably just another Gemini employee. If she continues as she has, doing her thing quietly and efficiently, they might ignore her. She's still listed in the employees' roster as an unassigned rover because someone hasn't kept those records current. I'll see to it those records stay that way for now."

"That's a bit of good luck we can use. I'd better get back to my apartment. Why don't you drop me off a couple of blocks away? Then I can sneak back in the way I got out and they'll think I never left. I certainly appreciate your acceptance of what I've done. I wasn't sure it was the best thing to do, but now I'm glad you know. I don't feel quite so underhanded about it as I did before."

Angus dropped payment and tip on the table when they got up and left quietly. Once they were outside, John became very talkative. "I'd like to meet the rest of our inner circle of those *in the know* soon. We may have to wait until this OSI thing calms down, and that could take some time. By the way, why don't you call me about twenty minutes after you get back to your apartment? I'll be home by then and you can apologize for missing our meeting. I can be indignant at being stood up. If they're listening, they'll think you never left."

"Good idea! I'll do just that. We had better be patient. We can get together when this OSI thing dies down. For the time being, I don't think we should discuss any of this on the phone. I've got a lot of bases to cover with Ali in the hospital and Mom forty miles south at the Namahoes'. Tomorrow and Sunday will be very busy days. I hope things come together by Monday. Here! Just drop me off right here."

John stopped the car where Angus indicated, said good-bye and drove away. Angus retraced his steps through the alley and into his apartment after checking carefully for any observers. It was nearly two when he called John who acted angry. He apologized, but John wouldn't let him off the hook. He sounded so convincing Angus even felt guilty. He laughed out loud after he hung up the phone and then thought, *What if my apartment is bugged? I'd better be careful even talking to myself.*

After making a quick but unsuccessful search for a bug, Angus decided to go over to the trauma center to see how the girls were doing. He turned the lights out in his apartment, went down to the main entrance and whistled as he walked to Lani's car. He watched his rear view mirror carefully to see if anyone followed. Sure enough, soon after he started down the street, a pair of lights flashed in his mirror and a car followed about a city block back. He turned right at the first cross street and then left at a main thoroughfare. The car followed his turns at a respectable distance. As he passed an all night filling station on the left side of the street, he made a U-turn just past it and pulled up to the pumps. He watched out of the corner of his eye as the dark, four door sedan drove past the filling station and turned right at the first crossroad. He could see there were two people in the car who both looked his way as they passed. He was definitely being followed. He filled the car with gas and stepped inside to pay.

The two young men behind the counter were discussing the shift change. One was leaving to go home as Angus came in.

"Are you heading home? I couldn't help but hear your conversation."

"What's it to you?" The young man who was leaving asked in a surly tone.

"I don't mean to interfere, but I could use some help and there's a hundred bucks in it for you."

The young man's demeanor changed immediately. "We get a lot of strange people in here late at night, so we're kinda suspicious. For a hundred bucks, I'll do almost anything legal."

"What I'd like you to do is drive my car back to my apartment and park it in the garage in stall 219. It's only about four blocks, and I'll give you directions. Just stick the keys in the ashtray, leave it unlocked and walk back here. I'll be gone by the time you're back. Then you can go home a hundred bucks richer. Oh yes, walk out the back of the garage away from the apartment and down the alley to the next street. You can probably do the whole thing and be back in ten minutes."

"I don't know, mister. How do I know the car isn't stolen or even worse?"

Angus took out his driver's license and showed it to the young man. "Look! You can see by the picture that it's my license and there's the address and my apartment number."

Noticing the name, the young man's eyes grew wide. "You Angus Thomas, the famous running back?" As Angus shook his head, he grabbed his hand and shook it. "I'm pleased to meet you, Mr. Thomas. I used to watch you on TV when I was in high school. You were one of my favorites. Wow! Buddy, this is Angus Thomas, the football player," he announced to his coworker.

After some animated conversation with the two young men, the deal was struck. Angus called a cab from the pay phone and asked to be picked up across the street from the station at the bus stop. He watched carefully as the dark sedan pulled back out of the side street in pursuit of Lani's car. They stayed some distance back, the two occupants' eyes glued on Lani's car as they passed the station. Maybe, they would not be close enough to see who got out of the car.

In about twenty minutes the cab arrived and took him to the hospital. He headed straight for the small waiting room where he found Lani and Leinaala sound asleep on the two couches. After just a moment of indecision he shook Lani softly and woke her. Holding his finger to his mouth to indicate silence, he motioned her to follow him. He didn't want to waken Leinaala. "We've got to talk. Let's go to the main waiting room. There's no one there and we can have some privacy."

As they started walking, Lani looked at him. "What's happened now?"

"It's a long and complicated story, so we need to find a place to sit and discuss some things. How's your dad doing? Have you gotten any more news?"

"Haven't heard a word. I walked in to see how they were doing around one and they were both sound asleep. I went out without disturbing them and slept until you woke me."

On the way to the waiting room, Angus gave her a brief synopsis of what had happened since he left. As soon as they found a quiet corner, they sat down facing each other in a pair of chairs on either side of a corner table. Angus related the entire happenings in as much detail as he could remember. Lani had many questions as Angus told her what had transpired, including John's idea about Chile. They talked for more than an hour and a half.

Finally, Lani sat back and slowly shook her head, deep concern for all the unknowns in the future controlled her expression. "Wow! My head is spinning. I haven't the foggiest idea how to proceed at this point. Well, I sort of *know* what's going to happen, but there is so much up in the air. Where do we start? We'll have to have most of it in place by the time we arrive at the Op Center on Monday morning."

"One thing we must do is to keep our relationship purely professional for the time being. We've done a good job so far. John is quite certain there are no rumors about us at work. If at all possible, we must keep you out of this OSI thing. With John's help I think we can do that OK. Right now we've got to get my mother back to my apartment and your car back in your hands without arousing suspicions. My trackers surely think I'm now back at my apartment sound asleep, if that kid got away without being seen."

"Why don't you go back to your apartment before it gets light and try to get some sleep? I'll call you between nine and ten to ask about retrieving my car. I can mention I loaned it to you to take your mother to visit friends. You can thank me for lending it to you and ask if I can drop you off at the car rental office where you have reserved a car. I'll agree to do so and ask if your mother arrived safely at her friend's house."

"All right, OK, OK. I get the picture, but what about my mother at your folks' house? They'll surely follow me there in the rental car. We've got to find another place for me to pick her up."

Lani's eyes grew wide. "I know just the place. It's perfect. I'll call Pastor Ruth and ask her to come over and pick up Serena. She could easily be the friend Serena came to visit. I know Ruth would be glad to help. She's one of the conspirators too, remember? I have to call and tell her the latest about my dad anyway."

Angus smiled. "Great idea! We've taken care of your car and my mom. Now what?"

Lani clasped her face in her hands, elbows resting on knees and returned a questioning shrug, Angus continued wondering and thinking aloud. "We can't make any more specific plans until I hear from OSI. What if they don't show up on Monday? I can make a row about my records and computer, but with whom? If they don't show up, I won't know what to do. I suppose I could call somebody official to complain, but the ball is definitely in their court. I will say one thing, good fortune prompted us to get that laptop and download those files when we did. We'll have to keep that in a safe place until this blows over or until I leave for Chile."

"It's safe at my place, at least for now. That is unless OSI gets suspicious of me. Maybe we can find a safer place."

"We'll have to give that some thought. Right now I haven't a clue."

She dropped her hands in her lap and set up straight. "Can the hard drive be removed from that laptop? If so, it would be a lot easier to hide. My cousin Joey's little brother Sandy is a real computer whiz. He works all kind of magic for a software consulting firm in Hilo. If anyone could help us with the laptop, Sandy could. He wasn't at the Luau, so you've never met him."

"Let's get hold of him and find out how best to deal with this laptop." Angus scratched his head in the instinctive expression of mental wheels spinning. "Why don't I pick up another laptop, identical to the one I have? I can pay cash for it and give another name if asked. That way, even if they find out about the first one and take it, we'll still be OK. I can download my files to the new one and no one will be the wiser."

Lani leaned forward and looked hard at the table for a moment, her brow furrowed by intense thought. She sighed and looked again at Angus. "It's hard to believe how paranoid we have become since this all started. Our lives seem to be getting more complicated every time we turn around. Now we're talking about fleeing the country to another part of the world. Do you realize I've only been off this island a few times in my entire life? And those times I just traveled to other nearby islands, Oahu and Maui. If we do this thing, it will be a real stretch for me, Mr. World-traveler."

Angus took one of her hands in both of his, trying to reassure her. "You've really had a lot come down on you lately, hon. All the cloak-and-dagger and your dad hurt as well. I know it hasn't been easy, but we've another bigger challenge facing us a few years down the pike that makes our other problems seem minor in comparison. Maybe

Monday this whole OSI thing will be solved and we can get back to the bigger problem. I'm sure we won't have to wait long for it to come to a head. Then we can get on with our lives."

Lani patted Angus' hands with her free hand. "I suppose you're right. At least I hope so." She paused for a moment, silent, looking once more at the table. Withdrawing her hands, she sat erect, a look of determination and decision on her face. "OK, let's get on with it. A couple of questions come to mind. If you pay cash for that computer, won't the cash transaction, your withdrawal, show up on your bank account? Won't that look suspicious?"

"No problem! I picked up a rather bad habit when I was playing football. I began keeping a rather large sum of cash around, some inside my belt, the rest in a number of hiding places. The guys did it for a number of reasons. I did because I often went to auctions to pick up art for my mom's Mohawk Inn. Cash always worked and some of those paintings were pretty salty." Angus patted a very fat section of his belt. "I've got five grand tucked inside my belt right now."

Lani's face registered a look of amazement. "I can't believe you're carrying that much cash. I'd be scared to death."

"You get used to it. That money's been there for at least two years. Do you suppose if we gave him the cash, your cousin Sandy could buy the laptop computer for us? I'm afraid OSI would follow me if I did it."

"I'm sure he'd help us out. I'll call him later in the morning. Incidentally, how are you and I to communicate? With your phones probably tapped at home and at the office, it will be extremely difficult. They probably placed a bug in your office as well. We know you are being followed, so personal meetings are out of the question. Once you return to your apartment, we're cut off."

"We both know that, but for now, they are probably quite sure we don't know it. We can use that fact to our advantage by deliberately planting misinformation in my office and during phone calls. If we do it carefully, we can find out positively if the phone's tapped." Angus grinned as he finished his comment. It had become a game with him, a game he intended to win.

"Let's have a communication plan in place by the time you pick me up in my car. You don't suppose they've bugged my car do you?"

Angus sat back and shook his head. "I certainly wouldn't put it past them. For all I know, they may think it's my car. Incidentally, whenever we aren't completely certain we're not being overheard, we should talk in *protected mode*. You know, speak as though we know someone is listening."

"That's a thought. I can't believe all this intrigue. I suppose we'd best get on with it. Why don't you head for your apartment and we'll put our plan into effect? I'll call you between nine and ten as I said and we can take it from there."

"One more thing, call and reserve a car for me. If I do it over my phone, they may know where we're going and could conceivably bug the car I'll be driving. Use the rental car company Gemini uses. Aren't they just outside the University Park Complex?"

"I know exactly. I reserved cars for people there several times while working at the Op Center. I've got your credit card, remember? They'll have the car ready to go by the time we get there."

"Sounds like a plan," Angus joked. "I'll call a cab for my trip home. Tell Ali I hope he's better and that I'm sorry we can't visit. In the morning you can fill them all in on what's going on."

They stood near the door talking until the cab appeared. After they kissed good-bye, Lani watched regretfully as the cab drove off.

*   *   *

Angus directed the cab to drop him off a block away on the next street from his apartment. Again, he walked down the alley and into the apartment by the back door. He noticed Lani's car was in his garage parking space. When he entered his room, he moved slowly and silently so no noise would be heard by any bugs that might be there. He crossed the living room and stood carefully near the window and peered out at the street. The dark sedan was still parked on the other side of the street, somewhat away from and facing his apartment. It was too dark for him to see if there were anyone inside, but he was quite sure there was.

He then crept into his bedroom, dodging the pile on the floor and crawled silently onto the bed. As soon as he was on the bed he moved about noisily finally getting up and heading for the bathroom making loud, normal noises. After flushing the john and turning out the light, he headed back for the bed where he flopped down and then became quiet. It was after three, but as busy as his mind was, he went off rapidly to sleep, fully clothed.

The nerve jangling ringing of his phone startled him awake after what seemed like a very short time. As he opened his eyes and reached for the phone, he noticed it was bright daylight. A quick glance at his watch told him it was ten o'clock. That would probably be Lani. He picked up the phone with a sleepy hello.

"Did I wake you, Dr. Thomas? This is Lani. I'm just calling to arrange to get my car back."

"That's quite all right, Lani. It's been a long night with much excitement. I should have been up a long time ago."

"What kind of excitement, Dr. Thomas? Were you out on the town?"

"No! It's nothing like that, just a little mess I've got to clean up now before my mom comes back. I want to thank you again for lending me your car on such short notice. When my mom wanted to visit her friend and I couldn't get a rental car in time, you were a real jewel to step in and let me use yours. I can be over there in about half an hour. Do you suppose you could drop me off to pick up my rental car? It's not far from your place and it would save me some time."

"I'll be glad to drop you off, only I'm not at my apartment. I'm at the hospital trauma center. My father was injured yesterday afternoon, and we've been here with him all night."

"I'm so sorry. Is it serious? How is he doing?"

"Yes, it's serious, but not life threatening. He has several bruises, cuts and broken bones, but the doctors expect full recovery. We were all relieved when the doctor gave us his latest report just a few minutes ago. He's now sitting up and talking with us. Last night he was so doped, he was hardly coherent."

"Are you sure you can leave? I can call a cab you know."

"I've been here since early last evening and would like to get away for a while anyway. My mom and sister are here, too, and the rest of the family should be here any moment, so he's well cared for."

"OK! As you wish. I know where you are. Remember? I was there myself a few months back. I should be there in about forty minutes."

"I'll be out front waiting for you. Bye."

As he hung up the phone, he thought to himself, *She's sharp. No one would think they were anything but coworkers.* He took a shower, got dressed and started to pick up some of the pile on his bedroom floor, then dropped them. *I might as well wait until later. Better get going.*

Walking to the garage, he looked for the dark sedan, but it was nowhere in sight. He looked again as he exited the garage into the street. The only vehicle parked there was a construction van in front of the next apartment building. *Is that another surveillance vehicle?* He wondered. As he headed up the street, he watched the van in the mirror until it was out of sight. Maybe they were no longer following him.

When he reached the trauma center, Lani was standing near the door. As soon as he stopped, she walked around the car to the driver's side. Suddenly it dawned on him that she was going to drive. When he got out, she pointed to the rear of the car. As they both stood behind the car looking at the trunk, she said softly, "Don't look up, but there was a dark sedan with two men inside that drove by the door several times while I was waiting for you. Could be the guys who were following you last night. They've been parked for at least ten minutes just back from the corner on that side street to the east of us. I'll drive by when we leave and you can check them out. Now get in the car and follow my lead."

"I'm sorry," Lani said in a normal voice as they got back into the car. "It must have been the way the light struck the trunk. I could have sworn there was a new dent there. I didn't mean to accuse you of anything."

"That's quite all right. No offense taken. If I did do any damage, I would gladly pay to have it repaired. That's only right."

As Lani drove past the intersection, Angus stole a sideways glance at the car. It certainly looked like the one he saw last night. He watched as they drove away and sure enough, the car pulled out of the side street and followed them at a discrete distance. He pointed behind them and silently mouthed, "Yes."

They headed to the car rental engaged in small talk. Angus asked Lani how long she had worked there and what her goals were. She asked him if he really had been a football star and, if so, why had he become an astronomer. All in all it was a good performance. As she drove toward their goal, she turned several times, taking a zigzag path to their destination. The dark sedan had dogged her every turn and pulled to the curb a block away.

Angus looked at Lani and winked as she parked. "Do you always take the long way?"

"I thought you might like the scenic route," Lani quipped in reply.

After stepping out of the car Angus turned and leaned back into the door. "Have you had anything to eat yet? The least I could do would be to buy you breakfast. There's a nice place about a mile east of here. Why don't you follow me there?"

Lani at first said no and then agreed after a little persuasion. *Another stellar performance for possible listeners,* she thought.

His car ready and the papers filled out, it was only a moment before Angus pulled out in a small bright green coupe. He honked and waved as he went by and headed east with Lani and the sedan in pursuit. They parked together in the restaurant parking lot facing the front windows, went inside and took a table right by that same window so they could watch the car. Angus did not want a bug or tracking device attached to this car if he could help it.

Lani pulled her chair up to the table, leaned in toward Angus and spoke softly. "Do you suppose we can talk safely now?"

Angus followed her lead to keep their conversation quiet. "I'm sure of it. At least until those guys come in for breakfast, too."

"Are you kidding? Do you suppose they would do that?"

"I have no idea, but one thing's for sure. They knew where I was going when I left my apartment, so my phone must be bugged. They probably did that while they were searching. I'll bet there's a bug on the phone in my office too. They may come in, so let's get our plans into action before they do. What have you found out?"

Lani looked intently at Angus as she explained, "First of all, Sandy is on his way to our house to get the original laptop. You remember we left it there before leaving for the trauma center. He's going to remove that hard drive and switch it with the new one. Then even the serial numbers will match, just in case they check. He's going to pick up an additional hard drive and duplicate your first one for a backup. If we lose the second laptop, we'll still have all the data intact. He told me about a bunch of other technical stuff I didn't understand. It means you will have a method of absolutely secure transmission of data to anyone who has the key and code. That key is a device for what's called a 'spread spectrum radio transmission encoder.' There's a little card that goes in the computer and does all the magic. The code is a set of numbers and letters that you must enter into the computer whenever you send or receive a transmission. Sandy says the code changes according to a pattern which you must memorize, but that the memorization is easy. He'll explain it to you when you two meet. The resulting code is sent, via the Internet, in complex frequency patterns that virtually defy detection. To anyone seeking to intercept your transmission, it looks just like common background noise and would be ignored. In the unlikely event someone did find it, the encoded pattern is so huge it is impossible to break. Provide the key and the code pattern to anyone with whom you want to communicate and presto, absolutely secure transmission."

"How's he going to do all that in such a short time? I'll need to get him the money for the laptop as well."

Lani smiled smugly. "No problem. With his job, he buys lots of computers and components all the time. They know he'll pay them. You can get the money to him at any time."

The waitress interrupted with water, coffee and menus. They placed their orders quickly and the waitress whisked away.

"OK, genius, how are we going to handle the rest of the problems between today and tomorrow?" Angus asked as soon as the waitress left.

Lani raised her chin in an attitude of feigned superiority. "Very carefully. I've arranged for Pastor Ruth to pick up your mother and the computer stuff around noon. Sandy should have it all there by then. The new laptop containing the hard drive with all your records, the backup hard drive and the papers we secured will go with Ruth as well. She will keep them until we need them. When you go to get your mom, you can pick up the original laptop, case and standard set of programs from the new hard drive. I'm assuming you will do that sometime this afternoon or evening. Everyone's been briefed on what's happening, so unless there's a slip up of some sort, it'll all go down without a hitch."

"Where will Ruth hide the laptop? She has such a tiny house. Suppose they search there."

Lani displayed that superior look again. "All taken care of, thank you. It's nice to know one's efforts are appreciated. How about this? We're going to hide your computer right out in the open. Ruth has a desktop computer she uses for writing and keeping her records. She'll use your laptop instead of the desktop. Plug in the monitor, keyboard and mouse and she will appear to have a professional workstation. No one would ever expect that to be anything but her own. She has tons of papers, manuscripts, sermons and letters as well as a huge collection of books. They're all in a bookcase that covers an entire wall in her living room. Believe me. Your papers would never be found hidden in that bookcase. I think it's perfect."

"I hope this doesn't get anyone in trouble. We're dealing with a department of the U.S. government. I'll bet they can get quite rough if they want to. Maybe we can find out what OSI wants and get them off our backs on Monday. I've had about all the cloak-and-dagger I can stand already."

Taking a fat envelope from his pocket, Angus slid it carefully across the table to Lani. "Here! Take this and put it in your purse. You can reimburse Sandy with it and keep the rest for emergencies. You'll find thirty-five one hundred dollar bills and what looks like two packs of cigarettes. Each cigarette is a paper tube with two one hundred dollar bills rolled tightly inside. It's a little trick I learned from some of my football buddies. You can carry them in your purse for emergencies and no one will know. Just don't try to smoke one."

She looked at Angus in astonishment. "Angus, that's almost twelve thousand dollars. I'd be terrified carrying that much money."

"Just act as if they're cigarettes. You'll soon get used to it, only never open one in front of another person. Open the pack from the top. The bills look just like some fancy filter on the top end, so you can safely leave the partial pack in your purse. There's a little trick to opening each tube. Hold it tightly in your fingers and twist it firmly. Usually the paper pops right apart and the bills can then be opened. I've done it inside my pocket and come out with two loose, but some-what curled up bills. You can fake digging deep into your purse as you pop one of the tubes. That's one way. Otherwise, go where you can be alone, a restroom for instance. Whatever you do, don't let anyone know what those cigarettes really are."

"But why so much money? After I pay Sandy, I'll still have more than eight thousand dollars," she asked, pleading.

"Just consider it insurance. Don't ever use it unless you must. You may find times when it's very comforting to know you have cash handy, even if you never have to use it."

As Angus finished talking, he noticed two men walking slowly toward the door. As they passed his rental car, one man bent over as if he dropped something right in front of the car. He was sure the man had placed a tracking beacon on his car, probably a magnetic one. They came inside, sat at the counter and ordered coffee. Angus and Lani changed to small talk while they ate the breakfast that mercifully appeared just as the men sat down.

The two men finished their coffee, left and drove off. By the time they were gone, Lani and Angus finished eating. They made arrangements to meet at Pastor Ruth's when Angus came to pick up his mom.

When they stepped outside, Angus got down on his hands and knees and looked under the front of his car. He pulled a small box off the front cross member of the frame. It was slightly larger than a quarter and had an antenna about two inches long at one end. Showing it to Lani he said with a chuckle, "I'm going to send the OSI men on a merry goose chase." He leaned over to the car parked next to him and placed the beacon in the same position, under the front end. Just to make sure, he looked under Lani's car and came out with another one.

"They'll soon know you found those beacons, won't they? Then they'll know we're onto them. Is that such a good idea?"

"Maybe you're right." Angus juggled the beacon in his hand as he thought about it. "I know! There is a rough stretch of road just south of town where they're doing some construction work. Remember?" When Lani shook her head yes, he continued. "When you head back to your folks', drop this in the road as you go over that rough spot. They will think it was jarred off by a bad jolt."

Leaning over, he retrieved the one he had placed on the neighboring car and put it back on his. "I'll take the car back to the rental place and ask for another on some pretense. Should they check at the rental agency, the records will show I didn't like the first car."

"Brilliant! Those clowns will find that Serena's boy is not one to be messing with. They still may not know we're onto them."

"I don't know. They'll probably be suspicious, but at least they won't know for sure."

"I've got to get back to the hospital soon. The boys should be back by now, and Mom will be ready to head home for a shower and some fresh clothes. She may stay with me for the time my dad's in the hospital, though she hasn't decided for sure yet. I'll probably be seeing you between one and two at Ruth's if all goes as planned. Your mother can call you on your cell phone should anything change."

"Good idea. They are probably monitoring that as well, but a call from Mom would be normal. I haven't had to deal with so much subterfuge since my football days. We did all kinds of weird things to confuse and mystify our opponents with our new plays. We went to great lengths to keep them from learning about them. Coach had a shredder in his office, and any written copy of a play had to be fed through that shredder. We even went so far as to make up fake plays that looked like real ones and slip paper copies into the regular waste-basket. We knew there were those that would search our trash, so we accommodated them. One of the guys even sold a fake play to a gull-ible spy for five hundred bucks. We had a big laugh over that one."

Noticing Lani's anxious appearance, he said apologetically, "You've got to get going and here I am rambling on. Remind me to tell you later what happened to that play." After a good-bye hug and kiss they headed off in different directions.

Angus exchanged the car for another slightly larger one and re-turned to his apartment, carefully parking in a guest space. He spent the next few hours picking up the mess, repairing the pictures and packing a few things in a small suitcase. Startled at the sudden gnaw-ing clamor of his phone, he jumped to pick it up but then decided not to. He knew the answering machine would identify the caller without revealing his presence. It was Joey Namahoe leaving a brief message asking him to get in touch as soon as possible and leaving his beeper number. *I wonder what that's about?* he said to himself. Remembering Joey was to stop and see Ali today, he decided to try to catch him there.

Repeated glances in his rear view mirror on the way to the hospi-tal told Angus there was no one following him. He parked near the emergency entrance and went in.

Pilau was surprised to see him. "Lani left a long time ago and Charlene went with her."

"I was sure of that. Would you do me a big favor? I'm going to call Joey's beeper and leave the number here and your name. When he calls in, tell him he should get over here ASAP, only don't mention my name. He should understand."

"Sure, Chief! Any chance you can let me in on what's going on? Lani gave me a quick run down before she left but didn't have time to provide much detail."

"Just as soon as you make that beeper call."

Within a few minutes of the call, the responding call came through for Pilau.

Pilau reported to Angus, "Joey sounded puzzled at first but then said he'd be right over. Fill me in while we're waiting, OK?"

"Gladly, but first, how's Ali doing?"

"That tough old bird's doing just fine. We had him walking around the halls outside his room a little while ago. The doctor wants him to walk as much as he feels comfortable doing. Says it should help his recovery. His arm is bound up to keep his broken collarbone in place and his hand is in a cast, but otherwise he looks fairly good."

While waiting for Joey, Angus told Pilau as much as he knew about what was going on. "I still don't have any idea why OSI is involved. It makes no sense to me whatsoever."

"It's a real mystery. From what you've told me and Lani's rough explanation, I'd say you're handling things quite well. That sister of mine is one very sharp cookie, but I guess that's no surprise to you."

A breathless Joey flew in the front door and spotted Angus and Pilau almost immediately. "Man! There's a hornet's nest buzzing down at the station. There were three federal agents asking for . . . no . . . demanding all of the records on you and Dick Rumley. My guess is they're the ones who worked over your apartment. Would you please tell me what's going on? I couldn't get a thing out of Hiakawa. Then my brother Sandy said he was doing some computer stuff for you but I'd have to talk to you to find out what it was."

Angus gave him a quick rundown and explained his suspicion of Dick Rumley. Joey agreed it was a lot of supposition with few facts. He chuckled at the treatment of the beacons. "Incidentally, I'm sure Hiakawa will be getting in touch with you. I know he's been asked to keep this completely confidential by OSI. He's bound to want his own slant and will continue to investigate unless ordered to stop. In spite of being rankled by them meddling in his domain, he will comply with their orders."

Pilau looked at Joey. "Won't they give you the same orders?"

"Nah! They won't bother with a lowly uniform. My guess is Hiakawa won't say anything to me either although he'll think about it. He'll leave the door open for a little information to flow through me. I won't hear about anything sensitive though. He's got Angus pegged as a straight shooter, and he treats people like that quite well.

Still, I wanted to get to you with this before they had a chance to muzzle me."

"If you want, I'll try to keep you posted on what's happening," Angus said to Joey.

"Maybe you shouldn't do that. If they questioned me for any reason, I'd have to answer truthfully. Why don't you let me ask Lani what I may need to know? As far as I can tell, not even Hiakawa knows about you two. I'm sure not going to tell them."

"Good idea!" said Pilau.

Angus tensed visibly, preparing to leave. "I'd best get on my way. I'm to pick up my mother in about an hour, so unless you two have more questions I'm outa here. Oh yes, give Ali my best wishes and that I wanted to visit but ran out of time."

Pilau patted Angus on the back. "I'll do that. He'll understand. You must know he thinks a great deal of you, don't you?"

"And the feeling's mutual. Tell him I promise to stop back. Now, I've got to go."

He left Pilau and Joey still talking and headed out the emergency exit to his car. As he headed south toward Pastor Ruth's, Angus began thinking through all that had happened during the last few days. He thought about Chile, Lani and her family, the ghost, OSI, Dick Rumley and what the next few weeks might bring. It was a mind-boggling mess of incomplete information and contradictions. He would try to sort it out during his drive. His orderly mind demanded he have a plan in place before Monday.

*   *   *

After kissing a much-improved Ali good-bye, Lani and Charlene headed for home. As they walked, Lani cautioned her mother. "Mom, there may be a bug in the car, so please be careful what you say."

"I know it's necessary, but I feel ridiculous with this play acting. I suppose we can talk about the family and of Ali's accident."

As she went through the construction, Lani dropped the tracking beacon out the window remarking, "I hope they finish this road work soon. I get my teeth jarred every time we go through here."

"It certainly is bumpy."

"You know, Mom, I love my job at Gemini. This new astronomer, Dr. Thomas, is quite pleasant to work with."

They had a hard time not laughing at that comment and couldn't look at each other for several moments. As they pulled up to the house, Serena and Sandy were standing on the porch, talking.

"How's your man doing?" Serena asked as they walked onto the porch.

"Really quite well, considering. He was sitting up, joking with my son when we left. I'm comfortable leaving him for a while now. He certainly has improved since yesterday evening."

Serena followed them into the house. "That's good to hear. I was quite concerned. Thanks for your call telling me he was out of serious danger. Though we've never met, I think of him as a friend."

Once inside, they all sat down in the living room to bring everyone up-to-date. After just a few moments of conversation, Charlene excused herself.

"If I don't get a shower soon, no one will want to be in the same room with me." She turned to Serena as she stood up to head for her bedroom. "When I come back, the two of us must sit down and get acquainted. We've already been through a lot."

While Charlene took her shower, Sandy went through the two laptops with Lani and Serena. He marked one with a large sticky label "DATA" and left the other unmarked. He turned over the one with the label and pointed to a tiny letter "D" engraved on the bottom. This would enable them to be identified after the label was removed. He handed Lani a tiny packet containing the spare hard drive and demonstrated its removal and reinstallation. Finally, he explained the function of the SSR network transceiver and showed her how to use the wireless network.

As soon as Sandy finished his explanation and demonstration on the laptop, Lani said coyly, "That's a lot for a simple little Hawaiian girl to understand."

"Hah! You bet," was Sandy's disdainful reply.

Serena looked at Lani and Sandy in turn. "Well, it's quite a bit for this Mohawk to digest. I use a computer at the inn, but the technical part is way beyond me. I'm glad you're the one who's going to use all this magic."

Later, Charlene emerged, freshly dressed in white blouse and pink slacks. "I feel like a new woman."

Lani, who was helping Sandy make sure all the computer equipment was in order, looked up. "I can hardly wait to do the same thing."

"Do you have any more questions?" Sandy asked.

"I think you've covered everything. Now let's get this financial thing settled."

After a few minutes, Sandy left, payment in hand. Serena and Charlene sat down to finally get to know each other while Lani took her shower and dressed. When Pastor Ruth arrived, they enjoyed a light lunch before getting into Ruth's car for the short trip to her house.

Ruth turned to Lani as they started. "Tell me what you can of this new mystery. I know there may be some details you can't share, just give me a rough idea what's been happening."

"Actually, Ruth, there's nothing we know of we can't share with you. We haven't a clue why the government is involved, only hints of a sketchy theory involving Dick Rumley. You remember. He's the one Angus had the run-in with."

"Yes, I do, but what could that have to do with all this intrigue?"

Lani reviewed the happenings of the last day and their ideas about it. When they arrived at Ruth's, Lani set up the laptop for her use and installed the programs according to Sandy's instructions. When she was finished, Ruth tried out the new system. As soon as she tried her own programs and found they worked well, she was satisfied. The three women then sat down to wait for Angus.

*   *   *

It was shortly after four when Angus arrived. He gave Serena and Lani hugs and kisses before sitting down at Ruth's desk.

He surveyed the desk carefully, touching the laptop. "Is this mine?"

Lani smiled. "Yes, the one with all the data. It's been set up as Ruth's word processor, but you can access all your data and programs as well. We've already hidden the spare disk and the papers in her book case and I'll bet even you can't find them."

"What about my data?"

"I downloaded all your data to three of those high capacity floppy disks. They're right there in that tray with Ruth's disks. They're the ones marked A, B and C. We can leave them there until we decide what to do. We're probably at a standstill until at least Monday, aren't we?"

"Pro-bob-ly!" Angus said emphatically, as he deserted the laptop, walked slowly over and sat next to Lani, his face beaming approval. "I've got to hand it to you. You did a great job setting all this up. I don't know how we could have done half as much without your cousin Sandy as well. And Ruth, how good it is to have your help in all this. I only hope it doesn't get anyone into trouble."

Ruth finally sat down. "My goodness, Angus, what are ministers for if they can't help their flock? I'm pleased to be of help in any way I can. If your data is correct, we're all in a whole lot more trouble than some little incident with the government anyway."

"Yes, I suppose you're right there. Our troubles look small considering the bigger picture. Now, I want to let you in on my plans for the rest of the weekend. I thought it might be a good idea to disappear for a while, so I'm taking my mother on a grand tour of the island. My rented car seems secure for the moment, so we'll take that and head over to the volcano. First, we'll tour volcano park and then drive to Kailua to spend the night. There's a great hotel there right on the beach. In the morning we'll drive south along the Kona coast and then back north to stop by the *Keck* headquarters facility in Kamuela. We can end up the day with a tour of the observatories on top of *Mauna Kea*. We'll take in the tourist attractions en route, and if OSI should follow us, they'll have a merry goose chase. We should be back at my apartment before dark and then I can plan Monday if no unforeseen events get in the way. What do you say, Mom?"

"I say, go for it. Sounds like a great idea."

"We might as well enjoy ourselves. There's nothing we can do until Monday, when it may all hit the fan. Can you think of anything we've missed, Lani?"

"Not a thing."

Angus rose to go. "Well then. Let's do it."

He took Serena's luggage from Ruth's car and put it in his trunk. He spent a rather long, private good-bye with Lani before getting in the car with Serena and heading out. Shortly after they had gone, Ruth left to take Lani home.

*   *   *

Angus and Serena inspected the harsh wonders of stark craters and steaming holes in the ground at Volcanos National Park before heading for Kailua. After checking into the hotel, they had dinner and took a walk by the ocean. The waves breaking on shore were spectacular. They took off their shoes and walked barefoot along the sandy beach, the wet sand crunching between their toes. Mother and son walked hand-in-hand and talked for more than an hour in the solitude of the beach to the rhythmic, reassuring soft sound of gently crashing waves. They gently reaffirmed their bond when together they stopped, kneeled on the beach and prayed for deliverance from the impending menace before turning in for the night.

Taking to the road after breakfast, they followed the coast south, sometimes between green walls of tropical foliage with flashes of yellow as native birds flitted through the branches and sometimes past barren, rock-strewn lava fields. After the usual tourist stops at macadamia nut groves and coffee plantations, Angus turned about and headed north. Lunch at Kamuela was their next destination. This was the home of the headquarters of the Keck twin multi mirror telescopes. Stopping at the headquarters, he made himself known to the Keck people, and he and Serena were given a tour. It was larger than the Gemini Op Center, but Angus felt right at home. They headed up the mountain so Serena could see the Gemini telescope before dark. Out in the chilly air, the two gazed at the spectacular panorama of the Big Island lying below them. Finally, the sun dropped below the horizon darkening the eastern slope of the Mauna Kea for the trip down.

Entering the outskirts of Hilo, Angus suggested, "Let's stop for a cup of coffee. We won't be able to talk freely when we get to the apartment, so we better get all our serious conversation over before we get there. I hope we can have a good night's sleep. Tomorrow's apt to be a bear."

"I could use a little coffee about now anyway."

They stopped at a little restaurant standing alone on a corner. There they spent the better part of an hour and a half getting their stories straight just in case they happened to be asked questions later.

"This is almost as exciting as some of those ball games you were in. I just hope nothing bad happens. Except for that chance, it's kinda fun."

"I hope so too. I just wish I knew what it's all about. It's driving me crazy not knowing. I hope tomorrow brings some revelations.

Let's bite the bullet and head for home. I have an idea our friends will be waiting for us."

As they pulled up and parked the car in Angus' spot, he asked his mom if she had any Scotch tape. She said, "No. What do you want with Scotch tape anyway?"

"I want to put some on the car door so I'll know if our friends have bugged it."

"Why not take a little piece of paper and close the door on it. Then tear off the exposed part. If anyone opens the door it will fall out and you'll know when you next open the door."

"Terrific! That'll fly! I knew you were a genius. Just didn't know what kind."

After setting the paper trap, they picked up their luggage and headed for the apartment. It was nearly ten after a full but relaxing day. They hoped to get a good night's sleep without interruption.

8

*A*ngus returned from his morning bike exercise, locked his bike and headed for his apartment. As he entered, a marvelous aroma of coffee greeted his nose, announcing Serena was fixing breakfast. He took a quick shower and joined her at the kitchen table.

Serena handed Angus his coffee, her face askew with stifled laughter. "Well, Son, I guess it's back to the old grind for you."

"Yes, it won't be as much fun as our island tour of the last two days. I took you to places I've never been before, myself. I really enjoyed it. What are you going to do today while I'm working?"

"I thought I might take the car and drive around Hilo to see what I can find. I may do a little shopping if I find an interesting place."

He handed her the cell phone from his pocket. "Why don't you take this phone with you? I won't need it today, and you could use it if you get lost."

Serena placed the phone in her purse. "Thanks. I'll walk you downstairs when you go. I may take a stroll after you leave."

"Well, I'd better get going, so let's do it."

As they walked into the open, Serena grabbed Angus' arm and looked at him. "Son, I know the situation with the ghost and OSI is very serious. Every time I try to talk, I have a real problem knowing your apartment is bugged. Sooner or later, I'm going to say the wrong thing at the wrong time and blow everything. This verbal caution

151

because of imagined bugs is a lot harder to handle than I thought it would be."

"So far you've been handling it well. With any luck we can put this mess to bed after today and get back to the work at hand."

"I certainly hope so. Well, off you go to the crisis center," Serena joked as Angus hopped on his bike and rode away, waving.

*   *   *

As Angus walked into the Op Center, Jenny motioned him to stop at her desk. "There are three government people waiting in your office. I wanted you to know before you walked in. They are very demanding and not friendly."

Angus actually felt anxious to meet them. He could handle nasty people, and maybe this would put all this business to rest. Nonetheless, he was a little apprehensive as he walked in. The three agents were seated around his worktable. He noticed his computer was back in place, and there was a large stack of his papers in the center of his desk. *All copied no doubt*, he thought to himself.

"What can I do for you?" Angus asked stiffly.

They all stood and the taller and older of the two men stepped forward, the eyes in his narrow face seeming to bore into Angus. "I'm Jan Lux. I presume you are Dr. Angus Thomas?"

"Yes. You presume correctly."

"This is Gerald Furman and Yvonne Techmeyer. We're from the U.S. Office of Strategic Intelligence and we have some questions we need you to answer."

Their tailored business clothing did not fit the local scene. Furman, shorter and stockier then Lux, was near thirty. He had the crinkly-eyed, deferring look of an underling when Lux spoke. Yvonne Techmeyer was a tall, slender, dark-haired woman, about thirty with a reasonably attractive face locked in a permanent, emotionless, nose-up sneer. Each exuded the same cold, hard-as-nails air of the hunting predator.

Angus grinned and relaxed in response. "I'll do my best."

"We understand you have discovered an object moving at nearly the speed of light and headed toward the earth. As part of our nation's first line of defense, we need to know exactly what you found out about this object. As you probably know already, we have accessed your data, searching for information on this object. So far, we have found nothing, and that disturbs us greatly. Why would an American citizen make such a discovery and then hide all references to it from the very people he supposedly works for?"

Angus' mind raced. *How did they know? Dick Rumley had been found out and disarmed before they measured the speed of the ghost. Was someone else spying on his work in Dick's place?*

He hesitated then finally asked, "Where did you get such an idea?"

Lux picked up a single paper from the small pile on the table and thrust it in front of Angus' face. "We are in possession of a communication from you to one Pat Yamaguchi at the University of Arizona. In this communication you state, *that sucker's coming directly at us at more than ninety percent of the speed of light.* I quote directly, your own words, hi-lighted on this paper."

Angus was astounded and dismayed. "Where'd you get *that* information?"

He didn't want to lie about it, but Pat would never have contacted anyone about this without talking with him first. How could they have gotten their hands on his message? He didn't remember exactly what he said to Pat, but those words were undoubtedly in the conversation.

Lux stood stiffly, looking directly at Angus. "We are the ones asking the questions here, Dr. Thomas. Just tell us what we need to know and we'll be on our way."

Angus' face began to flush as his anger rose. "I doubt that. The last time I checked, I was an American citizen and unless the U.S. is now a police state, I have every right to know what this is all about. If you want any answers to your questions, I suggest you get down off your high horse and level with me. I've done battle with hostiles before, and I still remember how."

Jan Lux bristled. "That's not a very cooperative attitude on your part. I would think a person in your position and with your fine reputation would want to cooperate fully with your government in every way."

"You break into my apartment when I'm not there, dump everything on the floor searching for God knows what and follow me all over the island. Then you come to the office where I practice my profession and remove all my records, bug my phones and who knows what else. Next, you quote me from a private communication with a friend . . . and *you have the guts to preach to me about cooperation and civic duty*? I wonder what the evening newsboys would do with that? I still have a few friends among the press. Suppose I call them right now. Do you think I wouldn't get some high-profile coverage on this in a hurry? If you really want my cooperation, stop the veiled threats, let me know why all this is going on and tell me just how you came to have that particular private communication with Pat Yamaguchi."

Lux glanced quickly at his two associates. "We can't reveal the information you want. You'll just have to cooperate with us anyway."

As soon as those words were spoken, Angus whirled, stepped quickly out of his office door and grabbed the first desk phone he saw. "Jenny! Get hold of Pete Radcliff of the Honolulu News Service as fast as you can and tell him Angus Thomas has the story of a lifetime for him and to get someone here ASAP! Then get in touch with the Gemini legal counsel and tell them to get over here, fast!"

By this time, the two men caught up with him. They grabbed him by his arms, one on each side and started forcing him back into his office while the woman stood holding the door for them. Angus feigned a halfhearted struggle until they were inside his office. As soon as the woman closed the door, they relaxed their grip some. Immediately he jerked them around in front of him, catching them off-guard with a sudden surge of force from his powerful arms. In one surprise motion he slammed their heads viciously together with a loud thump. They both slumped to the ground. The woman lunged for her purse, but Angus grabbed her arm and forced her to the ground before she could get it. She tried a clever escape twist, but all she succeeded in doing was dislocating her shoulder as Angus held on. As she grimaced in pain, he forced her into one of the office chairs and dumped the contents of her purse on the table, still holding her arm tightly. He picked up her automatic pistol from the pile of things from her purse and released the safety. Holding her at gunpoint, he released her arm and backed over to where the two unconscious agents lay on the floor. After relieving them of their weapons, he checked their ankles and found two more small automatic pistols which he also removed.

"Take off your clothes!" he said sharply to the woman as he deposited the small arsenal on his desk.

She looked at Angus in pain and disbelief. "What? What did you say?"

"I said, take off your clothes! Now! Do it slowly and carefully with no quick moves and kick them over toward me. If you make a suspicious move, I'll put a bullet in your knee. I'm a crack shot with one of these and will hit what I want."

She slowly removed her jacket with her uninjured right hand. "You know, you're making things hard on yourself. If you will put down the gun, I'm certain we can work this out."

"Not a chance! You chose this way. I didn't. All you had to do was level with me and treat me like a human being. The skirt too, and the blouse. I want to make sure I find all your weapons." She stood up and removed her skirt revealing a knife strapped to the inside of one thigh and a duplicate of the two men's leg guns strapped to the other. There was no weapon hidden beneath her blouse. When she kicked her clothes his way, Angus picked them up and felt through them.

He straightened up when he found nothing. "Stand facing me with your right arm over your head and spread your legs wide apart." She complied with his order. "Now reach down slowly and unhook the straps on both weapons and let them fall to the floor. Remember, I've got this gun trained on your knee. I'll blast it at the slightest quick move on your part."

She did as she was told. When both weapons were on the floor, Angus motioned her back to the chair. He retrieved her weapons, added them to the pile on his desk and tossed her clothes to her.

"Put those back on," he ordered as he picked up the phone to talk to Jenny.

"Were you able to get hold of the people I asked for?"

Jenny stammered a bit and said, "We were told by OSI not to put through any irregular calls from you, Dr. Thomas. I'm sorry. No, I just couldn't."

"Did they say anything about not letting me talk to my mother?"

"No, they just said unusual calls."

"Then call my cell phone number right away. My mom has it. I'll hold until we're connected."

"I'll get your mother for you right away."

After a short wait Serena's voice came on the line, "Yes, Angus, what's going on?"

"Where are you?"

"I'm in the little shopping center down some ways from your apartment. Why?"

"I want you to call Peter Hiakawa immediately and tell him to get to my office right away. Then I want you to call . . . "

Serena interrupted. "Hold on a minute till I get paper and a pen." There was a minute or so of silence while she secured writing materials. "OK, now, who am I to call in addition to Hiakawa?"

"Call Senator Sukai's office and tell them to get someone over here as well. After that, call Pete Radcliff of the Honolulu News Service in Honolulu. Tell him I'm in deep trouble and have a big story for him. If he's got some local people, tell him to get them here ASAP. Oh yes! Use a pay phone. I'm sure our little friends are listening in. As a matter of fact, they probably already know from the bug in my office so hurry. No telling what will happen next."

"Consider it done."

Angus cradled the phone and faced the now fully dressed agent. "All right, Miss Techmeyer, now that I've got the ball rolling, how about a little information. I already asked the questions. You supply the answers."

"You just don't seem to know who you're dealing with. I can't answer your questions even if I knew the answers."

While she was talking, Angus was removing the mouthpiece from the phone. Finding nothing there, he removed the two screws from the plastic cover of the phone cradle and took it off.

"What have we here?" he said, finding a cylindrical object that looked like a microphone on one end and attached by four wires. Taking her knife off the desk, he cut the four wires and dropped the object to the floor where he crushed it under his heel. He then put the phone back together. "Now you can speak freely. Your friends can't hear you, unless you have another bug or two around."

"You're making a big mistake. Nothing you can do will change anything, and you're going to be in a lot of trouble with your government. Don't you think you'd better get someone to attend to those two? They may be seriously injured."

"Answer my questions, and I'll call for medical help. Refuse and they can lie there until everyone arrives for all I care. I was surprised when no one came to the door after the noise of the scuffle. Then I remembered. These rooms are soundproofed so outside noises don't interrupt serious work within. Once you closed that door, folks outside couldn't hear a thing. What we do now is up to you."

"All right, I'll tell you what I can, but please get some help for those two. They've been lying there for quite some time, and I'm beginning to worry about them. In spite of what you may think, they are quite decent men."

Miss Techmeyer sounded quite concerned and conciliatory, her face transformed into a soft, imploring look. There was no hint of the earlier look of cold indifference. It appeared to Angus she was genuinely worried and her entire demeanor had changed.

Without lessening his vigilance, he picked up the phone. "Jenny, call the trauma center and get someone over here right away. Tell them there are some injuries in my office that may be serious. Don't tell it to another soul. Just make sure they are sent to my office as soon as they get here." Jenny was one who could be counted on to carry out directions precisely and efficiently.

"Thank you for that. I am worried about them."

"You may not think so, but normally I'm not so callous." His momentary concern quickly vanished, and he changed back to the tough, stony-faced interrogator. "Now, how about some answers?"

"You are right about one thing. Without the bug I do feel safer talking. Although I have been trained in the physical aspects of being an agent, I am just a computer consultant recruited into OSI. All I've ever had to deal with is computers and getting data, including hidden and erased data from difficult situations. For instance, I could tell you removed sensitive files from your computer and wiped the space that held those files with ones. That overwrites all data and was very clever. Many people merely delete files, leaving the data in place and recoverable. I could also tell you selectively edited a number of your records, although I couldn't figure out just what you changed. I also found small changes in a number of places."

"Very good. But just how on earth did you get hold of my private communication with Pat in Arizona. You surely didn't get it from him?"

"I don't believe I'm out of order in telling you this, but you probably do know about our sophisticated listening post on Oahu, don't you?"

Angus shook his head and muttered, "Huh-uh."

"It's where we monitor nearly all transmissions all over the world. Certain phrases in any transmission that pass through our listening post triggers a red flag and produces a copy of the entire transmission and its source and destination. I'm sure that is all public knowledge and no real secret. One of the triggering phrases is anything having to do with unusually fast movement of any object. That is primarily aimed at missiles and airplanes or space vehicles. When the Navy picked up your message mentioning ninety percent of the speed of light, red flags went up all over the place. When we found you were an astronomer and the object was coming directly at the earth, well, you can put two and two together and come up with advanced technology or alien space craft, can't you?"

Angus laughed so hard he almost fell off his chair. "That's what this is all about? Fear of little green men from space invading earth? I just can't believe you people. Why all the cloak-and-dagger? A straight question would have elicited a direct and specific answer. You are the ones who have no idea what this is all about. An errant message about a newly discovered celestial object three hundred light years away and all hell breaks loose. If the news services get hold of this, OSI will be the laughing stock of the world for years to come. What warped sense of reality ordered this investigation?"

"It may seem rather ridiculous from your position, but you know where you are. Try seeing it from our point of view. We discover your message about an object moving at fantastic speed in our general direction. Then, we find that you were involved in an assassination attempt by an agent of a foreign government and that the agent conducted clandestine surveillance of your work at a rather sophisticated level. Since we are one of the nation's first lines of defense, wouldn't you, in our shoes, have serious doubts and want to, at least, investigate?"

"I see your point, sort of. I still think it got rather out of hand. Gross overkill, I call it. I just went along for the ride. What else?"

"I think that about says it."

*   *   *

Peter Hiakawa hurried into the Gemini Operations Center and headed straight for Angus' office. As he hurried through the lobby, he glanced out the window and noticed two emergency ambulances pulling up to the front door. With a loud knock on the door, he announced his arrival. Angus opened the door a crack and then let him in, closing the door behind him. Hiakawa surveyed the scene: two obviously injured men lying on the floor and just beginning to stir and groan a bit, one disheveled lady sitting in a chair in obvious pain, a veritable arsenal of weapons piled on the desk and Angus standing, still holding the gun directed toward the woman.

Hiakawa held his hand out to Angus. "May I please have that?"

When he finished surveying the scene, he shook his head in amazement and a broad grin tipped the corners of his mouth. The damage visited on the OSI agents was a pleasant form of retribution to Hiakawa after their earlier treatment of the police. "I see you have been quite busy. Are you OK?"

Angus handed the gun to Pete. "I'm glad you're here. I was afraid I might have to use it."

Relieved some, Miss Techmeyer stood up. "It was just a little misunderstanding."

Hiakawa sneered, contempt oozing from every message of his body language. "I doubt that. It looks more like a rather large misunderstanding to me. Your people did a lousy job, couldn't even handle one man. If you had chosen to work with us instead of treating us like the enemy, this could have been done a great deal easier." He turned to Angus. "Do you mind if I call in the paramedics? They should be here by now."

"Bring them in. I hope these two aren't seriously hurt. They did take a rather nasty bang to their heads."

Hiakawa rolled his eyes as he opened the door. The paramedics were right outside, headed for the door as he opened it. "Head injuries," he said to the paramedics as they entered.

Angus pointed to Miss Techmeyer. "I believe the lady has a dislocated shoulder. I'm sorry about that."

The two teams of paramedics moved swiftly and efficiently, loading the two men into the waiting ambulances. A much-subdued Miss Techmeyer walked to one of the ambulances with a strap immobilizing her left shoulder. The Gemini staff watched in utter amazement. John Carroll was among those watching. As soon as the ambulances left, he headed for Angus' office.

Hiakawa stopped Dr. Carroll at the door. "Can you give me a few minutes alone with Dr. Thomas, say a half hour or so, then I'll let you have him. First of all, I need some important questions answered. Second, I want to minimize any damage that might be caused by this incident. I'm certain you will want that as well."

"Yes, I certainly do. Let me know as soon as you're finished with him. I must have the details of what happened here."

"You can count on it."

John headed back toward his office assuring the puzzled onlookers all was tranquil.

Hiakawa grinned as he closed the door and turned to question Angus. "Just what in the name of heaven happened here? Do you realize you have completely decimated and disarmed one of OSI's crack investigative teams? I assume it happened in just a few seconds."

Angus explained in as much detail as he could remember. Hiakawa roared with laughter when he told of ordering Miss Techmeyer to take off her clothes.

"I'll bet that nasty witch turned green. I'll say that was a far cry from when she was at the station ordering our file personnel around like a bunch of her personal slaves."

Angus defended her. "She didn't seem so bad. She was quite concerned about her fallen comrades."

"Trust me on this. That one is hard as nails. She may work you for sympathy as long as it's to her advantage, but the minute she gains the upper hand, wham! You're mincemeat. I still can't believe you took them apart the way you did. It's going to be interesting seeing what they do from now on."

"There's something else I've done that may not sit too well. I called the news media and Senator Sukai's office. They may be arriving at any minute. What do you think I should tell them now?"

"Why on earth did you do that? If there's anything OSI doesn't want, it's the news spotlight or political attention."

"I know that. That's why I did it. I figured the threat of publicity would drive them out into the open and get them off my back."

"Unless I miss my guess, it will do just the opposite. I'm afraid they'll be dogging your heels for quite some time, so you'd better watch your back. You've gone to war with an agency of the U.S. government that has a great deal of power. I doubt they will just walk away, no matter how well you explain the situation to them."

"Hope I didn't mess things up too badly. I think I can handle the press OK. I've dealt with them many times in the past and can give them a good story without it being too damaging. Got any suggestions as to how to deal with the senator's people? I could use a little help on that. I've never delved into the political arena, except for those guys wanting to be seen with me when I was playing ball. That's how I met the senator. It was the first time he ran for the Senate. He was at the Pro Bowl in Honolulu and was on the field for one of those publicity photo sessions. He had several shots taken of Willy Daniels and me with him in between. Later on, he invited us to a party. I had quite a talk with him while there. He seemed like a sincere and decent guy. When I came to Gemini, he made a point to be at the little welcoming party they had for me."

"I know him to be a decent type, for a politician, that is. His people will seek to make political hay over this, especially with the news media coverage. Whatever you do, be sure you tell the same story to both the news people and Sukai's. If both are here at the same time, they'll be playing to each other so keep them apart if you can."

"Thanks! That sounds good to me. I'm beginning to have some ideas of how to give the press a story they will like that won't put the OSI in a bad light."

"If you can pull that off you'll be a genius. I just had a thought. Try to get hold of Techmeyer by phone before the press gets here. Ask her for advice on what to tell them. You'll make big points with OSI. She may have some helpful ideas on that anyway. Just remember what I said about her. She may come off soft and friendly to get what she wants, but she's a hard case. I'll bet she can be mean as a junk yard dog when she wants to."

"That's a good suggestion. I'll do that as soon as I can get hold of her."

"Better yet, hand me the phone and let me call her. I may be able to catch her as she walks in."

Angus handed him the phone.

"This is detective Peter Hiakawa of the Hilo police. Would you please call the trauma center and tell them to have a Miss Techmeyer contact me as soon as she arrives? It's urgent she does so before they start treating her. It can't wait until after.'"

"Yes, sir!" was Jenny's immediate reply.

He handed the phone back to Angus. "I thought maybe they would be more apt to fill a request from the police than from a private person. It might even put Miss Techmeyer on the defensive as well. Do you suppose you could find a box to hold that pile of hardware on your desk?"

As Angus looked for a box in his storage room, Hiakawa removed the clips from each of the guns and made sure there were no shells in the chambers. Angus found a suitable box which still contained the bubble wrap from whatever it held previously and gave it to Hiakawa.

"This will do nicely," he said as he wrapped the guns individually in the bubble wrap and placed them in the box. He pulled a small plastic bag from his pocket and sealed the clips and loose shells in it before placing it in the box as well.

"Now tell me. What's this idea you have about what to tell the press?"

"It's actually rather simple. It was all a great big misunderstanding. When I found them waiting in my office, I assumed they were working with Dick Rumley. Then, when they took me back into my office and closed the door, I feared the worst and reacted accordingly. I'll tell the senator's people that I called to apologize for the mistake and they should get the rest of the story from the OSI. What do you think?"

"That's OK, but for one detail. We never released anything about Rumley except that he had tried to kill you. The press did that white knight bit on you with the evil one trying to take revenge. None of the information about the surveillance was ever released. Your story might seem to be quite a stretch to a clever reporter."

"Got any better suggestions in a hurry? The press may arrive any minute. I have no idea what my mother told them, but you can be sure it was convincing. Incidentally, where are the rest of the OSI people? I expected them to show up soon after I destroyed their little listening station. They are way overdue."

"I don't think there will be anyone here from OSI until they regroup. It wouldn't surprise me if the three you took out were the entire team here in Hilo."

The phone rang. Jenny reported, "It's your Miss Techmeyer on the line for Mr. Hiakawa. She sounds agitated."

Angus put on his friendliest manners. "Hello, Miss Techmeyer, this is Angus Thomas. Pete Hiakawa placed the call for me, and I'm glad you called back."

"I'm in a lot of pain, so please make it brief."

"I thought you might like to have some input as to what I say to the press and to Senator Sukai. I don't want to make any more problems for you people, so I'm offering to listen to any suggestions you might have about this."

Her voice became soft and friendly, "That's considerate of you. Let me think for a moment."

Angus gave her a brief synopsis of what he thought appropriate to say. "I'm open to other suggestions."

"How about a case of mistaken identity? Let's say we were given the wrong information about you and feared you were working for a foreign power. When you rushed out and grabbed the phone we assumed you were trying to warn your confederates, so we grabbed you. After we were in your office, you started the scuffle that resulted in the injuries. Then, when the police arrived, we realized you were not the man we were after. It was all a big mistake. I think we can live with that. There will be some overt punishments for those deemed responsible, and you will be issued a formal apology. It will all end right there, and no one will be the wiser."

"Sounds like a plan. That's what I'll tell them. Hiakawa will verify what I say and that will give the press their story."

"Now, if you will excuse me. I have a doctor to see."

"I hope you and your two associates are OK soon."

When Angus hung up, Hiakawa asked, "What's the story now? I take it she made a suggestion?"

"A good one too, I think."

When Angus explained, Hiakawa nodded in agreement. "That will keep us both off the hook and the Rumley angle from getting attention. I like that."

When the phone rang it was Serena. "I made all your calls for you. I had a little trouble finding the number for your press friend and just finished talking with him. Senator Sukai's office gave me a bit of a hard time at first. They probably thought it was a crank call. I reminded them of your support for his cause at the Pro Bowl and soon was talking with one of his staff, a Miss Dooley, who said someone would be right over to see you. Tell me what happened."

"Thanks, Mom. You do good work. Rather than talk to you over the phone, why don't you just drive over here. You're only a few miles away, and I'd sooner tell you in person. Is that OK with you?"

"Certainly! How do I get there from here? I'm a displaced New Yorker, remember?"

Angus gave her directions to the Op Center and told her he would leave instructions with the receptionist. After he hung up, the phone rang again. It was Pete Radcliff.

"Hi, Angus. How's the old knee holding up? What's this big story? Was that really your mother?"

"Hang on, Pete, one question at a time. For your information the knee's fine. The big story I don't want to talk about on the phone and, yes, that was my mother who called you. Do you have anyone trustworthy anywhere nearby?"

"Ginger Cari should be on her way there right now, probably be there in about twenty minutes. She's young, but she's sharp. She uses that innocent schoolgirl look and charm to disarm people she interviews. Make no mistake. She's a good, seasoned reporter who seldom misses a trick. Looks a lot younger than her thirty years."

"I don't think this is as big a story as I did when I asked my mother to contact you. It will still be worthy of your attention, though."

Angus chatted with Pete for a while longer and told him what he had done since leaving football. Pete was impressed and promised to stop in for a visit next time he was on the Big Island. As soon as he hung up, the phone rang again.

"I have a man and woman from Senator Sukai's office here to see you. Should I send them to your office with someone?" Jenny asked.

Angus thought for a moment about the number of people who would soon be in his office.

"Why don't you direct them to meeting room A. It's right off the lobby and is roomier than my office. I know it's empty, but check the schedule to be sure. Tell them I'll be there in just a few minutes."

"Certainly. It's not scheduled for use until tomorrow."

Angus turned to Hiakawa. "Can you stay until the press is finished? I'm going to need you to back up my story. They're sending a young woman named Ginger Cari for the interview."

Pete grinned broadly, with a look of extreme relish. "Ginger Cari you say? She's a clever little cookie. I wouldn't miss this for all the tea in China. My only regret is I don't have a recorder. This should be one to be saved for posterity. I already have enough for my official, confidential report. Now I'll have the information for public consumption."

"I've got to bring Director Carroll up-to-date on what's happened. He's probably as nervous as a long tailed cat in a room full of rocking chairs."

Hiakawa picked up the box of OSI weaponry. "While you're doing that I'll secure this arsenal in my cruiser. I'll see you later in room A."

They left Angus' office, each on his chosen path. When Angus arrived at John's office, he was standing by the door, waiting.

John closed the door as soon as they went in. "Tell me what happened."

Angus detailed the happenings while John sat listening in amazement.

"I think that just might work," he said of Angus' story for the press. "I certainly want to be with you when you tell it. We've far more difficult problems to deal with anyway, so the quicker we get this incident behind us, the better we'll be able to work with those bigger problems."

Angus was emphatic. "You've got that right! Now, if you're ready, let's head for the meeting room."

As they walked, Angus thought about John and the growing group of those who knew of the potential threat the ghost posed. "We need a meeting of the entire group shortly after we have the results of the next series of photos, data and spectra. We will have it in just three weeks. I hope this OSI incident will be over soon and we can proceed with the research unhindered."

John looked at Angus. "I agree wholeheartedly. Let's set that up as soon as we finish with this immediate problem."

They arrived at room A as Hiakawa was opening the door.

Nelson Napoka and Beverly Goldman were the two from the senator's office. Nelson was a local politician and long-time friend of the senator and ran the office on the Big Island. Beverly was a part-time statistician and managed their local poling. She was also a gradu-ate student in political science at the university. After introductions, Angus related his story and asked the two if they would convey his sincere apology to the government through Senator Sukai. They agreed it was an understandable mistake by all involved and that all parties regretted the incident. Hiakawa, who knew Nelson Napoka quite well, confirmed his part in the story adding that the police need no further involvement and considered the incident closed.

As they were finishing the conversation, Angus watched through the window as a young woman drove up in a small yellow convert-ible and parked near the entrance. She hopped out of the car, note-book under her arm and quickly headed for the entrance door. He was sure that would be Ginger Cari. He excused himself and picked up the phone.

"Jenny, I believe we are about to receive a visit from the press. If the young lady just walking in is Ginger Cari, please see that she waits for me in my office. Tell her I'll be there in just a few minutes."

"Right, Dr. Thomas."

Angus hung up and turned to the group. "Do you need any more information? If not, I'd like to get back to work as soon as I can. We dance to the dictates of the telescope schedule here, and I'm already running behind."

John immediately spoke up. "I can answer any other questions you may have. Dr. Thomas has a very important deadline approach-ing, and the stars won't wait. He was so concerned about the injured agents, he wanted this meeting to express his regrets and wishes for their speedy recovery."

The phone rang and Angus answered. Jenny reported quickly, "It was Ginger Cari, and she's on her way. She grilled me and wouldn't accept when I said she'd have to talk to you. She was persistent, but I stood my ground. Just thought you'd want to know."

"Thanks, Jenny. You do good work," Angus said before hanging up. Turning to the group, he asked, "Any last questions before I go?"

After shaking hands and exchanging good-byes, Angus turned toward the door saying quietly through clenched teeth to Hiakawa so only he could hear, "The press is in my office."

Thinking quickly, Hiakawa said, "One more question before I leave, Doctor. We can talk while we walk to your office." They left John with the senator's people and walked toward the meeting with Ginger Cari.

On the way, Hiakawa told Angus what he knew about Ginger. "I know this little gal. She will not be easily put off about anything. Don't let the wide-eyed, almost girlish act fool you. She can look like a teenager and act accordingly if she thinks it will help get her story. She did an undercover bit about two years ago at the local high school acting like a senior transfer student and fooled everyone. She helped us break up a drug ring in the school as a by-product of the story she went after. She's OK in my book."

"That's just about what Pete Radcliff told me about her."

"He told you straight then. If she thinks there is the slightest contradiction or discrepancy in what you tell her, she'll worry it like a bulldog does its prey. She'll be a lot harder to satisfy than Sukai's people."

"Would you rather handle her questions then? I could defer to you on any sensitive question."

"Not on your life! This will be your show. Anything I say would be suspect right off the bat anyway. She knows how guarded police interaction with the press can be. Just answer her questions and don't elaborate. She'll search out the details she wants. Oh yes, she will sometimes ask the same question several times from a slightly different angle. If you notice, say something about already answering. That's usually taken as indicating an honest answer. Liars will try to elaborate or repeat a previous answer to try to convince you of the truth of their story. That can be a dead giveaway."

"I appreciate the suggestions."

As they approached his slightly open doorway, Angus noticed a pair of attractive female legs crossed and bouncing nervously. As the two walked in, Ginger stood up.

"Hi, Pete!" Then she turned to Angus. "You must be the famous running back I saw in the Pro Bowl here a few years ago. You were really super in that game."

Angus could see immediately what the two Petes had said about Ginger. The pretty, wide-eyed, girlish face had to be seen to be believed.

"Thank you. I enjoyed that game myself. With no season record to worry about it was fun just playing football."

Angus pointed to the worktable and chairs. "Why don't we sit here to talk?"

Ginger produced a small tape recorder and placed it in the center of the table. "Do you mind if I tape this? It makes it so much easier for me when I go through my notes later."

Angus was a little nervous about the recorder but agreed it was OK. Hiakawa merely nodded in the affirmative.

"You can start by telling me in your own words what happened here this morning."

Angus related the story, adding he had never heard of the OSI before this morning. All he said was truthful. He merely left out what he did not want known.

"That's OK for starters, but let's get into the details. Why did you run out the door to get a phone? You have one right here in your office."

"Faced with an unknown danger in a nearly soundproof room, wouldn't you want to get out? Remember; someone tried to kill me just a few months ago. If you had been run over and left to die on a remote road by unknown persons, then spent some time in painful recovery, you might be just a bit skittish yourself."

"You have a point there. Whom were you trying to call anyway, the police?"

"I never got that far. They grabbed me shortly after I picked up the phone."

"You never tried to call anyone? No one at all?"

"I didn't say that. Before they grabbed me, I managed to ask Jenny to contact Pete Radcliff and the Gemini legal counsel. There were a number of others running through my mind, but I was stopped before I got to them."

"That seems a little strange to me. You'd think the police would be first on your mind, not some reporter. And why the legal counsel? They would be the last ones I would think about."

"When the situation first erupted and I felt threatened, something Pete said to me a long time ago came to mind. He told me, 'Faced with a serious threat, publicity and legal counsel can be your best help if you are in the right.' Maybe that's why I asked for them first. Who knows? People do strange things when they panic."

"I don't see you as one to panic easily, Dr. Thomas. Are you certain that was all that was going on?"

"Maybe panic is the wrong word to use. More like instincts taking over the way they did when I was running the football. You seldom had time to think. Instincts alone dictated those quick turns and twists. Survival instinct is a powerful force. And it's a whole lot easier to take apart and question those split second reactions now than it was at the time."

"You may be right on that. We can deal with it again later. Now tell me exactly what happened from the moment they grabbed you. Don't leave out a single detail."

Angus repeated a second run-through of the event, neither adding nor changing a thing. Ginger interrupted him several times for clarification. Angus began showing exasperation at the same questions being asked repeatedly.

"Haven't I gone through this several times already? The whole incident was over in just a few minutes. You can check your tape if you missed anything."

"Tell me about the attempt on your life. I'd like to hear more about that."

"That's an old story that your news service covered quite thoroughly when it happened. I doubt there's anything I could add now."

Hiakawa grinned at this statement. Angus was holding his own against a clever and persistent onslaught.

"My instincts tell me there's more to this than what I'm getting from your story. I'll just keep poking around till I find out."

She turned to Hiakawa. "Why is homicide here?"

"It's just part of the ongoing investigation of that attempt on his life. You know I can't make any comments on that. When Angus called, I decided to check it out myself."

Handing her card to Pete, Ginger asked sweetly, "Call me, please, when you do have information. I'd like to cover that story. Anything about this man is going to be worthwhile news for a while now. Big sports heroes make for excellent copy."

Pete grinned as he pocketed her card. "I'll see to it you get any information that's OK to release to the public,"

"Dr. Thomas, you don't mind if I poke around here for a while do you? I'd like to ask some of your people just what they saw and heard."

"It's not for me to give you an OK on that. We do some very serious research here involving people from a number of nations. You'll have to get permission from our PR people who handle that. Ask Jenny at the reception desk to contact them for you."

"Lots of secret stuff, is there? That's another angle I'll have to look into."

Angus laughed and shook his head. "Nothing like that at all. It's just that no researcher wants his or her raw data and preliminary conclusions made public before being double-checked for accuracy and confirmed by additional research. Even then, later, more accurate findings can revise or even reverse erroneous conclusions. In addition to that, there are seven nations involved in the Gemini project. Each nation has its own protocol for dealing with the release of information to the news media. We all do our best to honor each nation's policy."

"Did I hear you say scientists make serious errors? Isn't science supposed to be exacting? That sounds rather disturbing to me."

"Astronomy is a science dependent on exact measurements taken at unbelievable distances of an unimaginable number of objects. Our most powerful telescopes, most of them here on Hawaii, show all stars as mere points of light. Imagine measuring the thickness of a human hair with a kitchen yardstick. You could only make an approximation, an intelligent guess, with such a measuring tool. As powerful as our newest telescopes are, they would be akin to the kitchen yardstick in measuring some celestial objects. As a result, we are forced to make guesses and approximations in developing theories about many objects out there."

"I feel certain the public doesn't understand that at all. How can we rely on releases of information from your group here if we know you are only guessing? When we pass the information to them, they wouldn't have the slightest idea of whom or what to believe."

"Very good thinking. You now have an idea of what researchers on the outermost fringes of knowledge deal with all the time. Look at it another way. Supposing our telescope could resolve, or see, an object the size of a quarter on the moon. On photos, that quarter would appear as a light, fuzzy dot against a darker background. What we need is a telescope that enables us to read the words on the face of that quarter."

"I'm beginning to see what you're saying. It would be like one of us trying to write a news story based on the sketchiest data. We just couldn't release the story until the information was verified. Sometimes, when we do release bad information in a news account, we pay a terrible price for the error."

"Then there's the sales appeal question. You people won't even write a story unless you think it will sell papers or catch the evening news watchers."

"Come on now, please give us credit for some effort in the non-commercial news. We frequently do in-the-public-interest stuff."

"I wasn't being critical, merely factual. Most of the public has no interest in what we do here, except for the most bizarre or startling discovery. A good example would be the discovery of metal-rich stars in some of the nearby globular clusters. This new discovery was quite startling and significant to the entire astronomical community. It was reported in detail and read with great interest in scientific publications and news. I doubt any general news service even listed the story. Should it happen to be printed in a newspaper, how many people do you suppose would even notice it? Given the information about this new discovery, would you have come here to check it out? Would you be interviewing those who made the discovery? Be honest. Aren't you here because of an altercation between a once well known sports figure and some government agents? Would it be as newsworthy were I merely an unknown astronomer?"

"You got me there. The main thing that piqued my interest was Angus Thomas, no question about it. And I don't have an inkling of what a globular cluster is. I do appreciate your giving me a better understanding of your position on releasing information. I will definitely get with your PR people to finish my story. I still have a gut feeling that there's more to this than what I'm hearing."

"Maybe the OSI people can give you a different slant when you interview them."

"Fat chance! Those cats are so tight lipped, I'll be lucky to get a 'hello' out of them. They'll refer me to their public information people for any answers. OSI agents do not talk to the press, period."

Angus put on his best PR manners. "I would appreciate it if you would say some positive things about Gemini in your article. If you could emphasize this had nothing to do with our work here it would also be helpful. I will see to it you are the first news person to learn of any startling discovery I might make in the future."

"Why don't you meet me for a long lunch soon? I can do an interview for an article titled, say, 'Football Star Turns Star Gazer' or something catchy like that. Your name would get a lot of people to read the article and gain information they would never learn otherwise. It could be either a PR puff piece or straight, positive information about Gemini and your work. I could run it through your own PR people to make sure all the information is accurate and acceptable. I prefer good, solid, positive reporting over the sensational. Unfortunately, we sometimes need a gimmick to get John Q. Public to read something that's important. That's just the way it works. It's the news media version of the old saying, The squeaky wheel gets the grease."

"Pete Radcliff said several good things about you. I can see now he was right. You know, I've dealt with many news people over the years, some of whom could get very nasty. Your way goes a lot farther with me than theirs. I'll gladly give you that interview after all this excitement dies down, and I can catch up on my work."

Ginger rose to leave. "I'll definitely be in touch. Right now, I've some PR people to see."

She handed Angus her card as she left, adding, "You call me if you think of anything at all that slipped your mind."

When she had gone, Hiakawa rose to leave, a big grin on his face. "I have to hand it to you. Looks like you did a good job, but that wide-eyed little gal knows she's not getting the whole story. She'll keep digging for a while. OSI will give her nothing but a blank stare, so she'll rely mostly on what you said. She'll dig around at the trauma center for details on injuries and get what she can from your PR people. I'll wager her article will center around one man destroying a small army of federal agents and build on your sports hero status. It will be cleverly written and you'll probably like it. I can tell she likes you, and that could be a good influence on how she puts things. Just keep in mind to be careful of what you say. Despite her appearance, she has the killer instincts of a seasoned reporter with integrity to boot.

Now I need to get back to write my own report, a job I don't relish. Just keep me informed about things."

*   *   *

Shortly after Hiakawa left, Serena walked in with Lani as Angus finished straightening his desk and worktable.

"Look whom I found in the lobby," Lani said as they walked in. "I understand there's been a bit of excitement in your office. I ran into the doctor that fixed you up when I was leaving my dad's room. He told me you put three government agents in the hospital. One fractured skull, a concussion and a dislocated shoulder. What happened?"

"Yes, tell us what we missed. I can hardly wait to hear this story," Serena added.

They sat down and Angus related the morning's happenings to them in detail. When he had finished his tale, Serena said to Lani, "You see? You leave him alone for just a moment, and he gets into all kinds of trouble. It's been going on like this since he was just a little guy. Somehow he manages to wriggle his way through and come out OK, but he'll worry you while he does it."

"Mom! You're exaggerating." Turning to Lani with a pained expression he said, "Don't pay any attention to what she says. Like most mothers, she likes to brag about her offspring. This is probably the most real trouble I've been in. Ever!"

"I don't know about that. In the short time I've known you, there's been the incident with Dick Rumley, the accident or attempt on your life, the running around avoiding bugs, homing beacons and trailing agents, and now this latest altercation. You'll have to admit that's an extraordinary amount of excitement."

"When you look at it that way, I suppose there has been a little more excitement than normal."

"And now, we may be headed for South America, and who knows what that will lead to, not to mention the real problem of the ghost."

Angus tried to mount a weak defense. "Those are all things that are completely out of my control. The two of you seem to take great pleasure beating up on me. How can I fight back against two determined women?"

"Son, I don't see a single mark on you." Turning again to Lani, smiling, Serena added, "You're doing quite well. Keep him on the defensive at all times, otherwise, he'll run over you like he used to do to those line backers."

The two women were truly enjoying this moment. Angus merely shook his head in resignation and then, finally, chuckled a bit at himself.

"You seem to be enjoying this, but just remember, I've a very long memory, and paybacks can be vicious. How about we go for an early lunch then get back to work. We've a great deal of preparation for those measurements coming up in about three weeks."

While at lunch, Lani told them her dad was doing quite well and should be going home in a day or two. They discussed the problem that brought them together and to this place, concentrating on the next steps to take.

Serena's eyes went suddenly wide open as she recalled a forgotten phone call. "I completely forgot to tell you about talking with Chelton. You remember we were discussing him just before we found out about Ali's fall? Well, I went ahead and called him while waiting at the house. About three hours after I left a message with his office, he called me back. We had a nice talk and he told me all about his work. I explained as best I could the problem we face without the specific details. He knew I was quite serious and understood a face-to-face meeting would be best. He's going to rearrange his schedule and fly out as soon as he is able. He promised to call and tell us when he would be coming. It will be about three weeks before he can get here since he has some commitments he can't postpone. He would cancel those if it were that urgent. I went ahead and told him it wasn't and that three weeks would be fine."

Angus nodded and smiled. "Great! By then we should have better information on the ghost, including a tighter grip on the actual path and timing of its passage. I hope and pray the new information is less frightening. I'm just afraid that no matter how far it goes from the most probable path, it will still pose grave dangers. Incidentally, it feels good to be back on track and not have to dodge OSI agents."

Serena continued, "I called Kat and gave her an idea of why you brought me out here and that I may be gone for quite some time. She seems to have everything under control at the inn, so I'm relieved about that. I've never been so far away or for as long. When I told her about Chelton, she realized this was quite serious. I promised to come back just as soon as I could to give her the whole story, but it would probably take at least a month."

"Things seem to be shaping up again. Mom, why don't you stick around the office this afternoon? I've some rather tedious work to do on the computer, and Lani can give you the grand tour and explain how we work down here while the telescope is thirty-five miles away on top of the mountain. Then maybe we can have a relaxed dinner and evening for a change."

"Sounds good to me, but doesn't Lani have her work to do? She doesn't need to take time to show me around. She's probably behind as much as you."

"Part of my job is to show visiting VIPs around and explain what we do at the Operations Center," Lani explained. "You certainly qualify as a VIP, so I will be doing what I'm paid to do. Besides, I won't have much of Angus' work to do until he gets that computer ready. That's something only he can do for the present. When that's ready to go, I'll be very busy."

After lunch they headed back to the Op Center. Angus went to work on his computer and the ladies made a tour of the entire center. When they passed John Carroll's office, his secretary stopped them.

"John heard you two were touring the facility and asked me to catch you as you went by. He'd like to see you."

In moments they were ushered into his office. John came out from behind his desk to meet Serena.

After Lani's introduction, John indicated a small conference table with four chairs.

"Let's sit over here. A desk can be such a barrier to conversation, and I need to have a serious talk with both of you. I am quite apprehensive about this information release, which has us all so concerned. I understand we are all part of the select group that knows about this, correct?"

Lani and Serena agreed and expressed their apprehension as well.

John then continued, "What I need to know is just who knows and how far the information has gone at the present. Next, what plans have you considered for limiting the size of this group so we can better control the information? I personally think we should consider limitations until we reach a consensus on the best way to release it to the public."

Lani answered, "As of now it's almost strictly a family affair. My mother and dad were the first Angus and I turned to. Mom suggested we get some spiritual input, so we brought Pastor Ruth Malikalohe to our house and explained the situation to her. She's a long-time family friend and confidant, a real gem. She gave us some positive input. Then we brought Serena here from New York and told her about it. You are the latest member to join us. So far that's it."

"Good! It's still a small group. Are there any others you plan to include?"

"Only my nephew, Dr. Chelton Chum. He's a truly remarkable person and could add another dimension to the group. He's been involved in a number of humanitarian organizations and is currently with UNICEF," Serena said.

John looked at Serena in amazement. "He's your nephew? I've heard many great things about him. Have you talked with him?"

"As a matter of fact, he'll be coming here in about three weeks. We haven't told him what it's about. We want to do that in person. Who knows who might overhear our phone call?"

"How about meeting right here in my office soon after he arrives? It's convenient, three members of the group are here already and it should be fairly secure. I can schedule it as soon as we know when he's coming."

Serena smiled in agreement. "I know that will be fine."

The three stayed in John's office for several hours, discussing plans for future activities. They developed a tentative agenda for the first meeting with Chelton and a plan of action involving the new information to be obtained in the six-month observations and measurements due in three weeks. They talked at length about possible methods for release of the devastating information. By the time Lani and Serena left John's office, finished the tour and returned to Angus' office, it was a little past five.

Angus looked up and smiled, joking as they entered his office. "I was wondering if you were lost. That must have been quite a tour."

Serena immediately acted the haughty, stern matriarch. "No smart remarks. While you've been here playing with your computer, we've been meeting with your director and discussing plans for the future, including our meeting with Chelton. John knows about him and was impressed he's coming here. Among other things, we decided to meet in his office here at Gemini. He suggested it and we thought it was a grand idea. Now what have you accomplished while we were working so diligently?"

"My! My! I'm impressed," Angus responded with mock amazement. "You have been busy. Seriously, I'm glad it worked out so you could meet with John. Sounds to me as though you accomplished quite a bit. You three are all good organizers and will probably work well together. We're going to need a great deal of that kind of talent to do this thing right. Once the new data is in and analyzed, we'll have to get to work. Anything we can do before that will be a big help."

They sat in Angus' office for a time, informing him fully of the details of their conversation with John. They decided to stop and visit Ali on their way to dinner.

Ali brightened as they came in and told him they were going to dinner. "Take this woman with you. She's been cooped up in here all day. Besides, she's been driving me crazy."

Charlene scowled in response. "Who has been driving whom crazy?" Turning to the rest, she grinned. "I can tell he's a lot better. All he does is complain about having to stay here."

"Will you go with us?" Lani asked.

"I suppose. If I don't, he'll grumble at me for the rest of the evening."

It would be ten before the three left Charlene with Ali and returned to their apartments.

*   *   *

The rest of the week through Saturday passed with relative peace and quiet. Angus continued working diligently at computer instructions for the upcoming event. He brought his new laptop in and Lani entered all the programs and data required to duplicate his work at the office. When necessary, they could work using the laptop almost as well while away from his office. All mathematical references to the speed of the ghost were left as they were with the decimal point moved two places to the left. When needed, Angus could easily transpose data to the actual number in his head. Lani backed all new data and program changes to large capacity floppy disks. All could then be transferred to the other laptop to keep that one updated. The critical spectral files would be kept on the second laptop only. They would not be returned to his office computer or to the first laptop. Angus decided some data would be best kept secreted away from any prying eyes.

Ali left the trauma center, grumbling about being unable to do anything, one sure sign he was feeling better. He wore a back brace and was not to pick up anything weighing more than five pounds for two weeks. Charlene was glad to have him back home. She would have to help him for a while as he regained strength and as his back healed. She promised the doctor he would behave. She would definitely enforce the doctor's instructions.

The three agents were released, one at a time. Furman, who had a slight skull fracture as well as a concussion, was the last to leave. He returned home to the mainland for his recovery. Lux, with a concussion, was ordered to restrict his activity for a time and Techmeyer, shoulder put back in place, was to wear a sling for about a week and then take physical therapy for her shoulder. Lux and Techmeyer remained in Hilo.

9

Sunday, Angus, Serena and Lani drove to the Namahoes' place where Pastor Ruth joined them, bringing the laptop for Angus to update. They huddled in the living room where Angus and Lani brought them all the latest on the ghost, Chelton's coming visit and the meeting at John Carroll's office.

After the brief exchange, Charlene announced, "Dinner's ready. If you'll each grab a plate and some silver, we can move outside to the patio. We'll not feel so cooped up and can enjoy the warm, sunny weather."

"If this old cripple can make it that far," Ali groaned, exhibiting a grossly overdone limp as they headed for the patio. "My lovely wife has become a cruel dictator who watches me like a hawk. I can barely do a thing."

"Don't give me that business," Charlene chided, then turned to Ruth, "He's recovering quite rapidly. So much so I have to sit on him when he starts doing something he shouldn't. He seems to be experiencing little pain even though he still moves a bit slower than usual."

When Ali reached his chair at the table, he turned to Charlene. "You don't have to keep me from doing something once in a while."

"Just helping you remember what the doctor ordered." She turned toward Lani. "Your father complains a lot but otherwise is behaving himself rather well. I'll really have to ride herd on him in a week or so when he begins chaffing to get back to work."

With dinner finished and the table bussed and cleaned, they sat around for a serious discussion of their options. Ruth kept a record of important items of the discussion. Less than an hour into the discussion, it became apparent Serena had unofficially taken charge.

Ali extended his hand in Serena's direction. "Let's have a little organization here. I move we name Serena as chairman and Ruth secretary. We don't need much organization, but there are some jobs that need assigning so we can move efficiently. Serena seems to be taking charge and Ruth's already assumed the role of secretary. Why don't we just make it official?"

"Sounds good to me," Lani replied as the rest affirmed Ali's proposal.

Serena looked around and nodded in acceptance. "I'll gladly let anyone have the job at any time."

"Come on, Mom, you're a natural leader," Angus said, then turned to the others, "She gets elected to lead every group she joins. It's been that way as far back as I can remember. She's a very unassuming little powerhouse."

That settled, the group continued all afternoon. They decided to delay planning how to release the news until the meeting in John's office with Chelton. The results of the six-month measurements should be in by then, along with the latest calculations of the path and timing of the ghost's passage.

Charlene turned to Angus, questioning, "Explain to us the possible results in terms non-scientists can understand. Also, how sure are you of the nature of the danger we are facing? It sounds as though it's really quite indefinite at this point. That's hard for an ordinary person to understand."

Angus repeated the explanation he had provided Ginger Cari when she posed nearly the same question. "It may be several years before the path can be predicted with enough accuracy to begin computer simulations on what might happen. We're dealing with things on the fringes of knowledge. It's difficult to comprehend the distances and speed of celestial objects, even those close by. We've been tracking asteroids for years, calculating their paths so we could predict a collision with the earth and take preventive steps. Even though we can accurately measure these relatively nearby objects for size, mass, speed, distance and trajectory or orbit, we can only make approximations or intelligent best guesses as to whether they will strike the earth at some distant future date. The greater the length of the path, the less accurate our predictions will be.

"It's rather like shooting a rifle at a target. In aiming the gun, you are predicting the path of the bullet. At close range, a marksman can put bullet after bullet through the same hole in the target. As the range increases, the bullet holes begin to spread into a group that gets bigger and bigger. At extreme distances, the bullets may miss the target entirely, even if the gun is held in a fixed position by a vise. The longer the path, the more variables can affect the trajectory. Wind, differences in the power of the charge in the cartridge and of the shape and weight of the bullet, even slight differences in gravity along the path, all these and many more variables can change the path slightly. Does that make it more understandable?"

They all nodded their heads affirmatively. Ali added, "It must be difficult to explain these measurement problems to those of us who are not normally exposed to physics and astronomy. Your gun analogy helps me a great deal."

"Good!" Angus continued. "You're quite right. It is difficult to explain what we're dealing with here. With the ghost, we are trying to predict a trajectory, or path, in precisely the same manner, but on a scale billions of times larger than the trajectory of a bullet. It's also thousands of times larger than the path of an asteroid. The problem is compounded by the need to make precise measurements over huge distances of objects moving at unimaginable speeds. We take measurements six months apart using the diameter of the earth's orbit as a baseline for the most accurate distance measurement, a process called parallax. Even then, at a distance of three hundred light years, that measurement is near the limit of practical accuracy. We could be off by ten percent or even more and still consider it a good measurement. Then to calculate its true position, we must factor in its speed. That speed measurement, roughly ninety percent of the speed of light, is quite accurate and is based on measurements of the shift of spectral lines toward the blue.

"Taking that into account, we estimate its true distance at this moment to be only about thirty light years away. In the three hundred years it has taken the light we now see to reach us, the ghost has traveled an incredible distance of two hundred and seventy light years. Our view and our measurements will remain far behind its actual position until it is almost upon us. Adding to the problem, is the fantastic speed at which it is moving. At speeds approaching the speed of light, relativistic effects can become quite powerful. These are effects that Einstein predicted in his theory of relativity and that have since been proven by experiment. As far as I know, no one has ever considered an object as large as a star moving at relativistic speeds. We are in completely uncharted waters, and it will take a great deal of work to find the answers we need. It may even take a breakthrough in the application of relativity theory to obtain those answers.

"That's why it is so hard to pin down the path of the ghost. When we do obtain a path prediction, one tiny error could mean the difference between a prediction of total annihilation and merely the view of a bright and rapidly moving star with little or no consequences. That's why I think it will take years to obtain an accurate path prediction. Once the path is accurately determined, we must study the gravitational effects, and that is, clearly, unknown territory. It is even conceivable gravity will function completely differently than what we expect. Maybe there will be no effect at all. It is likely we will not know for certain until it actually arrives."

"That's amazing," commented Charlene. "It's hard to conceive it is not where we see it. How soon will we be able to see it without using a telescope?"

"Not until it is quite close. I'm guessing just a few dozen light years away. I haven't even thought about that calculation."

Lani squirmed a bit to find a more comfortable position on her chair. "It's going to be difficult to explain to the public about a danger they can't even see. For many years they will be completely dependent on powerful telescopes wielded by astronomers for any information about the ghost. That can create a lot of doubts and fears on the part of the general population."

"Unfortunately, the news media will likely play up the danger and hardly mention the better possibilities," Charlene remarked. "For that reason we had better be quite certain of what we say in any release. It will have to be accurate yet use the widest possible range of consequences. That might minimize the fear reactions. I wonder just how long it will be front-page news? You know how even the biggest stories are soon relegated to occasional small news clips."

Ali obviously thought otherwise. "This may be different. I have an idea as soon as the truth is out, this story will dominate the news for a long time. I just wonder how long it will take for things to settle down once the reality sinks in. Maybe they won't ever settle down. We may have ever-increasing chaos right up to the end, no matter how close that wild star comes."

Ruth looked around with a worried frown. "I'm really concerned about the effect on religions and religious institutions. My guess is many will turn to religion for answers. It will be a comfort to most but also an opportunity for all kinds of kooks to make hay. Prophecies in the Bible and other religious records will be searched thoroughly for answers. Some will interpret passages said to have predicted this as the end of the world. Interpreters of the book of Revelation will have a field day. Who knows what will come out of the other great religions of the world. In addition to the thoughtful consideration, there will probably be wild speculations of all manner and levels and hordes of cult-like leaders using the opportunity for pure exploitation. I can imagine the wild ravings of many fraudulent 'saviors.' I only hope calm heads will prevail."

Lani shook her head in wonderment. "It's mind boggling trying to guess what people will do when faced with this catastrophe. I'm also concerned with what heads of states and governments will do. Will they try to hide the facts from the people as some say they did about the incident in Roswell? Will news reports be branded as sensationalism with no basis in facts? Given that only a few people on earth have the technical know-how and instrumentation to find and define the ghost, it would not be hard for a government to control that information. At present, other than on this island and a few other observatory groups you could count on one hand, there are no installations located anywhere in the world capable of finding the ghost for a number of years. The Keck telescopes, the Japanese Subaru and our Gemini are all right here on the mountain. A few mountaintops in Arizona and Chile have the rest and many of those are not yet on line. Our own government could very easily control the entire astronomical community if they wished."

"After my experience with the OSI, I'm a bit worried about the U.S. government as well," Angus added. "The tiny bit of information they took from my communication with Pat in Arizona triggered the response we know about. What governmental reaction would the real information bring? That really worries me. And what's Dick Rumley doing? He's back here in Hawaii now, but what's going on? We're dealing with a lot more unknowns than just the data on the ghost."

Serena stood up and took the floor with her quiet forcefulness. "I'm quite concerned about the makeup of our group. We're people who have little power or contact with power in the world sense. Don't get me wrong. All of you are important parts of the group with good minds and caring hearts. It's just that we may need to have some people with more power in the media and political arena. John Carroll is one who has wider contacts than anyone except Angus. Those contacts are mainly in the scientific community. Angus has a few contacts in the media as well as political. They are from his career in football and may be useful only in leading us to those we really need. Chelton has many valuable contacts on the world's political stage, so he could be our international person. We can consider that after we have his reaction to our problem.

"It is my opinion we need two more outsiders in the group, a news media person and a politician or public servant of some kind. They must be chosen carefully since those cultures are loaded with self-centered, self-serving egotists who would sell their mothers for a story or political position. We need those who care a great deal about the people they serve and who will risk their professional necks to do the right thing. They will be most difficult to find, but I'm sure they're out there. Why don't you each try to come up with the names of possible candidates? We can tell John about this and ask him for suggestions as well. Let's try to find, select and contact those people so they can attend our meeting in John's office when Chelton gets here. We've less than three weeks, so we need to move quickly."

While she was talking, the group's positive reactions indicated their acceptance of Serena's suggestions. She was proving to be an effective leader.

When the discussion lagged, Angus stood up. "If we're finished for the moment, I'd like to take this laptop inside and test the SSR transmission encoder. I trust Sandy knows his business, and this message is secure. We can only test to make sure the message goes through. It's impossible to test for security."

After he finished and the message was on its way, Angus came back outside. He gave the laptop back to Ruth as she left to go home. Shortly after Ruth left, Angus, Lani and Serena headed back to Hilo to get a good night's rest in preparation for a busy and hectic three weeks.

*   *   *

Monday morning, as Angus entered the lobby of the Op Center, Jenny motioned him to stop at her desk. "Miss Techmeyer is back and waiting in your office, alone. I tried to stop her, but she waved her badge at me and kept on going."

Angus looked dismayed. "Thanks, Jenny. That's all I need, more interruptions."

"What's up now? I thought that OSI business was all over and done with. They said in the news it was all a big mistake."

"I have no idea, but I will probably find out shortly," Angus added, then headed for his office.

When Angus walked in, Yvonne stood up and smiled, airily. "Good morning, Dr. Thomas. It's certainly a lovely day, isn't it?"

Angus faced her disdainfully. Anger helped form his words. "I thought so, too, until you showed up. I'm way behind in my work as it is. I don't need any more problems from you people."

"Don't be so hostile. I want to thank you for the story you gave the news media. Even the senator seemed satisfied it was all a big mistake. You did very well. We confirmed your story for them, so it's all behind us now."

"I appreciate the thanks, and I hate to rush you away, but I really do have to get to work."

"Actually, I'm here to help you in your work. I'm your new research assistant. Miss Namahoe will be reassigned elsewhere."

Angus bristled and remained standing. "That's not even funny. I'd appreciate your leaving right now."

Yvonne wore a look that was cold, superior and haughty as she planted herself firmly back in the chair. "I suppose we'll have to do this the hard way. As you well know, except for the small part contributed by the other six nations involved, Gemini is a U.S. government-funded operation. As such, it has been placed under our jurisdiction until we know all there is to know about your work and this new discovery. Putting it bluntly, you are now working for me."

Angus clenched his fists and gritted his teeth. His face radiated hostility. "Not in this lifetime. The next part of this project requires considerable knowledge of astrophysics and the workings of our equipment. You're no physicist, and you certainly know nothing about our equipment. If you stay, I go. It's as simple as that."

"You mean to say you would give up your career and walk away from what could be one of the greatest discoveries of all time? I think not. You may bluster and threaten, but in the end you'll do just as I say. If not, we'll turn your project over to someone else. It may cause a slight delay, but we'll get what we want."

Angus stood glaring at her, eyes wide. "That's where you're wrong, Miss OSI. When I'm in the right, I don't give up, ever. Most of this project and what is to happen in the next two weeks is in my head. If I walk away, that goes with me. There's not another person in this world who could make those measurements with this equipment within the two weeks' time during which they must be taken. If you could get the best people in the field, it would take them at least two, maybe three years to catch up to where I am right now. Can you afford to do this? I think not." Angus knew Lani was capable of taking the measurements and running his equipment, but John Carroll was the only other person who knew that, and he certainly wouldn't tell.

Yvonne backed off just a bit. "You may be right. If it comes to that, we'll just have to deal with it. I really doubt you are willing to walk away. If it takes a few years' delay, we can wait. I'm sure we can find another astronomer to fill your shoes. Why not try working with me for a while to see how it goes. I've a quick mind and took enough physics to get a master's in computer science. Your Miss Namahoe is just a sort of roving secretary isn't she?"

Angus finally sat down at his desk, still boiling inside, but calming himself and forcing the practical scientist in him to take control. "Lani Namahoe is a highly skilled astronomer. She has been trained in the use of my instruments and has operated them for nearly six months. We work well as a team and she is an integral part of this operation. As bright as you may be, it would take years for you to reach the level of knowledge and skills she has. Without her assistance for the next three or four weeks, the project will be delayed for a year until the earth is again in position for the needed measurements. Are you hearing anything of what I am trying to tell you, or have you been rendered deaf and stupid by your OSI masters?"

"We can be flexible when it's in our best interest. Perhaps your Miss Namahoe is essential to the immediate problems at hand. I'll take care of the arrangements. Just remember, you and your assistant will be working for and reporting to me. Your office is large enough to accommodate another small desk. I can work there and monitor your work."

"No way!" Angus replied caustically, gripping the edge of his desk so hard his nails dug into the top. Anger and determination made up his face. "Sounds to me like Nazi Germany or the U.S.S.R. under Stalin. This is still the U.S.A. What you are asking would scuttle the project anyway, so I have no interest in continuing without complete freedom and the people and technology I need. Now you listen and listen good. Everything goes back to the way it was before you and your fellow goons came on the scene. I get to pursue my profession in complete freedom the good old American way. I'll see to it you get copies of all my reports as soon as anyone. If you must have a presence here, let someone find you a place where I never have to see you. That's as far as I go. Otherwise, I walk."

"You're being quite unreasonable. I could force the issue you know."

Angus stood up and pointed to the door. "Right now I want you out of my office. You have my terms, so take them to your boss. I want an answer today, before I raise another finger. End of conversation."

"But . . . "

"Out! Now! Or I'll heave you out the door," Angus said angrily, leaning toward her like an animal about to attack.

"I'll be back," she shot over her shoulder as she went through the door.

And I won't be here, Angus said to himself as he tried to cool down. He left his office and walked quickly to John's. "Is John in?" he asked John's secretary, Ani'i Pohaku.

"Yes he is. He's quite upset after coming in early to meet with that OSI agent, Miss Techmeyer. He said not to disturb him for anyone but you. I'll let him know you're here."

As soon as she announced Angus, John opened the door and called him in. "I assume you've received OSI's ultimatum? Tell me what happened. I would like to have been there to see your reaction."

Angus provided a detailed description, finishing with, "I think I'm ready for Cerro Pachon. I wonder if the OSI would hound me there?"

"Unfortunately, they probably would unless we could provide some fancy footwork." John leaned forward and looked intently at Angus. "For some time I've been thinking of a plan that's quite bizarre. It wouldn't take much to activate and would solve many of our problems in one step."

John sat back, slowly drumming a pencil on his desk. "For some reason the British want Rumley back in their hands. I know because they approached me to drop any charges the Op Center might be considering. This came up right after he was returned to the Hilo Police. They discovered something involving their security, something very hush-hush and they want him desperately. They are pressuring the Hilo prosecutor's office to drop their charges as well. I've gotten to know their man Conrad and I think he will aid us in order to clear the way for Rumley to be sent back to the U.K. This worked out better than I could have dreamed possible with my escape plans for you."

"You're really serious. So what's this bizarre plot?"

"Briefly, here's the program: They take Rumley back in secret, you assume Rumley's identity and head for Cerro Pachon. That's it in a nutshell."

Angus grinned, still a bit dazed. "You know, that's just crazy enough to work."

"The British are one of our partners in Gemini, so Conrad would certainly help. He thinks a lot of you anyway. There is no one at Cerro Pachon who has ever seen Dick Rumley, except the man who headed our startup here, Matt Hillman. He's managing the startup there and can be counted on to help us out."

"How would we handle my disappearance and the travel to Chile? I'm still recognizable, you know. Does any Chilean airline come to Hawaii?"

"We'll have to work out the details immediately. The best I could come up with is putting you two on the same plane out of here to Canada under your true names. Sometime after you reach British Columbia you will switch identities. Angus Thomas will disappear into nowhere while the Brits whisk the real Dick Rumley off to England in secret where he can rot, for all I care. As Rumley, you will head for Chile and Gemini South. Done carefully, no one should be the wiser."

"Won't that take a lot of high-level cooperation from the British? Do you think they will go along with this? I mean, with OSI and all. It might get messy."

"I've worked closely with the British on the Gemini Project. Done them quite a few favors as a matter of fact. I called one of my official friends in their consular office while Conrad was here asking us to drop any charges we might be planning so they could get Rumley back. They want him badly, so I knew we were in a great bargaining position. I agreed to drop all charges on their promise to assist me in this little deception. I didn't even have to say who was involved or when it would be."

"I'll have to depend on you for that. I do have a friend in the states who might be able to help with emergency transportation. He has a charter service and is quite reliable."

"Once you assume Rumley's identity, you'll have to fly commercial. That way there will be no doubt where you, as Rumley, are going. My hope is OSI won't make the connection. They'll be a little off balance by your departure even when you made things as clear as you did to Miss Techmeyer. My bet is they'll count on you to knuckle under and do their bidding. Your leaving will put more egg on their faces. It will take a few days for them to regroup. With luck, we can delay this as long as possible."

"I'm sorry, John. I gave them this afternoon as the deadline. Maybe they'll be the ones to knuckle under. What do we do if OSI goes along with my demands?"

"If that happens, you can be sure it's just a stalling tactic. They may leave you alone for a few weeks only to swoop down on you as soon as those readings come in. Once they get those readings, they'll be back in force. I don't see a chance they will leave you and your project alone to wait for your reports."

"Incidentally, is the fiber optic link to Chile ready yet? I know it's ready at this end. I haven't heard of it being operational yet. If it isn't, when will it be ready?"

"The cable is in and connected at both ends but has yet to be tested. There are thousands of amplifiers along that cable, and each one must be turned on individually and tested. It's my understanding that won't be completed for a couple of months, at the earliest. The satellite link is far too slow and sloppy to handle what you're thinking of. I'm quite sure there's presently no way to do a direct data feed from the telescope instrumentation to Cerro Pachon. We'll have to find another way to get the data to you and keep it out of OSI's hands at the same time."

Angus leaned forward, smug and triumphant. "I've a way to do the entire thing and even hand the results to OSI. It will take me eight or ten hours of reprogramming, but it will work, at least on OSI. I'll wager they have no one capable of doing a spectral match on *red dwarf* stars. Even with the special program I wrote, it took me forever to match the ghost's spectrum to find out its speed. They won't have the benefit of my program because I'll rewrite it to compress the area of the spectrum in the wavelengths that provided the speed confirmation. It's all math anyway, so I'll just use a fudge factor in the critical program calculations. To get the correct information, I'll use that fudge factor in my own calculations. I've already set it up to move the decimal place to the left two places. Without that specific knowledge, no one could get the correct information, even with the best possible data from the telescope. No matter how they tweaked it, all they would get is an interesting star with an unusual spectrum moving our general direction at 0.9 percent of the speed of light. An unusual body moving at an astonishing speed, it's true, but nothing earth shattering. It would take them months, maybe even years to discover the deception using a qualified astronomer and one of the three big telescopes on Mauna Kea. By that time, we should have our group in action and the news released in the manner the group sees as best."

John sat, chin in hands, elbows on desk, listening and thinking carefully until Angus finished. "That brings up another question. What about our meeting in my office with Chelton? We will really need your input and the latest data. We'll have to consider that."

"I need to tell you a bit more." Angus paused as a momentary thought brought a minor look of panic to his face. "Is your office secure? If not, the cat's out of the bag for sure by now."

"You are jumpy, aren't you? Don't worry. I'm quite sure it's safe. Since the Rumley incident, we've screened everyone who comes into the office. The OSI operatives are the only ones who got past the office door since then and we know they were only in your office. Besides checking service people to be sure they are legit, we have a staff member with them at all times when they're here. I'm quite sure my office is clear. Did you notice Andy standing in your door when you went in to meet Miss Techmeyer? We certainly didn't want to leave her alone in there."

"I'm relieved to hear about your security measures. I didn't realize those steps had been taken."

"It was done rather quietly for a purpose. No need to stir up fears and concerns among the staff. We've nearly a hundred people here now, and we've run positive IDs and background checks on each of them. We need an open workplace to do our research, so we're balancing openness with steps we can take to protect everyone from being spied upon. We used a local security consultant who made recommendations to prevent another Rumley experience. Those have been implemented, and I feel rather secure since they have. Now then, what's this I need updated?"

Angus told John what had transpired at the Namahoes', "We selected Serena as chairman and Ruth as secretary. We discussed expansion of the group and wondered what you thought about it."

"I rather like the idea of Serena as chairman. She's definitely a take-charge woman. Regarding the other, we must use extreme care in selecting any new members of the group. It will certainly be helpful if we can find the right people."

By the time they finished, another meeting of the group was scheduled in John's office the next day. Angus would have to hustle to get everyone contacted. In the meantime, they put the Chile plans on hold until they knew the OSI's next move.

STALLING TECHNIQUES

As he walked to his office, Angus thought just how much he would prefer to do the telescope work and the calculations right here in familiar territory. He hoped the OSI would agree to his demands, at least until the crucial work was done. If not, it would be a wild ride.

Lani was waiting for him in his office. She held a large sheaf of papers in her hand and shoved them at him angrily as he walked to his desk.

"Do you know what those OSI clowns have done? They kept all our originals and gave us these lousy copies, even of the photos. They're absolutely useless. I didn't realize what they did until I started setting up the comparison photos for next week's sessions. They've also changed something in your computer. It's much slower than it was before, and I can't access your program to run the preliminary settings."

Angus sat down slowly at his desk. "Calm down, will you? I've never seen you so agitated. We have all the original records of the photos we need for comparisons. We can have new prints made in plenty of time or just view them on the computer."

Lani stood, hands-on-hips and stared straight at him. "I understand you practically threw that female agent out of your office. I doubt I'm any more agitated than you were then. What about your computer? This is the first time I've used it since they had it, and it is definitely much slower."

"You can blame me for the computer being slower and for not being able to run my program. I added a bit of security which slows it down and made it impossible to access any of my programs without a password. With all that's been happening, I forgot to tell you about it. Want to know what my password is?"

"Of course," she replied as she sat on the chair beside his desk.

"Guess!"

"How could I?"

"Try my Hawaiian name."

Lani smiled broadly. "Sitting Duck?"

"You got it! Only all lowercase and no space."

"That's quite clever. No one would ever guess, except me."

"And everyone at the party."

"Care to tell me the latest on the Dragon Lady? What did she have to say, and what's she up to?"

"Miss Techmeyer?"

"Of course! I know she didn't stop by to exchange pleasantries. What did she want?"

"Your job. She is replacing you with herself as my assistant."

"Come now, seriously. What did she want?"

"I'm not kidding. She told me she was replacing you as my research assistant, and from now on, I would be working for her. Honest, those were her very words."

Lani looked stunned. "She can't do that, can she?"

"She thinks she can, but I told her she can't. I said I would walk out and leave them all hanging unless you stayed on and she left me alone."

"Are you serious? How did it end up?"

"It's still up in the air. I gave her until this afternoon to agree to leave me completely on my own with your assistance. I said it would take someone else at least a year, maybe two to get to where I am with this project. She said she thought I was bluffing, but I guarantee she is quite certain I'm not."

"Are you? Bluffing I mean?"

"Not one little bit. I'll go over the hill permanently before I'd work for that witch. John and I talked it over, and we have a contingency plan just in case she presses the point for OSI. I'm guessing she has to run this by a superior or two before she answers. Even if she steps back for the moment, she'll come on in force as soon as the data is in. We have to stall the data transmissions long enough to get them out of here. I've moved it up one day on the calendar already. By the time we run the critical data, we'll be three days ahead. We can have the data out of here and in safe hands before they know we even have it. Here's what will happen when push comes to shove."

Angus explained their plan for him to assume Rumley's identity and flee to Chile. "Execution of the plan depends on what Techmeyer does. John thinks she won't back off a bit, and I'll have to leave. In that case, you'll have to handle the telescope work by yourself. Then, after an appropriate wait, you will be transferred to Cerro Pachon. Several people have already been transferred, so there will be little chance your transfer would raise any eyebrows."

"I'm going to South America?"

"Only if it becomes necessary for me to go. I will precede you by at least two weeks."

"It seems so ironic."

"What?"

"I'll be going to Chile to be with Dick Rumley. Don't you think that a bit ironic?" Lani said with a smile.

Angus grinned and chuckled. "I see what you mean. And I'll be turning all my research over to him as well. In any event, let's do nothing drastic until we have to. I should have my answer from OSI sometime this afternoon. My guess is they'll go along with me as long as they feel sure we're not pulling anything on them. We must cooperate with them fully up to the last minute. As long as they feel certain we think they have caved in completely, we should be quite safe. I'll lord my tactical victory over them and rub their noses in my superiority. They'll be so sure my ego is in control, they can manipulate me to do their bidding. That should gain us the three or four days we need to obtain the proper data and provide them with the doctored information."

"What if they won't go along and insist on running things?"

"Then you, my dear, will take the measurements and do the same thing right under their noses. Miss Techmeyer has a low opinion of you and has not connected us in any way. This will provide you with a huge tactical advantage. Just play up the innocent young assistant to her dominance and you can get away with murder. I will walk out in a huff and disappear off the face of the earth. You can express amazement at Dr. Thomas walking out. Several weeks later, you, the proper data and the fake Dick Rumley will be joined at Cerro Pachon to finish what we started. OSI will be left with no one who can tell them their data has been doctored. It will take them months to discover the deception, and by that time, we should be releasing the information."

"I hope nothing happens to thwart those plans. You never know what might come up. Remember Murphy's law?"

"You bet I do. I also remember many a broken play where I was able to make a big gain by using my instincts in a completely new and unplanned sequence of events."

"And how many times did you lose on a broken play?"

"Too often, unfortunately, but we just can't let it happen here. The stakes are a lot higher. Have faith. I'll bet the good Lord is on our side. If everything falls apart, we'll just have to regroup and try another plan. Remember, most of the critical information is stored in our heads. There's no way they can get their hands on that unless we let them."

"That's true. In addition, they are looking for something specific and different from what we know is out there. As long as they are expecting space invaders, the truth will evade them no matter how hard they look."

"You have that right," Angus replied. "Now, all we can do is to wait for their call. Meanwhile, we've lots to do no matter what happens. Let's proceed as though this is my last day here."

Lani shook her head. "I'm nervous about this. There will be days of intense work with the telescope, so you've a lot to teach me in a short time. I hope I can get it all down before you disappear."

"Relax! It's a piece of cake. I've already programmed the computer to position the telescope for both the photos and parallax measurements. You will only have to check the results and rerun any part that doesn't come out right. The hardest part will be taking the spectra we need to determine the ghost's exact speed. I've rewritten the special spectra program to download the information directly to those high-capacity floppy disks. You'll only be able to get six readings on each disk, so you'll need to be prepared to change disks after every six readings are recorded. The program will pause, and a message will be displayed to remind you after every six readings. That will be approximately every forty-five minutes. You must change the disks within a minute of when the message appears, or we might lose some of the data."

"That means nearly six hours of constant attention during the middle of the night. Guess I should have tried to get a day job," Lani added with a smile. "How will I get those disks out? Surely OSI will be watching closely during this entire process."

"You remember what I told you about moving the actual schedule ahead three days?"

"That's right. It slipped my mind. They still may start searching anyone leaving your office by then, even though it will tip their hand. How will we get around that?"

"Jack Mercer will be our ace-in-the-hole, so to speak. He is helping me with the adjusted schedule because he handles all scheduling for the use of the telescope and would have to arrange the real times. Jack's one of the good guys OSI turned off when they questioned him just before our little altercation. Should you be at all concerned about being searched, put the disks back in the box with the blank disks and leave them right in the cabinet. Jack can pick them up during his late night sorties and either pass them on to you outside or ship them to us."

"I always carry my purse. I'll be quite sure they won't search me that particular night if they don't do it routinely. Besides. I'll be leaving about five in the morning. They might not be up then."

"Don't count on that. You'll be leaving at that hour two days before you have the data disks. They'll know your schedule by then."

"Maybe I should start working nights a week early. They'll be used to my new schedule by the time the data is in, and if they're going to search me, I'll know. The chances of them stopping me on that one night would be extremely slim."

Angus shook his head. "I still don't like it. Too much of a risk."

"Suppose, in addition to my purse, I start carrying the laptop when I go to and from work. If anything would make them suspicious, that would. If they stop me to examine the laptop a few times and find nothing, they may get tired of spending the time to do so and quit. That would give me a clue as to their search procedure. When I start working nights, I'll wear those loose fitting Hawaiian outfits I wear at home. I can slip those six disks inside my undies before I leave. They'll be well hidden, and I doubt OSI will search there!"

"They danged well better not. I still want you to leave the disks for Jack if there's the least suspicion in your mind you will be searched. That will remain our plan even if they leave us alone, and I am still here. I don't think they have any suspicions about you except possibly as an unwitting ally. I would be surprised, though, if they didn't test you somehow. Our best chance would be if they continued to see you as just another Gemini employee. Should they discover or even suspect the truth of our relationship, it would disrupt all our plans."

"Let's not even think about that. Some contingency plans are in order, just in case, but let's hope we never have to use them."

"My guess is they will lie low until the first scheduled night of telescope use. Then they will appear in force to monitor all that goes on. By then, the horse will be stolen, and the barn doors won't even be disturbed."

"What does that mean?"

"It's just an old expression. You've never heard that before? Locking the barn door after the horse is stolen? I just rearranged it."

"That's a good one. Never heard it before."

"We learn something new every day."

"I hope your plan holds them off, so you can do the telescope work. I feel a little insecure about doing that by myself."

"You'll do OK. Just practice what I show you today. Once you've run through it a few times, it'll all come to you. Oh yes, one very important thing. As soon as all the data is in, you must erase my program. I don't want anyone else to be able to use it. I've written a batch file that will not only delete the program, but will overwrite its sectors on the hard drive where the program code had been. No one could tell the program had ever been there. If we don't do that, a clever computer person, like Miss Techmeyer for instance, could *unerase* the program and track what we did. I used your name for the batch file, so all you'll have to do is enter 'Lani' at the DOS prompt. After it does its dirty work, the Lani file will erase itself completely and leave no trace. Do the same thing with the laptop at the same time. I'll bet they grab that laptop at some point and work it over big time. They'll find nothing, and that will help keep you above suspicion."

"What if they take it before I get a chance to clear it?"

"You won't be using it for anything, so I booby trapped it with fake programs and false information. If they take it away from you, it will lead them off on a wild goose chase. If they don't, clearing it will remove those fake parts when the data is secure, and that will make for even more guesswork on their part."

"Sounds like you've thought of everything."

"I certainly hope so, but we know something unexpected is bound to come up sooner or later. We'll have to stay on our toes and be ready to change course at all times on short notice. The first test should come this afternoon when we get our answer from OSI."

"Suppose nothing happens, they don't call or give you any hint about their thinking on the subject. What will we do then?"

"We'll just play it out here until we know I must leave. I'll feel better when I know John has made all the arrangements with the British. As soon as that plan is in place, I can leave at almost any time. I doubt the OSI will try to stop me. There's no way they can force me to do their bidding. All they can do is threaten to end my career, and I seriously doubt their ability to do so."

They continued working on preparations for the upcoming events for the rest of the day. The tension created by the waiting for the OSI call made it a long day, indeed. Shortly before four, John called Angus to come to his office. Lani continued working.

Conrad Has a Problem

When Angus arrived at John's office, Weldon Conrad was already seated in the chair next to John's desk. After exchanging greeting pleasantries and returning to his seat, Conrad stated, "We've a bit of a problem, old boy. The plan for you to assume Rumley's identity has run into a snag. We can solve it all right, but it will take as much as a week to do so."

Angus exchanged glances with John and asked, "What problem? I might have to leave at any moment. If so, we'll have to come up with a new idea in a hurry."

"Our barristers warned us, should the local authorities drop the charges against Rumley, he is, in effect, a free man. Our need to have him back in England carries absolutely no weight without extradition papers, and getting them could take several weeks," Conrad replied.

"Are there any alternatives?" Angus asked.

"There is one, but unfortunately, it requires backing up through several layers of legal actions. It means reversing actions we've taken to get him back here in the first place. Our attorney has started that process, but it will take nearly a week to complete. To worsen matters, he's not sure it can even be done."

"That sure chucks a monkey wrench into the works," Angus replied.

"I beg pardon?" Conrad asked.

"Just an old American saying about anything that destroys a plan," John explained. "For the time being, we must hope our friends leave us alone. If they do, there's even time for getting the extradition order. That would be cutting it close."

"Hope and pray Rumley's barrister doesn't get wind of this, or you can jolly well kiss your plan good-bye. He could use delaying tactics for months."

"What if Rumley asked to be returned to England? Wouldn't that work?" Angus asked. "Tell him all charges here in Hawaii will be dropped if he agrees to return to England to face a much lesser charge. Couldn't you leave the charges in place, to be dropped only when he was back on British soil? Even his attorney would want to go for that. Or does he know you have a new reason for wanting him back there?"

"You may have it, old boy. The chap knows nothing about us even wanting him back. I'll run that by our barrister as soon as I can get hold of him. We'll leave the other options in place to be certain."

"You're a good man, Conrad," remarked John. "I'm sorry we can't tell you more. I appreciate your confidence in the two of us."

"If it wasn't for your fine reputations and our joint interests in the Gemini project, I wouldn't consider doing what you ask without knowing why. I don't really *want* to know at this point for obvious reasons.

The less I know, the less I must worry about. Just promise to provide me with a full explanation when it's all over."

"That we'll gladly do as soon as possible."

Conrad called their attorney with Angus' latest suggestion and was promised a speedy reply, probably early the next day. The three men chatted for a while about the details of their various options. There was an obvious camaraderie among them, bolstered by mutual trust and respect. After Conrad left, Angus brought up the possibility of Conrad joining their group.

John shook his head no. "It's not likely. His oath of office probably requires him to inform his superiors of anything he learns. That would create great difficulties. We could approach him, but I'm relatively sure of the outcome. Let's run that by the others at our next meeting."

"OK, I'll second that."

"It's difficult making any decisions with so much still up in the air. We'd best stay in close touch for the time being, so we don't take conflicting actions."

"That's a big must-do. I'll let you know about any changes or new information either in person or through Lani."

"Everything's moving so fast we never know where or when a new factor could pop up."

"I wish we'd hear from OSI. I don't like this waiting."

"I'm with you on that."

"I'd best get back to my office. They could be there at any moment."

Angus headed back to his office at a brisk pace. He was disappointed to find no OSI visitors. Lani sat alone at his desk, working on preparations for the upcoming telescope work. It was a quarter after five.

Noticing the way her long hair tumbled over her shoulder onto the desk as she leaned over to look closely at a photo, he stopped, smitten and took in the view of her. "Wow! You are certainly one beautiful lady."

Lani looked up and smiled softly. "Thank you. What brought that on?"

"I don't know. It just came over me as I walked in and saw you sitting there, your hair lying curled on the desk." He walked around behind her and leaned down. "You smell delicious."

Lani turned slightly, raised her hand and gently pushed his face away. "Don't you start now, Mr. Sitting Duck. We've got too much going on. One of us has to keep their head."

It was not a rebuff, just a gentle reminder.

Angus straightened, slowly letting her hair slip through his fingers. "You're right, of course."

Lani was immediately back to business. "The phone has not rung once since you left. What do you suppose is going on?"

He sat down in the chair beside the desk and stared off into space, looking perplexed. "I don't like the situation at all. I haven't a clue as to what OSI will do. My deadline passed with no word from them."

"It's as though they are playing with you. It's maddening, just waiting and waiting."

Suddenly Angus turned to Lani and said, "I'm outa here. I just can't wait any longer. If they were going to cooperate with me, they would have been back to me by now. I have to assume they are going to force the issue. Here's the routine. I'll make a scene as we leave and then you beg me to stay. Later on, John will come to my apartment to try to talk me into staying. Nothing will work. I'll spend a few days here, getting my things in order until our British friends will be able to ship Rumley off and then we'll make the switch. John's got everything in order, so except for a little hitch in our British friend's plan, I should be in Chile within the week."

Lani sat forward, highly attentive after his last remark. "What's this little hitch?"

"The Brits have a problem getting clearance for Rumley to be shipped off to England. It's a little complicated, but everything's under control."

"That doesn't sound like a little hitch. It sounds to me like a huge problem. What will you be doing until they get Rumley on his way? I don't like it at all. Why not wait until the OSI does something? Maybe Miss Techmeyer is having trouble getting approval to do what you ask. Why don't you give it another day at least?"

"If I stay and they trump up some reason to hold me, it will scuttle my whole project because they'll be watching my every move. In Chile, as Dick Rumley, I can continue my work without interruption. In addition, I could always return for meetings with our group, almost at will."

"What about your mother?"

"Dang! I momentarily forgot she was here. I'll call and arrange to run this past her for a quick check. She'll be back in my apartment by now."

As Angus picked up the phone to call, Lani said in a worried voice, "You appear to be almost in a panic. I'm glad you decided to call Serena. She may help you calm down, so we can think this through carefully."

As soon as Serena answered, Angus said, "Get ready to got out for dinner in . . . "

Serena cut him off, saying sweetly, "There's someone here waiting for you."

"Oh, yeah. Who?"

"Your friends from the OSI. Miss Techmeyer and Mr. Lux. We've been having a nice chat while waiting for you to come home," Serena replied sweetly.

Covering the mouthpiece instinctively and turning to Lani, Angus whispered, "It's the OSI. They're waiting at my apartment." Returning to the phone, he said, "What are they telling you? Why are they there?"

"They want to apologize for the way they've treated you. They decided to come here rather than cause any more disruption of your work. They seem to think it is quite important."

"Those lousy . . . I don't trust them one tiny bit. They're up to something. Don't tell them anything."

"Of course you are," she replied sweetly. "I've been telling them what a terrific son you've been and just how much you love your country. We'll continue our visit until you get here. No need to rush."

"OK, Mom. I got the message. I'll be there as soon as I can."

Lani took Angus hand. "What's going on? Was your mom upset?"

"Both OSI agents are there, and, no, she's not upset. She acted cool as a cucumber on the phone. She'll keep them in conversation till I get there, and they won't learn a single thing. Those two have no idea what they're up against. That Mohawk warrior's mother will pick their brains without their knowing. She won't reveal anything of value. She's a master at that."

"What will you do now?"

"Go home and face the music. That's about all I can do. I'll try to figure out what they're up to. Mom will be a big help there. She's a hard one to fool because of her uncanny instincts in situations like this. I'll probably learn more from her after they leave."

"I'm glad you've calmed down a bit. I was concerned you were acting in panic."

"No. I was just reacting with the old running back's quick instincts. When those instincts work, it's amazing. When they don't, it can be a disaster. They're both a blessing and a curse, depending on the results."

"I much prefer thoughtful consideration, but there are times when only good instincts will work, when there is no time for consideration, and a decision must be made in an instant."

"We're all wrapped up here for the present. You head for home, and I'll go face the enemy."

"I wish you wouldn't say that. We may be at odds with them, but they are still on our side. At least they're supposed to be. They're not the enemy. Ignorance is."

"I hate to admit it, but you are right on. I'm going to do battle with ignorance. Does that sound any better?"

"Oh, all right! But you call me and let me know what's going on as soon as you can."

"I'll run right over and whisper it all in your sweet little ear," Angus said, leaning over and saying softly. "Then we can pick up where we left off a few moments ago."

They headed for the exit together, Angus grinning with delight. "I'm glad OSI finally made a move. Not hearing from them after they received my ultimatum was driving me nuts. I much prefer facing an adversary to guessing in the dark."

They parted at Angus' bike. Her car was just a few steps farther. "Drive carefully. I'll be over as soon as I find out what's going on."

As he rode the mile or so to his apartment his mind went through the recent happenings. Things were moving so rapidly and changing direction so frequently, it was difficult to follow. By the time he locked his bike, he had it well sorted out in his mind. He would be ready for the waiting OSI agents.

*   *   *

Serena opened the door at Angus' knock. The two OSI agents rose from the couch and greeted Angus pleasantly. Angus noted a stack of papers in some disarray on the cocktail table in front of the couch. They were the originals of his work OSI had taken from his files.

After Angus greeted them all, Serena directed them to be seated. "I was just telling these folks how proud I am of what you've been doing and how you have been searching for planets around nearby stars. They think your work is very important. They showed me some of the photos you took with the telescope. They just look like fuzzy dots to me."

Jan Lux commented, "That's what we see as well, nothing but fuzzy dots. That's why we're calling off this entire operation. It's been rather a comedy of errors. From the information we received and made you aware, OSI feared you might have captured on film some highly classified information. After first fearing the worst, foreign power intervention that is, we realized you would have done so quite by accident. We did still have to check it out. We all made some errors in judgement until things were completely out of hand. We hope you will accept our apology and not think too badly of us."

Angus remained apprehensive. "Apology accepted, but it may take some time to get over the anger. My work has been seriously impeded at a critical time. Fortunately, we won't miss these next critical observations. If we missed that schedule, our effort would have been delayed a full year."

Lux rubbed his still pained head, "I'll have to say you are a tough and resourceful adversary. I'm glad you are on our side. No hard feelings over the bump on my head. That was definitely our fault."

Techmeyer offered her apology as well, adding, "That trick I pulled trying to get away from your grip was a painful surprise. You have the most powerful grip of anyone I've run into, and I trained with some muscular agents."

"You had to train for a strong grip in order to keep the ball in the NFL. There were some very rough guys trying to rip it out of your hands on every play. I didn't mean to hurt you. I just couldn't let you loose."

They stayed for about a half hour more, explaining what they did to protect the nation from foreign espionage. They would look forward with interest to any new discoveries Angus would make and told him if he ever needed their help to call on them. They were gracious and almost effusive with their good-byes.

As soon as the door closed behind their visitors, Serena and Angus looked at each other in stunned silence for a long time. Angus opened the door and peered down the hall. Seeing no one he stepped out into the hall and motioned Serena to follow. As soon as he closed the door, he asked, "Do you believe anything they said?"

"Not a word! They are quite certain you are hiding something. They haven't a clue as to what it is, but want that information desperately. They think it is vital to their interests to find out. They spent the entire evening laying down a smokescreen."

Angus chuckled. "Yeah! It was a little thick wasn't it. I'm glad you're on my side. I'll bet they have no idea what went on in your head. Now all we have to do is put into action our best plan for dealing with their apparent withdrawal."

"My guess is they will pull away until your new readings are finished, maybe even a little longer. Then they'll watch you like a hawk and do what they can to get hold of any information. They may even bring in some new agents, undercover perhaps."

"We'll still have to watch our phone conversations. Phone taps are the easiest to use and they will probably have them all over the place. The one thing about phone taps is we can use them to our own advantage by planting misinformation. Done carefully, we can confirm the existence of the taps. Once confirmed, we can use them to our purpose and lead the OSI on a merry chase. We'll make that a top priority. I doubt they will be following me anymore, at least for the present. I'll keep my eyes open anyway, just in case."

"We'd best let the others know as soon as possible."

Angus headed for the phone. "I'll call John. He'll be glad to know and I'm sure he'll see through them as clearly as we. Then I'll ride over to Lani's and tell her in person. She's really worried, and this should put her somewhat at ease."

"You better treat her well. That gal's a real keeper."

"Don't I know it."

As soon as they stepped back into the apartment, Angus called John and relayed the information about the OSI visit.

"I'm certainly glad to hear that. It's one big problem with which we no longer need to contend." John obviously understood the truth of the situation.

After concluding his conversation with John, Angus turned to Serena and said, "Why don't you grab a bite to eat? I have no idea how long this will take, and I can eat something with Lani at her place."

"There you go, dumping poor old me for a younger woman. I'll just have to struggle through finding and fixing my own dinner and eating alone," Serena said with mock resignation and a couple of fake boo hoos.

"Life's really hard in this modern world," Angus replied in kind, with feigned concern. "You'll just have to bear up under all that pain."

"Seriously, Angus, you know I'm no meddler, but that young lady is a rare jewel in this day and age. I rather get the idea where you're headed with her, but you've never said anything to me about it. You remember those other two ladies you were a little serious about? They were OK, but I never uttered a word for or against them when you said you were thinking of marriage. Lani's a wonderful, kind woman and quite wise for her age. She comes from a warm, friendly, gracious family. She's almost too good to be true, and I like her a great deal. There! I've said my piece and will say nary another word about it."

Angus laughed, almost incredulous. "Mom! I can't believe you said that. Lani must have woven the same spell over you she used to trap me. Since I first dated in high school, you never expressed an opinion about any of the women in my life. I know you're not a meddler, but you came close this time. If I had a recording of your comments, I could blackmail you forever."

"I was just expressing an honest opinion. That's all."

"Opinion noted and I heartily agree, so don't worry. I'm not about to let her get away. Wait till I tell her what you said."

Serena became stern and scolding. "Don't you dare."

"Gotcha!"

"Oh, I should have known you were teasing. Now get over there and let her in on what's happened before I let you have it."

*   *   *

It was still light when Angus arrived at Lani's apartment and locked his bike into the rack under the entrance canopy. He chuckled to himself as he pressed her doorbell, remembering what Serena said about her.

"Who is it?" came Lani's pleasant voice over the intercom.

"Joe's Pizza delivery with the four pizzas you ordered," Angus replied in a high-pitched voice.

"Hah!" was all that came from the speaker as the door buzzed open.

After a long, lingering kiss, Lani asked, "What happened? I'm dying to hear about it."

"They explained they were wrong and apologized. They appeared to accept our position and most likely thought we believed everything they said."

"That's a plus for our side, but how can you be so sure they weren't sincere?"

"Mom's instincts are so good in cases like this, I wouldn't give that the chance of the proverbial snowball in hell. They'll back off and watch from a distance for the present. Sometime after our data is in and calculations are complete, they'll be back in force. At least, that's my guess. They'll probably bug my phones from a remote location. I doubt they will bug my office. A sweep would reveal any transmitter."

"We've done a good job keeping our relationship confidential so far and must continue to do so. As long as I remain just one of fifty or so female Gemini employees, we have a big advantage. I smile inwardly every time I say 'Dr. Thomas' in my most respectful manner. That has become a fun game for me. I hope I don't overact."

"I think you should bow and scrape a bit more. Display more subservience to the great scientist."

"Don't push your luck, *Dr. Thomas*. I have a hard time playing that role as it is. I've already been chastised by a couple of the more militant feminists who believe in the meat ax approach to relationships with male fellow workers. They have no comprehension of the power of the real female in these situations. They merely assume masculine attitudes, concentrating on the most unpleasant and uncivilized of those."

"Wow! I didn't think my little joke would put you on a soapbox. You don't have to convince me. I've always admired strong women. You, your mother and my mother are all strong women. You all have the power that comes from inner strength. You don't have to bluster and posture in imitation of some imagined macho male figurehead to make a point or master a situation. I really admire that in a woman. It certainly wins more important battles than the silly, macho male approach. I could never stomach that in either men or women."

"We certainly see eye to eye on that. Sorry about the soapbox. It wasn't aimed at you, of course. I just get so sick of people insisting hostile aggression is the only way to be assertive. All that does is demonstrate their inability to cope with the situation. Rather like the small child destroying its toy in a fit of anger because it can't get the toy to do what it wants."

"Well now! Since we've solved the battle of the sexes, I've a serious proposal to make."

"Oh! What's that?"

"Let's get married."

"What?"

"Must I get down on my knees? I just asked you to marry me."

"That's what I thought I heard."

"Well? Do I get an answer?"

"This is all so sudden and unexpected. Where's the two carat diamond ring?"

"First time I have ever proposed to a girl, and I get a smart answer. Maybe I should ask your father."

"You want to marry my father?"

"And your mother and the whole darned Namahoe clan. That's what I'll be doing isn't it?"

"Absolutely! It's a package deal."

"Well?" He waited, his face a half smiling question.

Lani stood up, took Angus' hands in hers, looked straight into his eyes and said softly, "You know the answer. We've both known the answer to that since a few days into this new millennium. I couldn't conceive of my life without us as the center. If you hadn't asked me soon, I would have asked you. How's that for feminist assertiveness?"

Angus hugged her tightly. "That's my Lani. Sorry about not having a ring. It came to me so suddenly, at this particular time I mean, I never even thought about a ring. We can pick one out in the next few days."

"And blow our cover for the OSI? Not on your life. You know I was joking about the ring. Let's hold off on that and on telling *anyone* until after this OSI thing is over and we can live a near normal existence."

"Even our families?"

"Especially our families."

"Even my Mom? Your folks?"

"I don't think we should breathe a word of this until OSI is out of the picture completely. Let's not even mention it to each other until that's behind us. It will only be a few more weeks anyway."

"You're right, of course. What a bummer. I want to shout it from the rooftops, and I can't make so much as a peep."

"We both know, and that's all that really counts, for the present anyway."

"How did I ever find such a smart lady?"

"Just lucky I guess. Are you hungry?"

"Just a bit. I'll ignore the last wisecrack."

"I just finished preparing a rather large spinach salad when you showed up. Eggs, bacon bits and all that other good stuff you like. Want to join me?"

"Have you anything a little more substantial to go with the salad? Say a steak or some of that great Hawaiian ham?"

"I do have a nice piece of ham left. I could stand a bit of that myself."

After eating, they sat and relaxed in Lani's small living room. It would be the last relaxation they would have for some time.

10

It was ten o'clock Wednesday morning when Jenny called Angus to the phone. "It's a Miss Ginger Cari on the phone. She wants to talk to Dr. Thomas," she oozed in a mocking, syrupy voice. "Isn't she that wiseacre reporter who tried to pump me a week or so back?" Jenny finished in her normal voice.

"Draw those cat's claws back a bit there darlin'," Angus drawled in his best cowpoke voice. "That little lady wants to do a promotional piece on Gemini for us. We'd better put our best foot forward to show her we're a great professional organization. Just be your normal, gracious self in spite of any misgivings you may have."

"I'll do my best, but you be careful. I've a funny feeling she wants more from you than information on Gemini. My sixth sense is standing the hairs up on the back of my neck, and those hairs are usually reliable." Jenny was genuinely concerned.

"Warning noted and appreciated. You ladies can feel things we poor males never notice. I will be careful, so put her through."

"Dr. Thomas?" Ginger asked sweetly.

"Speaking!"

"How about that lunch we spoke about when we met? I'd like to get started on the piece about Gemini and their football legend. Today or tomorrow would be great for me. Otherwise, it would have to be the latter part of next week. How's your schedule?" Ginger spoke quite professionally yet with just a touch of innocent femininity.

After a moment of thought he realized today was probably the least busy day he would have for several weeks. "Actually, today would be fine. It's probably the slowest day I'll have for the next few weeks."

"Great! Unless you have a better idea, I have a favorite spot where it's quiet; the view's spectacular, and the salad bar is awesome. How does the top of the Mokuloa Hotel strike you?" she asked with obvious enthusiasm.

"I've never been there, but I'll take your word for it. Sounds fine to me. How about meeting there at 11:30? Is that too early for you?"

"No, 11:30 sounds good. I'll arrange a window table where we can see all of Hilo Bay. I'll be there a little early to prepare some notes on things to ask you."

"Anything I should bring? Special information? Gemini propaganda?"

"Just your brain and your appetite. I've already obtained the nuts and bolts from your PR people."

"OK! See you at 11:30."

"See you. Bye."

A quick plan had him leaving at ten after eleven. He guessed it would take him fifteen minutes to bike to the Mokuloa and five to find the restaurant. Angus was seldom early for an appointment and never late short of a major disaster en route.

When he told Lani of his lunch meeting, she replied, "Sure you don't want me along for protection? I understand Miss Cari is quite a dish. Maybe I should go along to protect my interests."

"What is it with you ladies? Along comes an attractive outsider and all the claws come out."

"Oh! Who else is suspicious?"

Angus related Jenny's conversation and his own reply.

"Maybe I should be concerned. Jenny has a really good read on people. Suppose she and I just happen to have lunch there at the same time."

Angus' face showed a pained expression. "Are you kidding? Surely you're not serious."

"I'll have to ask Jenny what she thinks. Besides, we haven't gone to lunch together for months. It might be fun."

"Come on! Don't play games. This is supposed to be a serious, professional interview. It's for the good image of the Gemini Project."

"Using a handsome, eligible, famous athlete as bait and at one of the most romantic restaurants on the island, of course I'm suspicious . . . not of you but of little Miss Reporter. No, I won't be spying on you, but I think Jenny's right, so you watch yourself. And yes, my claws are out. I think that's normal when another cat's sniffing around my man."

"Since I still enjoy living, I don't think you've a worry in the world. I'd not only have Jenny and you to contend with, but big tiger cat Serena would be right in there with you. Right now I've the three of you on my side, and I'd like to keep it that way. The groupies and hot-after-an-athlete babes never got to me when I was playing ball, so I think I can handle whatever this one throws at me, even if she does throw a curve or two. I'll keep things on a professional level. Now, I've got to leave. I wouldn't want to be late for my tryst."

"OK. Off you go. I hope the interview goes well. I know I don't have to worry about you. Seriously, be gentle if she does something stupid. A crushed female ego could spell a nasty PR piece or even worse," Lani warned with obvious sincere concern.

"That's more like my lady," Angus said with a smile as he kissed her good-bye and left for his luncheon appointment.

*   *   *

It was precisely 11:30 when Angus stepped off the elevator into the restaurant. The lunch crowd was just beginning to arrive, but there were still a number of empty tables. A quick look around and he spotted Ginger sitting at a table by the center window overlooking Hilo Bay. As he reached the table, he knew Jenny was right on. Ginger was dressed in a rather short, white skirt and a brightly colored blouse with small ruffles down the front. The ruffles around the low-cut neckline framed her ample cleavage. Her hair had that slightly messed up I-just-got-out-of-bed look. Ginger obviously had much more on her mind than the interview. Angus was surprised at the animal attraction he felt. This was going to be a challenge.

As he sat down and they exchanged greetings, Ginger leaned forward. Angus had great difficulty keeping his eyes from focusing on the low-cut neckline of her blouse. The light, heady fragrance of her perfume was just perceptible over the pleasant aromas of the restaurant. Two glasses of a white wine were at their places on the table and soft music was playing in the background. Ginger had pulled out all the stops.

"I took the liberty of ordering a light German wine for us. I hope you like it," she said softly.

Angus was rather stiff: "I'm sure I will. Is this really conducive to the type of interview we talked about? This is not what I expected."

"I think it's important to be relaxed for this kind of interview. The view, the music, the food, the wine, the ambiance all contribute to relaxation. I may get you to tell me things you otherwise might keep to yourself. It's all part of the strategy of my interview."

"I've been interviewed by the press many times, but never in an atmosphere like this. How about we get some food from this legendary salad bar."

"Why don't we have a little wine and talk for a while first? I want to peek into your soul and find out who the real Angus Thomas is. I feel a depth there, the dedicated scientist searching for his own special Holy Grail. Let's drink to your finding whatever you're searching for." She raised her glass.

Angus picked up his glass in answer to her toast and gently tasted the wine. It was light and dry yet with a hint of fruit, an excellent choice for a lunch wine. "This is quite good," he said as he returned the glass to the table. "Now about this dedicated scientist stuff, I think you'll find I'm not mysterious. I'm very much a what-you-see-is-what-you-get kind of person. I'm an astronomer because I have always been fascinated by our universe and enjoy the search for more knowledge about it. You might say it's my first love. My financial success at football enables me to do whatever I choose, and the frontier of astronomy and cosmology is where I choose to work. You might try to romanticize it, but it's really quite simple and straightforward."

"Maybe that's how you look at it, but the general public won't ever see it like that. When it comes to sports legends, and you are certainly one of those, they like mystery and intrigue. I've done a little research on you and found some interesting information. You had a reputation for being a moral and honorable man, a real straight arrow among the group of rues and womanizers who were your football buddies. They all had good things to say about you, including what a fine example you set for young people. That's unusual. How did you maintain that kind of reputation and still keep some real rounders for close friends? Most men would be cut from the group as a goody-two-shoes, yet you remained. I find that fact alone fascinating."

Angus smiled as he thought of the close friends he had among the team. Some were really bad dudes, yet Angus found something to like in each of them. "I suppose that's hard to understand, but character, morals, honor and lifestyle are powerful forces at work in each of us. I just happen to believe these are individual choices for each person and shouldn't be thrust down the throats of other people by anyone. I also believe example is the best sermon for those who are moldable. Really bad people won't be reached by anything, so why bother?"

"In my research, I ran across a Cy Dooley who is now a minister in L.A. Isn't he the one who had such a bad reputation both on and off the field?"

Angus laughed. "Cy was a really hard case and quite a challenge. I still felt there was a decent man with a kind streak beneath all that anger. His first remark to me when I joined the team was, 'Another white boy wonder. I'll dump your pasty face in the mud our first team scrimmage.' When I pointed out I was a Mohawk and not a 'white boy' he muttered something about an Oreo cookie and stomped off. Cy was not usually a pleasant person, but I decided to find out how to get beneath that tough and angry exterior."

"Apparently you succeeded with truly amazing results," Ginger replied, smiling genuinely. "When I talked to him on the phone, he said you were the one responsible for his change. He laughed as he said over the years, the angrier he got with you and the meaner he treated you, the kinder and more helpful you became. Finally, he couldn't take it any longer and gave up his anger. That triggered his turnaround. He says he's been getting even with you for that by using the same tactics on angry, inner city youths. He says you were the single, most powerful positive force that changed his life. That's quite a testimonial."

Angus chuckled, remembering his experience with Cy. "Cy tends to exaggerate some, but he was a hard case all right. It took me three years to get through to him. I can still remember the day he broke down in the locker room. He walked up to me at my locker, dirt and blood from the game all over his craggy face, tears in his eyes and a somber look. 'I give up.' he finally said. 'I just can't be mean to you no more. Will you be my friend?' He stood there for a moment, then kind of awkwardly, he wrapped his huge arms around me, gave me a bear hug and began sobbing. We stood there hugging and crying and laughing at the same time. It was a truly magic moment I will never forget. Finally noticing several members of the team watching in disbelief, he turned and said, 'One peep or laugh outta you, and I'll smash your face.' Those were the last angry words I ever heard that man say."

"That's an amazing story. It certainly caps the information I dug up from news reports and from talking to him. The turnaround in his behavior, both on and off the field, was noted by the press on numerous occasions. He went from one extreme to the other almost overnight. You must be pleased with your effort."

"Yes, pleased, but even more than that, thankful . . . thankful I never gave up. Maybe it was just my Mohawk stubbornness that kept me at it. That three-year battle with Cy was one of the toughest I ever faced. He's the one person from my football days who keeps in constant touch. It's a rare month that goes by when we don't have a long talk on the phone. He tells me about the young people he's working with, his kids he calls them. I tell him about the stars. We laugh a lot and cry a little. He's a really good friend."

"He told me the same about you," Ginger paused thoughtfully. "May I change the subject? There was mention of several ladies you were going with for a time. How come no one ever bagged you? I mean, you're quite a prize. What woman wouldn't want a relationship with an intelligent, good looking, wealthy football legend with a really good reputation? Why is it you never found the right woman?"

"I don't really know," he answered quite truthfully. "I just haven't met the right woman." He would have liked to tell her about Lani, but the present need for secrecy stilled his voice on that subject. "The ladies I went with for a time were all decent women, but we just didn't click for a lifetime commitment. There were three I remember well. I parted company with each of them in a friendly way. None of those relationships really went anywhere and were best ended."

"I wonder if those ladies felt the same way? Do you think they felt the same as you about it?"

Angus shook his head sadly. "Angie, the first one, certainly didn't. She pestered me off and on for almost a year after we broke up. That made me a little gun-shy for a while. I was a little more cautious with the other two."

"Do you presently have any love interest?"

Angus felt uncomfortable lying about it and squirmed inwardly as he answered. "No, just my work."

"Then there's a chance for me," Ginger said smiling intently. "I can be a bit forward, but I am attracted to you. I think it's your mind.

I meet so many drooling dolts in this business. I really have a hard time finding a man who's interested in anything but sports and hopping in bed. I seldom go out anymore. I hate dull conversation and protective wrestling, and that's about all I've done my last few dates."

"Dressing like you have for our interview, I can see why you have those wrestling matches. You're a very sensual, sexy lady, and my physical attraction for you is strong. Acting on physical attraction has never been my style. I really think we would be a poor match."

"I hope I haven't blown it with you, but I have a confession to make. As a reporter, I have played many roles to get the real story. I even played a coy teenager at the local high school for one investigative report. When I researched you for this interview, I found all this almost *sainthood* around you in the press reports and from those I talked to, including some of your detractors. I decided the location, the atmosphere and playing the seductress would give me an answer on the reliability of the data I had. I found out what I needed to know. No, I don't normally dress like this. In fact, it makes me uncomfortable, and I would like to change into something more appropriate as soon as possible."

"You certainly had me fooled. You played the role convincingly. Right now, I don't know what to believe about you."

"Check with your friend, Pete, if you can't take my word for it. He knew all about my plan. He even chuckled and said he'd like to be here watching your reactions. In the meantime, I'd like to change. I have the clothes I wore here in the room I used to change into this ridiculous outfit for the act. It will only take me a few minutes, and then we can have lunch and get on with the interview."

"I can take your word. There's no need to check with Pete. I'll just hold down the fort until you get back. Incidentally, you have both the mental and the physical attributes to carry off your act quite well."

"I'm not sure, but I think I have been complimented and slammed at the same time. Sorry I had to do that to you, but I did have to know the truth, and now I do."

Angus smiled as he watched Ginger walk toward the elevator. Every male in the place stopped to watch as she walked by. No doubt about it, act or no act, she could be one very sexy lady. With the act explained, Ginger was turning out to be a woman of substance. If not for Lani, he would definitely have been interested.

In about fifteen minutes a transformed Ginger stepped off the elevator, a picture of the professional woman. The crisp, grey slacks were topped with a tailored, white blouse that couldn't quite hide her figure. Her hair was now neatly in place and Angus noticed a number of male eyes still followed her as she approached the table.

"Now then, I feel much more like me," she remarked as she sat down. "I wonder if people will think you are having lunch with two different women?"

"I like this one a bit more than the other," Angus said with a grin. "Ready for the salad bar now?"

"Let's go. I'm famished!"

*   *   *

The lunch and interview lasted until after two. As they were getting ready to leave, Ginger said, "I want to thank you for all the information. I now have a much better understanding of what's going on at Gemini and your part in it. I think you'll like the article when it's finished. If it's good enough, it might be picked up by a magazine section for papers all over the country. At least, I hope so. I could use a great byline story. It could do wonders for my career."

"I'm sure you will do an excellent job. Just remember, I'm as serious about my science as I used to be about football, maybe even more so. I hope you can get that across in your article. It's also important to show Gemini in a good light. People like to hear at least some of their tax money is going to serve humanity in a positive way."

Ginger was emphatic. "You can count on it. One more thing. I really would like to see you again, personally I mean."

After a moment of tense silence while he again struggled with a necessary lie, Angus replied thoughtfully, "Under normal circumstances, I'd like that. Unfortunately, these are not normal circumstances for me. Off the record, I will probably be leaving for another position halfway around the world within a few months. Please don't breathe a word of this to anyone. I wouldn't say a thing if I didn't feel I could trust you. For that reason I don't think it fair to either of us to start a relationship now. This whole thing is very hush-hush, and I've already said more than I should, so, please, don't ask me about it. When the time comes, I'll see to it you get the story first. I can at least do that."

"I will have to say, that was one of the nicest turn downs I've ever heard. Just remember, should things change, please get in touch. You never know what might happen."

They walked in silence to the elevator. When it stopped at Ginger's floor she leaned over quickly and gave him a kiss on the cheek. "That's to remember me by," she whispered in his ear, then stepped off the car.

Though there was not the least doubt in his mind about Lani and him, Ginger Cari would be hard to forget. She, too, was quite a woman.

PARALLAX AND SPECTROSCOPY

Preparations for taking photos, spectra and other measurements of Barnard's Star and the ghost were now proceeding at a feverish rate. Angus took particular care in selecting the grating angles and dispersion for the spectrograph. Since the motion of the ghost toward the earth had moved the visible light spectrum far into the ultraviolet, virtually all of that light would be absorbed in the atmosphere. The visible light spectrum to be captured would actually originate from the ghost as near infrared, reaching the telescope as visible light because the entire spectrum is shifted so far into the blue. The spectrum would be captured both on photographic plates and digitally by use of a charge-coupled device or a "CCD." By this time, the ghost should be viewed separately from Barnard's Star making both parallax measurements and spectrographic analysis easier and far more accurate than those of six months ago.

Angus was particularly anxious about the data transmission from the instruments on the mountaintop to the Op Center. This raw data would be first recorded by the Op Center's computer and held there for his use by his own computer. He planned to modify the new data as he did before, so the ghost would appear to be traveling a hundred times slower than its actual speed. Because of the huge amount of data and because doctoring the spectra would require a great deal of meticulous work, he knew it would require several days to complete. This would have to be done before downloading to his computer, or it would be obvious to Miss Techmeyer something was amiss. Angus would have to doctor each night's data as soon as it was in. That would mean several days with little or no sleep, during which time the original data would be vulnerable to capture. If the OSI appeared before the changes were completed, the fat would be in the fire for certain.

Having the use of the telescope three days before it appeared on the schedule was cutting it close. Angus guessed the OSI would be on the scene the first night they expected his readings to be done. They would have some pretense for being there and would probably have their own astronomer along to observe. It would be necessary for Angus and Lani to fake some activities to make it appear the actual telescope work was being done as they watched. Fortunately, Angus had written most of the programs they would be using, and he and Lani were the only ones at Gemini who knew how to use them.

To avoid suspicion, they followed Lani's plan and started working nights during the week before the actual readings were to take place. By the first night of actual telescope work, they were well accustomed to working through the night and sleeping in the daytime. The day before the actual telescope work was to begin, Angus remained at the office to see if this would trigger OSI to show up. They were relieved when no one appeared while they were working on the telescope or doctoring the data. Each morning, as she left for home, Lani carried out the disks with the actual, undoctored data without incident and hid them temporarily in a cereal box in her cupboard.

By four o'clock in the afternoon of the third day, a weary Angus finally finished and collapsed into his R-and-R chair. He was anticipating three nights of work on the newly acquired data while acting as if he were doing telescope work for the benefit of the OSI. This would not be much fun.

As he was trying to relax, Angus had a sudden fear-inspiring thought that brought him out of his chair. *Could OSI tap the fiberoptic link between the telescope and the Op Center and intercept his raw data?* he wondered. If so, all the efforts at hiding the true information would have been in vain. He grabbed the phone. "Jenny! Get Jack Mercer on the phone for me."

In a few minutes Jack answered, "What's up?"

"Tell me if there has been any work done recently on the fiberoptic link between here and the telescope, any kind of work at all."

"Why? Are you having problems getting your data?"

"No, not any problems I know, but can you stop by my office? I've something to show you."

"Be there in about five minutes."

"I'm a bit concerned about our suspicious friends," Angus remarked when Jack stepped into his office. "Could they have put a tap on our fiberoptic link and captured the data stream from the telescope?"

"Not without digging up the cable and cutting into it. I can guarantee you, if that happened, we'd know it. The only junction boxes on that cable are inside the telescope building and inside the Op Center. Even the amplifiers are sealed inside the cable cover and buried. Any disruption of that cable would have raised a huge red flag right here."

Worry still showed on Angus' face. "Is there any way at all the data stream could be copied or otherwise obtained?"

"The data is fed directly from the instruments on the mountain to the computer here in the Op Center. That raw digital data must be converted to usable information by our computer. You worked with that enough to know how difficult it would be to deal with the raw data. Without the programs and knowledge of how to use them, the raw data would be absolutely useless."

"You remember, OSI took one of the network drives when they raided us don't you? They have all of our programming and old data. Wouldn't they be able to use that to make the raw data usable?"

"I seriously doubt it. We don't have very high-tech security on our data, but we do some things to keep our scientists' information fairly secure from prying eyes until it's ready for publication. There is one way data being manipulated by any PC could be obtained. A sensitive radio frequency receiver within a few hundred yards of a PC can capture the RF signal emanating from the electronic processes in the PC. It's a weak signal since most good PCs are well shielded to prevent RF interference. The right equipment can convert that digital signal and enter it into another computer as an exact duplicate of the data being processed by the CPU."

Angus cursed in frustration. "I'll bet that's what they're doing. Could it be done from a vehicle near the building?"

"Yes, it could. As long as the vehicle was within about five hundred yards of the PC. It would take considerable time and effort, but it could be done."

"They could do it from the visitor parking lot or even from the street for that matter. I'll bet we've been had."

"Think positive, Angus. We moved your work schedule back three days. If they bit on that, they will only be copying your data starting tonight. All they'll get if they copy the transmissions for the next three days will be the infrared survey results the Australians are doing. I am assuming your data has been downloaded into your PC by now and only the raw data remains in the main computer. They won't be able to obtain anything you don't copy from one place to another or use in making calculations. Just don't handle any sensitive data for the next few days, and you'll be home free."

"I hope you are right."

"What is it about your data that interests them? I don't mean to be nosy, but I am really fascinated by what it could be. I don't care for their tactics, but OSI is a rather significant operation, and there must be something important to have triggered their attention."

"I just can't give you the details right now other than they made an extremely erroneous assumption based on a single, offhand remark I made to a colleague and which they intercepted. It's all a big mistake on their part. In a month or so, when I publish the results of my findings, it will all be explained. Until my findings have been confirmed, they must be kept confidential. You know the routine."

"Sure do. I'm still quite curious about what you've discovered. It must be something very unusual."

"Let me assure you, you'll be among the first to know as soon as it can be made public. I'll personally place a copy of my findings in your hands."

"Couldn't ask for more than that. If I were you, I wouldn't handle any sensitive data for the next few days, just in case your friends are listening."

"Thanks for your help and your confidence. Your work in keeping all this computer equipment humming is important and maybe not as appreciated as it should be."

"Thanks for that. Frequently, when I'm called into an office, it's by a frustrated scientist whose computer is not doing what they think it should. Then I get yelled at when I can't fix the problem immediately. It just goes with the job. I do get a lot of apologies, though, after their frustration cools down."

"I'll bet you do face some frustrated people. High-powered scientists are not known for their patience in matters that interfere with their work. I'll bet some can be quite testy at times."

"You've got that right."

"I don't need to hold you anymore. I know you're busy."

"Anytime, Angus. Anytime I can be of assistance, just holler. I leave you to your fun and games with OSI."

With that parting comment, Jack headed back to his office, and Angus returned to the work at hand. He smiled as he looked at the box of high capacity disks where duplicates of all the new data had been copied as they were downloaded to his own PC. As he was considering what would be safe to do with the PC, the phone rang. It was Jenny.

"Your friendly OSI man, Mr. Lux, is at my desk and wants to see you. He has another man with him. Should I send them up?"

Angus thought, *Here they are, right on cue,* then said, "Sure, send them right up."

He scooped the box of backup disks off his desk and dropped them into the wastebasket, covering them with the papers in the basket. A quick check around the office revealed no other obvious problems. He would be ready for the OSI. They seemed to be doing exactly what he had predicted by appearing on the scene just as the scheduled telescope work was to begin. He much preferred facing them to wondering what they were doing behind his back. When he opened his door, Lux and an older man appearing to be in his late sixties were headed his way through the outer office.

"I hope you don't mind if we stop by for a short visit," Lux began as they walked into his office. Turning to the other man, he introduced him to Angus, "This is Professor Hans Schuman from Cal Tech. He's an astronomer associated with NASA and is currently working here in Hawaii at the Keck telescopes. Professor, Dr. Angus Thomas."

The two men shook hands, eyeing each other carefully as they exchanged greetings. Angus was quite aware of Professor Schuman's work, remarking, "I understand you are tracking a number of earth orbit crossing asteroid trajectories for possible collisions in the future. Found any we should worry about?"

"So far, none that will concern us for less than a few thousand years. I understand you have discovered a most unusual object."

Lux interrupted. "We asked the Professor to examine your data for us some time ago. He is aware of the concerns we had early on and has confirmed much of what you told us. There are a few questions remaining unanswered which are best posed by an expert in your field. If you could answer his questions, we could then close this entire investigation and be on our way."

"Actually, I've been working day and night for the last four days. I haven't showered or shaved for the last two; I'm extremely irritable, and I still have a great deal to do. If you can wait for three or four weeks, I'll see to it you get a complete report of my findings.

Professor, you know it is not proper to release information without confirmation and it will take those few weeks to complete our research and confirm our findings."

Professor Schuman nodded his head in acknowledgment. "We're both headed back to California tomorrow. There are just a few points we would like clarified. I know you will have a lot to do for the next three days, but this will only take a few minutes. Actually, just three questions are all we ask."

Angus was still obviously agitated. "Well, let's get it over with. Shoot!"

"What is the exact nature of the object you have been studying? What are its position, size, speed and path?"

"That sounds like five questions and not three, but I'll answer as best I can. I don't know its exact nature. It appears to be a small, class-G star, similar to our sun but about half its mass. It's somewhere between three and four hundred light years from the earth and approaching our current position at around 0.9 percent of the speed of light. That is a phenomenal rate of speed. Undoubtedly the fastest moving object ever found within our galaxy. As a fellow astronomer, you, especially, should understand why I want this kept under wraps until I get confirmation."

"I most certainly do understand. I look forward to your results. In fact, I would greatly appreciate the opportunity to confirm your findings for you if you will permit me."

"Are you sure there's nothing else that you need to know, Professor?" Lux asked.

"Nothing that can't wait until he publishes. I see no need for concern. Dr. Thomas is a well-known and respected member of our fraternity. A few weeks or even a few months of waiting for his results to be published won't change a thing." Turning toward Angus, he continued. "Keep on with your work and good hunting. I have to admit a bit of professional jealousy. If your speed calculations are correct, you'll go down in history as the man who discovered the fastest moving celestial body in our galaxy. Then you'll have a real project, developing a theory on how it attained such a remarkable speed."

Angus decided Schuman was OK in his book, a real professional. If he read him right, he would probably try to confirm his findings as soon as he could get time on the Keck telescopes. By the time that was done, his information would be public knowledge. He chuckled inwardly at the thought of a distraught call he would probably receive from the professor when he discovered the truth.

"Thanks, Professor Schuman," Angus said as he stood to usher them to the door. "I appreciate your confidence and will keep you informed."

They stood at the door talking for several minutes before leaving. Angus could tell Lux was not pleased with Schuman's performance. It was apparent Schuman was not under OSI's control. Angus couldn't even guess what OSI's next action would be, but he was certain they weren't through with him yet. He watched as Lani passed the two on her way through the outer office. As she approached, Angus thought of another ploy he could use with the data to confuse OSI.

"Who were those two?" Lani asked as she walked in.

"That was Jan Lux from OSI and a Professor Schuman from over at the Keck operations," Angus replied as she shut the door.

"So OSI never left. They came back just when you said they would. It's a good thing we played games with your schedule."

"The professor seemed an all right guy. He's probably the first competent astronomer OSI could find on short notice. I doubt they have him under their control. Unfortunately, Lux is going to stay on our case, and what they do next is anyone's guess."

"You have that glint in your eye. What are you thinking of?"

"Just a little game with the spectra we just took. I think they fell for our rescheduling. As soon as they discover we already have our data, they'll be back. I'm going to tweak the records of the spectra on both the main system and on my PC to show the object moving at 100.9 percent of the speed of light. If they get hold of that information and turn it over to any kind of expert, they'll be laughed at big time. Everyone knows nothing can move faster than the speed of light."

"Won't they know they've been had?"

"I certainly hope so. By the time they get Schuman to schedule the Keck and obtain new spectra, it will be several months. By then, we should be able to release the real information to the public. I'll bet Schuman will drag his heels for the OSI. He seemed more interested in protecting our findings than in aiding them. My bet is as soon as he realizes the truth about the ghost, he'll understand exactly what we're doing and go along with us. He seemed to be a savvy old codger, not under OSI's thumb at all."

"I hope you're right. What's next?"

"Right now, I'd like you to run down to John's office before he leaves and see if the Brits have found a way to spring Rumley, so we can do our switch. Tell John OSI is still on our case, and we'd best implement the plan for going to Chile. In the meantime, I'll get busy tweaking some spectra."

"On my way."

As he sat down to the keyboard, Angus said a silent prayer the Rumley switch would work and work soon. He was convinced the OSI would take over as soon as they believed he had all the data. He would not be comfortable until he and the correct data were safely hidden. Many unresolved questions went through his mind. *How would the Rumley switch work? Would his move to Chile go as planned? When and where would their growing group meet next? How would Lani handle the move to Chile? What would it be like there?* He hadn't the slightest knowledge of the location, the country, or the people at Cerro Pachon. There was one thing he knew for certain. Gemini South was a year behind Gemini North, and much of the instrumentation he needed would not be installed for several months.

As he returned to the task at hand, he guessed it would take him a couple of hours to change the records and hide the fact they had been changed. He chuckled, thinking of how Miss Techmeyer's explanation of how she could detect modified files taught him the way to hide those changes so they couldn't be discovered. In addition to changing each file with spectral data to show a shift to his newly chosen speed of 100.9 percent of the speed of light, he would have to find and change all written references and conclusions to the actual speed to show 0.9 percent of light speed. He was certain this erroneous data would convince the OSI and any expert they used, the instrumentation had been in error. They might also assume he missed the 100.9 percent figure and erroneously assumed it to be indicating 0.9 percent.

He then went through and reset all the file date and time stamps to show their original date and time. Next, he wiped all the empty drive space clean and defragmented the drives to shuffle all the data into completely new sequences to prevent the possibility of any reconstruction of the old data and hide evidence of his tampering. His last step was to create two new complete backups of his own hard drive and the network drive, overwriting all existing records that could possibly hold any *undoctored* data. He chuckled to himself as he glanced at the wastebasket holding the two sets of backup disks. They would remain there until he could figure the best way for Lani to smuggle them out undetected.

As Angus began the defragment process, Lani returned and plopped herself down on the chair beside him. "John tells me the British have convinced Rumley to ask to be returned to England. They can move him out anytime during the next few days. All you need to do is arrange for your own reservations on the same flight to British Columbia."

"Great! I can leave at anytime. I was beginning to get a little nervous with OSI back in the picture. Now I've got to decide whether to put in these last three days to finish our little deception or leave tomorrow. Incidentally, we'd better find a place and a method to meet or at least communicate if I find it necessary to avoid OSI."

"What do you mean?"

"OSI could decide to take me into custody on some pretense as soon as they are sure I've completed my measurements and have the data. I don't think they would try anything until they are quite certain I've finished. My bet is they will try to grab me and my data on some trumped up charge and hold me until they find out what they want to know. If they do, they'll probably try to get me to run all the calculations necessary to make conclusions for them. If I don't cooperate, and I'm quite sure they know I won't, they'll have to get an astronomer who's up on the physics of this project to do the calculations. That will take them more time than they know, because none of my latest calculation programs will be available anywhere but on my safe computer, and the data is all cued to those programs."

"That's why you took time to set up the instruments when you first arrived, to make it difficult to convert to usable data. I wondered about that."

"Actually, it wasn't meant for that purpose. I set the instruments to feed data directly to my program to make it easier for me to convert the data to usable form. It just happens to make it extremely difficult to use the output of the instruments unless you have my computer programs available. It is just blind luck it works so well to hide the true nature of the information from anyone who might want to get their hands on it."

"Let's hope and pray luck stays on our side. What about this meeting place you think we'll need? Do you have any ideas?"

"Right now I'm drawing blanks. Do you have any ideas?"

"I know an absolutely perfect place," Lani exclaimed suddenly. "How about that doctor who took care of you when you were injured? He sounded as though he idolized you. I'll bet he'd be willing to help."

"I don't know. We'd have to level with him about OSI. He might not want to take the chance. I don't suppose it would do any harm for you to contact him."

"Maybe I could feel him out with a phone call. Why don't I do that right now?"

"Good idea! I might have to find a place to stay for a while on really short notice. It isn't quite time yet to make the move to Chile, though I fear it will be within the next few days."

"When am I to see you again? This will be the first time we've been apart. I'll miss you terribly."

"And I'll miss you as well. I don't relish running off to another part of the globe to a place I know nothing about. Other than it being a mountain in Chile, I don't even know where Cerro Pachon is. I understand it's near La Serena, a seacoast city. My one great comfort is that you will be there with me in a few weeks, and we can brave this new adventure together."

"Do you realize, Mr. World-traveler, I've only been as far away from here as Honolulu? This will be quite a step for a little Hawaiian girl to take. I'll be making the entire trip by myself, and that's a little scary. I talked to several of the Chileans here at Gemini, and they tell me few people in La Serena speak any English, and I don't speak Spanish. They say it is a beautiful little city that draws a great many tourists in the summer who come for the warm, sandy beaches and the ocean."

"Sounds like a nice place. Don't worry, hon. We'll be so involved in our project you won't have time to worry about anything. Besides, it will only be for the few months until our information is released."

"Something tells me it's not going to be quite that simple. Look how complicated things have become already. And we haven't even started to work on the latest data. What about that meeting with your cousin Chelton? How can you possibly get here for that?"

"Well, one thing's for sure. There's quite a bit of planning to be done. The interference of OSI has kept our plans in turmoil. Do you think you could get everyone together for a meeting in John's office tomorrow evening, say about six?"

"It just so happens that was the next thing I was going to tell you. John decided the same thing. While I was with him, we called the rest of the group and asked them to meet in his office tomorrow at five. I worried about a possible tap on your phone, so I didn't call your mother. I'm sure you can handle that."

"Great minds, eh?" Angus remarked with a smile. "That will be quite a meeting. We've a great deal of planning and many hard decisions ahead of us. I will soon have some preliminary results about the path and timing of the ghost's passing. Maybe none of this will be necessary."

"Could we be that lucky?"

"It's possible."

"But not likely."

"No, not likely."

"How are you going to do those calculations? Won't the results show up on the computers? Won't Miss Techmeyer be able to find the results of your calculations?"

"Hold it! One at a time. I won't use the main Gemini computer. I'll use the laptop. It's much slower, but for preliminary results it will work quite well. You remember, I told you about a little program named Lani that would completely clear the laptop?"

"OK! That's the one you told me to use if I was ever afraid OSI was going to take the laptop. I remember now."

"That will delete all traces of sensitive data and calculations in just a few minutes. As soon as I provide the group with my findings, I'll run Lani."

"Very good!"

"Now, let's get busy," he said firmly in that commanding voice. "If you'll align the photos and take the parallax measurements, I'll run the preliminary calculations. Let's just see where that wild star is now."

"Yes sir!" Lani replied, saluting smartly, "Your wish is my command."

Angus shook his head in exasperation. "Come on . . . you know what I mean. You can't be that sensitive."

"Just keeping you on your toes, Dr. Thomas. I wouldn't want you to think you can walk all over me, you know."

"Keep that up, and I'll turn you over my knee," he replied, grabbing her around the waist and dragging her off her chair onto his lap. Soon the two were in a passionate embrace.

As they finally stopped to catch their breath, Lani whispered in his ear, "If it wasn't so incredibly enjoyable, I'd be screaming 'sexual harassment' after that. You'd better behave yourself, or I will," she added with a grin, teetering precariously on his knee.

"Sorry! I just got carried away. I can't imagine why," he replied slyly as he placed her back on her chair. Becoming serious he added, "It's a good thing no one came through that door while we were busy. That would hit the office grapevine with a vengeance."

"Yes, *Dr. Thomas*, it's best we get back to work. It's not too late, so I'll call Dr. Lane to get that ball rolling."

As Angus began the initial calculations, Lani called Dr. Lane from her desk phone in the outer office. After an animated conversation of nearly fifteen minutes, Lani returned, a huge grin on her face.

"You'll never guess how good my idea turned out," she related. "Not only would he be thrilled to help you, but he said he had some experience eluding people himself. He has a complete guest suite in his home with its own phone. You're welcome to use it as long as you need to. He gave me all the phone numbers he uses, as well as his beeper. What a fantastic break."

"Did you explain it was the OSI we were trying to elude? That's different from just anyone."

"Of course! I told him as much of what was going on as I could."

"Great! That solves one more possible problem. Did you find out exactly where he lives? We may need to find it in a hurry."

"You know those four or five big homes on the curve in the road leading to the hospital? The ones with the beautiful pond in front?"

"Yes! How could you not remember those places? He lives in one of those?"

"The last one on the drive around the pond, the one farthest from the road is their home."

"That shouldn't be too hard to find, even in the dark. You certainly do good work," he added with a broad smile.

They began a long night of intense work. Lani used electronic overlay comparisons to view the star, which could appear in two different relative positions. Precise measurement of the difference in positions and a careful plot of the positions of the star since it was first discovered provided the basis for the projection of its future path. The latest path projection proved to be frightening.

11

The group of seven conspirators gathered in John Carroll's office shortly after five on Wednesday, June 20, 2001. Everyone but Angus was there by five o'clock. Lani explained the situation carefully.

"Angus is completing his latest calculations of the path of the ghost and will be here within an hour. In the meantime, I can tell you of our plans to escape the clutches of OSI. John has arranged with Weldon Conrad for Angus to switch identities with Dick Rumley when they ship him off to England. The trip is not scheduled as yet, but here's the plan: Dick will be in custody when they leave for Vancouver and Angus will board the same plane. There they change planes for Toronto. Angus will leave the plane in Toronto and become Dick Rumley while the Brits sneak the real Rumley off to Britain. Angus Thomas will appear to disappear in Toronto and go who knows where. Then Angus, as Dick Rumley, will spend the night in Toronto. The next day, he will fly to Mexico City, overnight there and then continue to Santiago, Chile. From there he will travel by bus to La Serena where he will join the staff of Gemini South. Sometime later, I will move to Cerro Pachon as part of the transition team."

"You're going off to South America?" Ali said, looking a bit shocked.

"Only if it becomes absolutely necessary, and we hope it doesn't," Lani answered. "We will have to wait and see what OSI does before making the final decision. If they force us, we will go."

"Let's hope it doesn't come to that," Charlene added.

After Lani brought them up-to-date on Angus' activities and plans, Serena took charge of the meeting and provided an agenda. The next meeting was scheduled for tomorrow at the same time and place as today's. Everyone in the group would be there, including Chelton Chum who was arriving the next day around two. They were discussing several suggestions for new members to the group when Angus arrived.

"I've the usual mix of good and bad news," he began. "The good news is the possible variation in the path of the ghost has changed for the better. It could pass as far as four light years from the sun. The bad news is the most likely path still passes right through the solar system. Its closest approach to the earth will be early in the year 2031. The precision of these latest measurements is in the range of ninety percent, much higher than the eighty percent accuracy of the earlier measurements. We've adjusted the cone shape of all possible paths to better account for all probabilities resulting in a slightly larger intersect space about eight light years in diameter."

"Can you tell us in laymen's terms just what that means?" Ali asked.

"I'll do my best," Angus replied. "The solar system will move quite a long way during the next thirty years due to the rotation of our Milky Way galaxy. While the path it will take is nearly straight, it is affected by the gravity of all the mass of the entire galaxy. Since the solar system is quite far from the galactic center, the effect of the *lumpiness* of our galaxy could cause the solar system to move in a very slight arc for the same reason the earth follows a nearly circular path around the sun. We can predict this path accurately, but not exactly, providing us with an egg shaped space within which the solar system will be at the time of closest passage of the ghost. This space represents all possible positions of the solar system. In the same manner and for the same reasons, the ghost will move in a not quite straight line through the galaxy. We can predict this path much less accurately than the path of the solar system because our measurements of the ghost are still inaccurate in comparison. The resulting egg shaped space where the ghost will be at the same time of passage is much larger. The intersect of these two spaces represents all possible positions of both the solar system and the ghost relative to each other at the time of passage. We will be able to shrink the size of this space and better predict the two paths and their point of closest approach as time passes. With present instrumentation and measurement techniques, it will be ten to fifteen years before we know the star's path with a high enough degree of precision to begin calculating the gravitational effects."

"Can you give us some possible scenarios?" Pastor Ruth asked.

"There are many possibilities, from no effect at all to a major disruption of the solar system," Angus answered. "Should it pass a light year or farther from us it would only disrupt the Oort cloud possibly sending numerous comets and meteorites coursing through the solar system. This would greatly increase the possibility of a cataclysmic collision of a large object with the earth, but there would be little chance of any disruption of the orbits of the planets. The danger of disruption of these orbits increases the closer the intruder comes to the sun. The type and amount of disruptions could vary up to being thrown free of the sun's gravity for any planet close to the path. We will be unable to accurately predict the positions of the planets relative to the ghost's path for at least a decade, so the range of scenarios is extremely broad."

John commented, "There are several other major unknowns at work here as well. Because of the unusual speed of the ghost, we are dealing with a completely unknown gravitational effect. It is even possible the ghost could pass directly through the inner solar system with little or no effect. Imagine a small ball floating on a calm lake as a large boat goes by at about ten miles per hour. The large wake created by the boat would change the position of the ball considerably as the waves passed. Should that same boat pass at say ninety miles per hour, the wake would be much smaller and move the ball much less. Imagine the size of the wake if it passed at ten thousand miles per hour. There would be almost no wake at all. Considering the boat wake as a representation of the gravitational 'wake' of the ghost you can visualize the possibilities. Unfortunately, we don't know if this is a valid comparison. To my knowledge, no one has ever even considered the relativistic effects of any object moving at this speed. Particle physics can provide us with the effects of subatomic particles moving at such speeds, but that is a far cry from a star-sized object moving through space."

"It surely boggles my mind," Ali added. "I liked your example. It gives me a better idea of what we're dealing with. You said there were several other unknowns. What else don't we know?"

John continued, "The path of the ghost from where it appears to be until it approaches the solar system is at least three hundred light years long. Any star sized object near that path could change the path by gravitational attraction. We are currently searching for such stars. This should not take long since there are not a lot of stars near the apparent path of the ghost."

Ali commented, "Maybe we'll be lucky enough to find a star that will divert the ghost away from us and we can all get back to our real lives."

"Wouldn't that be a blessing," Pastor Ruth remarked hopefully. "In any event, all these unknowns will make it extremely difficult to come up with anything accurate to tell the public. No matter how it is presented, the nut cases will have a field day with this, don't you think? I fear even the faith community will have extremely varying reactions, all the way from cries of 'Armageddon' to complete denial. The reactions of the radical fundamentalists of all the worlds' religions could pose a real danger to us all. Maybe even a worse danger than the ghost."

"That's why our work in this group is so important," Lani said. "Just how and when this news is released will surely have powerful and wide-ranging effects on all of humanity. For that reason, I feel it is vital we broaden the group to include a wider spectrum of viewpoints and that we do so soon."

Serena asked, "Have any of you thought of others to include in the group? After suggesting Chelton I haven't thought of another."

"How can we best select a broader group without risking inclusion of one person who might leak the information for personal gain?" Angus questioned. "Most of the people in this group are much like us and can be trusted. Sheer numbers of people will only compound the problem. What we need is a wide variety of viewpoints with the common denominator of genuine concern for humanity as a whole. I've thought of a few possibilities, but I don't know them well enough to pass on their integrity or concern for humanity."

John replied, "I think we should continue to think of possible new people, but wait for Chelton Chum's inclusion and counsel tomorrow. With his experience he should be a great help with this challenge."

Ruth looked around the gathering and said, "We're not a group with the typical ethnic and religious makeup. There are we four mostly native Hawaiians, you two Mohawks, three including Chelton, and one lonely Caucasian American. All of us are basically Christian Americans with the influence of native culture and a touch of our ancient religions. In a world sense, we're not very diverse. I see lots of genuine integrity and concern for humanity here. That should be the most important consideration. Diversity, while somewhat desirable to help project reactions of differing groups of people, is not nearly as important as unity of purpose. What do the rest of you think?"

After voicing general agreement with Ruth's comments, they decided to meet in John's office every Wednesday evening at 5:30. The next meeting would be tomorrow and would include Chelton.

"While I'm thinking of it, here are the duplicate sets of data disks holding all the latest readings from the last two nights' telescope work," Angus said as he handed one set to Ruth and the other to Charlene. "Take these with you and store them in a safe place. There are two sets in the unlikely event one should get damaged. I'll bring the data from tonight's work to the meeting tomorrow evening. Let's hope OSI doesn't get into the act before then."

"You still think OSI is going to come down on this?" John asked. "Even after they bowed out so carefully at your apartment?"

"What do you think?" Angus said directly to Serena.

Serena was adamant. "You can bet on it. My instincts tell me they were bowing out as a ruse to make us think they were leaving us alone and so to disarm us. You can be sure they'll be back as soon as they think you have new data. That whole scene at the apartment was a con job."

After they spent time discussing OSI's possible actions and how to counter them, Lani explained, "We have arranged for a hiding place for Angus at Dr. Francis Lane's, just in case. He's the one who treated Angus after the accident. We know we can count on him. However, we still have no safe method of communication between Angus and the group while at Dr. Lane's. If there are any ideas about that, let's talk about them."

Several ideas emerged, but final effort was put off until the next meeting.

Serena took the floor again. "I suggest we begin drafting a news release immediately. Then we will know better what to do when the time comes and we need it. After all, isn't that our basic purpose for the group, to decide how to tell the world about the ghost? I think we had better get to it as soon as possible."

After they spent nearly an hour discussing several different approaches, Charlene summarized. "Let's make sure we are all together on this. We've decided to create a series of news releases. The first will be a release about a newly discovered star with a projected path possibly bringing it as close as the present nearest star. There will follow a series of increasingly alarming revelations of the possible consequences of the ghost's passage, concentrating on the dangers of new comets and meteorites. By the time the astronomical community confirms the existence and possible path of the ghost, the full story will have to be released. That will be at least six months after publication of Angus' first report. OK, now who's going to write those releases?"

Charlene's question was greeted by a stony silence. Serena stood up and smiled. "No volunteers? OK, now you are all going to get some homework. Each person will draft a series of information releases using their own knowledge and viewpoint to present at the meeting a week from tomorrow. We'll use your work to create the final series. Those final releases will be edited as time goes on and more information is gained. This series of news releases will be the backbone of the group's efforts, as well as its main purpose. Remind yourselves just how important this could be and you'll come up with some good ones."

They soon agreed and the meeting ended about seven; most headed home while Angus and Lani returned to their telescope work for the night.

*   *   *

Angus grew increasingly apprehensive as the last night of his readings drew to an end. These readings would serve to confirm his earlier calculations, a very important activity. He expected little difference in the results, knowing any substantial change would indicate a problem with either the telescope or the instrumentation. He completed the processing of the incoming data, copied it to the last of the series of removable disks and edited all new records on the computers as he had with the earlier data. With the key to the altered records in his head and the actual records safely on the duplicate set of removable disks he felt reasonably secure. He would process the new data tomorrow if OSI didn't interfere.

Just before they left for home, Lani took the new data disks to John's office and placed them in his desk drawer as planned. It was just too risky for her or Angus to carry them out with OSI certain to descend at any moment. Charlene and Ruth could take them tomorrow after the meeting. Using the key John had given her, Lani carefully locked John's office door as she left.

Lani felt a little uneasy as she returned to Angus' office. The threat of the intervention of OSI weighed heavily on her mind. *Are we missing something?* she thought. *We are amateurs at this intrigue compared with the OSI professionals. Have we actually fooled them? I wonder what they are planning to do?* So intent was her thought she walked right past Angus sitting at her desk in the otherwise deserted outer office without even seeing him.

Angus gently grasped her arm as she swished by. "Whoa there, Miss Off-in-space. Don't you even acknowledge old friends?"

Startled back into the present, Lani stopped with a puzzled look, almost disoriented. Regaining her composure after a moment she turned and replied, "I was really spaced out in thought wasn't I? I can't believe I walked right past you. I'm just so worried about OSI, wondering what they might be planning. I can't imagine we rank amateurs can fool such pros at this kind of thing, at least not for long."

Angus grinned reassuringly. "Remember. They're people just like us. I'm counting on their overconfidence to make them lax. They most certainly believe their little act at the apartment was convincing and we think they've dropped out. They wouldn't expect such *amateurs* to see through them. That gives us a big edge. I'm more worried that our efforts to keep them out of what we are actually doing will seriously interfere with our prime objective."

Lani sighed. "You're probably right. At least I hope you are." Her eyes suddenly brightened. "Incidentally, what are you doing sitting at my desk?"

"I finished up while you were going to John's office, so I came out here to wait. I thought you might like to join me for breakfast at our favorite greasy spoon."

"That sounds like a prelude to a proposition to me. You'd better watch out. You're apt to be looking at a sexual harassment suit," Lani said laughing.

Rising from her desk chair he replied, "I take it that's a yes?"

"You got that right," Lani replied, taking his arm as they headed for the outer office door.

"Watch the touchy stuff," Angus chided. "We wouldn't want those folks out there to get the right idea."

With that she threw her arms around him and gave him a resounding smack of a kiss just as they reached the door. "That's for all those people watching," she whispered before letting go and regaining her cool professional demeanor.

Before they could open the door, it burst open at the hand of one of the secretaries who was momentarily startled. The morning crew was arriving, and the two lovers had returned to their usual professional appearance just in time.

"You two nearly scared the life out of me," were her first startled words.

"Sorry about that," Angus replied smiling. "We were rather startled ourselves."

The three were soon laughing about the incident and exchanging good morning greetings before going on their way. As they reached the parking lot and headed for Lani's car, Angus scolded, "You almost did us in, little Miss Risk-taker. What would you have said if she had opened that door just a moment sooner? How would you have explained that scene?"

"I'm just thankful I didn't have to. Are you angry with me?" she asked with that pouty-lipped hurt look women are so capable of showing.

"Nah! I thought it was rather funny. I wish I had a picture of the look on your face when that door opened. It was priceless. As it turned out, we were lucky with the timing. Better to be lucky than smart Mom always says."

"You're such a good sport," she replied, smiling. "I'm glad I found you."

During a leisurely breakfast they decided to arrange a visit to Dr. Lane at his home. Lani called him from the pay phone at the restaurant. When she returned, she related, "Not only was he at home, but he will remain there till he leaves for the trauma center in the afternoon. He suggested we stop over this morning. He and his wife will be relaxing by the pool and would welcome a visit. Are you too sleepy to go?"

"I'm game if you are."

After a stop at their apartments for a quick shower and change of clothes, they headed for Dr. Lane's. At Lani's invitation, Serena joined them for the visit.

As the three approached Dr. Lane's home on the driveway around the pond, Serena remarked on the beautiful setting, "Look at that beautiful pond. It's like a mirror set in green."

The pond was apparently created by damming a small stream which still flowed in at one end and out over a concrete spillway at the other. The stream continued into a large culvert under the main road and then wandered off on the other side. Lush tropical plants crowded the edge of the pond both on land and in the water. Several Hawaiian geese or *nenes* glided across the surface along with numerous ducks. White wading birds dotted the edge wherever the vegetation was sparse. To the east of the pond was a small hillside where the homes melted into the lush vegetation. Though they were rather large homes, they didn't stand out but appeared part of the hillside. Because of the viewing angle looking up the slope from the drive, all that could be seen of the homes was the edge of the hipped roofs and the upper part of some windows.

"Whoever designed this whole area is a master at making everything work in concert. It looks almost like a wilderness, undisturbed by human invasion," Angus remarked as they approached the small cul-de-sac in front of Dr. Lane's.

His driveway curved away from the far side of the cul-de-sac and disappeared as it rounded a small mound at the north end of his house. The three-car garage beneath the house was completely hidden. They parked by the garage and stepped out to the right side of the paved area. There was a doorway to the right of the garage doors and a stone walkway that climbed lazily up a slope between the garage and the mound that hid it. Both the side of the garage and the mound were faced with flat, casually stacked lava slabs. Plants grew profusely, drooping down the irregular stone faces and nearly closing the view to the sky above. At the top of the path there was a surprisingly large patio looking down on the pond and cul-de-sac. The patio and main entrance could not be seen from the drive below. The line of sight from the drive made the roof of the house appear to come nearly to the ground at the edge of the patio. The view west from the patio would be breathtaking at sunset.

The main entrance to the house consisted of two huge glass doors centered between two equally huge glass windows on either side, a wall of glass. The doors slid silently apart as they approached. The house opened itself to the outdoors and immediately became part of it as Dr. Lane stepped out to greet them, his wife Oona at his side.

"Greetings and welcome to our home," Dr. Lane offered with a broad, genuine smile. "This is my lovely wife Oona. We are honored by your visit."

"We are pleased and grateful to be here," Angus replied. "I'd like you to . . . "

Dr. Lane interrupted, "Don't tell me. I can tell from the eyes this lovely lady must be your mother. Am I right?"

"I guess those penetrating Mohawk eyes aren't too hard to notice are they? Yes, Dr. Lane, this is Serena Thomas, my mother," Angus answered.

"Enough of this 'Dr. Lane' stuff. I'd much prefer to be called 'Francis' or 'hey you.' If we're to conspire together, I think first names will do quite well," Francis replied with a laugh.

When the introduction pleasantries were finished, Oona led them from the patio to the pool just beyond the patio and hidden by a wall of vines growing on a large trellis. Entrance to the pool was through a two-gated arch in the trellis which almost hid the pool from view. The poolside lanai was ideal for casual entertaining with several wrought iron tables and chairs mixed with beach loungers. Like the entrance patio, it could not be seen from the drive. The same glass wall as at the entrance opened from a large recreation room to the pool area. On the far wall of the room was a huge picture of a football running back exploding through a group of would-be tacklers, the number "35" emblazoned on his jersey.

"When I said I was a fan of yours, I wasn't kidding." Dr. Lane turned toward Angus proudly, indicating the picture. "Do you have any idea when that was taken?"

"Isn't that during the one score I made in the Pro Bowl right here in Hawaii?" Angus leaned over to scrutinize. "At least I know it was during the Pro Bowl."

"Close, but no cigar. It was actually taken earlier during that same series of downs when you were about to be decked for a loss. Actually, it was the best picture Charlie Waters got that game."

Angus pointed to one of his pursuers. "Yeah! I remember now. Right over here is Wen Laughten, who really smeared me about a second after the picture was taken. I can still feel his shoulder smacking my chest. He was not a gentle man on a football field." He feigned being hit in the chest.

After a few moments discussing past football events in front of the picture, Oona led them out to a table near the pool. She offered them coffee, tea and other beverages and had several takers. After some conversation that included Angus explaining his move from football to astronomy, their talk turned to the immediate problem.

"Tell me more about wanting to hide from the OSI. Lani explained a little about it when she called. Does it have anything to do with your accident? I know it was no accident, but is it related?" Francis questioned, leaning forward in anticipation.

"That's the crazy part of this whole thing," Angus began. "We still don't know if it's related directly or if it's just incidental. OSI told us the attempt on my life was a factor in their interest after they intercepted my personal message to a friend in Arizona. In the message I casually mentioned to my friend Pat about the recent discovery of a strange, fast-moving object out in space. Conjuring up visions of space aliens and foreign involvement, OSI saw me as a central figure in a possible threat to the US."

"Couldn't you have easily dispelled their fears?" Francis queried. "What was the object anyway? Could it possibly be an alien craft of some sort?"

"Not a chance!" Angus said disdainfully. "It's a star about half the mass of the sun and it's many light years away. Of that there is no doubt. Unfortunately, even that information didn't dissuade the single-minded tunnel vision of the OSI. They finally came to my apartment and apologized for their actions and told us they were withdrawing from the investigation. We just don't believe they have or will."

They sat at the table while Angus explained as much detail as he dared about the ghost. For the next two hours the group discussed what happened, why the hideaway was needed and how it could be used. Care was taken to not divulge the true speed and path of the ghost or the possible danger to all life on the earth. Finally Oona suggested a tour of the guest suite where Angus could stay securely for as long as need be.

As they walked up the seven steps to the second level of the house, Francis explained the house was built on three levels over a basement and garage which were dug into the slope of the hill. Each level actually sat on the slope in stair step fashion up the hill from the main level. The living, dining, recreation and entertaining areas were spread over the first level.

The second level, smaller than the first, held the sleeping rooms and bathrooms. The third level included a complete guest apartment with a single bedroom with a full bath, living and dining room and kitchen. A hallway continued from the top of the stairs to a door leading outside to a walkway and steps going down to the driveway in front of the garage. Across the hall from the apartment was a large study and exercise room that both Lanes used for reading, personal office work and general relaxation. One wall of the study was a bookcase liberally supplied with all kinds of books, publications and memorabilia. A pair of stationary bicycles faced the one high window. It was a comfortable home.

"Francis and Oona, I don't know how to thank you," Angus remarked. "Are you certain you don't mind hiding me from the OSI? They might get nasty if they find out."

"You're welcome here for as long as you like," Oona answered. "In the long run, the OSI people will find out they're wrong, and the whole thing will vanish. Investigative government types seem to have more than their share of paranoia. They see spies behind every door and intrigue in every action. It's certainly no normal existence."

"Well said!" Francis added with a smile.

Turning to Lani and Serena, Angus said, "This is perfect: a lovely hideaway, gracious hosts and less than two miles from the Gemini Operations Center. Something tells me I'll have to use it. There are a few things to bring over right away. I'll pack a travel case with what I will need for my trip to Chile just in case that comes to pass."

"Chile? What's this about a trip to Chile?" Francis asked with great surprise.

"That's where the other Gemini twin telescope is located," Angus answered. "We've a rather complex plan in place where I will switch identity with another astronomer on my trip there and Angus Thomas will disappear from the face of the earth. I'll probably have to go to Gemini South, as it's called, to complete my work if the OSI people return. We think they are lying low until they know for sure all the new data are in hand. Then they'll swoop down on us like a hawk on a rabbit."

"This sounds familiar. I once had to hide under an assumed name for a number of years, myself. I'll have to tell you that story some-time," Francis said with a chuckle, remembering Chinatown. "Your situation sounds more intriguing with each new revelation."

"I really wish it wasn't so involved," Angus said seriously. "I'd like to get on with a normal life. I've too much to do to spend all this effort eluding OSI madness."

Serena interjected, "Hadn't we best be on our way? I really enjoy the Lanes' warm hospitality, but we've much to do, and you two haven't slept since yesterday afternoon. Chelton arrives about two and we have a meeting at 5:30." Turning to the Lanes, she added, "Chelton is my nephew, who is coming here for a visit."

"I think we have things well in hand here," Oona interjected. "You have a key to the door and know your way around. Come when-ever you need to."

As they returned to the main floor, Francis turned, smiling. "You can see who runs this house. I just live here. Incidentally, I wouldn't have it any other way. She does a superb job."

"He runs his practice. I run our home. I think it's an even division of responsibility. However, I'm certain you realize by your picture on the wall he has considerable input here," Oona added with a know-ing grin.

The three said their thanks and good-byes as they paused on the patio before continuing down the walk to Lani's car. As they drove past the pond, Lani remarked, "There are a lot of really sensational people in this world. It's those few bad ones, those 'rotten eggs,' they can really make a mess of things."

"My sentiments exactly. It's those few 'rotten eggs,' as you call them, that make the rest of us realize the value of good people," Serena replied. "They also show us the value of trying to lead a decent life by their misery. I've known some basically decent people who have done bad things as well as a few genuinely evil ones. The really evil ones lead a miserable life of deceit and fear. The others often regret their actions as long as they live."

Angus changed the subject by asking, "How about returning to our own current reality? Who's going to meet Chelton?"

Serena immediately replied, "I'm driving to the airport to get him in a rental car. I've already arranged it. Chelton will then have a way to get around on his own while he's here. You two are going to get some sleep. You will need to be sharp for the meeting tonight."

"How are you going to get the rental car?" Angus asked.

"Their driver will bring it over to the apartment. I'll drop him off on my way to get Chelton. Incidentally, I arranged for him to stay at the Mokuloa Hotel. It's only a mile or so north of the Operations Center. So, you see, everything's under control."

"I still need to pack some things for Chile. I'm not even sure of the weather, it's winter there you know. I would like to get the laptop to the Lanes' as well as a set of data disks."

"You think your Mom's just another pretty face?" Serena said with a smile. "I went through your closet and have already packed clothes for your trip. I found some winter things you must have brought for use on top of the mountain. They're already packed. All you will need to add are your toiletries and anything else I may have forgotten. I arranged with Dr. Lane to drop them off at the trauma center. That would protect your hideaway in case OSI is snooping around. I can take the laptop at the same time."

"Mom, you're amazing. You're way ahead of me. I guess I should have known you weren't just sitting around the apartment doing nothing."

"Your mom's just a very capable woman," Lani interjected. "I expect she has been one step ahead of you most of your life."

"There you go, ganging up on me again. How does a mere man stand a chance? I don't suppose you've tested out the SSR transmitter on the laptop as well," he said a little sarcastically.

"Watch it there, Buster," Serena cracked back. "You're treading on thin ice with that kind of comment. Besides, we have to leave something for you to do."

"Touché again," Angus replied. "I know when I've met my match. Seriously, I hope the Lanes' home is close enough the SSR will work from the laptop. Jack Mercer installed one network transmitter on the server, and if all goes well, I can access everything on the network with the laptop from Dr. Lane's apartment. If Sandy's right, there's no way OSI can find or interfere with transmission. We must keep the laptop out of OSI's hands. It provides a secure way to communicate in case I have to go into hiding."

"How's that?" Serena asked.

"Lani can get the laptop Ruth's holding for us and bring it to her apartment. We can communicate directly by SSR between the two laptops," Angus replied.

"Isn't that a bit risky? Suppose OSI decides Lani is involved and searches her apartment?"

"We'll just have to risk it. I still don't think she's under suspicion. Wait a minute. Why don't we have Ruth bring the second laptop to the meeting tonight? Better yet, why don't we have her drop it off for Dr. Lane at the trauma center? The one at my apartment has the same doctored information as the one in my office. It would work perfectly well for communication and if OSI should pick it up, the data would be the same data they would find on my office computer. The only thing that would have to be kept hidden would be the SSR card and transmitter. I'm sure you could find a secure hiding place for those. They're so tiny. What do you think Lani?"

"I don't know. It would depend on how thoroughly they searched, if they do. I could hide them in a cereal box or something, maybe wrapped in frozen meat in my freezer," Lani offered laughing.

"Let's not get carried away," Angus replied.

"You two are so bushed you're going looney on me. You'd better concentrate on sleeping the rest of the day. Let me take care of things for you. I'll call Ruth and make the arrangements," Serena suggested earnestly.

"Do you think my phone's secure?" Angus asked.

"I'll use the phone at the car rental place. Surely they won't have that one bugged. Is that OK with you, Mr. Paranoia?"

"Come on, Mom, we really can't be too careful. One slip and who knows what OSI will do."

"I suppose you're right. I'm beginning to be seriously annoyed by these people and what they are forcing us to do. I'll be glad when it's finally over."

As they stepped out of the car at Angus' apartment, Serena ordered Lani, "You get some sleep now. There's a lot of work ahead of us, and you'll need a sharp mind. I want to see those bright eyes stay bright. OK?"

"OK, Ali'i!" Lani replied as she left.

"What was that she called me?" Serena asked of Angus as they entered the building.

"Ali'i! It means chief or boss. Take your pick, but you definitely are one today."

"This is the first day you've been home this week. Do you get any sleep there at your office?"

"Astronomers learn to catch sleep when they can during the night. When clouds interfere with viewing and there is no computer work or calculations to make, I stretch out on the couch in my office and take a nap. Sometimes you have to wait for hours. Sometimes the subject of your study is only visible part of the night. When an object is close to the horizon, it is seen through a great deal more air than when overhead. The same air that makes the sun turn red as it nears the horizon changes what we can see through the telescope. It can interfere with viewing to the extent some objects are distorted and may even disappear from view entirely. The best viewing is directly overhead through the least air. Large telescopes have stops preventing them from pointing too near the horizon. They are not designed to point too low since the viewing is so poor."

As they entered the apartment, Serena remarked sternly, "Now that I've had my latest lesson in astronomy, I'm going to tuck you in bed, and I don't want to hear a peep out of you. I can run my errands and get Chelton settled in his hotel while you sleep. We'll be back here by five—in plenty of time to make the meeting."

"Somehow, no matter how old I get, you'll still be my Mom," Angus said with a grin.

"Yes, but today I'm your ali'i as well. And don't you forget it," Serena stated in a firm but joking manner.

Angus made a quick check of the suitcase Serena had packed for him and added only a few small items. He closed it and placed it in the living room with an approving comment. He then went dutifully to bed, glad to be able to catch a few hours of needed sleep in his own place.

Serena made her arrangements with the car rental company. The car would be delivered by noon providing time to call Ruth, drop the suitcase at the trauma center and still make it to the airport in time for Chelton's arrival. So far things were moving along smoothly.

CHELTON ARRIVES

Serena waited at the gate as Chelton's flight from Honolulu arrived at Hilo Airport. He walked down the stairs with just a hint of a twisting limp, a leftover from his childhood condition. Several people were talking with him as he walked toward Serena. Chelton made friends everywhere he went.

As he approached, he shouted, "Hello, Sunflower," a name he had given her when he was a child. "This is my mother's cousin and dearest friend, Serena Thomas. I call her Otsitsakowa in Mohawk or Sunflower in English because she is so pretty and strong. I'd like you to meet some new friends from the flight. This is Sandra Yu, Mike O'Leary and Diedra Long. We've had quite a discussion cut short by the end of the short flight."

"I'm so pleased to meet you," Serena replied. "Chelton is such a miraculously different person. All his life, Chelton has been full of surprises for those around him."

"We certainly enjoyed his company," Sandra commented.

"We were all talking like old friends just a few minutes after the plane took off from Honolulu. He really has a way with people," Mike added.

They continued talking until they reached the luggage carousel and their luggage finally arrived. After a few moments for good-byes, they each went their separate ways.

When they were in the car heading for the Mokuloa, Chelton asked, "Can you give me an idea of what this is all about? I know you wouldn't call me out here unless it was serious."

"I'll give you the general idea of what we're facing, but Angus will have to provide the technical details. He's discovered a star moving at tremendous speed toward a rendezvous with the solar system in about thirty years. It's about half the size of our sun and will pass within four light years of the sun. According to Angus' latest path prediction, the most likely path will bring it right through the solar system. Should its path be a light year or more from the sun, it will still cause many more comets to enter the inner solar system with the increased possibility of a catastrophic collision with earth. In the worst case, should it pass through the solar system, it could disrupt the orbits of the planets with the probability that life on earth would be obliterated. We've decided to hold back the news of this discovery until we find the best way to release the information to the general public."

"That is dreadfully frightening," Chelton replied, a concerned look on his face. "I'm certain Angus' information is reliable. He always was a stickler for accuracy. What are the chances of someone else making the same discovery? Isn't that a major concern?"

"I don't know just why, but Angus thinks it would take another astronomer six to twelve months just to confirm his findings. He doubts anyone else would be looking exactly where he found the 'ghost' as he calls it, but there is that remote possibility."

"Assuming he is correct, I see the absolute necessity of devising a well-considered plan of divulging his discovery to the public, at least the potential danger. Who knows what the general reaction would be once the danger became apparent? That's a serious psychological, religious and social bombshell. To use a common, but in this instance appropriate, expression, all hell could break loose."

"Isn't that the truth," Serena responded in firm agreement. "We have formed a group specifically to formulate just such a plan for informing the public. We want your expertise and instincts added to the group."

"I feel honored you want me included and will gladly contribute what I can. Finding the right way to release such frightening information will be a major challenge. When will I get to meet the rest of the group?"

"There's a meeting tonight at the Gemini Operations Center. The entire group will be there, and they are all looking forward to your joining them. Incidentally, your reputation has preceded you, so be prepared."

"I value that reputation and the attendant notoriety for the many ears it gains for my message of peace and common sense. Every conflict I can lessen or stop completely is another victory for people everywhere. Large or small, feuding nations or small groups of people, all desperately need to find ways to settle their differences peacefully. While that is the message of all major religions, it is not the actuality. Do you know why I have this overpowering drive as a peacemaker?"

Serena thought for a moment, then replied, "I haven't a clue."

"You, Sunflower, are the one who set it in motion. As a small boy, I watched you settle a number of arguments and fights between boys on the reservation. I remember one occasion when Michael and two other boys were having a heated argument behind the inn. You stepped in, cooled them down by asking each one to state his position precisely and proceeded to listen intently to each in turn. Within a few minutes they were walking off arm-in-arm. Remembering that incident and others like it eventually brought on my drive to become a peacemaker. Maybe my childhood infirmity was a blessing because it prevented me from being involved in fights as a boy. I learned to stay out of verbal battles that might escalate. I had to become a peacemaker. I certainly couldn't fight."

"That's amazing! It only goes to show how a single action of one person can affect another's life. I don't remember the time you describe, but I know I learned that way of settling arguments from my mother and her mother, your great-grandmother. So you come by that naturally. You have taken it to another, much higher level for the benefit of a great many people. How proud we are of you."

By the time they reached the hotel, Serena had given him a rundown on the rest of those in the group. After unpacking, taking a refreshing shower and getting dressed, Chelton decided they should relax for a while and chat. As they sat in his room overlooking Hilo Bay, Serena filled him in on Lani, the Dick Rumley affair and the OSI intrusions.

"So Mr. Loner finally met a female to tame him did he?" Chelton joked. "She must have some powerful medicine to handle him. I always wondered if he'd ever meet his match."

"She's an incredible person," Serena replied. "Much wiser than her years might indicate. We hit it off really well right from the start. And you know how mothers can be about their sons and other women."

"She must be very special having you speak of her that way. I'm anxious to meet her. Incidentally, what time is the meeting? Shouldn't we be going?"

"We've plenty of time. It's just a short distance to Angus' apartment and that's right near the Gemini Op Center where the meeting is being held. He will probably be gone by the time we reach his place. He always rides his bike to work, still the stickler for exercise and keeping in shape. We'll get to his office about five. You can meet Lani and visit with them both for a while before the meeting. Angus is just tying up loose ends on his latest readings, so he is not as pressed as he was a week ago."

"I haven't talked to him since he moved to Hawaii. It'll be great to see him again. I hope he's not too busy to spend some personal time with me."

"Knowing how much he thinks of you, I'm sure he'll make time. He's proud of you and what you've accomplished, you know," Serena said with a warm smile.

"I really miss those long talks we use to have when he came home for visits before I went away to school. We were very close. We still have occasional long talks on the phone when we can catch each other."

Realizing how late it was getting, Serena called Angus' apartment to make sure he was up. After hearing his answering machine message she guessed he had gone to the Op Center. "We might as well go directly to his office," Serena remarked. "There's no reason to stop at his apartment now. I've everything I need with me."

12

S erena and Chelton arrived at the Gemini Op Center and stopped at the reception desk where Serena introduced Chelton. "Sometimes I think this is the one who runs this place," she said of Jenny. "At least she's the one you call whenever you want to find someone or get something done."

Jenny's bright smile, courtesy and quick wit were ready as usual. "Tell my boss that, will you? Lani, Angus and John are in Angus' office right now. You might as well go right on in. I'll let them know you're here."

As they walked through the outer office, Angus opened his door to greet them. When they reached Angus, he and Chelton grabbed each other in a long bear hug. The two men obviously cared a great deal for each other. After Serena closed the door, she introduced Lani to Chelton, who immediately took her hand, bowed at the waist and kissed it in an exaggerated ceremony.

"Greetings, fair lady," he said stiffly and then broke into laughter. Opening his arms wide and looking at Angus, he asked, "May I?"

Angus smiled, "Silly question. Of course!"

Chelton gave Lani a big hug and said, "Welcome to the tribe. And just how did my Neanderthal cousin manage to entrap such a beautiful lady as yourself?"

"Just good luck, I guess."

"And such a glorious sense of humor as well," he replied in pleasant surprise. "Angus, you are indeed a very lucky man."

Angus grinned and looked proudly at Lani. "You got that right."

Smiling broadly and reaching his hand out to John, Chelton remarked, "You must be John Carroll, the head man around here. I understand you run a tight ship with a difficult crew."

"Difficult, but dedicated. A pleasure to work with most of the time," John replied with a wry smile. Switching to a more serious look, he continued, "It's quite an honor to have you visit us. I've been an admirer of your work for quite some time. It must be rewarding."

"I'd place frustrating right up there with rewarding. In my line of work, the successes make the headlines. Political barricades to so many humanitarian efforts erected by immoveable people create monumental frustrations which rarely make the news. When you do win one of those battles, it is extremely rewarding to all those involved in the effort. Unfortunately, those workers in the trenches who do all the hard work rarely get mentioned by the media. They are the ones who should receive the accolades."

The four visited for a while, discussing everything from astronomy and politics to football in the coming season. Serena, in her usual role as leader, finally said, "Isn't it about time we head for John's office? The others should be arriving there soon."

"I can see why we chose you as leader, Serena," John said with a smile. "I only hope you're not after my job."

"Thank you. Maybe I should look into it. Just where does one apply?" She answered, smiling as they stepped through the door.

As they walked down the hall to John's office, they ran into the Namahoes and Pastor Ruth. Introductions were made in the alcove by Ani'i's desk in front of John's office door. Ruth informed Angus the laptop had been delivered to Dr. Lane at the trauma center without incident. As soon as they entered the office and sat down around the conference table, Serena started the meeting.

"I'm not much on meeting formalities with a group like this, but I will try to keep us on track and moving along. Lani, if you will pass out those short agendas we prepared, we can get started. Notice Angus' latest information is the first item. Angus, please run through what you have for Chelton and then give us all your latest information."

Angus ran through the high points of his discovery for Chelton, repeating the scenario he had described to the group at the last meeting. He then repeated his best case and worst case scenario for the passage of the ghost.

Angus continued, "One more day of calculations produced no changes in the projections. It will likely be ten to fifteen years before the path and the relative positions of the planets to the ghost can be predicted with a degree of certainty. The ghost will probably pass through the solar system within the orbit of Jupiter in about thirty years. It definitely will pass within four light years of the sun and that does not bode well for life on earth. The chance of the star passing with little or no serious effect on the earth is almost zero."

"So we're looking at a long period, years actually, when we won't know for sure exactly where the ghost might go? Is that what you're saying?" Chelton asked.

"You are quite correct for now," Angus answered. "With the rapid growth in all technologies, a major breakthrough in measurement techniques is a definite possibility. Should that happen, it could shorten the period substantially. Unfortunately, it is also quite unpredictable."

"That brings us back to the next item on the agenda," Serena pointed out. "Whom we should add to our group if, indeed, we need to add anyone?"

"I, for one, would like to find a member of the news media we could trust. That might be a tall order," Ali suggested. "I certainly don't know anyone in that category."

Angus immediately thought of Ginger Cari. Among all the news people he had met, she seemed the most likely. Her boss, Pete Radcliff was another possibility, but something he felt about Pete made him uncomfortable. Likeable as he was, Pete would probably sell his mother for a great story. Angus would remain silent for the moment and see who else was brought up.

Chelton suggested, "I know a few press people I could trust, but they are all in Washington and New York. I doubt it would be practical to bring them out here for meetings unless we just couldn't find anyone closer. Angus, you have had lots of experience with the press. Do you have any possibilities closer to Hawaii?"

Angus had to adjust his thoughts quickly. He had shared his interview experience with Lani, but with no one else and would like to confer with her before suggesting Ginger. Before he could formulate a response, Lani spoke up.

"What about the reporter that interviewed you, Ginger Cari? You seemed to think she was bright, dedicated and trustworthy. Do you think she could fit in and not betray us?"

Lani's question caught Angus a little off guard. He knew she was still a little suspicious of Ginger's motives, so he stumbled, tongue-tied for a moment. "She's a possibility. Hiakawa seemed to have a lot of respect for her integrity, and he's sharp on that. I'd like to check with him before we make any overtures to her."

"I think it important we check out carefully any prospective new members before bringing them in," Charlene commented. "One mistake and the cat's out of the bag for sure."

"Any more suggestions?" Serena asked.

After a period of silence, Lani spoke up again, "I hate to make all the suggestions, but I know another good one. Dr. Francis Lane would give us a new dimension. He grew up in the Detroit inner city and is half African and half Chinese. He has a unique background in both cultures. His wife, Oona, is part Korean and part Japanese. She brings even another dimension and should probably come along with her husband if we choose him. They are right here in Hilo."

Ruth made note of their names and asked for addresses and other information for her minutes. "That makes a total of eleven members if we bring in all three. I think we should limit the group to a dozen. More than that and things may get unwieldy. There were twelve apostles, remember?"

Angus chimed in, "And one of them was a betrayer. Maybe we'd better stop at eleven. We certainly don't need a Judas."

Charlene made a suggestion. "Why don't we leave it open in case we run across someone we need later on? Let's not limit ourselves. We can just stop actively looking for new people. Besides, after investigation, we may decide not to invite one or more of those people suggested. I think a negative vote from any member should remove a person from consideration."

John thumped his desk and smiled. "Excellent idea, Charlene. Could we bring them in to meet the group and then decide if we want them? I'd rather like a chance to talk with these people before deciding."

Ever in charge, Serena said, "With your approval, here's what we'll do. Check them out as best we can and, if we don't find any negatives, invite them to our next meeting under some innocuous pretense. We'll all get a chance to talk with them and form our own opinions. Should anyone get a negative impression, that person could veto membership for the person they felt posed a danger to the group."

"Sounds like a plan to me," Angus remarked. "Who's to conduct the investigation?"

"Charlene and I could do it," Serena replied. "We both have the time. I know Pete Hiakawa, and Charlene has a nephew who could provide her with at least some of the information we need. How about it, Charlene, are you game?"

"I've never tried *sleuthing* before, but why not?" Charlene answered. "Sure! I'll grill Joey and you can do the same with Hiakawa. If there's any dirt out there, we'll find it."

"What about the time?" Ali asked. "Shouldn't we invite them right away? It's only a week until our next meeting. We may not be able to check them out in time to invite them."

John made a suggestion. "Why not have a short reception here in one of our meeting rooms. We could do it Saturday or Sunday afternoon and describe it as a thank you from Gemini for what has been done for us after Angus' accident and the OSI affair. An hour or so of socializing would give each of us a chance to meet our new prospects and form our own opinion. Then, unless someone gave a thumbs down, we could invite them to our next meeting on Wednesday."

"Great idea!" Ruth replied. "If we could do it Saturday, it would be a lot better for me. My Sundays are always so crowded."

Lani offered, "Why don't I try to call all three right now? I can invite them and find out if they can attend Saturday. If we get confirmation, we can start the ball rolling right away."

"Do you still have Pete Radcliff's number?" Angus asked. "He'll know how to get in touch with Ginger."

"It's on my desk. I'll run over there now, make the calls and be back in a few minutes," Lani replied as she rose to leave.

"While she's making those calls, let's get on with the next item," Serena requested. "I doubt anyone has done anything toward our news releases since yesterday, but Chelton wasn't here, so we'll have to explain it to him. Everyone was asked to prepare press releases for us to view and to help find the best wording. So far as I know, only Charlene has done any work on this."

Chelton agreed to start working on this immediately. "These press releases and the message they will convey are the main purpose for our entire group. In fact, they may actually be the entire purpose," he remarked. "I suggest we start working seriously on them immediately."

All agreed wholeheartedly and began discussing a number of possibilities while waiting for Lani to return.

After about half an hour passed, Charlene wondered out loud, "What could be taking her so long? She must be having trouble finding someone. Maybe one of us should go see what the delay is."

Reaching for his phone, John said, "I can just ring her line. If it's busy, we'll know she's still trying."

After a single ring, Lani answered. "The Lanes would love to come, but may not be here until nearly four because of a previous commitment. They're free for the rest of the afternoon. Ginger is a little harder to find. Pete left for the day, and I had to persuade the man who answered to give me Ginger's pager number. I'm waiting for an answer to her page. If she doesn't call back in the next few minutes, I'll forward my phone to yours and come back to the meeting."

"At least the Lanes will be here," John replied. Hanging up the phone, he asked the group, "Do we have anything else of importance to discuss while we're waiting? If not, I'd like to hear Chelton's fresh view of the problem."

Serena replied, "I have nothing more on the agenda. If no one else has anything to bring up, I'll turn things over to Chelton. I, too, would like to hear his comments."

After a moment of silence and anticipation, Chelton began, "I guess that means I'm on. First of all, I am truly honored to be invited to join a group with such a noble and compelling purpose. At first I thought the problem was a little out of my league, but then I realized each of you could say the same thing. Although what we do will have no effect on the physical reality of the interactions of the celestial bodies, it will have a powerful effect on the lives of billions of people. Released carelessly or without due consideration, the information we possess could trigger riots, mayhem and many deaths throughout the world. I am certain we will create our communications and make our decisions with great concern for our earth. In all our efforts, we must weigh the possibilities of deliverance from this monstrous threat with the realities of what we know for certain. As I understand it, Angus, there is a possibility this wild star could pass without incident. It could miss us by enough distance, or its great speed might lessen or even eliminate the effects of its gravity. The latter possibility is apparently a complete unknown at this time. Am I correct?"

"Right on the money," Angus answered. "That's an accurate description of our problem. Very well put."

Chelton continued, "Then one of the first things we should be doing is researching the effects of the star's passing in the worst case. I'm not sharp on scientific things, but shouldn't we be arranging for computer simulations of that situation to see just what might happen? Do you have that capability right here?"

"I wish it were that simple," John answered. "We have some computer facilities here, but not with enough computing power to do what you suggest with the degree of certainty we need. We'd have to go to NASA, Cal Tech or another university on the mainland for that level of computing power. Then there's the relativity problem with an object moving so fast. We might need a particle physicist or someone with an understanding of the math of such an object to help program any simulation. I know of no research work using an object as large as a star moving at relativistic speeds. We may be on completely unchartered waters here. Professor Botkin at Cal Tech would probably be our best bet for some answers. I sat with him at a seminar a few months back. This is definitely in his field, but how do we enlist his aid without letting the cat out of the bag?"

"Might he be one to invite into the group?" Ruth asked. "Do you know enough about him?"

"Charlie Botkin is sort of a maverick genius. He graduated from Purdue at seventeen with degrees in physics and math. He then went to Cal Tech for his doctorate and has been there ever since. He's a genuine wild card, an unconventional thinker and personality. A capable rock musician, his hair and dress make you think of him as anything but a serious scientist. He works actively against drugs and alcohol abuse in the community. You wouldn't call him religious by any stretch of the imagination, but he regularly lectures to troubled youths on the real value of morality. All this while putting in many hours teaching graduate students and researching at the forefront of quantum physics. I believe he is one of the pioneers in the application of quantum physics to cosmology. That's what the seminar was about. He was one of the presenters. Most of what I know about him is by reputation and the blurb on the seminar program. I only spoke to him for a few minutes, not enough to get much of a personal feel about him."

"I've heard of him from some of the people I work with," Chelton replied in realization. "All I remember is some talk about a crazy scientist from California who was working wonders with troubled young people and whom we should investigate. I don't know if anyone did check it out. That came up just a few months ago. He could be one we could use."

John spoke up, "I can give him a call and ask him a hypothetical question about a star moving at relativistic speeds past another star. I can tell him it came up here after a discussion of that seminar. We should at least find out how to go about finding an answer. Then we can decide if we need to proceed with him or find someone else."

Ali looked up, searching for straws. "I hope he tells us it will blow by without a ripple."

"At the very least, that kind of answer would certainly change things for the better," Ruth said. "How reliable would it be? I mean, it's all quite theoretical, isn't it? Couldn't the theory be wrong or at least in error?"

Angus replied, "I'm sure we would get another best case/worst case scenario. It's unlikely we'll know for certain until it actually happens. The difference between theory and actuality can be all over the map. We'll have to prepare for the worst and hope for the best."

"We'll just have to go with our best shot and pray a lot," Ali remarked.

"What's this about praying a lot?" Lani asked as she walked in, just catching her father's last remark.

"We can tell you what you missed after we hear from you. What did you find out?" Serena asked.

"Ginger called just as I was about to give up and come back. I told her four o'clock since the Lanes won't be here until then. She said she'd be delighted to come, then asked if there was a story in it for her. I said it was just a social event, no big story. So all of our prospects should be here. Now, what did I miss?"

"We brought Chelton up-to-date, then he pushed us to work on the press releases right away. John offered to call a physicist he knows at Cal Tech to see about running simulations of the star passing through the solar system," Serena explained. "That's all you missed."

"Why don't we record our meetings in the future so anyone who misses anything can catch up?" Lani asked. "We have several tape recorders available, and I'll gladly set it up."

When they all agreed, she continued, "I'll get with Jenny to arrange for the room for the reception."

Serena stood up. "Unless there's an objection, I declare this meeting adjourned."

For at least an hour after the meeting was adjourned, the group continued informally discussing many aspects of the situation.

During the conversation, Angus suggested, "We need to find an appropriate name for our group, a name that will give a reason for meetings without arousing suspicions of anyone, including OSI."

Ruth's spoke up, "What about Gemini Community Action Committee? That should be innocuous enough."

When everyone agreed, Serena added, "We can start using it in the announcement of the reception. Now, I think we should all head out."

John looked relieved. "Good idea. I've got to get home."

Leaving in an upbeat mood, the rest stopped for dinner at a nearby restaurant. Those who didn't know him became well acquainted with Chelton at dinner. By the time they headed for home, many life histories had been shared.

CRAZY CHARLIE BOTKIN

Friday morning, John called Jenny. "Find Dr. Charles Botkin at Cal Tech and get him on the phone. Don't make it sound too urgent, just important."

John knew Jenny was good at filling these kinds of requests with pleasant, but persistent efforts.

About an hour later, Jenny called. "I have Dr. Botkin on the phone. Is he nuts? After tracking him down and talking to him for just a few minutes, he asked me to marry him. Weird!"

John laughed. "That's Crazy Charlie all right. You never know what he's liable to say. Put him on."

"How's the old fogey, John? You still the stuffy old guy in the fancy suit?" Charlie was not known for being diplomatic. He usually said just what came into his mind.

"You still the kid with the pony tail and the tattered jeans?" John shot back with a laugh.

"You betcha! What's this about? It must be important for your Jenny to track me down in the gym. She's obviously good at finding people. I'm usually impossible to find."

"Well, it's important for our group here. I don't want to bother you while you're busy. Would a later time be better?"

"Nah! Now's fine. Shoot!"

"Our query is right up your alley. When it came up, I immediately thought of you. During one of our brainstorming sessions, someone came up with this scenario: We have a hypothetical star moving at near the speed of light, say eighty to ninety percent of light speed. Should this star pass quite close to another star with planets around it what would the effects of gravity be? Would its speed be relativistic, and would that change the gravitational effect and how much?"

"Now that's a tall order. I've never heard of a star moving that fast. Is it possible?"

"I've learned, as far as celestial objects are concerned, next to nothing is impossible, unlikely, but not impossible."

"That's an interesting question. I would have to give it some thought. I don't think anyone has ever looked at that kind of event, at least, not to my knowledge. How'd you ever come up with a question like that?"

"As I said, it came up during an open discussion right after the seminar, and the idea caught our interest. We just couldn't leave it without trying to find an answer. Remembering your presentation at the seminar, I called you. I'll understand if you can't help us. Some of these hypothetical situations can be quite bizarre."

"I'm fascinated. Now you've piqued my curiosity, and I'd like to know the answer as well. It may take me some time, but it is a valid question that should have an answer."

"I know you must be busy. Are you sure you want to tackle it now?"

"I can set it up as a problem for some of our grad students. They can create a computer simulation of the event. The ones I'm thinking of are sharp. This would be a real challenge for them and a worthwhile learning effort."

"That's great! I thought maybe you would like the challenge. Do you have any idea how long it would take? I'm not trying to press you. It's just that my people will want to know."

"I'd say at least a couple months. By the time we set up the simulation and can schedule time on the computer, it will take that long. Give me some more details about the star, so we're on the same page. How big is it? How fast is it going and how in creation did it attain such a speed?"

"Make it half the mass of the sun, a red dwarf and have it moving at ninety percent of the speed of light. I haven't the foggiest idea how it reached that speed, maybe from the mind that originally posed the question. We can address that one ourselves in the future."

"OK. I've the size and the speed. I'll have it passing through the solar system. We have real information there and wouldn't have to create anything new."

John gulped when Charlie proposed the solar system. That was a stroke of luck. "Sounds good to me. Do you need any more information?"

"Just the exact date of the closest point of passage and the path, so we can position the planets."

Again John hesitated, then said, "Try April 1, 2031. April Fool's Day would be appropriate if not significant. Have it coming from eighteen hours right ascension and about five degrees up."

"Got it! If I need any more info, I'll give you a call. This is exciting. A new dimension to relativity. Pardon the inside joke, please. By the way, how's Gemini performing? As I remember, you were just about finished with testing and were to turn the telescope over to the astronomers shortly after the seminar."

"Things are going even better than expected. The delays are all behind us and all seems to be running smoothly. It's made my job easier in the bargain."

"Glad to hear it. I'd like to come out and visit some time. Astronomy has always interested me."

"Come out any time. We'd love to have you."

"I'll let you know. Now I gotta get back to makin' sweat. I'll keep you informed on how things are progressing. Meanwhile, try jeans and a tank top. That would blow the minds of all those stuffy scientists you work with."

John laughed heartily as they said their good-byes. *Crazy Charlie is a unique person*, he thought as he hung up the phone.

THE RECEPTION

By 3:30 Saturday afternoon, everything was ready for the reception, and the entire group was there. All that was needed now were the guests. At about a quarter to four, they watched as Ginger Cari drove up and parked her convertible right in front of the window of the meeting room. Seeing the faces as she walked past the window toward the door, she waved.

This will be interesting, Angus thought, wondering how Ginger and Lani would get along. Lani knew about Ginger, but Ginger did not know about Lani, yet. If she joined the group, she would know, and that would relieve Angus greatly. He did not enjoy even small deceptions.

John greeted Ginger at the door and did the introductions. By the time Ginger had met everyone, the Lanes drove up. As Angus went to the door to greet them, he noticed Ruth, Serena, Charlene and Lani were already in an involved discussion with Ginger. He was sure they would be quite thorough in their investigation. He was equally certain Ginger would hold her own with the four women.

After introductions, the group hung together for a few minutes and then drifted into smaller, mixed groups. Everyone made a point to talk to each of the three prospects to help make their decision. At one point Angus found himself in a discussion with Oona and Lani about career women and their problems with marriage. It was a light-hearted discussion until Oona left to join John and Chelton in a discussion of youth problems and Ginger walked up and replaced Oona in the continuing discussion.

"I think it is difficult for a career woman to have a successful marriage," Ginger stated. "Few men can put up with the hassles, let alone the competition of a career. It's no wonder two-career marriages have such a poor record."

"I don't know about that," Lani replied, standing beside Angus and facing Ginger. "Insecure people of both sexes must deal with problems created entirely by their insecurities. Secure people are mostly free of these handicaps. A marriage between two relatively secure people might be enhanced by two careers. I, for one, feel insecurity of either or both partners contributes to the downfall of many marriages, especially those having two careers. What do you think, Angus?" she asked, looking straight at him.

"I don't know. Sometimes I feel married to my work. I know there are times when it takes precedence over everything else. Few women could handle that well and it is probably even more difficult for a man. I'd say it takes hard work and some occasional sacrifices for any marriage to work. That would certainly be true of a two-career marriage as well. In any event, I haven't had to deal with the problem."

"I haven't either, but there are times when I'd like to," Ginger remarked, staring intently at Angus. "Just haven't run across the man yet." She then turned to Lani. "I take it you're in the same situation."

By this time Angus was worried about where the conversation was headed.

"Not really," Lani answered coolly. "If a warm, decent, intelligent, secure man comes along and if there's some magic there, I might be inclined to marry. If not, well, I have a life right now that's full and rewarding. The wrong man could mess it up. I'm not about to let that happen."

"In spite of my earlier remarks, I'm inclined to agree with you," Ginger answered. "The wrong man could certainly wreak havoc in my life. I rather like how it's going the way it is."

"I couldn't agree more!" Angus said with conviction. "The same could happen to a man who picks the wrong woman. I see no difference at all in our positions on the subject." A strong flash of body language and nonverbal communication sent hidden messages through the three people. Angus felt uncomfortable, a man standing unarmed directly between two expert sword fighters beginning to skirmish.

Lani rescued him with, "Who's kidding whom? With that instinctive need for a mate deep within us, we'd each go for it if we ran into another who attracted us and met most of our criteria. We would probably give serious and thoughtful consideration before taking the plunge. I know I would anyway."

Ginger smiled, looking first at Angus and then at Lani. Something fleeting in their faces tweaked her feminine instincts. "Well said! A hunk with brains, heart, intelligence, a sense of humor and high moral character would certainly cause me to think twice, as long as he wasn't one of those stupid macho characters. I just can't stand the macho male and his ridiculous posturing. They may appeal to air headed little girls, but a woman wants a real man."

"Likewise, a man wants a real woman," Angus said, trying to move the conversation to safer ground. "I have serious problems with the macho male's female counterpart. Those *feminachos* can be equally ridiculous."

Suddenly Ginger's eyes flashed back and forth between he and Lani. Her instincts, reading their body language and other subtle clues, clicked with her mind. "Now I get it! The two of you are an item or are about to be. Why didn't you just say so during our interview?" she shot sharply at Angus.

"I . . . I didn't . . . " Angus stammered.

Noting his expression of panic, Lani mercifully rescued him by interrupting. "Yes, we are definitely an *item* as your clever observations have discovered. It is important this doesn't become common knowledge. I can't tell you why, but a great deal, even lives, may depend on that. Angus thinks you are an honorable person. I had my doubts, but since we've talked tonight I feel the same way. There is a real story for you here, and you will be first to get it when it's safe to release. It's much bigger than two people in love. I feel certain you can be trusted and hope I'm right."

"Wow! My instincts were right. There is something newsworthy going on here, and, suddenly, I feel as if I'm right in the middle of it. That's why you were so evasive about those personal comments I made. Why is it the good ones are taken when I find them?" Ginger remarked with a sigh, looking straight at Angus.

Angus turned immediately toward the rest of the group and announced, "Something has just come up making it imperative for the Gemini people to have a huddle. If our guests will excuse us for a moment, we can step out of the room, confer and then return in just a few minutes. I know it's irregular, but it's quite important."

As soon as he finished, Angus opened the door and they followed him out, closing the door behind them. Ginger and the Lanes stood dumbfounded wondering what this might mean.

"What's this about?" Serena asked as soon as the door was closed.

"I hate to rush things, but a delicate situation has come up with Ginger, Lani and me. It's become necessary to decide on Ginger and maybe even the Lanes right now. Mom, have you and Charlene finished your checking?"

Charlene spoke up, "Joey said he couldn't find anything negative about any of them. That's only from the police records that are public knowledge. A credit check turned up nothing negative. That's about all I have had time to do."

Serena added, "Hiakawa had nothing but good words for Ginger and told me Dr. Lane was well known for his cooperation with police in many instances over the years. Why the rush to judgement?"

After Lani explained how Ginger had uncovered her relationship with Angus, creating a rather delicate situation, Serena asked, "If any of you have negative feelings about any of the three, get them out. If we can, I suggest we make our decision now."

Many questioning looks passed between members of the group before John finally asked, "Did everyone get enough time talking to each of them to feel confident having them join us?"

A general positive shaking of heads was his answer. Lani then commented, "I think each of them will bring a special presence to the group. They all come across to me as honorable, intelligent and concerned people. I say we go for it."

As the nodding of heads and short comments indicated, everyone seemed in agreement. Serena announced, "In view of the absence of vetoes and the general agreement, I propose we go in and tell them what this is all about right now. Anyone voting no?"

At the absence of nos, Serena said, "Done! Why don't we have Lani explain to them what the situation is? Chelton, you explain what the group is all about, and, John, would you please explain Gemini's part in this?"

Upon agreement with Serena's suggestion, they rejoined the three new people in the meeting room. Serena asked the three to be seated and then began. "This is a most unusual request made under extraordinary circumstances. You three are being asked to join our group, all of whom are present, for a noble purpose. We ask nothing we divulge here be revealed or even discussed outside this group whether or not you decide to join us. If each of us did not see each of you as honorable, trustworthy individuals, we would not be revealing to you the awesome secret we now share. If any one of you cannot agree to this request, please let us know and we can part friends without sharing what we know. Ginger, as a news reporter, you may find it impossible, so consider your answer carefully."

After glancing at the Lanes, Ginger spoke up, "Under ordinary circumstances, I would feel obligated to excuse myself since it is virtually impossible for a news person to sit on a story, and I see a big story here. In looking at this group and seeing the caliber of its members, I feel honored to be asked to join. That you have asked me to join for a specific purpose is quite obvious. Under these circumstances, I can forgo my obligation and willingly agree to keep your secret. As you probably found out if you did any checking, I keep my word."

Oona then spoke up, "I'm overwhelmed by your request. You can count on me. Francis will have to speak for himself, but I think I know the answer."

"My wife knows me quite well," Francis replied. "I, too, feel honored to be asked. This is an extraordinary group. For whatever purpose you have, I'm with you. Now, before we die of overwhelming curiosity, tell us what this is all about."

The three sat spellbound as Lani proceeded to explain Angus' discovery and the terrible consequences threatened by the event thirty years in the future. The new members had many questions, but Serena asked them to defer until Chelton and John had explained their part. Chelton explained the group's purpose and just how important secrecy would be. He asked Angus to explain how the group started and grew to its present members. When Angus was finished, John explained how Gemini was involved and that all their capabilities were at the group's disposal.

"Unbelievable!" Ginger remarked when John had finished and asked for questions. "I only have a few million questions, but that's the reporter talking. Maybe I should defer to the Lanes while I try to cut that million down to just a few important ones."

Francis then spoke. "At the moment, I have one question above all others. What in the devil has OSI got to do with this, and what really happened to those three agents we treated?"

Angus explained how it happened and gave them a run-down on his plans to escape to Chile should they return. When he finished his story, Francis replied, "It makes a lot more sense than the rumors that percolated through the trauma center. It was the talk of the place for several weeks." Turning to Ginger he said, "I'd rather like to hear your questions. Why don't you ask away?"

Ginger stood up and began pacing in a small area. "I think better when on my feet," she explained, then continued: "Just as I suspected, there is a great deal more to the story than I was told. I now understand why. All those things that just didn't add up before are now making sense. I have a good idea I've been asked into the group to help with press releases and the like. I will gladly perform that function. I have started a story on Angus and Gemini. This should provide a good reason for my involvement with you, so no one at the news center should wonder what's going on. I'm completely awestruck at the enormity of both the challenge and the menace. It is exciting to be part of what could go down in history as a very important group of people. Unfortunately, it could be a short history. My first question is, who else do you plan to add to the group?"

"No one else, unless we run across someone we think we must have," Angus answered. "With the three of you added, we've a diverse cultural, social and racial group and have decided we can do the job with the present members. Too many people and it might become difficult to make a decision."

Ginger continued, "I heartily agree. I have a number of technical questions, but I can take those up with Lani and Angus later. Do you have a schedule of the kinds of news releases you are planning? I'd like to begin work on it right away. I feel your sense of urgency in this."

John explained, "As yet there is no schedule, but each of us is to present suggestions for releases at the next meeting on Wednesday. Now that we have a news person in our group, I suggest we give her those suggestions and place her in charge."

"I'll be glad to handle the news releases," she replied.

They continued with questions and answers, taking time to bring the new members up to the group's level of understanding as best they could.

When the question about OSI came up, Angus explained, "I am certain OSI will be back on the scene soon. Should I have to go into hiding, I'll be at the Lanes' guest apartment in their home. We must be careful about communication and will work out procedures as quickly as practical. Lani is the one to contact if you can't reach me."

At shortly before seven, Serena said to the group, "Let's adjourn until the next scheduled meeting. In the meantime I have a few suggestions. Please, everyone, remember, as far as the public is concerned, our group is a Gemini P.R. effort. We'll try to keep the regular meetings in John's office low key. Don't mention them to anyone outside the group. We don't want OSI to get wind of these meetings. Also, we are concerned about phone calls to or from any of Angus' phones. They and possibly other phones may be tapped, so act accordingly. Please leave all meetings, including this reception, one at a time or in small groups normally expected to be together. Let's try to keep OSI guessing."

13

As the group left the meeting room, Ginger came up to Lani and Angus. "Do you two have any plans for this evening? If not, I'd like you to join me for dinner. I have some technical questions about this ghost of yours."

Lani looked at Angus. "You have any plans? I don't."

"Let me check with Mom and Chelton. I don't want to leave them hanging."

After a few minutes conferring with Serena and Chelton, Angus returned and said, "They're OK. They'll head down to Chelton's hotel. This could be the last opportunity for us to talk for some time. I feel the impending, ominous intrusion of OSI into our process. I can't see them standing back much longer."

"Just to be safe, let's go our separate ways now and meet at the top of the Mokuloa in thirty minutes," Ginger suggested.

Angus looked at Lani with a wry grin. "I think we can handle that. My chauffeur will take me there in good time."

Lani crossed her arms and glared defiantly. "One more remark like that and you'll be riding your bike."

Ginger laughed at the pseudo battle. "I can see knowing you two is going to be an experience. See you in a few."

Ginger headed out the front door while Lani and Angus went out the side entrance to her car in the parking lot. As they neared Lani's car, two men stepped out of the shadows and stopped them. One was

Jan Lux and the other they had not seen before. Angus thought of bolting from the scene, being sure he could outrun them, but he couldn't leave Lani. He would play out this episode before making any moves.

"Dr. Thomas, we've some questions for you and we want you to come with us to our office to answer them. Now!" Lux stated emphatically.

Angus' mind raced. "Can't this wait? Miss Namahoe was going to drop me off for a date with a lovely young lady who is waiting for me as we speak."

Lux smiled, barring their path. "You'll just have to stand her up. Your friend here can tell her you had an important date with your Uncle Sam. Now let's get going."

As he finished, he took hold of Angus' arm. It was a bad mistake. Angus twisted quickly out of his grip, stopped, crouched, arms spread parallel to the ground and glared at Lux like a tiger ready to spring. "Keep your hands off me. One more move like that, and I'll deck you and your goon."

Lux and the other man froze facing Angus. All stood unmoving yet poised for action. Angus continued, forcefully, "I'll talk to you, but it will be according to my rules. Try anything and you'll be going down, so don't move. Here are my rules. We go inside and talk in the lobby. There will be people there who will see what's happening, but won't be able to hear our conversation. Miss Namahoe can let my date know I'll be delayed and where I can be reached. The only other place I'll talk to you is at Hilo Police headquarters with Pete Hiakawa present. He'll come here to get me. I won't get in a car with you two. I don't trust you at all."

As he finished, he began backing toward the door motioning Lani to step back. Lux moved slowly in the same direction, following his move. "That's not practical. We have some confidential questions for you that can only be asked in private. You understand?"

"There's absolutely nothing you can ask or I can answer that can't be handled in the presence of the police. You and all the rest of your idiot comrades at OSI, who are looking for space invaders or other such nonsense, are so far off base you'll be the laughing stock of the whole world when the truth is made public. That's exactly what I plan to do as soon as possible."

At this point, Angus had nearly reached the door when the other man lunged for him. Angus responded with a Karate kick that all but took the OSI man's head off and dropped him to the ground like a stone. Lux stood back and drew his gun, aiming for Angus' shoulder. A searing pain shot through his left arm. Instinctively he reached for his shoulder and found a syringe dart which he yanked out. He had been shot with a tranquilizer gun. Lani, who was now behind Lux, swung her heavy purse with all her might at Lux's head, stunning him momentarily. Angus jumped forward and hit the faltering Lux in the head with another kick, downing him.

Angus moved quickly toward Lux. "Look for other syringes. I don't know how long before that shot takes effect. I just hope we can find the antidote syringe before I pass out."

Angus' head quickly started buzzing. He headed for Lani's car and barely made it inside with Lani's help before passing out completely. Lani returned to Lux and searched his pockets. She found another dart gun and an automatic pistol, but no syringe. With a sudden inspiration, she searched the other man. There were four syringes in a plastic packet in his pocket. He had no gun. Taking the items she had collected, she jumped in her car and headed for the Lanes' hoping they had gone directly home after the reception. Angus lay silent and limp on the seat as she drove calmly out of the parking lot. She would drive normally so as not to draw attention in case other OSI operatives were around.

She drove up the Lanes' driveway just as they were getting out of their car inside the garage. *What good luck,* she thought as she jumped out and called to them. Within a few minutes, Angus was stretched out on a furniture pad on the garage floor being examined by Dr. Lane. His breathing was labored, his eyes were open and he was limp as the proverbial wet dishrag.

Dr. Lane examined the pouch of syringes Lani handed him. There were two types in the pouch, all unmarked. "I would guess two are filled with tranquilizer and two with the antidote. Unfortunately, we don't know which is which, and a lab analysis would take too long. Did you happen to pick up the syringe he was struck with?" he asked Lani.

"No, but I did bring another tranquilizer gun I found, will that help?"

"Excellent! Get it for me. I have an idea that might tell us which is which."

Taking the tranquilizer gun Lani brought, Francis gingerly removed the syringe dart. He squeezed a small drop from the dart onto his fingertip, smelled it and then touched it to his tongue. "Not familiar to me," he commented as he reached for one of the other four syringes. Taking a drop from this syringe he repeated the tests and announced, "This is definitely not the same as the dart. I must assume it to be the antidote. What do you say? Shall we try it?"

"How safe do you think it is?" Oona asked. "Let's not cause any more damage."

Francis raised the syringe and cleared the air with a slow press to the plunger. "Safe enough. All of these tranquilizers act about the same way. The greatest danger is in not administering the antidote. I can tell by the taste this is not another tranquilizer. I say we inject about a third of the syringe and keep tabs on his vital signs. I wouldn't suggest it if I thought there was any danger. Were we to take the time to transport him to the trauma center, the delay could be damaging."

Lani, visibly shaking, her face drawn taut from the tension, looked at Francis. "Do it! I know you wouldn't take any unnecessary chances."

Within about ten minutes of the injection, Angus began to move. In another five his eyes began to wander and he began moving his tongue against his lips. Lani got down beside him, cradling his face in her hands and wiping his now profusely perspiring forehead. "Can you hear me?" she said, looking into his now less vacant eyes.

Angus sat up slowly with Lani's help. "Did I have an accident? My head feels like it's about to explode. What's going on?"

"Let's get him inside on the couch," Oona suggested. "That concrete floor can't be very comfortable."

Angus was still dazed and unsteady as they half-carried him on wobbly legs and sat him on the couch. He sat there for nearly an hour, slipping in and out of consciousness. Finally noticing the unfamiliar surroundings, he looked through blurry eyes at the fuzzy image before him and asked, "Francis, is that you? How'd I get here?"

Lani was pleased to finally hear him talking. "You had another run-in with OSI. They shot you with a tranquilizer gun. You've been out for almost an hour. I brought you to the Lanes', and Francis gave you an antidote to bring you around. Do you remember anything that happened?"

"My head's still buzzing like mad and hurts like blazes. Feels as though it's been that way for many hours. My thinking is beginning to clear up though. The last thing I remember is hitting Lux. It's coming back. How'd I get here?"

Francis arose to get something for Angus' headache. "You'll probably be woozy for another hour or so. I'll get you something to relieve that headache. You'll be back to normal before long."

Still in a fog, but beginning to be able to focus, he looked in Lani's direction. "Did you call Ginger? She'll be thinking we stood her up."

Lani stood up in response. "I was so concerned about you, I forgot all about our dinner date. I'll call her right now. She'll probably want to come here. Is that OK?"

"It's OK with me if the Lanes don't mind."

"Of course not," Oona said. "She will be most welcome."

It took Lani some time to reach Ginger, who went down to the lobby to inquire when they didn't show up. Lani gave her directions to where they were when, as expected, she asked if she could come there. She relayed the information to the rest of the group as soon as she hung up. "Now, I wonder what OSI will do next?" she added as she sat down next to Angus.

Angus looked at Oona and said, "Well, for one thing, it looks like I'm here to stay, for a while at least. After what happened tonight, I had best disappear. Your anonymous house guest has moved in." He turned to face Francis. "It's a good thing we were prepared. They caught me by surprise. I didn't think we'd see them until Monday. I wonder what prompted them to move tonight?" He then moved his bleary-eyed gaze to Lani. "You don't suppose they knew what the reception was about do you?"

Lani looked more and more relieved as Angus' eyes grew clearer. "I doubt it. The reception notice was posted on the main bulletin board in the lobby for several days. Anyone who walked in could have read it and known you would be there. They must have decided since the scheduled readings were complete, now would be the best time to move. They did catch you off guard, didn't they?"

"I'll have to admit they did. I only hope they don't know much more than we think they do. Like where I am right now for instance.

I'll bet they're scurrying around looking for me by now. You don't suppose Lux is back at the trauma center do you?" He grinned weakly as he finished speaking.

"Wouldn't you like to be a little bird watching what they're doing?" Oona commented. "How about your mother? Won't they be looking for her first?"

Growing stronger each moment, Angus reached for the phone on the table by the couch. "I had better call and warn her. I hope she is still with Chelton at his hotel. I doubt they have made that connection as yet."

Angus was relieved when Chelton answered his phone and said his mother was there with him. When he suggested she stay there for the night and then drive to Ruth's to stay out of OSI's hands, she replied, "Not on your life! My things are all at your apartment and I'm going to have to face them sometime, no matter what. I'd like to do it now while they're still off balance after messing with you. Besides, the more normal and unsuspecting we act, the more confused and unsure they will be. I'm going back just as soon as Chelton and I finish."

Angus agreed reluctantly. "Maybe you're right, but be careful. Those creeps might get nasty. This is the second time I've manhandled them, and they could be getting mean. You are the closest one to me they are sure about, and they could use you to try to get me to come out of hiding. I'll not rest easy until this whole ridiculous mess with OSI is cleared up."

"I'll just be the sweet, innocent mother who knows nothing of what her son is doing. I'll kill them with kindness, sympathy and mother-love. I'll bet they buy the whole thing, lock, stock and barrel."

"I'll bet you can pull it off at that. Just remember what I said. They are not nice people."

After finishing with his mom, Angus lay back down on the couch. He was still a bit shaky from the effects of the tranquilizer, and the pills Francis gave him hadn't started to relieve his headache. After lying on the couch for just a few minutes, he suddenly sat bolt upright.

"We've got to notify the others right away," he blurted out, looking at Lani almost in panic. "Call your parents and Ruth right away and tell them I've gone into hiding. Call John also. They may be tracking everyone that was at the reception."

Lani reached over and forced him back down on the couch. "Will you relax? That tranquilizer must have turned your paranoia up several notches. I called everyone while you were sitting on the couch, dazed. John said there was no one outside on the walkway to the parking lot when he left about fifteen minutes after we did. Apparently Lux and the other OSI man came to and left without going inside. I called my folks and Ruth was there, so everyone knows."

Angus rolled his eyes up to look at her from his supine position on the couch. "I should have known you'd be on the ball."

After a time, the pills began to work and his headache faded considerably. He stood up to walk around and then sat back down without taking a step. He was still a bit dizzy.

Francis suggested, "You had better stay down for a while. I may not have given you enough of the antidote to completely remove the effects of the tranquilizer. I don't want to inject any more since we're dealing with some unknowns here. You're quite lucid, but just a bit wobbly. Let's leave things as they are and let your body clear the remainder on its own. You should be completely back to normal within a couple of hours."

"Whatever you say Doc, you're the boss," Angus replied with a smile.

"I think we had better plan to use alternate means of communications for the present," Lani suggested. "Have you tested the SSR network enough to know if it will work from here?"

"Not from here, but it worked like a charm from my apartment and from your car here in the city. I tested connections with the other laptop, the computer in my office and the network at Gemini."

Lani was noticeably relieved. "Good! I don't think anyone in the group should communicate about any of this over our telephones. With Angus out of sight, they may spread a broad net to find him. I wouldn't be surprised if they tapped each of the phone lines any of the group might use, at least for the present."

"Maybe you should get back to your apartment right away," Angus said to Lani. "Laptop one is there and you can use it to contact me over the SSR network. Whatever you do, keep the network card and SSR transmitter well hidden except when you have to use them. My bet is OSI will eventually find out about that laptop and start searching for it."

"Like I suggested, those two items are frozen in a package of hamburger in my freezer right now," Lani said with a straight face, looking directly at Angus.

"Always the comedian," Angus said with resignation. "All right, where are they really?"

"I slipped them under the edge of the bathroom carpet where it goes under the cabinet door. They're both so flat the door still closes easily and you can't see even a hint they're under there. They're easy to reach and replace. As long as OSI doesn't see them or find them by accident, in my purse for instance, they wouldn't even know they exist anyway. Just to make sure, the laptop is hidden behind one of the back cushions on my couch. Satisfied, Mr. Worrier?"

"Just double checking. I knew you had things under control, but it doesn't hurt to make sure."

"You're probably right, but just remember what you said when I start double checking on some of *your* actions!" she replied to Angus emphatically. "I'll head for home and call Serena at your apartment. To throw them a curve, I'll ask if she knows your whereabouts and give her a doctored version of what happened with OSI. We know OSI will be listening on your phone and I've a lot more to let them hear that will surely get me off the hook over that incident."

When she quickly explained her plan, they all laughed. Then she looked back at Angus. "After the call, I'll try the SSR network. If you set up the laptop in your new home, we should be able to communicate."

After she left, the three headed up to his new suite. Oona stopped at the stairs and suggested she put together something light for them to eat because none of them had eaten since lunch.

*   *   *

When Lani arrived at her apartment, she took a careful look through the entire place, closets and all. It wasn't only Angus with a touch of OSI-induced paranoia. After checking the couch for the laptop, she sat down by the phone. Satisfied things were as they should be, she gathered her thoughts before calling Serena, who should be home by now. After a few rings of the phone, Serena's voice put Lani's plan in motion.

"Have you heard from Angus? I'm afraid something terrible has happened," she said in a breathless, worried tone.

Caught a little off guard at first, Serena quickly regained her composure. "No, I just walked in the door a few minutes ago. He's not here and there are no messages on his answering machine. Why? What's happened?"

"We were on our way to my car when two men stopped us in the parking lot. They wanted Angus to go with them and he didn't want to go. There was a scuffle and he knocked the first man out cold. The second one shot him with some kind of dart. The dart just grazed his shoulder and stuck in his shirt. I was so afraid for him, I hit the one with the gun over the head with my purse. Angus knocked him out too and proceeded to go through both their pockets. He took several guns and a small black packet from the men while they lay on the ground. At this point, he suggested I head for home and not drop him off to meet his date as we had planned to do before the men stopped us. He took off at a run and I headed for my car. I was so upset I started out to go to my folks' place, but halfway there I remembered they would not be home. I decided to head for my apartment and call you to let you know what happened."

"I'm glad you called, but I'm afraid I can't shed any light on where he could have gone. Was he hurt?"

"I don't think so. The dart that stuck in the shoulder of his shirt looked like one of those you see in animal shows on TV. You know, the ones they use to tranquilize large wild animals so they can work on them without danger of being attacked. Apparently, it just grazed his shoulder and didn't inject him. He seemed fine as he jogged off out of the lot."

Serena quickly caught onto what Lani was doing. "Who was his date? Maybe I should contact her to see if he's there?"

"I have no idea. He said she wasn't far from the Op Center and he'd direct me when we got in the car. I have no idea who she is or where I was to drop him off. Angus is quiet about his personal life."

Serena sighed. "That's Angus. He'll show up sooner or later, and when he does, I'll give you a call. What's your number?"

They talked for a while, laying down a confusing smokescreen for OSI's benefit. Serena told how proud she was of her son while Lani explained how nice he was to work with. Just as Serena returned the phone to its cradle, the door buzzer startled her, announcing someone at the outer door. She pressed the button on the intercom. "Who is it?"

"Jan Lux from OSI. We need to talk to you. May we please come up?"

"What's this about? I thought the last time you were here was to be the last time. If you're looking for Angus, he isn't home yet. He had a date and I don't expect him until late."

"We'd like to talk to you. Just a few routine questions."

Serena didn't want them to be in the apartment while Angus wasn't there. Then she remembered the game room. There were always a few people there on Saturday evenings. "I'll meet with you in the game room. It's at the end of the hall to your right after you enter the door. I'll buzz it open for you now and be down in just a few minutes."

Without waiting for an answer, she pressed the button and immediately stepped out into the hall. The door locked behind her as she walked quickly to the back staircase which led directly down to the hall with the game room entrance. The two men were midway down the hall as she entered the game room. Fortunately, she entered first, and there were two couples shooting pool as well. She sat down at a card table in the corner away from the pool table. The men soon came in and walked over to the table where she invited them to sit. Lux introduced his new partner, Jack Wells. As the two sat down, Serena noticed the unmistakable signs on their faces of the recent altercation with Angus.

"What's this about?"

Lux fastened his cold look on her eyes. "We've had another misunderstanding with your son, Mrs. Thomas. We need to find him to get some important questions answered. Do you know where he could be?"

Serena was not intimidated and expertly played the innocent mother, weaving her own web of deception. "I understand there was some trouble. Angus' research assistant, Miss Namahoe, called just before you arrived. She was frightened. She said you shot at Angus and he knocked both of you down, went through your pockets and then took off running. That poor girl was scared to death. She told me she was so scared you were going to shoot Angus she hit one of you on the head with her purse."

Lux rubbed the back of his head. "Is that what she used? She sure packs a wallop. It felt more like a baseball bat. Where is she now?"

"I believe she called me from her apartment," Serena replied, then continued in a stern voice. "It seems to me there was more than just a misunderstanding. Why did you have to shoot at him? My son most certainly would not have reacted as he did unless he feared injury to himself or someone else. He is definitely not a hot head. What was this dart you used to shoot him and what was this all about anyway?"

Lux looked a bit exasperated. "The situation became violent when we tried to get him to come with us. I used the tranquilizer dart to try to subdue him. It normally injects a harmless chemical that knocks a man out for several hours. He should have been lying right there beside the two of us when we came to. He certainly couldn't have gone more than a few dozen feet after being injected. Someone must have picked him up and taken him away."

Serena laughed. "Miss Namahoe said the dart missed his shoulder and stuck in his shirt. Apparently he didn't receive your tranquilizer. She also said things didn't happen the way you say. Angus asked you to come inside and talk where there were other people around. As he was heading for the door to go inside, your man here tried to jump him. Angus does not take kindly to force. He reacted to protect himself in the only way he knows. You just came off second best again. I think you were dead wrong. Angus does not trust you, and neither do I. That's why I met you here, with those people present."

Lux was not deterred. "We believe Angus has information vital to the security of our country. In this circumstance, we are authorized to use force if necessary to obtain information. It is unfortunate it has come to this, but your son has refused to cooperate with us when . . . "

Serena interrupted, exploding in anger as she stood up and pounded the table. Glaring at the two men with fire in her eyes, she spoke very deliberately. "I'm furious! Don't tell me he has refused to cooperate. You come on like a bunch of storm troopers, forcing your demands on people as if their own personal business didn't matter a whit. You act more like the gestapo or KGB people than agents of our own government. Were you refused any information when you asked Angus in a civilized manner? No! Not once did he refuse to answer any of your questions. You chose not to believe what he told you. I know because we talked about it. What's the point of asking him questions if you aren't going to believe what he tells you? My son has a fine reputation as an honest, moral man. If you haven't already found that out from your checking, you're even more stupid than your actions indicate. I know absolutely nothing about his work, except it is important to him, and he is dedicated to excellence and truth."

Lux answered Serena's tirade. "We understand all you say. We know your son is a fine, upstanding citizen and a great scientist. We are just as certain there is something important he is keeping from us, something vital to our interests that we must know. He is being less than honest with us."

Serena stood her ground. The fierce anger she felt controlled her face but not her mind. "You have the audacity to talk to me about honesty? Right here in his apartment you handed us a string of bald-faced lies just a few weeks ago and you can still talk about honesty? I say this: My son has more honor, more courage, more dedication to his country than your whole organization put together. He never knew his father, who died in the service of a country that for centuries mistreated his people, the Mohawks. He holds the principles of this country sacred, in spite of past mistreatment. I won't speak for Angus, but I now have a great deal of contempt for you and your organization. To me, you represent those things our American revolution fought against. This interview is now over. Unless you feel the need to beat a helpless Mohawk woman, I'm leaving."

The two men lurched to their feet, stunned and helpless as Serena marched out of the room to the applause of the four pool players who had stopped and listened to her lecture.

"That's what I call a big-time put-down," one of the male pool players commented.

His female partner watched gleefully. "That's some awesome woman. You guys look as if you've just been run over by a verbal tank. I love seeing men in suits get run over by a little woman."

The two OSI men left the room like two dogs slinking away with their tails between their legs. The Thomas clan had once more trounced them severely. They would head for Lani's where they hoped to do better.

As soon as Serena reached the apartment she called Lani to tell her what happened. "Those OSI people were just here and will surely go directly to your place, so be prepared."

She was certain they would hear her phone conversation, so she played the role of the indignant mother to the hilt.

Lani played the frightened, intimidated waif. "Those two scare me. I don't want them in my apartment. I'm going to head for my folks' right away."

"Before you go, are you sure you have no idea where Angus might have gone or who his date was?"

"He didn't get the chance to tell me before those men stopped us. I only know it must have been close by because he told me he'd give me directions when we got in the car. He said it wouldn't be out of my way." Thinking to add more confusion to OSI she added, "He did say something about a late dinner in Kailua. If he mentioned the place, I didn't catch it."

"That's clear across the island, isn't it?" Serena asked.

"Yes, it is. I've got to go. I don't want those men to find me here. I'll talk to you later," she said quickly and then hung up the phone.

In a moment of inspiration, she retrieved the SSR cards from the bathroom and grabbed the laptop from the couch. She would try to contact Angus with the SSR network from her car. She hurried out of the apartment, fearing any moment she might run into Lux and the other man. She placed the laptop on the passenger seat and drove out the rear entrance and down the side street. Fortunately, there were many small, red coupes the same model as hers on the island. Once away from her apartment she would be quite safe.

After driving about two miles, she pulled into a restaurant parking lot that was mostly hidden from the street. She connected the SSR card and transmitter to the laptop and booted it. When it finally finished the boot process, she opened the network communication program and attempted to make a live connection to Angus' laptop. She only hoped he had it in operation as he said he would. "Are you there, Sitting Duck?" she typed.

"It's about time you tried to get me. I've been sitting waiting for nearly an hour. Did you have a problem with the system?" came up on the screen after just a few minutes. The SSR network was working well.

She typed where she was, a description of her conversation with Serena about the OSI visit and her reply about his date. "That will teach those clowns not to mess with my women," popped up on her screen, shortly followed by, "They'll probably be headed for your folks' house. I doubt they would go to Kailua without more information than they have. What do you plan to do now?"

"I thought maybe you might have an idea. I can head for my folks. They will probably be home by the time I get there. Maybe you could call and warn them OSI might be coming for a visit. You don't think they have my folks' phones tapped yet do you?"

"Even if they intend to, I doubt they will have that done for a few days at least. I know how you can test your folks' phone. Is there a gas station in sight of the parking lot you're in?"

After a quick walk to the street and back she typed, "About a block away and on the other side of the street."

Back came, "Good. Walk down to the station and use the phone there to call your folks. Tell them you were on your way to see them when your car broke down and you are stranded at a service station. They'll want to come and get you, so say it will be less than an hour for them to fix your car and you'll be on your way. Next, tell the people at the station you broke down several blocks from there and you have called a repair service who promised to come and fix your car where it sits. Pick a spot where you'll be out of sight, but can watch the station and recognize Lux if he shows up. If your folks' phone is tapped, Lux will be there in about fifteen minutes. If they don't show up after a half hour you can be quite certain it's not. We know they're hot on your trail and will try to catch you if they know where you are."

"I'll have to go closer to the station. I couldn't recognize him from here. I don't see any place I could wait that wouldn't be out in the open. Maybe I'll find one on my trip there. I'll let you know when I'm back." As soon as she finished typing, she shut down the laptop and headed for the station. Lani stopped at the pay phone in the station lot and called her folks. It went about as planned. After explaining to the station attendant, she started walking the opposite direction up the street, crossed to the other side a block away and started walking back toward where her car was parked. Right across from the station she entered a bookstore that provided her an excellent view of the station. She stood behind a rack of books providing her a view through the front window. She explained to the shop owner she was watching for a friend and would browse through the books on the rack while waiting. When no one appeared after she had waited for more than thirty minutes she left and returned to her car. Her folks' phone was obviously not bugged as yet.

When the communication program finally came up, she typed, "No one showed. I'm heading for my folks'."

After a moment, "Have a safe trip. Be careful. I love you. XOXOXO," rolled across the screen.

She typed, "Me too. XOXOXO," before closing down the laptop and heading for her folks' where she was sure OSI would catch up with her.

Angus was a bit sad as he read those last words from Lani on his computer screen. It could be some time before they were together again and already he was missing her. Just then Oona's voice called to him from downstairs.

"Come down as soon as you can. Food's ready and Ginger is here."

"I'll be right down," he called through the open door. He had been there nearly two hours and already felt like a prisoner. With Lani headed for her folks' and his own phone off limits, he suddenly felt alone. He was temporarily cut off from all of those closest to him, an entirely new condition, which he didn't like one bit.

He joined the others in the den where Oona had prepared crackers and cheese along with vegetables and fruit with bowls of dip. Decanters of both red and white wine graced the center of the table along with four wine glasses. He greeted Ginger and apologized jokingly for standing her up earlier. They sat snacking and talking for some time. Angus gave Ginger the details of the incident with OSI, and Francis filled in the details of his recovery from the tranquilizer. After they thoroughly discussed the situation of Angus' hiding out, Francis told them the fascinating story of his flight from Detroit as a youth when he was condemned to death by a young drug pusher named Ahmed who was once his friend.

He stole the pusher's car in a bizarre escape from the pusher and his gang who were killed in a police pursuit when they tried to catch him. He found several hundred thousand dollars in cash in the car as he drove across the country to California. There he assumed a new identity and hid out for years in San Francisco's Chinatown, passing as Chinese. He used some of the money to make anonymous donations to inner city youth charities in Detroit. After a number of years, he returned to Michigan, went to college and then medical school, paying for it with the remaining drug money.

When he finished, Ginger said, "Wow! You never know what secrets are hidden within the lives of the people you meet. I'd like to write that story some time if I may. I'll bet it would sell to some magazine. I could change the names of course. That might not be a tale you would want identified with, Dr. Lane."

Francis laughed and replied, "Use it as you wish. I doubt there would be any problems with the use of my true identity. That was more than thirty years ago, and as far as I know, everyone directly connected is dead."

"I don't know," Ginger said thoughtfully. "That guy Ahmed could have some family out there who might come looking for revenge. It isn't worth the chance. I've heard of some bizarre happenings as the result of the publication of a true story. Maybe you should save it for your autobiography. I'm certain your life story would make fascinating reading."

Just then the phone rang. Oona answered and handed it to Angus. "It's Lani."

"What's up?" he asked.

"Everything is quiet here at home. No OSI as yet and with luck they won't show up until tomorrow. I'll let you know if and when they arrive."

"I'm certainly glad to hear all is OK and that you arrived safely. At least now we have a usable communication link. I feel much better knowing that."

After some chitchat, a much-relaxed Angus said good-bye and hung up.

"Now, astronomer, how about explaining to us laymen where you are with this ghost of yours?" Ginger began as soon as Angus returned to the table. "I'd like as much technical information as you can hand me in layman terminology. I'm sure our friends here have some questions as well."

Angus was good at describing technical information in a way normal, intelligent people could understand. He spent the next few hours explaining his discovery and answering their questions. It was nearly one when they finally decided to call it quits. There were some solemn faces around the table as the terrible realization continued to sink in.

"Can we meet again tomorrow?" Ginger asked as they wound up their discussion. "I'd like to work on those releases with the three of you, and I have nothing planned for my usual day of rest."

After conferring briefly, they agreed to meet in the morning. Then Oona suggested, "Why don't you stay here tonight? No need to run home and right back. I'm sure we can supply anything you may need, and we still have two spare bedrooms."

"Are you sure it won't be a bother? I only live about a half hour away."

"Of course not. We love to have guests," Francis commented with a smile. "Oona will even lend you one of her fuzzy nightgowns and slippers if you want."

They all laughed as Oona led Ginger off to show her the bedroom. Angus and Francis sat at the table for just a few minutes before heading off to their own rooms and a night's rest.

*   *   *

About eight in the morning, the phone next to his bed woke Angus. It was Lani calling from her folks again and reporting no OSI so far. He told her about the evening's discussion and that Oona had invited Ginger to stay the night.

Lani feigned anger. "I no sooner leave you alone and you spend the night with another woman. You men are so predictable."

Angus cracked back immediately. "It was a fantastic night, too. What was the song? 'If you can't be with the one you love, love the one you're with.' Isn't that how it goes?"

"Ooh! You're terrible! If I didn't know better, I would really be upset. Just don't push your luck, mister." With that, the two broke out in laughter. By now they knew each other extremely well. That bond of comfort and trust had been forged strong and resilient.

Angus remarked, "I had this almost painful feeling of isolation until your call when you arrived at your folks' last night."

"I felt much the same way during the drive. It was so good to hear your voice."

They talked for some time, the warm talk of lovers apart.

Finally, Lani brought them back to business. "I will return to my apartment early evening and contact you at eight via computer. I'm afraid to come to the Lanes' for fear of being followed, and I certainly don't trust my phone line." Before she hung up the phone she ordered, "You be sure to be by your computer at eight this evening."

"Yes, boss," he replied with a laugh as he hung up.

After returning the phone to its cradle, Angus lay back, gazed at the ceiling for a while, then drifted off and slept soundly.

*   *   *

Waking far later than his usual hour, he thought about his bicycle still back at his apartment. He would miss his morning ride. Maybe he should jog for a change. Then he remembered his warning from the doctor who rebuilt his knee that jogging was not a good idea. Somehow he was going to get some exercise. Just then Francis knocked lightly on his door.

"You awake yet?" came through the door.

"Come in," he replied. "I just finished putting on my sweats. Thought I might go for a brisk walk since I don't have my bike."

Francis walked in. "I wonder if that's such a good idea? This is a normally nosy neighborhood and you might not want to be seen, or your hideout could be discovered. You'd best stay inside during daylight hours. After dark you'd be invisible, but even then we might want to drive you away from here for any outside activities."

"I guess you're right. I don't think I'm going to like hiding out."

"Why not join me in our exercise room? Oona and I ride stationary bikes while we catch the morning news. You're welcome to use hers if you wish. You're a bit larger than Oona, but the bike's easily adjusted to fit your size. She'll probably sleep for another hour."

"I'd like that. If you're sure she wouldn't mind."

The two men headed for the bikes where they rode for a half hour, chatting occasionally. Sounds from the kitchen let them know Oona was up and about.

"I'd better head upstairs for a quick shower," Angus said as the aroma of Kona coffee gently caressed his scent organs. "Smells like breakfast is about ready."

As Angus reached the top of the stairs near his room, Oona called out, "Breakfast in ten minutes."

The two men arrived at the breakfast table almost simultaneously after a quick shower and change of clothes. Ginger and Oona were already enjoying coffee. As soon as they finished breakfast, Ginger suggested they work on a series of press releases to gradually let the public know about the ghost.

Ginger stepped into her reporter persona, notepad and pen ready. "How long after you release the first information will other astronomers be able to confirm your findings?"

Angus showed a concerned face. "I've thought quite a bit about that. If we released the information right now, it shouldn't take more than a few weeks to confirm the ghost's location. Calculation of the speed might take an additional week or ten days, but the trajectory will be much tougher to plot."

"When could they learn how close your ghost might come to the Sun and the threat it could pose to humanity?" Ginger asked.

"That's the big question. The most likely path of the star will take computer simulations to measure and calculate. That could take several weeks or even months. Given the fact other astronomers will not have the benefit of our parallax measurements, the accuracy of their results will be much poorer than ours. If we waited about four months, it would take an additional three months since the star would be hidden behind the sun, out of sight of all telescopes for those months. The Hubble space telescope is the only exception, and with their schedule already in place, I doubt it could be brought to bear on our star for six months or more. Stalling the release those four months would gain us seven to nine months in which to prepare the actual releases. While I think it important to try to stall any release for those four months, perhaps we should prepare a series of releases for immediate use, just in case."

"Sounds like a reasonable idea to me," Francis remarked.

Ginger scowled and shook her head. "I strongly disagree. News of this kind is hard to keep under wraps. It is an absolute must for you to be the first to release the information. Should someone else do so, we would all be out of the picture and all our efforts would have been in vain. How long would it take for another astronomer to accurately predict the path of your ghost and duplicate your work to date?"

Angus replied by verbally diagramming the parallax process of distance measurement. He explained how several measurements would have to be taken six months apart to most accurately determine distance and path. He explained further that even after readings were taken six months apart, the path would be accurate only to within a few light years. Several years of measurements would be required to pin down the path with a high degree of accuracy. He added his own measurements were over a period of a year and were only accurate to within a little more than three light years at best. He finished his explanation with, "So you see, we're still just making intelligent guesses. Anyone starting off right now would take at least a year to get the results we have."

"On second thought, I think Ginger is right," Francis said thoughtfully. "It would be better to word releases carefully and get them out soon to preempt others from gaining control. We could time all releases to the best schedule you could provide for others duplicating your work. As long as you are the first source of any new information, the news media would continue to turn to you for the latest news about the ghost while others merely confirm your work."

"You may be right, but from my standpoint it seems extremely unlikely anyone will run across the ghost on their own," Angus replied, sticking to his guns. "Once we announce the new findings, many eyes will be trained on our ghost. I'm concerned we might lose control that way. Some astronomers are not careful how they treat new findings. There's always the possibility a sensation seeker could grossly exaggerate the danger making it seem worse than it is, if that's possible. I like the idea of having the series of news releases ready, but I still think we should hold off as long as practical. If we could delay until the end of November, it would be this time next year before anyone could possibly get a handle on the path."

"OK," Ginger began, "Let's work out a series of releases that would work in any case. We can then place the proposal before the whole group and see what they think. We could begin the sequential release of the news any time we feel it necessary. Angus, you know much more than I do about this field and how information is given to the press. I only know how easily one can be burnt sitting on a story for any length of time."

"We still have one joker in the deck that could jump up and bite us when we least expect it," Angus warned. "From the get-go, Dick Rumley obtained a lot of the information we had. We have no idea whether or not he saw the whole picture. My guess is not. I believe he focused on my work because of my move from Arizona. He knew I wouldn't have made that move unless there was something unusual I had discovered there and needed to have use of the Gemini telescope to confirm my findings. I doubt he had enough information to know the speed or position of the star. If he had, he'd be blabbing it to everyone. His lack of comment convinces me he hasn't a clue about the ghost."

"What about the Rumley incident?" Francis asked. "I thought that was a personal thing. At least, that is what was in the news. I take it there is a lot more to the story."

Angus spent the next few hours telling the newest members of the group all the most recent happenings related to the group's formation and purpose. During this time, he answered the many questions they asked. He shared all the information that hadn't been in the news about his run-ins with OSI and why they were pursuing him. He explained how Rumley had spied and how the police found out about it. He told them about Weldon Conrad and how the British were cooperating to the point of letting him switch identities with Rumley if he had to go to Chile. When he finished, they had a much better understanding of the whole situation.

Ginger looked thoughtful, then shook her head as if in doubt. "That's quite a story. I hope I can put it on paper some day."

Francis' wide eyes and open grin displayed his amazement. "We all hope you can. Between Rumley and the OSI, your story about an amazing and threatening discovery has been turned into one of danger and intrigue as well. I have an idea that's more than you bargained for."

"You can say that again!" Angus said emphatically. "We had enough of a problem just trying to decide how to release the information. We could certainly do without having to dodge OSI. Rumley has been a minor inconvenience by comparison."

They worked through the day on the news releases, pausing only for meals and relaxation breaks. By early evening they had carefully drafted a series of seven news releases designed to gradually inform the public about the ghost. Angus worked out a timetable of the most probable course of confirmation by other astronomers. By planning the wording and scheduling of the releases to fit the timetable, they would put off sharing the most frightening news until the last possible time. This would provide a window of at least a year and possibly two during which time the ghost's exact path and time of passage could be determined. It would also provide time for calculations to be made of the ghost's gravitational effect on the sun and planets. They would present the news releases to the entire group for approval at the next meeting.

14

The two OSI men, Lux and Wells, walked silently back to their car after the tongue lashing from Serena. As they entered the car, Wells asked, "You don't suppose she's right do you? I mean, this guy is definitely Mr. All-American-hero. We checked him out thoroughly and he comes up squeaky clean. From looking over all the reports of your earlier work when I was assigned to this case, I can clearly see we've drawn nothing but blanks."

"I don't care what we've found out. There is something he is keeping from us, something very important. Somehow we are missing it and it's probably right there in front of our eyes. Yvonne found evidence of massive selective deletions from his computer. Selective deletions meant he was changing parts of his data, probably to hide something. In dealing with data on a computer, you either run calculations from it or delete it when you don't want or need it any longer. You don't selectively change it. No scientist would change the data taken by his instruments unless he didn't want anyone else to see the data. There's something there all right. We just haven't found it yet."

"I don't know," Wells said quizzically, "Maybe the other astronomer, Schuman, was right. He said any astronomer who made a big, new discovery would want to keep it to himself until he was quite sure he was correct. A premature release of information later proved to be in error could be a career-ending fiasco. Weren't those just about his words?"

"And don't you think we should find out what this new discovery is, just in case? Better to discover it's not a danger and have egg on our face than to drop the ball and later pay a terrible price. Our efforts are certainly warranted. If it turns out we're wrong, no harm done. In addition, we've taken an inordinate amount of abuse on this case, both physical and mental. Why would he resist our efforts so strongly if he isn't hiding something?"

"You're right there," Wells answered, rubbing the side of his head. "Shouldn't we check in to see if our taps have found anything before we get to his assistant's? I don't think we need any more surprises."

"Definitely! Get Yvonne on the phone. Let's find out if we've had any more activity," Lux answered quickly.

In just a few moments Wells said, "She's got one call from his assistant to his mother and one back from his mother right after we were there. I'll put it on the speaker so we can both listen."

The men listened intently to Lani's call to Serena and then the call back. When it was over, Lux asked, "What do you think of that? I was sure I hit him in the shoulder with the dart. I don't see how I could have missed. He did grab the dart and yank it out immediately though."

"How accurate are they anyway? Maybe it twisted in flight and missed the target," Wells suggested.

"I guess it's possible," Lux replied. "They are not nearly as accurate from a pistol as they are when fired from a long gun. That would explain his not being there when we came to. No, I take that back. I'm sure it injected. I remember clearly seeing the dart sticking in his shoulder. He definitely grabbed it and pulled it out."

"What's your read on his assistant? She's a good-looking woman and apparently a good scientist as well. Otherwise, she seems a bit scatterbrained."

"I think you've got her tagged," Lux replied. "She's highly intelligent in science, not very bright about the real world. That incident in the parking lot scared her almost to death. And him, having a looker like that drop him off for a date. I'd be hot on her heels if I were in his shoes. I think we can cross her off our list of possible accomplices. Now his mother, there's another story completely. That's one wily female if I ever saw one. She has no scientific background at all, runs a motel of some sort for fishermen. She can't be involved technically in what's going on, but I'll bet she knows about it. He probably told her when she came for a visit. She's a sly cat who knows how to handle herself. We won't get anything from her, even if she does know."

"Back to his assistant," Wells interjected. "Are we going after her tonight? She's probably left to visit her parents by now. Do you know how far away they live?"

"I was just thinking about that. It's almost an hour's drive and she's so frightened she'd probably go off the deep end if we tried to question her. I doubt she has any idea where he is by now anyway. You heard what she said to his mother. Let's regroup with Yvonne and plan our next moves carefully. We didn't do well tonight, so maybe we should go over what information we have and plan our next series of moves, including how to find our missing astronomer."

Wells added, "I'll bet his mother knows where he is. There's no chance getting her to tell us though." After a long pause he asked, "What did you make of that meeting tonight? Did it have anything to do with our problem? He was there and so was his mother. Do you have a run down on any of the others?"

"I doubt there's anything significant about that meeting, even though Thomas and his mother were there," Lux replied. "They have similar meetings or receptions frequently. Our new guy on the inside reported it was in honor of people who had helped Thomas's work at the Gemini Project in some unusual way in recent months. It was set up by their PR people and was a public reception. Yvonne can probably get us a list of all who were in attendance from our man at the Op Center, if she doesn't have it already."

"Speaking of him, how has he been doing since he finally got a job there?" Wells questioned. "He's been there how long, a week? Ten days? I don't know just when he started."

"Tony started with their night cleaning crew on Monday. He hasn't been able to snoop much yet. He says this night guy Anaaka watches them like a hawk. Yvonne may have his latest report by the time we get there. I'm sure it will have the list of people at the reception. We'll see if anything unusual pops up."

As they entered the garage at the federal building, Wells was rubbing the side of his head. "My head still hurts where he kicked me. I can't believe how fast he moved. I'll bet he could still do some fancy stepping on the football field in spite of his age."

As he parked the car, Lux confessed, "He is definitely quick and effective. I hate to admit it, but that's twice he's gotten the better of me, and he's at least ten years older. I don't like it, but you have to admire a man that stays in such great condition. I wish he was on our side."

"According to his mother, he is. I still wonder if we're in the right."

"Don't be going soft on me, Jack. We've a job to do. Our country depends on us."

"Yeah, I know. What happens to us if this blows up in our faces and we do become a laughing stock? Ever think about that? We'd end up with sweeper jobs like Tony's, only for real."

"Enough of this nonsense. For our peace of mind, let's get to the project board and do a complete update of what we know and what we suspect, then run some probabilities. We may have some time before Dr. Thomas shows up, so let's put it to good use. I doubt his assistant will do us any good. Let's forget about her for the time being. We can always talk to her later."

"I like that," Wells commented as they entered their office.

The two men walked over to Yvonne's desk. She was busy at her computer and paused as they approached. "Have any luck finding our elusive astronomer?" she asked. After they shook their heads no, she continued. "What happened at his apartment? When you radioed in to get the phone calls, you said you had just left. I take it he wasn't there?"

"No, but his mother was," Lux answered a little sheepishly. "You remember that pleasant, gracious lady we talked to when you and I were last there? Well, she turned on us and delivered a verbal tongue-lashing. Said we were like the Nazi gestapo or Russian KGB and that her son was a loyal and patriotic American. Typical proud mother stuff. She'll certainly give us no help."

"Why, Jan, I do believe you've met your match. The master agent foiled again and by a woman," Yvonne said with a smile in obvious satisfaction. "Maybe now you understand my failure to force my way into working with Dr. Thomas. You raked me over the coals for that one, remember?"

"So, they're a tough bunch to deal with. It only makes for a greater challenge," Lux replied in defense, then changed the subject. "Do you have any new report from Tony? By now he should have a list of the people at the reception."

Yvonne retrieved a paper from her desk and handed it to Jan. "Is this what you're looking for? He phoned it in about ten minutes ago. Said there was nothing new to report, except he had a hard time just making the phone call. I guess the night manager stays right on him much of the time. He has to be extremely cautious whatever he does. He had to tell him he needed to call home about some minor emergency just to get permission to use the phone."

"Do you have a run down on this Gemini Community Action Committee or the names on this list?" Jan asked as he glanced down the paper.

"Not yet," Yvonne answered. "There's Thomas and his mother, his assistant and an older couple also named Namahoe, John Carroll, who is the director there, and a reporter named Ginger Cari. The rest are complete unknowns to me. I should have information on them in an hour or two unless they're outside all our databases. So far, I've found nothing unusual. I'm running a computer search on the Lane couple even as we speak. I should have information on them in just a few minutes."

"Good! We're going into the war room to update the board. Join us as soon as you have it," Jan commented. "We need to update our information there and maybe have you run some probabilities. We can review what we have now and see if we can come up with any fresh ideas on this whole project."

"There's one thing I need help with," Yvonne added. "What do I do with all the data downloaded from the telescope transmissions to their computers? It's a whole lot of numeric data with few words. I have been unable to make heads or tails of it. We'll need an astronomer to decipher it for us for sure."

"We'll have to forward that to Washington," Jan replied. "Maybe they can come up with some answers or find an astronomer here that will cooperate with us, not like that guy Schuman. He was more loyal to his colleague than to us who hired him. I don't want to do that again."

"I can send that data as soon as the present search is complete. It will take an hour or so to do, but I can join you as soon as it is set up to transmit."

The two men headed for the conference room appropriated for their use while they were in Hilo. They had dubbed it the war room as it was where they held briefing and brainstorming sessions. The war room was a bland twelve by eighteen-foot, windowless office with whiteboards covering three walls. It had the ambiance of a police interrogation room. There was a small table with six cheap wooden chairs. Next to the entrance door was a cabinet with a sink, coffee maker and small refrigerator. All showed evidence of careless use by many people with things on their minds other than cleanliness. A cabinet above the sink contained a jumble of mugs, plastic cups and other supplies. Some sessions could run for extended periods, so drinks were available without leaving. It sometimes doubled as a lunchroom, albeit an unappetizing one. There were liberal quantities of colored markers in trays running along the bottom of each of the whiteboards, which no amount of scrubbing could get clean. One of the larger boards was nearly half-covered with notes about the current case, loosely organized around the names of the various people being investigated. The names were in four columns labeled from left to right, Principal, Minor, Suspect and Unknown. There were no names under Unknown and under Principal were Thomas and Rumley with a number of bits of information about each of them. Under Suspect were three names, Lani Namahoe, John Carroll and Pete Hiakawa. The only name under Minor was Pat Yamaguchi and it had a line drawn through it.

The two men entered the war room and Jan immediately began listing the names from his paper under Unknown. He placed a red asterisk by the name of each person already on the board. Yvonne entered just as he finished writing the last name.

"Here's the run-down on the Lanes," she said reading from the paper she held. "He's been a physician at the trauma center for many years. His wife is a semi-retired nurse there. They are both active in other community service groups dealing primarily with teens. There's no hint of any problems or trouble. They show up as model citizens. I should have the information on the rest in an hour or so."

"Looks to me like one of those PR groups organizations use to improve their image to the local community," Wells commented. "Gemini is new to the area isn't it? Using a popular sports figure to get attention and bringing in others who do community service seems natural enough. I'll bet we find the others fall in that same category."

"I don't know about that," Yvonne remarked, looking at the list. "These two, the Namahoes. That's the same name as Thomas's assistant. It isn't a common name. Maybe they're related. And the reporter, Ginger Cari, what's she doing in this group?"

"That name strikes a bell somewhere. I just can't put my finger on it, but I've heard of her before," Lux remarked, his face skewed in thought. Suddenly he remembered. "She's the one who did that exposé on drugs at the high school. Went undercover for several months as a student and got away with it. Works for the local news service. What would she be doing in this group?"

"Probably her job," Yvonne replied quickly. "You're the only one of us from Hawaii. You'd be the only one to know about her or anyone else local."

Wells added, "Chelton Chum is a name I remember hearing, but I haven't the foggiest idea where. I've been wracking my brain and getting nowhere since I saw it on the list. You'll doubtless get the results of your search before I remember, if I ever do."

Sitting down at the table and motioning the others to join him, Lux suggested, "Let's review what we have. By the time we've done that, the results of our search on those others should be complete. Then we can get a better handle on that committee."

After several heated discussions, they decided to call it a day and continue in the morning.

*   *   *

Around one in the afternoon Sunday, the run-down on the people at the reception was finished. The group's common denominator was helping troubled youths and promoting the community image of the Gemini project. They planned to continue watching the group just in case there was a tie-in to their problem with Angus.

By Sunday afternoon, preparation of their plan of action was complete. When Angus arrived at Gemini on Monday they would pick him up and hold him until they had some answers. Jack Wells was not happy with the plan, but Lux was adamant and he was in charge.

"What do we do if he doesn't show up?" Wells asked. "It wouldn't surprise me one bit if he just lit out. He's the type."

"Then we'll just have to find him," Lux sneered. "This is an island, remember? There's no way he could get off without our knowing it unless he took a private small boat, and that is extremely unlikely. We've just posted Dr. Thomas at the top of our list of detainees, so everyone in law enforcement will be looking for him. We've all the airports under surveillance, and our U.S. Navy people are watching the seaports. Unless he has vanished from the face of the earth, we'll find him in the next day or two."

As they left to go home and when Lux was well out of earshot, Jack Wells suggested Yvonne meet him for a few minutes at the all-night coffee shop where they often had breakfast. It was a short walk down the street from their office. Yvonne didn't like the idea, but agreed. She wondered what this was about.

Jack and Yvonne waited until Jan had driven off from the parking lot before heading for the coffee shop on foot. As soon as they started walking Yvonne asked, "What's this all about? If it's personal, I'd just as soon not have any discussion. If it's about Jan and this case, I think we should not talk about it without his presence."

"It's a matter of OSI policy I'd like to discuss with you. It does involve Jan and this case, but I'd like you to hear me out. After you've heard what I have to say, you can do what you want."

Yvonne didn't like this at all. In silence, she thought about it for the few moments it took to walk to the coffee shop. Both she and Jack Wells were relatively new to the OSI. She had been with OSI for nearly two years after being recruited from the FBI where she had been a computer crime expert for six years. She liked the new job because there was a lot more fieldwork than she had while at the FBI. At nearly six feet and relatively muscular, she liked the more physical aspects of her new job and didn't want to hurt her chances for advancement. She would listen to what he had to say, but would cut him off if she began feeling any more uncomfortable. She didn't particularly like Jan inasmuch as he was rather caustic and obviously felt OSI was a man's domain. Still, she was a loyal agent who tried to overcome those personal feelings. For a woman, Yvonne could be quite detached.

Jack Wells joined OSI about a year ago after his last stint with Naval Intelligence. OSI sent him from the mainland to replace Gerald Furman after Furman's skull fracture. A bright young man with a fierce sense of personal loyalty to his country, he graduated at the top of his class at Annapolis, the first African American to do so. Leaving the Navy to join OSI, Jack thought it provided a better venue for his talents and desire to serve his country. With personal ambition a step or two below his loyalty, Jack Wells was a company man and the USA was his company.

Jack waited until after their coffee was served before starting. "I am concerned with the direction this case is taking and don't know the best way to deal with it. I could resign from the case, but that wouldn't help OSI. You and Jan are the only people who can see the whole picture here and my talks with Jan have gotten nowhere. You have been present at one of those. You heard my objections to taking Thomas in and holding him. We have no legal justification for doing so, but Jan insists we do it anyway."

Yvonne interrupted, "Careful, you're getting on shaky ground. Jan's the boss and we do what he says."

"Even if it's illegal? Even if it goes against the oath we swore when we joined OSI?" Jack asked, a pained expression contorting his face. "Thomas still has legal and constitutional rights we seem to be ignoring. Maybe his mother was right. We are behaving rather like the gestapo or KGB and that makes me uncomfortable. There's been a great deal of evil done in this world by people who's only excuse was they were ordered to do it by a superior. Unless I'm mistaken, that defense didn't cut any water at the Nuremberg trials. Frankly, I'm amazed we haven't run into legal counsel acting on their behalf. I'd hate to think of the hubbub that might arise if we ever do get control of him and try to hold him. Didn't you tell me he asked for their attorney the first time you tried to detain him when Furman got his skull fracture? I wonder what Washington would say if they heard all the details of this operation?"

"I . . . I guess I never thought of it that way," Yvonne answered, almost stammering. "I mean the legal aspects and all. I'm mainly a technical person, not well versed in the legal aspects of what we do. I assumed Jan would not ask us to act illegally."

"Didn't you receive training in the legal aspects of our job? I remember that as one of the most emphasized part of the training I received both in the Navy and then at OSI schooling. We were told over and over we were to uphold and defend the law, not break it."

Yvonne cringed. She explained that her training had never been completed since she was sent on a computer emergency right after indoctrination and physical conditioning. She was to return to Washington to complete her training but was shuttled from computer emergency to emergency out in the field. This was her fifth field assignment in a row since leaving Washington. Clearly, someone had dropped the ball. "I . . . er . . . they must have skipped that part of my training. My indoctrination included only two months of concentrated computer training and then the physical conditioning course. I've been hopping from one field assignment to another ever since. Sometimes I think I'm the only computer savvy operative they have. They probably didn't worry about my incomplete training because most of my work has been with computers and not people. I was sent here just as I completed the computer work on the hacker that broke into NASA's computer system in Cleveland. What meager information we had on Thomas I learned from reading the reports on the plane on the way out here. This is the first assignment I've had that wasn't nearly all computer oriented. The day I arrived we hit the local police for all they had about Thomas and Rumley, and I've been running ever since. The only chance I've had to catch my breath was the three days after he put us all in the hospital."

"That's most unfortunate," Jack said resignedly. "If I were you, I'd request the completion of training as soon as this job is finished. As a matter of fact, I'd insist on it. There's a lot of valuable knowledge you missed and must have to be a complete operative. Unless I'm mistaken, you have at least four months of intensive training to catch up on. My guess is you have the talent and all the tools to be a top notch OSI agent. You'll not make it without that training however, so be sure you get it."

Yvonne became defensive instantly. "What makes you an expert on the makings of a good agent? You've only been with OSI for about a year."

"You might not know I was in Naval Intelligence for six years before I joined OSI. For the last two years, part of my job was evaluation of field performance of those I worked with. It wasn't a popular job and most of those few who knew what I was doing resented me. I had to keep a low profile. By the end of the second year, I had a bad case of burnout. It wasn't a job anyone could handle permanently. Since then, it's been difficult to get completely out of the evaluation mode so to speak. I try to look for the positive aspects of those I work with and by the way, I meant it when I said you could be a top agent."

"No, I didn't know that about you," Yvonne said with a smile. "I knew you had been in the Navy but not what you did there. I'm glad you shared with me. I feel a little better about our talk now. I was afraid you might be trying to undermine Jan to further your own career."

"Nothing could be farther from the truth," Jack replied with a broad smile. "Jan is a clever agent and an expert organizer. He's a forceful leader and works well with associates. We could both learn a great deal from him. My only fear is he may have broken one of the cardinal rules of the game and let his personal feelings influence his decisions. There's no question in my mind Thomas has severely challenged Jan. He has beaten him badly several times, both physically and mentally. I fear that has pushed him over the legal and ethical limits. Should it go the wrong way it could severely damage his career. If it goes badly and we do nothing to change the course of this investigation, the OSI could get some serious negative publicity. It could possibly damage both of us as well. That is a serious concern of mine, and that's why I wanted to talk with you."

Concern furrowed Yvonne's face. "What can we do to get things back on track? We certainly should handle this right here, within our own group."

"My sentiments exactly," Jack answered, smiling. "I'm certain the two of us working together can convince Jan to back off a bit, at least to get some semblance of legality back in control of our activities. We should pursue Thomas aggressively, but legally. I've been studying the part of the National Security Legal Code within which we operate. There are a number of ways we can hold and question a citizen legally when the nation's security is at stake. I see no reason why the police investigator Thomas asked for, Hiakawa, couldn't be present during our interrogation, at least during part of it. We could even conduct it at police headquarters if they would let us."

"I don't know. We were not well received when we went to retrieve those records at the beginning of this investigation. Being in a hurry, we were rather high handed and certainly didn't make any brownie points with the local police," Yvonne explained. "Local police can be difficult when we override their jurisdiction. Unfortunately, we don't seem to operate on the same time frame. We always seem to be pushing them and they often resent it big time."

"What we're talking about doing is a tall order. It will take the two of us working together to get Jan to back off. We're supposed to meet him here for breakfast at seven in the morning before we head to Gemini. Let's be here at six so we can plan our strategy. Are you game for that?" Wells asked.

Yvonne still had reservations, but replied, "Six is OK with me. I only hope this doesn't turn into a big battle and backfire on us. I don't see him giving in easily. He's determined to force Thomas to cough up whatever he has by any means possible. Wouldn't it be better to do this back at the office rather than out in public?"

"I don't know. We can take that table there by the window. It's not close to the booths or other tables and if we keep our voices down and talk in generalities—you know the routine for discussions in public places—that would help keep Jan's anger in check and maybe we could get somewhere. We can plan our strategy in the morning. Think about it until then."

"OK, I'll think about it," she replied as they stood up to leave.

They walked in silence back to their cars and headed for their hotel rooms. Yvonne's doubts were growing every time she thought about the situation. *Jack Wells is a convincing talker, but is he for real? Maybe he's just trying to feather his own nest. Could he be trying to discredit Jan to promote his own career? If that were so, he'd not be trying to work things out within our group. He'd more likely try going over his head or lying low until Jan made a serious error.* Thoroughly confused, she finally crawled into bed with strongly conflicting thoughts and had a hard time going to sleep.

*   *   *

Yvonne's five o'clock alarm awoke her with a jolt. She was instantly awake, renewing those conflicts of the night before. She thought of skipping the six o'clock meeting. She could call Jack and tell him she changed her mind. She reached for the phone several times, paused and then rethought the situation. She finally decided to meet with Jack as planned and let their discussion help determine her own course of action. She did not like being in this situation at all and rather resented Jack Wells for putting her there. The same troublesome thoughts went through her mind as she showered, dressed and headed for the coffee shop. Jack was seated at the table as she walked in precisely at 6:00 A.M.

He could tell Yvonne was not happy to be there. After the usual greetings he surprised her by saying, "I can tell you're not happy about this. If you want, we can drop the whole thing right now and let it play out like before. I don't want to involve you if you have the slightest misgiving about working with me. I can do what I feel I must do on my own, if necessary. It's a touchy situation. I'll think no less of you if you back out, but if you are going to do so, please do it now. There will be no turning back once the ball starts rolling. Acting alone, I will need to take a slightly different tack. One voice is not as persuasive as two."

There was a long pause as the two looked intently at each other. Somewhat disarmed by what Jack said, Yvonne thought for a moment before replying, "Why don't we work out a plan? Then we can decide whether to implement it or not. If what we work out makes sense to me, I'm in. If not, we'll have to play it by ear."

"Sounds reasonable to me," Jack replied. "Let's get at it."

For more than thirty minutes they tossed ideas back and forth. Yvonne was impressed at Jack's attitude about swaying Jan's mind without confrontation. *He was a team player with the best interest of OSI and the country at the forefront of his suggestions,* she thought. She now felt much more comfortable about what they were planning to do. By the time Jan arrived they had a well thought out, loosely knit plan of action in hand. They would let Jan lay out plans for the day and then question the details from a legal standpoint. For Jan, the day would be a near disaster.

15

OSI agents are trained to be adept at controlling the content of their discussions in public, using pseudonyms so nothing of any significance could be gleaned from their conversation by eavesdroppers. They never use a real name, situation or incident in conversation. Only those who were involved in any case and knew what was going on could possibly learn the truth of what they said to each other.

The three OSI agents met for breakfast to prepare for the coming day. Jack and Yvonne made their point about the necessity for legality of their actions while planning the day's activities. Jan was furious at their questioning of his judgement. Jack carefully avoided any hint of Jan's obvious personal attitude toward Angus. He and Yvonne concentrated instead on the legal issues and their fears about the investigation blowing up in their faces. They were quietly persistent in expressing their views and did not react to Jan's obvious anger. Jan was on the verge of exploding and knew it. He demanded they go to their office to finish the discussion in private where they would have no restraints.

Fearing a major confrontation if they did so, Jack said calmly, "We're trying to keep you from making a mistake that could seriously damage your career, Jan. I'm sure we can resolve this quietly right here and now."

"Jack's right, you know," Yvonne piped up. "We've been treading on shaky ground. If we don't stick strictly to company policy, it could backfire on all of us. We surely don't want to lose this sale. It could be a very important one for each of us."

Finally calmed by their persistent, low-key persuasiveness, Jan was beginning to regain his composure. He finally gave in a bit saying, "All right. We'll do this by the book for a few days and see what it gets us. I see what you're saying, but I still don't want to back off. If we lose this prospect there could be dire consequences for us all."

They talked for nearly two hours, planning a new tack in reaching Angus. Yvonne would go in to meet with him and try to reach him by trading on his patriotism and loyalty. Grudgingly accepting a cue from Serena's outburst of the night before, she would ask for his cooperation in sharing whatever information he had. They had tried intimidation and strong-arm tactics and gotten nowhere. Maybe the softer approach would work as Serena suggested. In any event, they couldn't be any worse off than they were at present.

Around eleven, Yvonne walked up to Jenny's reception desk and asked if she could see Angus. "I'm sorry, Miss Techmeyer, Angus hasn't come in yet and I don't know when he will. You'll have to try later," she answered,

Yvonne didn't want to waste any effort. "Is his research assistant, Miss Namahoe available? I could probably get what I need by talking with her."

"I'll check," she replied curtly and immediately rang Lani's line. "Miss Techmeyer from OSI wants to see you," she relayed to Lani, adding, "and she's alone."

"I don't relish the idea of talking to Yvonne alone or otherwise," Lani replied, then thought for a moment. "Tell her I'll be out to see her shortly."

When Jenny relayed the message, Yvonne took a seat in the lobby to wait. After about ten minutes, a somber looking Lani walked out of the office and over to where Yvonne was waiting. Yvonne stood up as she approached and the two women faced each other rather like two gladiators preparing to do battle. Without saying a word Yvonne sat down in a body language message of submission. She motioned for Lani to sit on the seat beside her. The submissive role was difficult for Yvonne. She was a dominant personality and this was proving extremely uncomfortable. Lani, neck hairs raised in the instinctive reaction of preparation for combat, would not help.

"I've come to try to make peace, real peace and to ask for your help," she began in her most contrite tone of voice. "We have been wrong in our approach to Dr. Thomas, creating animosity and suspicion rather than trust and cooperation."

"I'd say that was a gross understatement," Lani interrupted coldly. "From what I've seen I'd describe it as all-out war."

"I hear what you're saying, and you're right. What we want to do now is make peace—try to get things back on track to better cooperation, if possible. To that end, I'm trying to reach Dr. Thomas. Could you help me? I'm willing to do whatever it takes," Yvonne explained in her most apologetic manner.

"He's not here, and it's unlike him not to let us know when he is going to be away. I don't know if or when he will return. When he didn't come to work at his usual time, I wondered if you people were holding him," Lani replied, not softening a bit. "We have lots to do with the new data and I am at a standstill without his direction."

"Perhaps he slept in. Does he ever do that after a big weekend?"

"Never!" Lani spat out. "Maybe he carried out the threat he made to you when you tried to take over. He told me all about it. He was upset then and so was I. Just like him, I love what I do and worked hard to get where I am. Your high-handed efforts to replace me with no notice left a great deal of animosity. You've all of that to overcome before getting any help from me, and I have serious doubts about your ability to do so."

Yvonne was quickly revising her opinion of Lani. She was definitely not the scatterbrained, frightened science student the other OSI agents pictured her to be. She was a woman of substance who would stand up and fight if necessary. Gaining her confidence now would be difficult. In an almost begging voice Yvonne asked, "Would you at least give us the opportunity to try to make amends? I can't change our grossly misguided efforts in the past. I can only apologize and work to rectify the mistakes we made. I also remind you we are all working for the same national interest and our common employer is the U.S. government."

"How can I possibly believe you?" Lani asked disdainfully. "You've changed tactics so many times, even apologized before and it didn't mean a thing. You run over our people with all the compassion of a lava flow and then expect us to give you another chance? We're not fools you know."

"That is obvious," Yvonne remarked with complete sincerity. "All I can say is, give us a chance. We'll follow any ground rules you care to set up. We are willing to meet on your terms, on your turf and with whomever you want present. As soon as we feel assured our nation's security is not threatened, we'll disappear permanently."

"I'll test your sincerity quickly and easily right now," Lani said coldly. "I believe Dr. Thomas already explained to your people that he found a new and unusual stellar object some three hundred light years from us. It is what we call a red dwarf star, much like our sun, but about half its mass. It is moving in our general direction at an unusually high rate of speed. It is obviously not space aliens or their craft. It certainly does not represent a national threat OSI or anyone else needs to do anything about. Your astronomer, Dr. Schuman of Cal Tech and the Keck telescope was present and satisfied with the answers.

"We have just finished collecting massive amounts of new data about this star which will take months of dedicated effort to wade through in order to gain more knowledge about it. The interference of you and your comrades has greatly hindered that effort. I fear irreparable damage has already been done, particularly if Dr. Thomas has been driven from his project by your actions. Until he has analyzed this data and made new calculations, the information I just provided and that you chose to ignore in the past, is all that is available. The exact numeric data would not alter a single conclusion by anyone. Your ignorance of science, scientists, astronomy and astronomers is obvious and appalling."

Yvonne withstood the onslaught as her opinion of Lani continued its upward course. "I can see now why Dr. Thomas spoke so highly of you when I tried to force myself into your position. I admit to being disdainful of subordinate, secretary-type women. This was the image I held of you before our conversation. I admire forceful, perceptive women who will stand up and fight for what they believe, maybe a bit too much. Obviously, you are one of those women who developed strength and maturity. I find that a little unusual in one as young and attractive as you. Please believe me. I'm not saying these things for a purpose other than to tell you my true opinion and let you know I believe you to be truthful and forthright in what you say. My hope is I can convince my associates of this."

Lani was beginning to believe Yvonne might be telling the truth but knew it would take considerable time to confirm. She would stand her ground for the present, replying after a momentary silence, "Surely you understand I find these things hard to believe. You've a lousy track record with all of us here, and I doubt it's possible to repair the damage. I speak only for myself. I have no idea how the others might respond. I suggest you begin by removing all your surveillance people and equipment."

Yvonne didn't flinch at the revelation of Lani's knowledge of their surveillance. She continued explaining, "Like you, I'm only a member of an organization. I will relay your response to the others, along with my recommendations. Let's try to resolve this amicably and all get on with our work."

"When Dr. Thomas returns, I'll give him your message. The rest is up to him. I'd best return to my work now. We're far behind, and I'd like to be prepared when Dr. Thomas does return," Lani replied coldly, her suspicions remaining. She was certain Angus would doubt their honesty as well.

Handing a business card to Lani, Yvonne said, "Please contact me at this number should you want to talk further."

Lani watched as she left. She wondered what caused OSI to change tactics. She was absolutely certain of Angus' reaction to this new turn of events. He would believe none of it. She decided to tell John and see what he thought. She walked to John's office and asked Ani'i if he was busy. After checking with John, Ani'i sent Lani right in.

"I understand Miss Techmeyer met with you. I assume that's why you're here," John replied knowingly and with a broad smile. Jenny obviously had been keeping him aware.

"That Jenny doesn't miss a trick does she?" Lani answered pleasantly. "She stays right on top of things. Yes, I had an interesting talk with Miss Techmeyer. Apparently, they are trying a new method on us, sweetness and light. I find it hard to believe."

Lani relayed to John all Yvonne had told her and what she was certain Angus would say.

"It sure sounds phony to me," John agreed. "You had better tell Angus right away. We can inform the others as soon as it is practical.

If there is to be any change in our actions, we can make that decision at the Wednesday meeting. Take my car to see Angus, just in case OSI is watching."

"That's a good idea," Lani replied. "I'm certain the Lanes' phone isn't tapped, and we know your line is OK, so I'll call if Angus has any questions I can't answer. We'd best continue to be guarded in any method of communication we don't know to be secure."

Lani left John's office and headed directly for the private parking lot exit, John's car-keys in hand. As she drove out of the lot, she thought of how to pick up Serena on the way.

She parked in Angus' apartment garage and headed for the entrance looking around carefully for any sign of OSI. *Surely this one isn't bugged* she thought while picking up the intercom phone and dialing Angus' apartment.

"It's Lani," she replied to Serena's pleasant greeting. "Don't say anything and just listen. I'm going to visit Angus and give him some interesting new information about OSI. I thought you might want to go along. I'll wait for you in the garage if you're coming."

"That's fine," Serena replied. "Just leave it there by the door. I'll be down to get it in just a few minutes."

"OK," Lani answered with a chuckle. "I'll be waiting."

As she headed to the garage, she smiled at Serena's avoidance of informing any hidden microphones about what was going on. Her OSI-induced paranoia hadn't dulled her mind. In about ten minutes Serena joined her and they headed to the car.

"What's this all about?" Serena asked as soon as they met.

"I had a visit from Miss Techmeyer a little while ago," Lani began. "She, again, apologized for their actions and then came on with a new approach."

She related the entire conversation, her talk with John and her own feelings about the situation. She was stunned when Serena asked, "You don't suppose they mean it do you?"

"I thought you would be the last person to think they changed," Lani said in surprise.

"Well they certainly have not succeeded with their aggressive tactics. They may have finally realized those tactics didn't work and are trying another method. They're not stupid. Maybe they had a reality check and are trying a more sensible course of action. I still distrust them. I'm sure they'll quickly change to whatever tactic they think will work for their own ends whenever it suites them," Serena replied.

"Of that, I'm sure!" Lani stated emphatically.

*   *   *

A little past noon they parked in the Lanes' driveway. They made their way up the steps to the door to Angus' hideout and rang the doorbell several times. Finally, an anxious Angus answered.

"What the devil are you two doing here?" he asked incredulously. "Are you certain you weren't followed?"

"Yes, we're sure. We're here with some exiting news," Serena said with a grin as they walked into the apartment. "OSI has turned into quiet pussycats, waiting patiently for any information you might want to throw their way."

"Now I know you're kidding," Angus replied, a little less apprehensive. "They'll be snow skiing in downtown Hilo before that happens. What's this all about anyway?"

Lani related her conversation with Yvonne and then her talk with John. Serena told of her reactions to all this and asked Angus what he thought.

"What exactly did she say when you asked them to pull their surveillance? What kind of reaction did she have?" Angus asked.

"She didn't bat an eyelash, completely ignored what I said. She went on without pause or comment, quite deliberately."

"That's interesting," Angus replied. "I'll bet she made a mental note of it. I surely wouldn't hold my breath until they complied with your request."

"I'll second that!" Serena said emphatically. "Well? Where do we go from here?"

"I suggest we go downstairs. Oona and I were the only ones here and we were about to have lunch. Maybe there's enough for you two to join us."

As they walked down and entered the kitchen Angus asked, "Look whom I found on my doorstep. Do you have enough for a couple more mouths?"

Oona looked up and smiled at Angus. "Splendid. We've plenty. What brings you?"

Lani retold her story to which Oona commented, "I trust you didn't believe a word of it, did you?"

Serena replied, "We're all skeptical, but there is just that small chance she could be telling the truth. I'm sure it's just another tactic. I don't see them giving an inch on their main objective. If we play it out carefully, we can check their sincerity without giving any more information than we already have."

"If we're smart, they'll get their information from our press releases just like the rest of the public," Angus said. "I fear they will quash that information if they know about it before it's released to the general public. My instincts tell me to continue on our present course for the immediate future. The entire group can deal with this at our next meeting on Wednesday. I'll remain in hiding until then. I've been running my calculations on the laptop, and although it is a bit slower than the system in my office, the results are just as accurate. There are a few involved calculations of the spectra which must be run on the Gemini computers, but I can sneak into my office Wednesday before the meeting to run those."

"Are you sure that's wise?" Oona asked. "Won't they be watching your office for just such a thing?"

"I know it sounds a little hokey, but I plan on wearing a disguise when we leave for the trauma center to get Francis. If you could leave an hour or so early and drop me off at Gemini before you go to pick him up, I'm sure I can get in unrecognized and run those calculations before the meeting. I have the tourist outfit I wore at Lani's family luau. I'd look like some mainland tourist with shorts, a loud Hawaiian shirt and floppy hat that almost covers my face. I stuck those in my suitcase for that reason."

Lani grinned gleefully at him. "You will look ridiculous in that outfit, but you're right. It definitely would work." They all laughed when she described his appearance at the luau.

"Would you two mind if I stayed when Lani leaves to go back?" Serena asked. "I'm rather bored at the apartment. Chelton has the rental car and is visiting some people he knows in Kialua where he will probably stay the night. I was going to walk down to the mall and look around. I'd much rather be here."

"I'd love that," Oona said happily. "We can go shopping together. I've several places you would love to see and would never find on your own. It will also give us a chance to get to know each other better. Francis will be at the trauma center until nearly seven today. Perhaps we can join him for a late dinner."

"Sounds good to me," Serena replied.

"I've already discovered Angus can find his way around a kitchen," Oona said, glancing at him. "You think you could fix yourself dinner if we came back a little late?"

"No problem," Angus answered quickly, then added in mock sadness, "I guess all you women are going to desert me again. I'll just have to deal with my loneliness by myself."

"Ha!" Lani and Serena exclaimed in unified derision.

"It's plain you'll not get much sympathy from this group," Oona remarked with a chuckle. "Just remember, I'm with them."

When Lani left to go back to Gemini, Angus accompanied her out across the patio and down the steps to John's car. "None of that mushy stuff," Serena called after them as they left. She was proud of her son and of his choice in women. Inwardly she hoped there would be lots of mushy stuff between them in the years to come. Remembering her times together with Angus' father, she felt pleasant joy and then that sharp pain of loss as her eyes filled with tears. That pain was always hiding just beneath the surface. She dealt with it, but it never disappeared.

When Angus walked back from seeing Lani off, he sat back down at the table with Oona and Serena. "You don't suppose there's a chance OSI could be on the up-and-up do you? I find it almost impossible to believe, but their strong-arm tactics certainly got them nowhere."

"I say it's possible but extremely unlikely," Oona answered. "Is there any way we could check it out with any degree of certainty?"

"Maybe we should feed them a dramatic hoax via Angus' phone and see if they bite," Serena suggested. "The only problem is, they now know we know they have surveillance in place. It would have to be a casual slip in conversation they wouldn't suspect, maybe a simply coded message they could figure out. It couldn't be too simple or they might suspect."

"I have an idea that's been percolating in the back of my mind since I heard about this," Angus exclaimed. "It's risky, but it just might work, and we wouldn't have to rely on coded messages."

"OK. Let's have it," Serena requested.

Angus continued, "I'll go back to my apartment early afternoon Wednesday and call Miss Techmeyer to make an appointment to talk with her, alone. I'll give her thirty minutes to get to the meeting. We can meet at police headquarters with Hiakawa and two uniformed officers present, along with Gemini's legal counsel. She will not know who the officers are until she gets there. She's to enter with no papers of any kind. Before I appear, she will be asked to sign a legal document declaring OSI will not detain me at any time or for any reason on Wednesday. Gemini's attorney can prepare the document. She can ask any question she wants about the ghost, and I will answer to the best of my ability. If she wants to confer with her other operatives, she will have to do so by phone. Let's go on the attack."

"That sounds a bit risky to me," Serena replied. "Couldn't they just ignore the paper she signs and grab you as you leave?"

"They might order the police to hold you as soon as you walk in," Oona added. "It sounds like a dangerous chance to take."

"The beauty of this plan is its surprise," Angus explained. "I doubt on such short notice they can mount any kind of process to get the police to hold me without a warrant, and I'm certain they don't have one. We'll catch them by surprise and within an hour we'll know if they are sincere. I'll leave first in a borrowed police uniform so anyone watching will not recognize me. Joey can drive me out in a squad car. After a short delay, when I'm well away from there, Miss Techmeyer will be permitted to leave. If nothing happens, we can be reasonably sure they are not using their new tactics as a ruse to get hold of me. Any action of any kind on their part will put the lie to their efforts, and we'll be right back where we started and much the wiser. I don't think they can afford to do anything but comply. They'll know they're being tested. We will have done our part and placed the ball firmly in their hands. The next step will be up to them."

"It's a brassy idea, but it could do the job," Oona said smiling.

"We'll have to plan this out carefully for it to work," the always cautious Serena said. "I'd be interested at what Gemini's attorney will have to say. You'll have to contact him right away won't you?"

"I'll leave that up to you, Mom," Angus replied. "You could call him from here, right now, give him a rough idea of what we plan to do and then arrange to see him this afternoon if possible. His name is Frank Ito, and he is aware of both the Rumley situation and OSI from Gemini's viewpoint. I told him what we all know except the true speed and path of the ghost. I have no idea how busy he is, but do stress this could be important. Tell the receptionist John Carroll is calling. Don't use my name unless you are talking to Frank personally. If you get hold of him, have him call John to confirm what's going on. I'd do it myself, but I'm still a little leery of any phone."

Before calling Frank, they spent some time collecting Angus' idea into an organized plan. When they found Frank would not be available until after three, they decided to stop by then on the chance he would be able to see them.

"Surely you could use the phone in the guest room, Angus," Oona commented. "I don't see any possibility of that being bugged. Why don't I call Ito's office right back and give them that number? Then Mr. Ito can call you as soon as he's available."

"OK. Tell them to ask for John Carroll. That should get his attention without leaving my name around for who knows who to see," Angus replied cautiously. "I still want you to go to his office after three as planned. You can fill him in on anything I missed should I talk to him before you get there. Incidentally, use a pay phone and call me before going to his office. Then we'll all know where we stand."

Oona called Frank's office. When they answered she said, "Please have Mr. Ito contact John Carroll at 555-4757 as soon as he can. It is urgent, so please get the message to him as quickly as possible."

She turned to Serena. "That's done, so let's go. We won't have a lot of time to shop before our appointment. We'll call Angus before we go. I can use my cell phone since pay phones are so hard to find now."

The two women left shortly and Angus returned to the waiting laptop and resumed his calculations. About a half hour later he jumped as the phone beside him rang loudly. After his surprised hello, a professional female voice said, "Dr. John Carroll please. Frank Ito calling."

"This is John Carroll," Angus answered.

After a second or two, Frank's voice came on, "John. What can I do for you?"

"This is Angus Thomas, Frank. I've a problem and need your assistance. When I finish, you can call John to confirm if you wish."

"No need," Frank replied. "I am fully aware of your situation as of a few days ago. How can I help you? I'm between things now and have as much as half an hour you can use before I'm needed here."

Angus explained the new OSI tactic and how he was going to test it. "If all goes well, we should know if they mean what they say."

"I can provide a document or two for them to sign that looks and sounds convincing but will actually have no teeth. Maybe it will stall them long enough. I'm sure I can come up with ideas of my own for the meeting. I'll check schedules to see if I or another attorney from the firm can be there Wednesday. I will definitely be back in my office by three and will gladly visit with two lovely ladies. Everything should be confirmed while they are here."

It took about twenty minutes to complete their conversation. Frank was efficient. Angus was pleased with the call and encouraged about his plan. As he hung up, he relaxed for a moment before returning to his calculations.

At five to three he was again startled by the ringing of the phone. It caught him concentrating on some complex calculations, which he had to set aside before answering.

Serena was on the other end asking, "Well, what's the good word? Will we be able to see Mr. Ito? We're now walking into his building."

"He's expecting you and I guarantee you will be charmed. He's quite the gentleman, not formal, just gracious. Don't let that gentle manner fool you. He can be hard as nails and meaner than a junkyard dog if he has to. I'm glad he's on our side."

"Did you get to tell him about our plan?" Serena asked.

"I explained to him all he needs to know. You should not have to tell him much. Just answer his questions. Remember, he's not one of the inner circle, but probably knows as much as anyone outside our group. I hope he's the one to go to our meeting with OSI," Angus commented. "Call me back if you run into any snags. Otherwise, I'll probably see you around nine this evening."

"If you're lucky," was Serena's retort. "Incidentally, Oona and I have gotten on fabulously. We discovered we're shopping soul mates— neither one of us wants to spend any money. We have enjoyed our time together."

"Great!" Angus answered. "She and Francis are incredible people. They're one of the good things that came of Rumley running me down. If it hadn't been for that, we would probably never have met. Now, go see Frank. You can bring me up-to-date when you get back."

Angus was beginning to feel a little more secure when talking on the phone. *At least on someone else's phone*, he thought when he returned to his calculations. It would take him several minutes to bring things up to the point where he was interrupted. He continued until after six when he took a break and went down to fix dinner for himself.

Just before eight he turned on the SSR program to wait for Lani's contact. Shortly, "Hi Sitting Duck," popped up on his screen.

His quickly typed for her, "You're not the only one on time."

His screen spelled out, "Boy, that was quick. I spent the afternoon comparing spectra. From the comparisons, not only is the ghost moving extremely fast, but it is apparently rotating rapidly as well. How do you like them pineapples?"

"Very good. I knew I could count on you."

Then began some back and forth small talk. When Angus sent, "We're as silly as school kids."

She replied, "Ain't it wonnerful?"

Their maturity gave them access to the children within them, no pretenses, no faking it, just two people in love. After an hour, the two signed off reluctantly. There would be tomorrows and more tomorrows for them till the ghost arrived.

*   *   *

It was nearly 9:30 when the three returned home from dinner. When they all sat down in the living room, Oona asked Serena, "Why don't you stay the night with us? I'm sure Angus will want to hear the details of our meeting and that way we won't be rushed and can all relax a bit."

"Sounds good to me," Serena answered. "You're sure it's no bother?"

"Of course not," Francis commented. "I'll fix us some coffee, and we can sit here relaxed and go through everything for as long as it takes."

Oona and Francis placed the small lamp she had purchased on a small table between two chairs. "There, that's perfect. I've been looking for a lamp for this table for more than a month since we accidentally knocked over and broke the one we had," Oona stated as she eyed her latest acquisition.

"It's lovely," Serena added. "Perfect for that table. You certainly have an eye for decorating. Everything in your lovely home looks as if it belongs."

"Thank you so much. It's so nice to have someone who appreciates one's efforts." Oona smiled in gracious appreciation. She turned to Angus. "Now I suppose you want a report on what happened at the attorney's office?"

"Yes. I most assuredly would," Angus replied.

"Well, to begin with, Frank is, as you say, quite a charmer. After a genuine Japanese greeting, in Japanese and which I interpreted for Serena, he asked us to elaborate on what you told him over the phone. He is sure OSI overstepped legal bounds in their treatment of you. He will try to get a court order to prevent any more actions of that type but doubts it can be ready before Wednesday afternoon. He thinks a court order would definitely have teeth, a lot more real power than an agreement for them to sign. He will provide you with a copy of the request for the court order which should have the power to deter them until the actual order is obtained. We both felt relieved when he told us that. He also explained OSI has some extraordinary power to hold people and question them when the nation's security is at stake. However, they probably would not be able to make a case for this kind of danger with your situation."

"I thought they might be overstepping their bounds a bit," Angus commented. "Did Frank say if he will be there?"

"He currently has a conflict. If he can change an existing appointment, he will. Otherwise, one of the senior attorneys will cover for him," Serena replied. "I'm sure you'll be well represented in any case. He suggests you give them more than thirty minutes to get to the meeting, at least an hour, two if possible. He doubts OSI would be able to do anything to put you in jeopardy with less than three or four hours. He also thinks you may be a bit over-cautious with the meeting place, all the police and only one of their people. He suggested you invite them all and change the meeting to one of the deposition rooms at their offices. They have a private parking garage beneath their offices where you could surely elude any efforts OSI might make to try and follow you. They use that procedure for an occasional high profile witness or client. With all three of them in attendance, you will, at least, know where they are, and they surely wouldn't try anything there. He also felt the presence of an office full of top attorneys was a more effective control than a police station but would welcome Lt. Hiakawa's presence. Frank has a great deal of respect for him. Says he is a great police officer."

After much discussion, weighing their options and Frank's suggestions, Angus shook his head and agreed. "OK, we'll meet at the attorney's and invite all three an hour and a half before the meeting. I'm a bit nervous about giving them that much time, but I'll rely on Frank's judgement. The court order sounds like a great idea. Frank's input has been valuable. I still plan to change into my disguise after the meeting before going to Gemini."

The next two days were fraught with anticipation, periods of intense activity and many important decisions. The meeting Wednesday would be the most important yet and would determine the course of their actions and maybe even the way the whole world would take the impending horrifying news.

*   *   *

After what seemed an eternity of anxious waiting, Wednesday morning finally rolled around. Rising early, Angus rode Oona's exercise bicycle hard for more than a half hour. Exercise always seemed to help clear his mind, and he definitely wanted a clear mind this day. After cooling down in the shower, he dressed and headed downstairs. Francis was fixing breakfast while Oona was dressing. "Help yourself to some coffee," Francis said in greeting. "Breakfast will be ready in just a few moments."

"I see you're the cook this morning."

"We share all the house duties fairly equally," Francis replied. "Although, I will say Oona does much more than I since retiring from working full-time. She seems to enjoy it, and she is definitely the better cook."

"When I was playing football, we ate at decent restaurants, but I relished those few home-cooked meals I did get. I even got restaurant food at home. With Mom running the inn, we usually ate what the customers didn't. It was very good, at least as good as the meals from those fancy restaurants the team used. Once in a while she'd fix something special for me when I came home for a visit, but usually we ate from the menu. After I quit football, I cooked for myself most of the time. There are some great restaurants in Tucson, so I did eat out a lot after I moved there."

Oona walked into the kitchen just in time for Francis to serve. "I timed that well, don't you think?" she commented as she sat down with them.

After breakfast they stayed at the table for some time discussing the coming day's activities. They had informed all members of their group about Angus' meeting with OSI.

The plan was for Oona to take Angus to his apartment where he would place the call to OSI. As soon as that was done, she was to drop him off near the Gemini Operations Center in his disguise. He would walk the few blocks to the Op Center. Once in his office, he would change into his normal clothes and work on what he had to do on the Gemini computer until time to leave for the meeting. He would go to the attorney's office with John who would join him in the meeting. After the meeting, John and Angus would leave while their attorney would question the OSI agents for the ten minutes it would take for them to get to the Op Center. At least that was the plan. They hoped things would go smoothly.

Angus changed into his disguise and packed his regular clothes in a small valise along with some data disks he would need for his work at the office. He booted the laptop and activated the SSR network program. He would now be able to access files on the laptop from his office computer.

When he came down, everyone laughed. Still snickering, Oona said, "You sure do look like a mainland tourist. No one would expect you to be under that crazy hat."

"Let's hope it fools any OSI agents waiting for me at the Op Center. Now let's start the ball rolling."

They drove to Angus' apartment where he was greeted with more laughter from his mother, who said, "I wish I had a camera."

Using the OSI card Lani had given him for the number, Angus placed the call at precisely one thirty. He waited nervously until a woman's voice answered. It was Yvonne.

"Our missing astronomer at last. Where are you?" she asked.

"Never mind where I am," Angus replied. "If you want to talk to me, here's your chance. You can bring as many agents as are involved in my case to my attorney's office, and I'll talk to you with him present. I will be there at three o'clock sharp and leave at precisely 3:30. You can ask anything you want relating to my new discovery. I will answer no questions about anything other than that. If you can't make it for any reason, it's the last chance you'll get. You can then read about it in the news releases in the papers."

After a long pause, Yvonne replied, "I'll have to discuss this with the others. I can't say what we will do until I confer with them."

"That's quite all right. I'll know your answer if and when you show up. In any event, I will be there." He gave her the name and address of Ito's law office, repeated it once, said good-bye and hung up. "Now let's get out of here before they can show up and grab me," he suggested. After saying good-bye to Serena he left with Oona for the Op Center.

OSI knew he was at home since they had not removed any of their surveillance equipment. They would not act but would honor Yvonne's commitment, at least for the present.

Oona dropped Angus far enough from the Op Center so he would appear to have walked there. As he passed a tour van near the entrance, a group of ten or so visitors tumbled out to visit the Op Center. *How lucky can you be?* he thought as he mingled with the group walking to the door. Once inside he stayed with them to the reception desk, then moved casually away from the group and toward his office.

"Sir! Wait Sir!" Jenny called after him as he approached the office. She quickly left her desk and ran after him, stopping him just before he reached the door to the outer office. When he turned, she recognized him and immediately burst into laughter. Quick to size up a situation, Jenny caught herself and said in a louder than usual voice while trying to keep from breaking up, "I'm sorry sir, I didn't realize you were the one who was to visit our inner office. Just go right through that door," she finished by pointing to the office door.

"Thank you," he replied, also trying to keep from laughing. As soon as the door closed behind him, he removed the floppy hat and headed for his office. As he approached, Lani stood up, joining the entire office in hoots and catcalls. He would be glad to get out of the outfit as soon as possible now that its purpose was fulfilled. "Don't you people have anything better to do other than ridicule a poor tourist?" he said amidst the outcry. This brought on another round of ridicule. They all knew Angus quite well and enjoyed the kidding.

Once inside his office, Angus changed into his regular slacks and shirt. He then opened the door and called Lani in. "What happened to that crazy tourist?" she asked, laughing. Changing into a more serious tone she asked, "How did it go? Are they coming to the meeting?"

"I won't know until I get there," Angus replied, giving her a rundown on the details of his conversation with Yvonne. "We'll just have to wait and see."

"I hope they don't try to grab you," Lani remarked, then in a more serious voice added, "Now, Dr. Thomas, you've much to do and had better get cracking. I have all your photos and spectral diagrams ready right there on the table. Your computer is up and your special program is ready. The printouts you requested are right there on your desk. If you need me, I'll be at my desk working on that comparison data you wanted for the meeting tonight."

Angus blew her a kiss when she turned to leave. Obviously tense about the upcoming meeting with OSI, she returned a nervous smile. Always the professional, her nervousness did not prevent her from being efficient at her job. Angus had never worked with an assistant quite so capable.

Angus knew he would not be able to complete the preparation for their meeting tonight before leaving. This placed him under a lot of pressure. If he got back to it before four it would be close. He wanted everything ready since the effort tonight would be crucial. It was anyone's guess just when they would be able to meet again. He tried not to think of OSI as he worked.

*   *   *

Yvonne hung up the phone after Angus' call, a stunned expression on her face. Both the others were out of the office and she didn't know whether she could round them up in time for the meeting. Jan was somewhere in Hilo trying to find more information on the members of the Gemini Community Action Committee. Jack had gone to Waimea to see if there was another astronomer connected with the Keck telescopes who could help them.

Yvonne called Jan's cell phone first. When he answered, she explained Angus' request as best she could. Jan interrupted her several times with outbursts of expletives.

"What's the clown up to now, I wonder?" Jan asked, not expecting any answer. "I'll have to cut short my business here and get back to the office. Have you gotten hold of Jack?"

"No, I called you first. I'll call him as soon as we finish."

"Don't bust your fanny to get him. He's so cautious it probably wouldn't matter if he couldn't make it." Jan was clearly unhappy with Jack Wells' cautious attitude.

"He should be at a meeting in Waimea with a Dr. Morris right now. Do you have anything else for me?"

"Nah, try to get Jack. I should be back there in about fifteen minutes."

When she finally reached Jack, he was waiting to talk to Dr. Morris about their problem.

"It will take me at least forty-five minutes to make it back to the office," Jack said. "If I wait to speak to Dr. Morris it could take another half hour or so, and I will just be able to get to the meeting at three if everything goes smoothly."

"Why don't you do that? Jan should be here shortly. We can get you on your cell phone if we need to."

"At least you could acquaint me with any plans for the meeting," Jack said before they finished the call.

At ten of two, an obviously angry Jan Lux stormed into the office. "I hope that jerk doesn't expect this meeting to be the end of it," Jan muttered furiously. "How does he expect us to learn anything in a half hour? I've a notion to skip this and go after him again. We know where he will be between 3:00 and 3:30. Did he say anything about bringing any data or documentation? That's what we need, photos, spectral diagrams and calculation results. Did he say he was bringing any of that?"

"No! All he said was he would answer our questions. He gave me the time and address and then hung up. The call came from his apartment and we have it on tape if you'd care to listen to it."

"No need," Jan replied, calming down some. "Let's decide what questions we want to ask him. If we're going to do this, we'd better be prepared. Did you get hold of Jack?"

When she told him about her conversation with Jack and what he decided to do, Jan grumbled, grudgingly admitting it was probably the best course of action he could have taken. Yvonne suggested they call him after they had written down a number of questions for Angus. They could relay the questions to him and ask for his suggestions. Jan didn't see the need to include Jack at all. He was openly antagonistic toward him. This was not conducive to a well-oiled team, and it disturbed Yvonne.

The first question was actually the same one Professor Schuman had asked, the nature of the object, its exact size, position, speed and path. In other words, what was it and where was it going. That would be the last question upon which they would agree without considerable argument.

"OK. What should be our next question?" Yvonne asked.

"How about asking why Dick Rumley was so interested in his work? I'd like to know the answer to that one."

"He stated specifically he would only answer questions about the new object he has discovered. I don't think he would answer that," Yvonne replied.

"And why not?" Jan shot back, "It's about that thing, what do they call it, the ghost? I'd like to know the significance of that name. It doesn't sound like any celestial object to me."

"Maybe we should ask why they call it the ghost. How's that for a question?"

"Nah! That sounds sort of ridiculous to me. This whole question and answer thing sounds outrageous. I doubt we'll find out anything of value from it," Jan said in frustration and disgust.

"We might as well get some more questions ready anyway. It's apparently the only shot we'll get before he goes public with it. At least, that's what I got from what he told me."

"Maybe I'd better listen to the tape of your conversation. I might pick up on something you missed."

Yvonne selected a tape from the small box on her desk and placed it in the tape player. They both listened intently.

"Not much to go on," Jan uttered with a sigh. "You've got to hand it to him. He knows how to call the shots. Giving us less than two hours to prepare for this meeting was clever. He knows it would take us more time to prepare a surprise for him. He caught us off guard again, blast him."

"Hadn't we better get on with the questions?" Yvonne pleaded. "We're short on time and have only one question ready after nearly twenty minutes."

"OK. OK. Let's get back to the questions. Why don't you write those two down, my suggestion and yours? Then we can use them as we see fit."

"I just thought of another. Ask if he sees any danger to our nation—any danger we at OSI should be aware of. If he'll answer that one, it could help us a lot."

"He'd probably lie about it if he didn't want us to know. I doubt he'll be truthful in any event. We'll not get anything of value from this," Jan remarked in a continuing negative reaction.

"We might as well try," Yvonne pleaded. "We won't find out anything if we don't ask. Try putting your anger aside for now and concentrate on what you would like to know."

"I'm not angry," Jan shouted "This clown has bested us at every effort we have made, and I'm tired of it. Now he's going to do it again. I'm not angry." After a long pause, he said quietly, "Yes, I am angry . . . and frustrated . . . and consumed by the desire to get even. That's not very professional of me is it?"

"You don't really want me to answer, do you?" Yvonne replied tentatively. It looked as though Jan may have come to his senses, and she didn't want to provoke him.

After a long pause while Yvonne held her tongue and Jan worked to regain his composure, Jan said calmly, "I nearly blew it. I finally see what you and Jack have been trying to tell me for some time. I can't believe I could have become so unprofessional. I almost forgot completely the thing I have stressed to so many new agents. Don't personalize. From the moment he manhandled us the first time, I have been on a personal vendetta. It's no wonder we've gotten nowhere. I broke the first rule of the OSI."

"That sounds like the team leader I met when I first joined this project. Where do we go from here?"

Jan brightened noticeably, rejuvenated by his realization and admission. "Let's get Jack on the phone and get some good questions ready. I know he'll have some. Maybe we can rescue something out of all the confusion."

The next twenty minutes were spent on the phone with Jack, preparing the list of questions to be used at the meeting.

Yvonne stood up, almost enthusiastic. "We have only a short list of questions. Possibly we can expand on them after Dr. Thomas answers."

"That's OK. I'm certain we'll have new questions once we get into the meeting. I now feel much better about the situation." Jan got up, picking up the one paper with the questions. "We'd better be leaving now while there's still plenty of time to get to their attorney's office. Incidentally, it feels good to be working like a team again."

HARD QUESTIONS, SOFT ANSWERS

Just before three, Angus, John and Frank stepped into the meeting room at Frank's office. The three OSI agents were seated at the table, waiting, along with a secretary, who was there to record the meeting. They all rose for introductions then sat down.

Frank sat forward, a number of papers in his hands. "As Gemini's legal counsel, I am here to observe the meeting and assist my clients. This is an information meeting only not a deposition and no one is under oath. With your permission, I have asked the meeting be recorded. If there are any objections please voice them now."

Jan immediately declared, "Should we venture into areas of national security where secrecy might be involved, I would ask the recording be stopped. Since none of you have security clearance, we will do our best to avoid that area."

"If no one objects, I think we can agree to do so," Frank replied. "Since you of OSI are the only ones who will know if it becomes a problem, we will rely on you for that information. Let us know, and the recording will be suspended. Now, let's get on with the questions."

It was precisely three o'clock as Yvonne read the first question, the one Schuman had asked.

Angus replied, "The object I have found is called a red dwarf star. It is about half the size of our sun and its light comes to us from a distance of about three hundred light years. It is moving at an unusually fast speed. At nearly one percent of the speed of light, it is the fastest moving object ever found within our galaxy. At some time in the distant future, its path may bring it within visual range of our solar system, at which time it should be visible to the naked eye. Red dwarfs are among the commonest stars in our galaxy. Our sun is a red dwarf star. They can be quite old since they have a very long lifetime. Does that answer your question?"

"Does this star pose any threat to our nation whatsoever of which OSI should be aware?" Jack Wells asked.

"This object poses no threat of any kind to our nation in the near future, certainly nothing involving national security or which OSI could affect in any way."

"I take it that was a no?" Jack asked.

"Correct," Angus answered curtly.

"Is your answer a true fact or only your opinion? Might others view it differently?"

"All astronomical objects are viewed at incredible distances by telescopes that are extremely tiny when compared to the objects being viewed and the distances involved. Careful as we are, we are limited to best guesses within the limits of accuracy of our instruments. At the distance we are viewing this object, the variations can be on the order of several light years. A light year is a very long distance. It takes light only eight minutes to cross the ninety-three million miles from the sun to the earth. Should the sun be a light year away it would appear as a fairly bright star. Another astronomer might view the data differently and report lesser or greater numbers than I. It is a fact within a range or an opinion. You make that decision."

"Are you absolutely certain this could not be an object made by an intelligent race of creatures, perhaps shielded in such a way as to appear as a star far away when it was, in fact, a much smaller object much closer?"

"Anything is possible in this universe, but the answer to your question is: I am absolutely certain this is not an object such as you describe. Should an intelligent race be able to do what you suggest, they would most assuredly not. The level of technical achievement required to do such a thing would be infinitely greater than to merely hide an object completely from our view. Since we can see it, it could not be a vessel as you describe."

"Why did you name it the ghost?"

Angus laughed at this. "It was a name put on an object that seemed to appear and disappear behind Barnard's star. Like what photographers call a ghost image that sometimes appears on a photograph. As a joke, my colleagues at Kitt Peak named the images I found 'Barnard's ghost,' after the star it appeared to shadow. The name ghost stuck and that's what we've called it ever since."

"Why have you been so secretive and hidden the data about your discovery? What is it you don't want us to find out?"

"A truly simple explanation, which I gave you before and which Professor Schuman, your own hand-picked expert, confirmed. You chose to ignore it then. I will repeat it for you now. Any astronomer who makes a new discovery, or even supposes he has made a new discovery, is extremely protective of his early data. I'm sure you found out that Gemini has some rather elaborate security measures in effect to help keep such data from being used by anyone other then the person or group that first discovers it. In fact, one of the reasons you are even involved is because Dick Rumley breached security at Gemini and gained access to some of my data. This protection is given so the original discoverer can check his data for accuracy and confirmation. Only when it is published is the opportunity given for others to confirm the original work. There are some rare exceptions to this with the permission of the original discoverer or in the case of a death. It will take at least a year and maybe two to confirm the data so far collected on the ghost. This is because confirmation requires parallax measurements, which must be taken at six month intervals in order to be useful. A complete duplicate confirmation series takes two years. I remind you it has been eighteen months since the first discovery and complete confirmation will take another year. In this instance, I am planning on releasing the data for confirmation within the next four months so others can confirm my findings at the preferred time of the next parallax position of the earth. I see no reason to provide you with the data I have until it is released to my colleagues."

"We can force you to release that data to us since Gemini is an agency of the U.S. government," Jan stated defiantly.

With that, Frank stood up and handed Jan a sheaf of papers, saying, "I have given you a copy of a legal request we have made to the federal court for a restraining order, which will prevent you from acting on any demand for those records for at least six months. I think you will find those papers in order. We don't have the order yet, but we will have it long before you can put together any kind of legal order to do what you suggest. By the time the restraining order runs out, the data will be made public, and we will be pleased to send you a copy."

After pausing for a moment, Frank continued, "You will note a copy of another request we made of the federal court for an order for you to return all data records obtained by OSI from Gemini by any and all means, legal or illegal. All copies are to be returned. There are to be none retained in any form whatsoever. You will note we have stipulated on the request, anyone who keeps such records in defiance of the order will be subject to both criminal and civil suit. Furthermore, there is another document that lists the various occurrences of battery and denial of civil rights against our client; namely, one Angus Thomas. This is to inform you we are preparing action against OSI and each of you individually. At our client's request, we are holding these actions pending future activities of OSI. He believes you have come to realize the errors of your previous actions and are now operating in a legal and ethical manner. He has no desire to file against you as long as you continue to act in this fashion. Rest assured, should you return to your previous methods, suit will be filed. Do you have any more questions?"

The three OSI agents sat in stunned silence. Jan thought much of this was bluff and bluster, but he would have to check it out with their own attorneys. He certainly didn't know for sure if what Frank said was true or not. These were only requests for court orders, not the orders themselves. Still, he decided they had best watch their actions until he knew for sure.

Jack Wells posed another question, "Is there any chance we could get to see the data before it is published? We are concerned there may be something of a classified nature in the data and, if so, would not want it made public."

Angus answered quickly with pointed sarcasm, "Does your request mean we may have accidentally recorded something of a classified nature in that portion of the sky? Perhaps a new type of spy satellite or ultra fast aircraft or the like? Maybe even our own flying saucer? I'll have to review the data and photos to see what else I can find. That's interesting."

"There's nothing like that at all. We don't know what you found other than what you told us here, but we would like to cover all bases, just in case. We're trying our best to cooperate with you. Could you possibly give us a little cooperation in return? If you can find a way to give us that opportunity without compromising your position or professional ethics, we would be most appreciative," Jack was trying hard to secure whatever ground he could for OSI. Even Jan was impressed.

Angus, surprised by Jack's request, paused and looked at John. "Maybe something could be worked out that would satisfy your needs. We've some time available to discuss it. We can meet with you at a later date to work out the details. I won't promise anything now except we will consider doing something for you. After all, we are all working for the same U.S. government."

It was now 3:30, and Angus and John rose to leave. True to his promise to hold OSI until they were out of the building, Frank walked over to the OSI people with additional papers in hand. "There are a few more details I want to go over with you before you leave," Angus heard Frank saying as John and he stepped out the door. His conversation would give them plenty of time to get away before OSI left. He had another order request prepared, which would direct them to cease any and all surveillance immediately. It listed the known and suspected bugs, phone taps and auto beacons. It also requested a list of all others and when they would be disabled. Frank would take at least fifteen minutes talking to them about this final order request.

"That seems to have gone well and without a single hitch," John remarked as they drove out of the parking lot. "Did you see the looks on their faces when Frank hit them with the explanation of those papers? They looked like three kids with their hand caught in the cookie jar."

"I was rather surprised with the new man, Wells," Angus commented. "He seems the most level headed of the lot. He countered my derisive answer to his question deftly and without rancor. His suggestion did make sense and just might work. Maybe we should ask for him to be involved in the early release of the data should we decide to do it."

"We can discuss that with the group tonight," John replied. "They'll be glad to hear the good news from our meeting today. At least it appears OSI will be backing off. What do you think? Should we let down our guard?"

"Let's run it by the group tonight. Let them decide," Angus answered. "I think you're right, but maybe we shouldn't let down our guard completely. I'd hate to be blindsided. We can relax a bit, but let's keep playing things cool till we know for certain."

"Maybe now we can concentrate on the awesome responsibility before us. That's a much bigger challenge than OSI."

"You're certainly right on that count," Angus replied. "We'll probably have a long session tonight developing and editing those press releases. I hate to think what might happen if we make a mistake. Our whole schedule could fall apart. This whole thing is a truly awesome responsibility. I almost feel we're responsible for the whole of humanity, holding the fate of everyone in our hands. It's scary and mind boggling at the same time."

"Well at least those hands are genuinely kind and caring. I'm sure of that. I doubt you could gather a more concerned group of people. I just hope we find the best way to share this terrible knowledge with the rest of the world."

"Right on, John, right on."

16

John and Angus drove back to the Op Center without incident. They both talked about the positive outcome of the meeting with OSI and what a masterful job Frank had done. "I can't get over seeing the looks on their faces when Frank was through," John said, his voice charged with amazement.

"Me too!" Angus replied. "The look on their faces was like that of a quarterback who's just been blindsided—total disbelief and dismay. I would love to have a picture of them at that moment."

"I only hope they stay in that mode, at least until we get our job done," John added. "Jack Wells certainly made a lot of sense. That's the first positive step OSI has taken in this situation. I've been considering it since we heard it and still think it is a reasonable request."

"That took me completely by surprise," exclaimed Angus. "We'll have to go through it carefully with the group tonight. I tend to agree with you on that, but we'd better give it some serious thought before proceeding. I just hope there's no hidden agenda behind it."

"Yes, it will take a lot of positive effort on their part to undo the damage they have done. It's difficult to regain trust once it's broken."

"I don't know if I can ever learn to trust them completely," Angus commented. "I'm not one to hold a grudge, but trust is a special and precarious thing. It's not earned easily and once broken, nearly impossible to regain. I approach these situations with cautious optimism, but not foolish abandon. Time alone will tell."

"I tend to agree," John replied. "If they are as good as their word, they have become a minor part of our problems. Dealing with the rest of the world—now there's the rub."

"With a borrowed phrase from Willie S. no less," Angus said with a chuckle.

It was a quarter to four when they arrived back at the Op Center. Angus headed straight for his office with Lani dogging his steps as soon as he passed her desk. "How'd it go?" were her first words. "What did they ask you?"

Angus gave her a quick run-down. He also related his and John's positive feelings but deferred a detailed explanation until the evening meeting. He needed to get right to his work in order to be prepared for the meeting. Lani understood perfectly, so the two tackled the work at hand. They would finish the calculations and the report just in time for Lani to run copies for each in the group. They were the last ones to enter John's office at just a few minutes after five.

Serena started the meeting and went through their most recent efforts. After a short question and answer period she asked John to report on the afternoon meeting with OSI. John gave a detailed account of the half-hour meeting. They all were pleased with the results and felt positive about Jack Wells' suggestion. Decisions on that would be deferred until after they had completed work on the press releases and their schedule.

Ginger was the only real skeptic about OSI. Incredulity etched her face and laced her words. "How can any of you even consider trusting them after they lied so blatantly and did what they did? I'm against ever trusting them, period!"

Serena replied, "You're comments and objections have been noted, understood and will certainly be considered." She next asked for Angus' report on his latest calculations, noting each of them had a copy of his report in hand.

Angus looked around the table at the group. "Before I start, we have another knotty little problem. It relates to the apparent new attitude of our friends at OSI. When I called Pete Hiakawa this morning about the planned meeting with OSI, he said he couldn't make it. He told me Conrad was all set for the switch with Rumley, so I could escape to Chile. I said I would contact Conrad on Thursday and give him a definite answer, one way or the other. He explained Conrad had gone out of his way for my benefit, and whatever I decide, I should tell him how much I appreciate his efforts. I'll certainly do that, but we must decide tonight whether or not I should go. What do you think?"

The consensus was he should stay. Even Ginger agreed. "You all know I don't trust them, but you've a good hiding place and maybe they have pulled their claws in a bit. Leaving now would set your work schedule back quite a bit, wouldn't it?"

Angus nodded affirmatively. "In that case I'll tell Conrad thanks but no thanks. I was most definitely not looking forward to trading Hawaii for Chile. You're correct. It would set my work back about six months, maybe more. Gemini South is a full year behind here. When they are on-line and the cable link is ready, I'd like to go there, but not now."

"That's one decision out of the way," Serena commented. "Now let's get to your report."

Angus picked up his paperwork. "It's nearly the same old story. Refinements to the rough calculations reported at the last meeting have not changed the projected outcome a bit in spite of a new view of the ghost itself. That's both good and bad news. The good news is it doesn't look any worse. The bad is it doesn't look any better either. In all honesty, it will take many years of work to have an accurate enough path and schedule for the ghost to enable us to develop a reasonable scenario for the future of the solar system. It could take as long as fifteen or even more. We will also need the report from the work Dr. Botkin is doing for us at Cal Tech. Should new technologies be developed relative to gathering and understanding this type of data, the schedule could be speeded up. How much is totally un- known. When Gemini South comes on-line and is coupled with our installation here, we will be working with a telescope with an effec- tive size hundreds of thousands of times the eight meters we have here. That could improve our accuracy enough to speed up the sched- ule as well, but we won't know how much until we do it. All I can say is we should plan for the worst and hope for the best. I don't think we should use anything but the best-case scenario in our press releases. Right now the worst case is annihilation of all life on earth as we know it. That option is not an option in my book."

They sat discussing the report and asking clarifications for nearly an hour. Ali, Ruth and Chelton expressed their frustration at dealing with such a broad range of possibilities. Many scenarios were brought up and discussed. At six, Serena asked them to break for ten minutes and then begin with the press releases.

After they reconvened, Serena asked Ginger to review the status of the press releases and explain what needed to be done. After Ginger distributed copies of the six releases to each member, she commented, "As you can see, these releases are rough drafts and we don't have a schedule as yet. Our job tonight is to edit at least the first few releases to convey only what we intend to let the public know. My guess is they will make few newspapers unless someone sees a possible story behind the release. I doubt very much that will happen. Angus and I have a difference about the schedule. We will settle that tonight with the group after discussing both viewpoints. The other release we must decide upon, is the one with the data for confirmation by other astronomers. I tend to agree with Angus on that one. Let's look at the first few releases and get some suggestions on editing."

They spent the next half hour or so editing and reediting the first three releases. When they had finished, three were ready to go.

News Release: Gemini Observatory, Hilo, Hawaii
Dr. Angus Thomas reported today the discovery of a previously unknown star which has been temporarily named the Ghost by some of his colleagues. It is a red dwarf, like our sun, but only half the size of old Sol. The latest measurements place it between 300 and 350 light years away. It is moving in our general direction and will pass within three or four light years of the sun at some time in the distant future. At that time it will be our nearest star and visible to the naked eye. Dr. Thomas will continue to study this newly discovered star, which is probably at least as old as the sun.

News Release: Gemini Observatory, Hilo, Hawaii
Dr. Angus Thomas reported today new measurements of his recently discovered Ghost star indicate it is traveling at a phenomenal rate of speed. It appears to be the fastest moving object ever discovered within our galaxy. The exact speed has not yet been determined, but it is definitely faster than any other known object in the Milky Way galaxy.

News Release: Gemini Observatory, Hilo, Hawaii
Dr. Angus Thomas reported today he has determined the speed of
the recently discovered Ghost star to within a few percentage points
and its speed is astounding. Pending confirmation by other astronomers, its speed appears to be an unbelievable 90 percent of the
speed of light. What circumstances caused such incredible speed
are a complete mystery. Its present true position and direction will
bring it screaming by in thirty to forty years to within three or four
light years of our sun. It should be able to be seen with the naked
eye and its motion detected when it is closest to us.

"The third release will doubtless make headlines," John commented. "I can't see any newspaper ignoring that one. The genie will
definitely be out of the bottle once that is released. What do you
think, Ginger?"

"I think you're right. The second one will make it in a few papers,
any of those with a sharp science editor, but it won't be picked up by
the news services except by accident. The third one will probably be
picked up by all the news services. I'll be surprised if it doesn't make
a few headlines. Your central phone here at Gemini will light up like
a Christmas tree. We'll have to be careful about scheduling these releases. We can schedule the second one after we see what happens
with the first and so on. We'll have to use Angus' best guess about
how soon other astronomers will confirm his findings and release
their own data. It could be tricky." Ginger was proving to be a valuable addition to the group.

Francis asked, "What about confirmation of Angus' work? When
could we expect that to happen? Who would be the ones to do it, and
how would they get the data to confirm? Shouldn't we know these
things before we schedule the release any of these?"

Then Charlene seemed a little confused. "The whole process looks
complicated to me. Am I missing something here? I would like to see
an outline covering all our activities and how they will dovetail with
Angus' work, not just of the news releases. We could figuratively shoot
ourselves in the foot without an overall plan."

"She's right, you know," Oona added. "We should put together a
complete calendar of all the events. There's Angus and Lani's schedule for data acquisition and conclusions, the schedule of the release
of data for other astronomers to confirm, the schedule for the news

releases, the best guess as to how soon the other astronomers will be able to confirm Angus' data, the tentative release of the data to OSI, any readjustments we might need caused by press reactions to the releases and even the public reaction to any of these things. Right now, I don't have much of a clue as to how they will follow."

When Oona finished, Ali suggested, "What we need is a CPM diagram for this project. That's a term from the construction industry which stands for Critical Path Method. It's a way of outlining all the various parts of a project including order, time to complete, dependence on other parts of the project, time needed for delivery of necessary items and anything else required before the project is completed. They are an absolute necessity for large projects and this is certainly a large project."

"That seems like a good idea. How do you develop one of these CPM diagrams?" Ruth asked. "It sounds complex to me, but then I'm not in the construction business. There must be hundreds of different parts to a large construction project, maybe even thousands. Just where do you start?"

"And just where do you suppose Mr. Namahoe learned about CPM diagrams?" Charlene said smugly. "From me. I took some extension courses on the construction industry a number of years back to help Ali when he first started his business. Mostly they were about bookkeeping and bidding, but I did take one on construction management and that's where I learned about CPM and CPM diagrams. It was fascinating for me, and I urged Ali to use it even on small projects. I've drawn up many CPM diagrams for him since. I'm his secret weapon in the bidding wars. It's become old hat compared with some of the newer methods, but it still works quite well."

Ali's face beamed proudly at his wife. "She's right, you know. I can use them, but she's the expert when it comes to setting them up. It got so I wouldn't touch a bid for medium to large projects without one of her diagrams. They kept me from quite a few mistakes and gave me a superior handle on cost and time management. We rarely had one trade waiting for another to finish. That can waste real money which you can't recoup."

Seeing the situation develop, Serena, the organizer, stepped in. "OK. We'll develop a CPM diagram. Charlene, I put you in full charge of creating this diagram for our project. You tell us what you need, and we'll do whatever you ask. Remember, your job is to see to it we get the best CPM diagram ready in the shortest practical time. We are all at your disposal. You manage, we'll do the legwork. Do I hear any objections?"

Heads turned and eyes searched, but no objections were raised, so Serena continued, "Now Charlene, what will you need?"

A little surprised at the turn of events, Charlene paused a moment, then responded, "OK. That sounds workable. Let's see, the first step is to list everything we will need in the way of labor, materials and information, preferably on a spreadsheet. Next to each item we will list a number of factors including: the time required to complete the item, the place in the schedule, that is what must be done before the listed item can be started, other items dependent on the completion of the listed item, materials needed and the order in which they are needed, the people needed to complete each item and the tools and equipment needed. Also, you can't have two items requiring the same person at the same time. That description may not be exactly what a CPM expert would say, but I've tailored my understanding to fit Ali's small business and it's in the language of that construction business. It should work well for this project with a few adjustments. I think you get the idea."

Chelton agreed. "That makes a lot of sense to me even though I know nothing about the construction business. It's a lot like developing a flow diagram for a multi tiered, multi faceted organization. I've worked with a number of those, strictly from the personnel standpoint. I was usually working to make peace between the various feuding factions. They used those flow diagrams as weapons to promote their own point of view. Why don't we start the list now? Ruth can list all the items we come up with and then we can add the things Charlene mentioned. She can organize the whole project. We can start with the three news releases, the release of the data for confirmation, the release of data to OSI. Come on, Angus. What things do you have to do?"

They spent the next two hours listing items and all the critical steps and dependencies in those items.

At this point, John stood up and stretched. "It's after nine and we still have no schedule for the news releases. We do have an amazing number of items on the list and which ones are dependent on others."

Charlene agreed, "I'll take a copy of Ruth's notes on the CPM process and work up a chart. It shouldn't take much more than two days, three at the most. There is a great deal of work needed to develop a reliable diagram, particularly one with so many unknowns."

"Why not meet again Friday at the same time and place?" Oona suggested. "I can provide us with snacks so we won't have to go out until we're finished."

"After office hours, we can move to the meeting room that has a sink and coffee pot and serve the snacks there," John offered.

By the time they broke up, they had been at it for nearly five hours.

Decisions, Decisions, Decisions

Charlene spent all day Thursday working up the CPM diagram for Friday's meeting. Ruth came over to help translate her notes from the meeting into an organized list. They made frequent calls to various members of the group, mostly to Angus or Lani. After their umpteenth call, Angus became frustrated at the interruptions.

Angus said, "Why don't you come to the Op Center on Friday. These constant phone calls are driving us crazy. Come early enough to complete the CPM diagram right here in the office. You can work at the empty desk right next to Lani's. We will have time then, so Lani and I can help without the bother of calling on the phone. Chelton and Serena could even help if need be."

"That'll work," Charlene replied. "We'll see you in the morning."

Friday morning Charlene and Ruth arrived at 7:30 and went right to work. At Angus' request, Serena and Chelton came over to help, taking some of the papers into Angus' office to work at the small table there.

The manual creation of a CPM diagram is a daunting undertaking. There are computer programs that make the job much easier and quicker. Unfortunately, no one had such a program available or knew how to use it. Charlene had always done them by hand.

By four, it was complete except for a few refining touches, so they headed for John's office with the diagram. Some of the items they needed to track remained unknowns. They used intelligent guesses for these items. *SWAGs* Angus called them. The schedule could be adjusted as new information became available in the future. They would have to make changes on the run, so to speak. After a few minutes to set up, the finished CPM diagram was displayed on a three foot wide by two-foot high corkboard.

Francis and Oona arrived before five to set up the food in the meeting room they would use later. Everyone was in John's office by five when Serena started the meeting. "We had better ask for help from the Great Spirit. We're going to need all the help we can muster for this meeting. Ruth, could you offer a prayer?"

"Certainly. Almighty God. Great Spirit. Master of the Universe. Hear our prayer this night we beg you. A fearsome menace approaches, to do what we know not to our world. The terrible knowledge of this menace, that we alone now possess, troubles us greatly. Help us find the best way to share this knowledge with the rest of your children throughout the world. We know there will be great terror among the people, both now and as the menace draws near. Help us all bear that fear in steadiness and not panic. Guide our thoughts and actions now and in years to come to be pleasing to you and of solace to our brothers and sisters worldwide. Help us make decisions that are honorable, helpful and encouraging in the face of ultimate destruction. We are a small group representing many races and cultures. Diverse as we are, we share a common mind and heart in searching for the best way to know what the danger is so we can best share that knowledge with others. Guide our scientists in finding what they need to know to determine our fate thirty years from now. If it is possible, let this wild star pass without damaging this beautiful earth you have provided for us. For those among us who are Christian we ask these things in the name of your most precious son, Jesus. For others, we ask in the special heart of their beliefs, whoever or whatever that may be. Amen."

There was dead silence for nearly a minute. John finally broke the silence with a hearty "Amen," which then echoed around the room. "I don't usually comment after a prayer," John continued, "but that was a complete picture of who and what we are and what we are about. Now all we have to do is live up to it."

Then an unusual thing happened. They all stood and began to applaud. It was a magical moment. As the applause died down, Ruth said quietly, "I had no thought for a prayer until I started. I believe we just received a message from the man upstairs."

"That is a tough act to follow," Serena commented as she began to get the meeting going. "With that inspiration, I expect we can get the job done. The first thing on the agenda is the CPM diagram. It's there on the easel, so let's get to it. Charlene, will you explain it to us?"

Charlene did a quick overview of the chart. "Actually, it is not finished since we have not set the dates for the two releases of information. Those two dates are critical to the full schedule. As you can see on the diagram, we set the first news release for July 15, less than a month away. With luck we will have Dr. Botkin's report by then. Maybe it will bring us good news. That makes the time for the second release in October and the third in December, after Angus makes his next readings and calculations. We chose the early date for this display since we will have plenty of time to prepare another should we select a later date. The data release is scheduled for November, a month before the third release. The data critical to calculating the path of the ghost will not be released until later, probably December when we should have a better handle on the path. Angus assures us the first possible confirmation and discovery of the true speed and path of the ghost could not be completed before the third release is out and probably not until February or as late as June. This maintains our control of the information. In addition, he will be taking another set of readings in December and should be able to further refine the probabilities of the path of our wild star. The fourth news release will be made sometime between January and April and will outline the possibility of an earthly cataclysm. The exact date will hinge upon what happens in the interim. Should we push the schedule up the four months that Angus wants, it will change all dates accordingly. The only problem being, what happens if someone discovers the ghost in the meantime and lets the world know? Angus doesn't think it's likely, but it is a definite possibility."

"I didn't know you were an astrophysicist," Ali said to Charlene with a sly chuckle. "You sound just like Angus or your daughter talking."

"There's lots you don't know about me," Charlene quipped back. "Never underestimate your little wife."

"Believe me. I never have and never will." Ali's answer brought a few chuckles from the group.

"If you look carefully, you'll note I have been reading from notes on the CPM diagram. Angus and Lani helped organize a lot of this information, but I have also learned a great deal from them for myself," Charlene commented with a cheery "so-there" attitude.

Smiles and chuckles here and there never hurt a serious discussion. A completely somber discussion sometimes dulls the mind. As a whole, they felt they were finally getting somewhere. Things seemed to be jelling. Threads of positive concepts were weaving through them from person to person; couple to couple. Their differences were melting into group consensuses without their realizing it. There were two critical decisions needed almost immediately. One was when the first news release would be scheduled, and the other was when the data would be released for other astronomers to confirm. Angus and Ginger were at opposite ends on the first one. Angus and John were the only ones who had a clue about the second. Once those decisions were made, everything else would fall into place, albeit a little roughly.

The bomb drop of the third news release would come in December if the first one was made within a month. If Angus had his way, the third release would not come until June of next year. They would have to work that out tonight if things were to fit well into the CPM schedule. Angus knew one of the linchpins of the entire schedule to be the time it would take for other astronomers to confirm his work. That would hinge directly on when he released his data for confirmation relative to the date additional accurate observations could be made. A small error in estimating the time or in scheduling that release could make a difference of at least three months in the date when the people would know the earth to be in danger, maybe even more. They continued discussing the release dates with Angus and Ginger stubbornly at loggerheads.

At about six fifteen they headed for the meeting room and refreshments. Serena announced, "I'll reconvene the meeting in fifteen minutes in the other room. While getting your food, which Oona and Francis have so graciously provided I might add, please do continue your discussion of the release dates. We'll try to get a vote on that as soon as we reconvene."

For the next quarter hour they all mingled, mumbled, munched and gulped coffee or tea. Minds worked and shared. Hearts communicated and soared. Eyes locked momentarily and spoke volumes. Ears picked nuggets out of the rumble of many voices. Egos dropped into low key and the group became almost as one individual with a single, noble purpose. That purpose was of the highest order, humanity at its best, helping others with little thought for self.

When Serena reconvened the meeting, Angus asked to speak. "I have been adamant about delaying this news release. Ginger has been just as adamant about getting it out as soon as possible. This has created a little stalemate between us and locked up our entire group. Now, I have a question for you. Who's the expert in the world of the news? It sure isn't old War Whoop here is it? I, therefore, defer to our news expert. Let's go with the early release date."

The entire group broke into applause. As it died, Ginger stood and bowed slightly and graciously to Angus. "It's nice to hear a man defer openly to a woman in public. That, I say, is a real man." There followed more applause and a few cheers.

Serena smiled proudly as she looked at Angus. "I'll wager your cousin Chelton had a hand in that change, but I won't press it. With that decision behind us, let's try to set a tentative date for the data release. Fortunately, we aren't at loggerheads over that one. Unless I'm mistaken, once the second date is settled, the rest of the schedule falls right into place. John, you're the one with the longest history in that area. When do you think the data should be released?"

"Angus and I have divided the data in two distinct categories. The first, tentatively scheduled for November release, includes the distance and location data. With that information, any astronomer should be able to find the star if he is using a telescope with enough power. The Hubble space telescope should be able to see it clearly. That is, after it gets worked into their busy schedule which would probably take many months. After this, the first one who takes a *diffraction grating* spectrum and studies it long enough will discover the tremendous blue shift and will know the speed. Fortunately for us, it will be too close to the sun for an accurate spectrum to be obtained until at least October. Our third news release should be out prior to any discovery of the huge blue shift by other astronomers. Actually, I doubt astronomers using any of the big telescopes will schedule time to look for our ghost until the third news release is out. They are the only ones who could find that high blue shift, and they probably won't be looking. Once the third release is out, everything will break loose. That information will set the astronomers of the world on their ears. Every major astronomical installation on the planet will be studying the ghost from all viewpoints and in all wavelengths. The first one to plot its path will blow the lid off our little secret and the whole world will know. We must be the first. Fortunately, without the data only we possess, it will take at least six months for anyone to obtain the parallax measurements necessary to get even the slightest knowledge of the path the ghost will follow."

"Can you add anything to that, Angus," Serena asked?

"John covered it quite well. I just want to mention that anyone who obtains our parallax data, including the three sets of readings we have thus far obtained, could immediately determine the path as accurately as we have. For that reason, we are not going to include our parallax readings in the data release. That is a bit unusual, but I think we can get away with it since we are releasing the other data rather early on. As you know, my friend Pat Yamaguchi in Arizona, is working to confirm our data. Unfortunately, delays on using the new, six-meter telescope have held him up. I sent an encrypted e-mail asking him not to relate any of what I've told him to anyone else and to keep all data fully encrypted. I didn't want to phone him for obvious reasons. He e-mailed me back saying not to worry, his lips were sealed and the data was buried securely in junk. Pat's reliable and can be counted on to keep his mouth closed. OSI has not bothered him, so our encrypted e-mail must be working."

Serena posed a question. "I take it we can make those tentative data release dates firm at this point, at least until something pops up to change our plans?"

Angus and John both agreed. The CPM diagram was beginning to be a real action plan. The ranges of dates for the various actions were narrowing down. If only OSI would continue to keep a low profile, and no new action would upset the apple cart. They loosened up quite a bit and several conversations were going on in small groups. The night's activities were winding down. Much had been accomplished, and everyone felt good about it.

It was nearly eight when Serena asked for their attention. "Chelton and I have been discussing how far we have come and where we probably will go in the future. We each need to get back to other obligations and would like to head out as soon as practical. We will both be here at least until Monday when we will fly to Cincinnati together and then go on our separate ways. Either of us can be back in a single day if necessary. I'm certain there will be much for us to do in the future, individually and as a group. We will keep in touch by phone or the Internet. As you all know by now, the Internet can be used with encryption so effective even our government cannot crack it. I suggest we all learn how to do this and that we use secure communication methods for all messages. Chelton can help set this up before he leaves."

After each of the group stopped to thank Serena and Chelton for their help, Francis stood up and announced, "Oona and I would like to invite you all to our home for a cookout Sunday afternoon at one. We've come to be such good friends that we'd like to say good-bye to these two in style. No business, just some good old Hawaiian hospitality."

There was general agreement within the group, and, apparently, all would be there. With Ruth, Ali and Charlene helping, Oona and Francis packed up what remained of the things they brought.

Angus, Lani and Serena were in a group talking when Chelton came over with Ginger to talk to Serena. "Would you mind terribly if I left now? Ginger wants to show me around Hilo a bit if you don't mind going home alone."

"Certainly. Go ahead. I think I can manage," Serena replied quizzically. "Have fun," she called after them as they walked away. Then, turning to Lani and Angus she asked, "What do you suppose that's all about? I wonder? They're definitely an interesting couple."

Lani watched with cocked head and a slight grin curling the corners of her mouth as they walked away. "How about that!"

Angus grinned knowingly at the two women. "What's going on in those two matchmaking minds now? You two lit up like a Christmas tree when Chelton asked his question about Ginger showing him around. Of course, I wouldn't mind being a little mouse listening in on their present conversations. That might prove to be interesting."

Lani looked at Angus, her hands on her hips. "Well for goodness sake! We women are not the only interested parties."

The three of them had a hearty laugh and began discussing Ginger and Chelton going off together. It wasn't long before the entire remaining group was speculating about the two absent ones. It was kind and loving speculation of true friends about an interesting turn of events, completely devoid of malice and evil thoughts.

Serena broke up the gab session. "Well, Son, are you coming home or are you going to your hideout in the hills?"

"Yes, where are you going? Do you think OSI is going to come after you now?" Lani asked.

"I hadn't even thought about that until you brought it up. I don't know. Do you two think it's safe?"

"I say you chance it," Serena answered. "What do you say Lani?"

When Lani agreed, Angus replied. "I guess I'll go home. There are already two votes for, so I'd be outvoted anyway. I guess I just don't have a say in the matter."

Lani looked knowingly at Serena. "Well, he's finally having a reality moment."

"It's about time," she replied.

When all the food was picked up and packed, Charlene started to clean the floor.

John reassured her. "We've all had a full day. Our cleaning people come in tomorrow. Let them earn their pay. It's a lot cleaner than after most of our other meetings, believe me."

Angus stopped and talked to the Lanes. "I'm going to chance it and head for home. If you don't mind, I'll leave my things there for a few days, just in case. I plan to unwind for a day or two with the two most important women in my life. We'll try to forget about the ghost for the weekend and just enjoy ourselves."

"Good for you," Oona said, smiling. "You will be at our little party, won't you?"

"Wouldn't miss it. I'm sure everyone will be there."

It was about 8:30 when they finally closed up shop and headed for home.

17

Ginger and Chelton walked from the center and got into her car. "Do you mind if we leave the top down? It's such a beautiful night, and we can see and feel so much more out in the open."

"I'd prefer it. It makes you feel so free, so much a part of what's out there," Chelton replied, making a broad sweeping gesture with his arm as they drove away. "Funny. It's been a long time since I've ridden in an open car. Years and years. I can't even remember the last time."

"I love top-down driving. The only problem here in Hilo is the rain. You can't park your car with the top down without the chance for a soaking. I often put my top up several times a day."

"It's still worth it."

"I take it this is your first visit to our islands?"

"Strangely, it is. As much as I've traveled around the world, I've never been here before. It's a truly beautiful place, almost magical."

"Well, sir, where would you like to go or what would you like to see: Hilo's night life, our oceanfront, maybe the lava flowing into the sea near where the city of Kalapana used to be? Sometimes that can be a spectacular sight at night."

"How about you taking me to see what you'd like to show me. I feel certain you have a few of those."

"Right you are, Mr. Chum. They won't be terribly exciting, but they are truly peaceful and full of beauty."

"That sounds just like my style," Chelton responded, thinking to himself there was more to Ginger than meets the eye, more even than the woman he saw powerfully arguing her point against two strong men. He would find more surprises before the night was over.

Ginger drove west from Hilo into the foothills of Mauna Kea, not a long distance from where Angus was run down. She rounded a turn in the road and pulled up on a parking area used by sightseers to view a wide panorama, including part of Hilo and the southern part of the mountain upon which the Gemini observatory stood. When the car stopped, they both got out and walked to the barrier at the steep drop of the hillside. Off to the right, the lights of Hilo gleamed brightly in the contrasting darkness. To the left, the mountain loomed. Its outline could just barely be seen by the absence of stars. There were almost no lights at all on the mountain. Overhead, the Milky Way was clearly visible splotched across a sky full of stars. They stood there a long time, drinking in the glorious silence, broken now and then by the chirp of a nearby insect. High overhead the red planet Mars glowed, not far from where the ghost was hiding. The sight and the silence were almost overpowering to two tiny creatures viewing the vastness of the universe.

Chelton finally broke the quiet. "I don't know that I've ever seen the night sky more beautiful. When I was a little boy, Angus took me out many nights to the banks of the St. Lawrence, where we would gaze in wonder at the stars. After the frosts came in the fall, it would be dead silent, except for the barely perceptible rippling of the river. Angus would point to stars and call them by name. He taught me much about the stars, even at such an early age. He frequently said he wanted to be an astronomer. Now look where he is. His youthful ambitions have been fully realized."

"And what did you dream of doing? What was your burning ambition? Did you have one then?"

"Mine were not as lofty as his. He always had just that one ambition. I wanted to be a pilot, an actor, a bus driver, and, for a short period, an opera singer. Mostly I just wanted to be able to walk and play like my friends. After the second operation on my legs, I spent a long time in physical therapy and some psychological therapy to help me adjust to my new mobility. I didn't know it then, but there was a much larger mental adjustment required than physical. A young body heals quickly, but an injured psyche takes more time. The young woman who helped me in that adjustment was the first crush of my life. I was fourteen at the time, and she must have been at least twenty-five. Unlike others I have known, my friends and schoolmates never teased me about my infirmity. That was a benefit of growing up in a community much like an extended family."

"You were fortunate in that respect. So many children can be cruel to those who are different, so to speak."

"You're right there. That's when I finally became focused and developed a real ambition. I found a burning desire to help people in pain, mental and physical. By the time I went to college I had chosen to become a minister. I thought about being a physician for a time but felt I could better serve in a spiritual capacity. To that end I majored in psychology for my undergraduate degree before going to seminary. I never really wanted to preach, thinking I would better serve by being a counselor or chaplain."

"That's fascinating. I never heard of a preacher who didn't want to preach. I have read many news reports about your work, but never knew you were an ordained minister. I would say that however you reached your present position, you have definitely carved yourself a niche, a large and successful one I might add."

"Enough about me. Tell me just how you got into the news business and came to be in Hawaii. I gather you are not from here originally. I notice a barely perceptible New York or New Jersey lilt to your speech."

Ginger laughed. "You sure have me pegged. I'm a Long Island girl. Grew up in Port Washington with all the perks. My father was a New York investment banker who lived a bit on the financial brink most of the time. Several times we moved from small houses to big houses and then back again while I was growing up, depending on how my father was doing. Usually it didn't take him long to get back on top again, so mostly we lived in big houses. He died in his early fifties of lung cancer from a lifetime of smoking. Unfortunately, he left us during one of the financial lows. Mom had to sell the big house we had been in for two years. She bought a small one nearby within the same community. Dad kept his life insurance in force, so we weren't destitute. It was a terrible blow to me since we were quite close. I was in my last year of college at the time with all the ambition of the cheerleader I had been since high school. I had no idea what I was going to do with my life. At fifty, my mom went back to work as a legal secretary and started writing a legal information column for the New York Globe. She invested the proceeds from Dad's insurance wisely and was able to retire several years ago. She now writes a column for the local newspaper and still lives in that same little house. I guess she's the reason I became a reporter. After my dad died, I realized I had no plans for my life. At my mother's urging, I went to journalism school for a year after I received my B.A. degree.

"When I finally started to look for work, she introduced me to her boss at the Globe, asking him where a bright young journalist might find a job. In about two weeks, I started at the Globe as a proofreader. I knew I wouldn't be able to last long in that job. I'm not built for that kind of work, and it would have driven me crazy. It wasn't long before Pete Radcliff, from the newsroom, asked if I could help him with a series of articles he was writing about the life of rock musicians. He said he was too old to go to those concerts, so he asked me to go and take notes to help him write the series. As it turned out, I ended up writing all the information about the concerts. Pete was so impressed, he saw to it I got a raise and was moved into the newsroom as a junior reporter. When he then took the job to head up the News Service operation here in Hawaii, he asked me to come with him. Now, Mr. Chum, we're current on each other's lives, so what should we talk about?"

"It's interesting how two people from such different backgrounds can see things in such a similar fashion. Like the others, you share my concern about what will happen to humanity when the news of this terrible thing comes out. I've known a number of news people who seem to have no compassion at all. They would sell anyone or anything for a good news story. Here you sit with information about one of the biggest stories ever without breaking down doors to get the story published under your byline. I am seriously impressed."

"We're not all ghouls with the only mantra being to get the story in print. I know a number of associates who care deeply for the effect their work will have on the people involved. I will sadly admit, though, many others I know would fit your description. There have been serious betrayals and much damage done in the name of journalism by reporters who use the excuse, The people have a right to know. These reporters create much evil instead of making a judgement that is kinder and less self-serving. When I was young, my grandfather taught me to be my own person and not sell my soul for a buck. He was an interesting man, not successful financially, but he could talk on nearly any level with most anyone he met. He loved to tell stories. There were many a tall tale he told me about his younger days. I'm sure many of them were grossly exaggerated but most were probably partially true. When I was in my early teens, we were close. I learned a lot about principles from him, and it has stuck with me. He was my mother's dad and she also kept those principles going while I went through my terrible teens. Personal honor laced with compassion was a strong force in my whole family. I guess it's their fault I became me," she said breaking into a broad smile.

"We are both fortunate to have been born into such wise and caring families. That has a lot to do with whom we become and what we do when we mature. That kind of family background opens us to kindness and wisdom from others who may cross our paths for the rest of our lives."

"You're certainly right on that point!" Ginger replied emphatically. "I can feel the input my family gave me more and more each day. They imbued in me a liking for and an interest in all kinds of people. You, for instance, are a fascinating person, a real spellbinder. I'm happy our paths crossed."

"So am I. Speaking of fascinating people, I'm reminded of an incident about two years ago while on a late night flight from San Francisco to Atlanta. An older gentleman sat down next to me, and during our first few words, we both admitted to planning to sleep all the way to our destination. After the usual pleasantries of who we were, where we had been and where we were going, we continued talking. Before long, we both said we would rather talk than sleep. He was fascinating, and we were like old friends in just those few moments of conversation. He gave me some new insights that have had a positive effect on my life. Needless to say, neither of us had any sleep, just several hours of interesting conversation. When I mentioned I was a minister, he told me the story of an experience that had changed his life.

"As a young and thoughtful scientist, he had a great deal of difficulty with religion, especially since he was raised in a family deeply committed to Christ. One day he realized that both science and religion were searches for truth. Shortly after, he was having a heated discussion with a fundamentalist friend, the evolution-creation battle, when a miraculous realization and idea came to him. The only thing they were arguing about was the method and the timetable. They actually agreed on the things that mattered. Think about it. Both the Big Bang theory of the creation of the universe and evolution theory are close to the creation story in the Bible. As far as the earth is concerned, both say all life on earth was created out of dust. Why, then, couldn't evolution be the method God used to create the myriad forms of life on this planet? The Bible doesn't define the method, just that he caused it to happen. As far as the argument some biblical *experts* make about creation happening some six thousand years ago, a little error in math by the ancients is understandable. After all, no one knew about dinosaurs back then and today it's hard to deny their existence or when they lived. When he first came up with the concept, he wanted to cram it down everyone's throat, and no one would listen. He has since softened his approach and been somewhat successful calling it 'reconciliation' in his efforts to get its message across."

"It makes lots of sense to me," Ginger said thoughtfully. "As a factual, thinking person, I rather discounted religion because of that conflict. I felt most religious people were either ignorant or in it for what they could get. I had little respect for ministers, especially those TV evangelists making big bucks and living the high life. I know many did kind things, but I was convinced they were merely taking advantage of vulnerable people. I know, there are many fine, honorable people in the ministry who do truly astounding and inspirational things, yourself for instance. However, most churches and ministers leave me cold. Now a religion or minister that followed the doctrine you just described, I could find very interesting."

"For you, that's a beginning at least," Chelton commented thoughtfully. "There are many out there, like yourself, who have become disenchanted with religion. They are good people who despise the hypocrisy, pettiness and downright cruelty they see in some churchgoers. The only way to change that is to get involved and become a positive influence. Usually all that is needed for evil to win is for good people to do nothing."

"I've heard that at home. My father often repeated those words," Ginger commented with a smile. She was beginning to feel a strong attraction to this man who was so different from most men she had known.

"Before we left the plane, my new friend gave me a card that now holds a prominent place on my desk. He told me he had written those words many years before. I will try to repeat them as written. 'When truth and belief come to conflict, it is better to change one's belief to fit the truth, than to change the truth to fit one's belief. Beliefs are the creations of men while truths are the creations of God.' To me, those are powerful words with much meaning that have been a valuable guide since I first heard them. Right out of the blue and from a complete stranger, I gained some precious knowledge."

"Those *are* well-chosen words. I'd like you to write them down for me if you would."

"Gladly." Chelton looked intently at her as they both grew silent. Warm feelings flowed through his entire being. The depth of her pleasantly intrigued him. "You are a fascinating woman. I was impressed by how you stuck to your guns against Angus about the news releases. Angus has strong opinions and doesn't give up easily, but you kept flailing away at him until he caved. Or should I say, realized he was dealing with a woman who knew her trade. Many a person, woman or man, would have given in to his dominant strength. I was secretly applauding your victory."

"Well, thank you. I've seen news stories that were suppressed sneak out the back door and bite the ones who suppressed them. I certainly didn't want that to happen here. I saw it as a victory for our group. If someone else beat us to the punch with any part of this, all our efforts will have been in vain. Pandora's box will be open for certain."

They walked slowly back to the car, leaned against it and looked up at the sky. Ginger leaned against Chelton and lay her head on his shoulder. The warmth of her body felt good in the cooling air. The smell of her wind-tossed hair was powerfully delicious, an intoxicating pheromone of attraction.

"What shall we talk about now?" she said softly.

Gently he turned her around until they faced each other. At that moment, he thought she was the most beautiful woman he had ever seen. Their faces grew closer until they were but a few inches apart. "I don't want to talk about anything," Chelton whispered, his eyes glistening.

No words needed to be spoken as their faces drew closer slowly and their arms circled their bodies until they were completely embraced. The thrill and rapture of that first kiss coursed through them in myriad waves, overwhelming their senses. They stood there for a long time, clinging like intertwined vines, sparkles of starlight shining in their eyes. They moved back from their kiss and looked at each other in silence. It was a surprising, magical moment that neither had expected. When they finally sat down in the car, they turned facing each other, holding hands. Their eyes were locked in their own special embrace. When Chelton opened his mouth to speak, Ginger gently closed his lips with her finger then leaned over and kissed him again and again.

It was much later when she finally said ever so softly, "Now, what did you start to say?"

"Nothing that my arms, lips and eyes haven't said already," he answered gently. "Except maybe, what a marvelous surprise."

"Most eloquent," she whispered, adding after a long pause, "I, too, was surprised. Incredibly surprised."

They sat in the car for a long time, savoring the precious wonder and excitement of tender, new passion. Kisses interrupted quiet conversation which followed each kiss. They shared many of their dreams, joys and sorrows with each other before finally heading down the hill toward Hilo.

Ginger drove carefully, a multitude of delicious thoughts coursing through her love-muddled mind. "I haven't quite put my feet back on the ground, but what about tomorrow? I had scheduled some work, which I no longer feel like doing. Since you will be leaving so soon, I would like to spend the day with you."

"Then I will instruct my social secretary that my calendar for the next day or so is filled to overflowing with a beautiful, intelligent lady. Everything else is to be set aside."

"Thank you, kind sir. I will be at your beck and call," Ginger said coquettishly, adding with a smile, "I'm not going to last much longer without a wisecrack. I hope that doesn't destroy the wonder of the night."

"Have no fear, milady. Laughter and love are the handmaidens of joy. It's impossible to keep one without having the other. There can be no love without laughter and little joy without them both."

"Very well said," Ginger answered, an amazed chuckle in her voice. "That doesn't happen to be a quote does it?"

"If I repeat it word for word, I will be quoting one Chelton Chum from the night of June 22, 2001," he replied, a twinkle of mischief in his eyes.

"I don't know," she replied, her tone rising in question. "That sounds almost Shakespearian."

"Not unless Shakespeare was a Mohawk," Chelton answered.

Though soft passion had given way to humorous conversation, the magic of the evening would carry over at least till tomorrow. They continued their light conversation all the way to Chelton's hotel making plans for the following day. Ginger would pick him up at eight for breakfast and they would take it from there. It was difficult for them to part, but after sitting in her car in front of his hotel for nearly an hour, they finally did. Two thoughts flowed through each of their minds separately, but almost in unison, "How did this happen? How long will the magic last?"

Neither would sleep soundly this night.

*   *   *

Lani, Serena and Angus walked into Angus' apartment and collapsed in the living room. This was the first time they had been able to relax for many days. The calculations and meetings were up-to-date, and OSI seemed to be off their backs. A schedule and plan of action were now fully in place and everyone seemed pleased with what had been done.

"I can hardly believe how much we have accomplished in the last few days," Lani commented.

Serena replied, "Definitely. It's been a productive week or so. As of this Monday, I couldn't imagine we would be where we are right now. I hope OSI doesn't come barging back in."

"You can say that again!" Angus replied emphatically. "If what Frank Ito did has real teeth, we may have seen the last of their interference. The next important bit of information we need is the results of the work Dr. Botkin is doing. We won't see that for at least a month or more and I'm quite anxious about it."

They chatted for more than an hour, mostly trying to decide what to do for the next two days. It was nearly ten when the phone rang and a startled Angus jumped up. As Serena answered, Angus admitted, "I've got to get over that. This business with OSI has me jumping at every little thing."

"It's your mother, Lani. She has invited us to go fishing with them tomorrow. They have friends who live on Hilo Bay who have a boat and a standing Saturday invitation for them to go fishing. It will mean lots of fresh air, relaxation and good company. I say we go for it, unless you have other plans."

"The Millers," Lani replied excitedly. "They're terrific people. They were our neighbors in Kalapana until the lava drove us all out. He and Daddy used to work together before he sold his plumbing business and retired. I've been fishing with them many times. There's plenty of room on his boat, and we'll have lots of fun. How about it, Mr. Sitting Duck? You game for a little fishing?"

"There you go. I'm outvoted again and I didn't even get a chance to speak. Sure. Go ahead. I say we go for it," Angus replied.

Serena received the instructions from Charlene. They would all meet at six sharp for breakfast at a little restaurant near the dock where the Millers keep their boat. Lani knew the place well since she had been there many times. Ali would bring some of his equipment and the Millers would furnish the rest.

After some discussion about the day to come, they decided to retire and get a good night's rest. Angus rode home with Lani, taking his bicycle to ride back. As they drove, Angus prayed silently that OSI would not interfere. By the time he arrived back home without incident, he felt more assured that they were finally off his back. He would find they were not completely done with him yet.

*   *   *

At a quarter to six in the morning, Lani stopped to pick them up for the fifteen minute ride to the restaurant. Angus and Serena had just finished packing their sweats and a few other items Lani had suggested when she arrived.

As they walked to the restaurant, Lani remarked, "Now, aren't you glad you brought those light jackets? The early mornings can be a bit coolish and a little damp here by the bay."

"Never thought to wear anything but a shirt," Angus replied as they entered. "I see everyone's here already."

They joined the Namahoes and Millers who were already seated at a large round table. Lani gave them each a hug and then introduced everyone. The Millers were both large people. Dan looked Irish, and Maria was obviously native Hawaiian.

"Where are you from originally," Angus asked Dan.

"I was born on a farm in Missouri, but grew up on Oahu," he began. "My father was in the Navy and stationed at Pearl for a number of years. He was on the battleship Arizona when the Japanese attacked. I was only ten when he was killed. My mother stayed on in Honolulu durin' the war, workin' as an aide at the big Navy hospital there. She met and married a local restaurant owner. I spent ten years in the Navy myself. When I had enough of seein' the world, I quit and became a plumber."

"My dad died in war too," Angus said, establishing a common bond. "I never knew him. He was killed in Viet Nam when I was a baby."

"Such a shame," Maria shook her head and looked sympathetically at Serena, then changing the subject she broke into a broad smile. "I guess you can tell where I'm from."

When Angus replied, "Ireland?" they all had a hearty laugh.

Maria looked to be about fifteen years younger than Dan. "I met this haole when he hired me to work in his new shop in 1966. I was just out of high school then. After a few years he asked me to marry him. He claims I was so expensive that the only way he could keep me was to marry me."

"Sure looks like it stuck," Serena said. "Do you have children?"

Dan's eyes dropped as his face changed into an expression of pain and sadness. "We have two boys. They moved to the mainland for work and rarely make it back to see us. Our grandchildren have never been here and know us only from pictures and phone calls."

During the silence that followed, Dan and Maria looked at each other, tears glistened in their eyes. Finally Serena broke the silence. "How sad for you and such a loss for them."

The Millers were friendly, down-to-earth people, a little rough-hewn, but real. After the momentary silent reflections, happy animated conversations returned again. In one of these, the subject of football and the past season came up.

Suddenly Dan paused. Looking intently at Angus, he said. "Darned if you ain't *that* Angus Thomas, number 35. I never put it together till just now. There can't be that many guys named Angus Thomas runnin' around. You sure look like him. I saw you in the Pro Bowl. When was that? Had to be seven . . . eight years ago. You were one unbelievable runnin' back. How'd you ever end up here in Hilo?"

Angus admitted his identity and gave a short rundown on what had happened to him since he retired from football. Dan couldn't get over it. He sat shaking his head, looking at Angus and then at the rest of them. "Maria. Don't you remember that guy I was so excited about back durin' that game? I kept yellin' about him every time he handled the ball? This . . . is . . . that . . . guy!"

Maria looked at Dan. Her broad Hawaiian face, almost blank for a moment, finally broke into a huge smile. "I'm sorry, hon, I just don't remember. You get so excited at all the games you go to. Even the local high school games. I'm not a big sports fan you know." She then directed her gaze at the rest of the group. "I enjoy watching, but I don't get into it at all like he does. We've been to several Pro Bowl games. They were thrilling, but I can't remember much about what happened at this late date. He's the football nut. I hope you're not insulted. I do remember hearing your name though. It's a hard one to forget, even for a Hawaiian."

Angus laughed. "I'm sure there are lots of good people who have never heard of Angus Thomas. I understand completely," he assured her.

"We'd best be on our way," Dan said as he pushed back from the table. "I can hear those fish barkin' all the way in here. Let's us go a fishin'."

With that, they headed out of the restaurant and toward Dan's boat. On their way Dan explained, "She's not a beautiful yacht, but she looks beautiful to me. She's got character. She's also good 'n sturdy with plenty of room. At thirty-five feet, she can handle just about anythin' that old Pacific can hand her short of a typhoon, and I'm not sure she couldn't weather most of those. She's got twin diesels that are in topnotch condition and can move us at a respectable speed while bein' stingy on the fuel. When we get there, you'll know how much I care for her because she carries my lovely Maria's name on her stern."

When they came to the boat, Angus could see what Dan meant. Obviously, she had been covering the waters for a number of years. In spite of her age, the boat was clean and neat, shipshape indeed. When Dan started the engines, their throaty growl spoke of smooth power and great reliability. It would be a safe and comfortable trip. Shortly after leaving the bay, a group of dolphins picked up "Maria" leading them toward the beckoning blue swells. It would be a marvelous day, a marvelous day indeed.

*   *   *

At breakfast Saturday morning, Chelton said he would like to see more of the island. Ginger suggested they drive around the island and visit a few tourist sights. They could easily cover the two hundred or so miles before nightfall if they didn't stop at too many of the sights or stay too long if they did.

After breakfast they stopped at the visitors bureau on Keawe Street and picked up some maps and other information before heading out. They drove north along the coast, where Chelton commented on the many coastal villages with their unpronounceable Hawaiian names. They left the coast and drove up through Waimea. There they passed the Parker Ranch, the largest individually owned cattle ranch in the United States. According to the information Chelton read out loud to Ginger, it had been founded in 1847 by a sailor from New England who married King Kamehameha's granddaughter. It now comprises 225 thousand acres, seven of which were donated for the site of the headquarters for the Keck telescopes. They went north on the Kohala Mountain Road to the northernmost point of the island where they visited Mookini Helau, a fifteen-century-old temple complex still considered sacred. As they walked hand-in-hand, their conversation constantly flitted from history to the beauty around them to their growing feelings for each other.

They next headed south along the Akoni Pule highway on the coast then continued south past miles of desolate broken lava rocks and into Kailua-Kona, where they stopped for lunch. Continuing down the Kona Coast and then east on the Mamalahoa Highway, they stopped for a leisurely, barefoot walk on the black sand beach at Punaluu. They marveled at the crashing surf and the many sea turtles they sighted. It was a delightful, romantic pause in a phenomenally beautiful day. They sat on the beach for some time listening to the surf and watching for turtles. After a long silence they began to talk about their growing relationship.

"I'm rather awestruck by this growing feeling about the two of us," Chelton began. "I have some idea where it's headed, and from your words, I take it you feel those same giddy heart-fluttering sensations. I now hate to think of leaving on Monday, but I must. Where do we go from here?"

"This has been at least one of the most glorious days of my life. Maybe the *most* glorious," Ginger replied. "Of course, I feel those same magical feelings. I, too, can see where it's going and dread your leaving as well. I have learned so much about you since last evening. It feels almost as if I've always known you. At the same time, it's a completely new and almost frightening feeling for me. I think this actually started when we worked so closely together with the group. Even then, I felt as if I had known you forever. How long can this state of delicious confusion last?"

"Maybe a lifetime. If we treasure these moments and work hard at being us, together. I have a favorite saying, the source of which I know not. 'Plan your life as if you would live forever and live each day as if it were your last.' I think that may be an excellent guide for us."

"I like that," Ginger responded, repeating his words slowly.

It was early for any but the most tentative kind of commitment. She knew it would take time for that excitement of new love to grow into a less stimulating but more stable, comfortable and longer lasting relationship. His coming departure loomed heavy in her heart. She would not let the growing pain of it alter her enjoyment of the remaining time they had.

Turning to him she said softly, "When do you think we can be together again? I have no idea of your plans for the future and you have no idea of mine. Do you ever take a vacation?"

"As a matter of fact, I haven't had a real vacation for years. What about you?"

"The last few years I've been going home to St. Regis for the few days between projects, long weekends mostly, and those were few and far between. I haven't taken more than a few days off at a time since I left seminary. When I was traveling out of the country, even those mini vacations were impossible. Hawaii is a long way from New

York, and that distance will make getting together difficult. We'll have to think a lot about that and what it means to us. This thing we are dealing with—this ghost—it puts a rather new light on future planning, doesn't it?"

"That thought has crossed my mind several times since learning about it," Ginger commented as they walked back to the car. "Between the ghost and now you, my world has been turned topsy-turvy. Talk about bad news, good news. One thing is for certain. I'm going to concentrate more on enjoying life and the people around me. Staring at ultimate doom makes you reassess your values, doesn't it?"

"I'll say. It also heightens your senses and raises your appreciation for what you have in the present. Should our worst fears prove to be the case, I will feel most sad about those children born into a world about to end. It's one thing to face your own doom. It's quite another to face the extermination of all life on the planet. Somehow, I just don't see that as part of God's plan. Maybe it's just the optimism within me, but I think the ghost will pass with little physical effect on the earth. It will, however, have a tremendous effect on humanity. Facing such a doom will truly test mankind. Maybe we will come through this far better managers of this fragile world."

They continued talking about their future as they drove north on Highway 11. They stopped to view the immense Kilauea Caldera, marveling at the huge opening in the earth and the craggy, moonlike appearance. They continued north, stopping to eat at a small roadside restaurant just south of Hilo. When finally they arrived back at Chelton's hotel, the sun was dropping behind Mauna Kea. They headed for the top of the hotel to watch the light disappearing from Hilo Bay.

They sat for a long time, slowly sipping some wine and gazing at the bay, hearts warmed by the luscious words of new lovers. When finally they started discussing the next day, Chelton suggested, "Why don't we head up to Ruth's church in the morning? It can't be far, and I would love to see her in action."

She looked at him with a sheepish grin. "I don't know. It's been a long time since I've been in a church. You don't suppose it would collapse, do you?"

The corners of Chelton's eyes crinkled as he laughed. "I think it can stand the stress. Do you know where it is and how to get there?"

"I know it's not far. We can check the church listings in the phone book. How many Methodist churches can there be between here and where Kalapana used to be?"

"I've a far better idea. I'll call Lani and find out from her. Maybe she, Angus and his mother would like to join us? That OK with you?"

"Then I won't have you all to myself," Ginger answered with an exaggerated pout. "I suppose I can live with it."

"You're kidding, right?"

"Of course, silly," was Ginger's immediate, laughing response.

"We'll stop by my room and call them now. Ten o'clock isn't too late to call Angus. We'll try there first."

Serena answered when he called. "Where have you been? We called to see if you wanted to join us for dinner, and no one answered then or several calls later. Did you get our message about going fishing? We called early and told the desk to give you the message after eight. We assumed you'd be up by then."

Chelton glanced at the flashing message signal on his phone and realized he may have other messages as well. "No. I haven't retrieved any of my messages yet. I left early this morning and just now returned. How did you enjoy the fishing?"

"It was a fabulous day. We didn't catch many fish but had a fantastic time on the ocean. We can tell you all about it tomorrow. Incidentally, we were calling to tell you that Lani, Angus and I have been invited to join the Namahoes for church in the morning. You've been invited too. Would you like to join us?"

"What a coincidence. I was just calling to find out the location of Ruth's church. Just a few minutes ago we decided to go there ourselves. We'd love to join you."

"We? Who's the *we*?"

"Oh. Pardon me. Ginger and I spent the most glorious day touring the island, and we just decided we would like to attend Ruth's church."

"Friday evening and then all day Saturday? You two must have hit it off well, quite well indeed."

"Yes. We found we have much in common. We've thoroughly enjoyed each other's company. We'll tell you all about it tomorrow, and you can share your fishing experiences with us. Where shall we meet you?"

After making arrangements to meet the others in the morning, the two sat down on the couch. They shared the soft words of two people falling in love. With Ginger snuggled warmly against his chest, they talked until almost two. Finally Ginger decided she would have to go if she was to get any sleep at all before she had to get up and get ready for church. They parted slowly, sharing the loss they now both felt when alone. This night they both slept soundly.

*   *   *

The five met in front of the Mokuloa Hotel and headed for church in two cars. At first, Serena wanted to ride with Chelton and Ginger to find out just what was going on there but thought better of it. She would let them pick the time to talk to her if, indeed, there was much to talk about. She was patiently curious, not nosey. When the Namahoes joined them at the small church, they were a happy, animated group of seven. Entering the church, the group quieted. Ruth spotted them talking to the greeters, an elderly couple with enormous smiles. She stopped long enough to say how pleased she was they were all there and gave each a hug.

Before the service began, Pastor Ruth proudly introduced each of the four visitors as they stood together. There was a noticeable stir when Angus and Chelton were named since many there knew of their fame. Ruth's sermon was on helping those who were dealing with fear and danger in their lives. It was obvious to the group, she was subtly beginning to prepare her congregation for the frightful menace to come. It was a warm and encouraging sermon. Chelton could see these people would be well comforted when the time to need comfort came, at least in the beginning. The response from the congregation showed how much they loved Ruth. As in many churches, there was a preponderance of older members and just a few children. Noticing this, Chelton thought how sad it was the secular world had been so successful at weaning young people from the churches with the resulting moral and ethical decay. He wondered how this would change when the awful news reached them and the realization of what that news meant sank in.

When the service was over, Charlene guided them into a room where coffee and snacks were being served and fellowship was encouraged. Most were eager to meet the visitors and some lively conversations sprung up. These were friendly people from a mostly rural area. They were just a bit out of the main stream of society. Life here moved at a slower pace than in Honolulu and much slower than in the other big cities of America. Most lived a far simpler, happier life than their big city counterparts on the mainland.

As they paused to talk about the Lanes' cookout, Serena, silently observant, noticed the telltale looks that occasionally flashed between Chelton and Ginger. Finally, she could bear it no longer, and, quietly guiding them away from the rest, she asked, "What's with it with you two? I don't want to intrude, but every once in a while you look like two moonstruck kids. Is it my imagination or is there something going on? You don't have to answer and I won't press you, but sooner or later someone's going to have the same suspicions I have."

Without hesitation Chelton replied, "Yes. There is something going on. It's all so new, and we don't know yet where it will lead us. Ginger will agree we found a great deal to like in each other the night before last and during our day together yesterday. We plan on continuing to see each other whenever we can."

"We were both surprised at how powerful that mutual attraction was when it struck," Ginger added, looking intently at Chelton. "It's still new, and we are both a little cautious."

"Don't you be too cautious," Serena quipped with a grin. "From what I've seen and heard you two have been bitten by the same bug that bit Angus and Lani. You'll get no flak from me."

Chelton smiled and replied, "Thanks, Sunflower. You're a jewel."

"Watch out for some merciless kidding when your cousin finds out. Of course, he'll probably be the last one to notice what's going on if you don't make a point of telling him. Lani will know what's happening long before he will."

"What will I know is happening before whom?" Lani asked as she joined them.

Deftly shifting subjects, Serena answered, "I just finished saying that you would have Angus all wrapped up before he even knows what's happening."

"We all know that," Lani answered disdainfully. Then, turning to Ginger, she said, "You look like the proverbial cat that swallowed the canary. What cooks?"

"What did I say?" Serena said pointedly to Ginger and Chelton. "He'll definitely be last."

"I'm lost," Lani confessed. "I feel like I just walked in on a joke and heard only the punch line. What gives?"

"It seems that the two of us are about half a year or more behind you and your astronomer," Ginger replied.

"Oh my. You two? That's absolutely fantastic. I thought you looked a bit cozy," Lani remarked haltingly, an incredulous look on her face.

"It's new to us, Lani, and we don't know where it is leading yet, so don't be over anxious," Chelton said firmly.

"I know just how you feel. I think it took Angus and me about fifteen seconds to decide to pursue our relationship after that first magic moment and three months or so before we realized we had something long lasting. Since then we've grown a lot, learned a lot and prayed a lot for a future."

"I hope we can be that fortunate. Sadly, we won't be able to be together as much as you two have," Ginger replied, a pained expression on her face.

"As much as I hate to keep these things to myself, I suppose it would be best to let the others find out on their own," Lani said.

"That will be enjoyable, watching and knowing and seeing just when others figure it out. My money is still on Angus to be last," Serena replied.

"He'll have a hard time outlasting my dad," Lani said with a smile. "Men can be so blind to such things, sometimes even when they are in the middle of them."

"My bet is that all the women in our group will know before the first man realizes what's going on," Serena commented haughtily. "Even if we never tell any of them."

As they all drifted slowly toward their cars, Serena thought to herself, *Chelton has always avoided women like the plague. Ginger is so much flashier and more worldly than my picture of the woman he'd go for. I hope it works out well.* She liked Ginger, so her thoughts were all positive about the two of them. She still thought it to be an unusual match.

"See you later," Ginger said as she and Chelton drove off.

The rest soon left and headed for home to change into more casual attire for the Lanes' gathering.

*   *   *

As the guests were arriving, Francis was busy barbecuing chicken and pieces of pineapple on the grill. A long table on the patio was covered with vegetable dishes and plates of fresh fruits. There were some traditional Hawaiian and Japanese appetizers as well. It was a splendid luau without the traditional pig. The Lanes knew how to throw a party. Finally Francis announced dinner was ready. After some complimentary comments were offered by several of the guests, Ruth offered grace. The next half hour was spent consuming the wondrous assortment of foods and drinks while warm conversations flowed freely. It was a fantastic party with a group of kind and gracious people who had become close friends because of a small, distant star. After they all pitched in and cleared the patio of empty glasses and dirty dishes, they relaxed for an afternoon of pleasant company.

A sudden silence gripped the group and all eyes were drawn to the patio entrance where two uninvited guests had appeared. It was Jack Wells and Yvonne Techmeyer of OSI. Anger and fear were a few of the emotions that ran through everyone in the group. *How did they know to come here? Why can't they leave us alone? What's going to happen now? What are we going to do?* These were a few of the many questions that coursed through their thoughts during several uncomfortably quiet moments. It was as if everything stood still, frozen in time.

The men all stood up in one common motion of preparation for action. The women tensed, but remained seated, their eyes riveted on the intruders. Jack Wells raised his right hand palm forward in the universal sign that said hold everything. His left hand held a packet of papers.

"Pardon the intrusion, please. I ask you to hear me out. We came because we agreed to do certain things. We chose this time and place to display our knowledge of your movements while helping to prove our agreement was sincere. The agreed upon information about our surveillance and our assurances of its cessation are contained in the papers we are delivering to you. By leaving peacefully, we hope to demonstrate our desire to cooperate and not interfere. We would like to learn more about the work of both your group and Dr. Thomas in the future. We are admittedly suspicious that there is something vital you are keeping from us. Your actions alone can dispel our suspicions. I know you are distrustful of OSI, and we regret the actions that fostered that distrust. We are not like the gestapo or KGB and truly regret your thinking so. That some possibly inappropriate actions triggered those thoughts is true. We feel some of your actions were wrong as well." As he finished, he walked over and handed the packet of papers to an astounded Angus.

Yvonne then looked directly at Angus. "We will leave now. Please accept our apology for interrupting your party. We did so only to underline our desire to keep our end of the agreement. We are assuming you will keep your part. There will be no more unannounced meetings."

When she finished, Yvonne turned and followed Jack down the walk to the driveway. Everyone was stunned. The OSI agents were well down the walk before it sank in and the group reacted to break the overpowering silence. Angus was the first to speak. "I can't believe my eyes and ears. You all witnessed that little scene. Can it be true? Do you suppose they actually meant what they said?"

After about twenty minutes of lively discussions of this latest development and the contents of the packet, Francis stood up and said, "Time alone will tell us if what they said is true. I say we've earned some personal time away from OSI and the ghost. Let's put this aside and get back to it. Do I have any dissenters?"

A general rumble of agreement passed through the group. There were no dissenters. In a short time they were back to normal with laughter and pleasant conversations again dominating their activities.

By late in the afternoon all the women became aware of the action going on between Chelton and Ginger. Those in the know were together in hushed conversation with occasional laughter for some time when Ali suddenly asked, "What's going on in that hen party over there? You sound as if you've all caught a case of the giggles."

"You men are so blind," Charlene replied.

"You are so oblivious to what's happening around you," Ruth added.

"Can't you see what's going on before your very eyes?" Oona asked a little contemptuously.

"You mean the goo-goo eyes between those two?" John asked walking over to the growing group and shocking all of the women into surprised silence.

"Well, yes," was all Serena could muster.

"We noticed that a long time ago. Angus said they reminded him of Lani and he right after the New Year's luau," Ali added. "We figured they had enough of a problem, so we didn't say anything."

"I can't believe it. They did notice," Serena admitted. "Just who among you was the first to comment about them? We'd all like to know."

"I think it was Francis who first said something to me," John answered. "I was wondering as well when he asked Ali and me about them."

Ali added, "When Francis said something about them, I realized I had noticed they were staying together most of the time. Shortly after that, Angus came over and wanted to know what we were talking about. When we told him he looked over at them and said he thought we were right. That's when he made the comment about them reminding him of Lani and him last New Year's Eve."

"Then I *was* right," Serena crowed triumphantly. "He was the last one to notice."

"What's all this hubbub about?" Angus asked as he and Francis finally joined the rest in the center of the patio. They all grinned and laughed looking toward the new couple who were totally engrossed in each other for the moment. They grew silent, watching intently.

Suddenly aware of the quiet attention from the center of the patio, the pair snapped out of their trance. Chelton was the first to speak. "I believe we've been found out," he directed to Ginger.

"No. They don't know a thing," Ginger said haughtily. "They just think they do."

With those comments they walked over to the rest just a bit nervously. It was a tense, but warm moment for them. The discovery and confirmation of a new love affair can be a very unnerving experience. Balanced precariously on an emotional brink, unsure, uncommitted, the unknown future full of pitfalls yet deliriously giddy from hormones and happy hearts, the two admitted to what everyone now knew. Laughter, hugs, kind questions and a few serious comments filled the next few minutes.

Chelton finally said, "Thanks so much for your kindness and encouragement. We both know this is only a beginning. We are dismayed at having to part so soon in our newfound relationship and are planning to spend more time together as soon as we can arrange to do so. I do not relish leaving tomorrow."

"I hate it!" Ginger added emphatically. "I had a notion to just drop everything and run off with him until my practical side took control. I've some vacation time due, and we plan to use that soon."

Excitement over the new lovers finally faded away as the party continued and then began to wind down of its own accord. It was still light when they all parted and headed home. Tomorrow would be a day of real partings.

*   *   *

Ginger, Lani and Angus took Serena and Chelton to the airport. They planned to fly together to Cincinnati where Chelton would change planes for New York. Angus arranged a charter flight to Watertown for Serena with his old friend, Warren. Serena was particularly anxious to get back to the inn to take the load off Kat. After some teary good-byes, the three headed back.

As they rode along to get Ginger's car, Ginger mused, "You're the first close friends I've made since I came here a year ago. I've been so immersed in my new job, I haven't taken time to meet new people socially. With family and other close friends so far away, gaining friends as close as you is a real treasure. I have several acquaintances at the news bureau in Honolulu and then there's Mililani Keo, the only other person in our tiny Hilo office. These were my only friends until I joined your group at Gemini. You've never met Mili. She's a jolly, roly-poly woman of about fifty who handles the phone, runs the computer and knows just about everyone and everything that happens in the islands. For years Mili maintained the office for many reporters before me. They seldom stay here in Hilo more than a year or two."

As she drove, Lani turned to Ginger. "Yes, we certainly have gotten close. Why don't we set a day each week to have lunch together? We can even let Mr. Football here join us occasionally."

"Great idea. Wednesday is usually my easiest. How does that sound to you?"

"OK with me. We'll also have to arrange times to maintain and implement the news releases."

"We could have those meetings right after we meet for lunch. Where should we go? My office or yours?" Ginger joked.

Angus finally chimed in. "I don't know, the two of you together sounds like a threat to all Hilo males. Who knows what evil lurks in the minds of conniving women?"

"I trust we can ignore the jealous comments from the Neanderthal," Lani quipped as they stopped behind Ginger's car.

After good-byes, they watched Ginger enter her car and head for her office. "I think it's so exciting about Ginger and Chelton, don't you?" Lani asked as they drove along.

"Yes. They're certainly an interesting couple. I hope they get to see each other once in a while. I would have hated leaving you a few days after we found each other."

Lani was almost teary eyed. "Yes, that's sad."

After a few silent moments, her face brightened. "Remember what you suggested several weeks ago when you thought you might have to go to Chile?"

"What? No, I haven't the slightest idea what you are referring to."

"C'mon, hon. You know what I mean. About us."

"What about us?"

"Don't be so difficult and obstinate. You know precisely what I mean."

"You couldn't be talking about my proposal of marriage could you? I withdrew that long ago."

"There are times, Dr. Thomas, when I could beat on you. I don't remember any withdrawal. I'll sue for breach of promise."

"Well. What do you suggest?"

"Let's do it, soon."

"Do my ears deceive me or did I just receive a decent proposal?"

"You proposed to me, you cruel monster. I've decided to accept your proposal—in spite of your cruelty."

"You waited until after my mother left. How are you going to get her approval?"

"You'll get a whole lot of disapproval from your mother if you don't marry me. Of that I'm certain."

"I'll have to agree with you there. You've done as good a con job on her as you have on me."

"Ooooh! You can be so infuriating when I'm trying to be serious. I think we're ready and so do you."

"How can I be sure you're serious? Last time you brushed me off like yesterday's newspaper."

"Angus," she announced sharply, pulling her car up to the curb and shutting off the engine. "Stop your darned foolishness and help me figure out a date and all the rest. We have much to do to find the best time and place for everybody and everything. I need your help."

Reaching over and grasping her hands, Angus said softly, "You surely know I'm right with you on this. It's just that your eyes flash so beautifully when I tease you. That must be Pele's fire in the back of those eyes."

Lani still acted a bit peeved. "Don't you think you can soft soap me with those words." Then her face morphed slowly into a girlish grin. "I'll bet you say that to all the girls."

With that she threw her arms around him and gave him a big kiss. They sat there holding each other in silence for several moments, oblivious to all the traffic and people around them. The magic of their love was still growing.

"What do you think, really?" she asked as she started the car and pulled back into traffic. "We've not talked seriously about this, at least not with any definite ideas in mind. Two families living so far apart pose much difficulty."

"Believe it or not, I have given that a great deal of thought. I even have a plan roughly in mind. I'd like us to talk it over with Ruth if you agree with me about it."

"OK, what's this plan? Have we time to get into it before we get to work or should we hold it for later?"

"I think I can outline it now. Then you can think about it and later we can hammer out any changes you might think of. OK?"

"All right, shoot."

With enthusiasm Angus began telling of his ideas. "We'll get married here at Ruth's church and with your family and friends. Then we will go to St. Regis for a Mohawk ceremony with my family. We'll have two weddings with twice the fun."

"I don't know. Won't your family feel slighted, not being there for the first ceremony? I would feel a little guilty."

"Nonsense. Any of my family that wanted to make the trip could come here. I'm sure Mom and Chelton would, maybe even Kat and

Peter. We could do the same thing in reverse from St. Regis. Anyone could go there as well and no one would feel slighted."

"Let me think about that. It sounds OK, but later I'd like to discuss it in more detail as you said. What about our honeymoon? Should we go to Niagara Falls? I'll bet I'd be one of few girls married in Hawaii who honeymooned there, maybe the first one."

"I'm sure between the two of us we can work out a great plan," Angus said as they pulled into the Op Center parking lot. It would take a while to get back into the swing of things at work after such an eventful, memorable three days.

*   *   *

Ginger was subdued driving to her office. The pain of being newly parted from Chelton gripped her heart. She knew she would miss him terribly, particularly until the time when she would know when they would meet again. Vivid memories of the excitement and wonder of the last few days flashed continually through her mind bringing both joy and pain. She knew she had never felt quite like this before.

Come on now, girl. You're a tough news reporter. Get back some of that hard objectivity, she repeated to herself. She had little success. Tears ran down her cheek several times before she stepped into her office.

When Mili greeted Ginger with her usual cheery, "Good morning," Ginger took one look in her face and burst into uncontrollable sobbing.

Caught totally by surprise by a Ginger she had never even imagined, Mili stood up and wrapped her ample arms around Ginger, trying to soothe her tears. "What on earth is wrong?" she asked in shocked amazement. "Can I help?"

"I've just fallen hopelessly in love, and he's left to go back to New York," Ginger spluttered haltingly between sobs.

"Who? What? I'd like to get my hands on a bum that would desert a girl and leave her in such a state."

"No. No. It's not like that at all," Ginger sobbed, just a little bit more in control. "He didn't want to go. He had to. We had three of the most glorious days of our lives together, and I don't know when we'll see each other. It could be a long time."

"Why don't you tell Mili all about it? We don't have to get down to work yet. It looks like a light day anyhow. Who is he?"

"It's Chelton, Chelton Chum."

"You mean *the* Chelton Chum? From the United Nations? The minister with all those awards for humanity or something like that?" Mili asked with rising excitement as Ginger affirmed her questions with a nodding head. "You don't mess with the small fry do you?"

"No, I guess not," she answered as she continued to calm down. Surprised and a little sheepish at breaking down as she did, Ginger continued, "I can't believe I broke down and dumped on you like I did. Now you know the terrible truth, don't you? I am human after all."

"I always knew you were. That tough reporter persona of yours couldn't hide the real you from old Mili. I knew there was a big heart in there and probably a soft, loving woman as well. You just proved I was right."

"Thanks Mili. You're a jewel. You've been the closest to family I've had since I left Port Washington. I needed that just now."

Ginger had always been closed-mouthed about her personal life, and Mili had never pried. Earlier, they had talked about a few personal things, and she was sure Mili was no gossip. She did not feel uncomfortable talking about the weekend happenings. Suddenly, Mili had changed from a casual friend to a close friend and confidant. They would continue talking and sharing until Ginger noticed the clock and was shocked back into reality.

"Look at the clock. It's nearly eleven. I've got to get to work. I thoroughly enjoyed our talk and appreciate your understanding, but we'd both best get back to business."

"You're right, but I don't think you could have done much in the condition you were in when you first got here. You needed to get that out. I'm glad we shared. Now we'll both work better because of it."

"I'm sure you're right—and we're both good at catching up."

With that, the two dug in. Mili had proven she could be a good friend in need. Ginger would learn to treasure that genuine friendship in the times to come.

18

As Warren's small jet touched down at the airport in Watertown, Serena decided she was ready to get back to work at the inn. During the trip, she relived all the happenings of the busy few weeks she was away. She was pleased she had the story of Angus and Lani to hide the real reason for her trip from Kat and her family. Eventually, she would find the best time to tell them about the fearful secret she held. For now, it would be a happy reunion with splendid experiences to share with family and friends. As much as she enjoyed her visit to Hawaii, Serena was glad to be home. As she walked down the steps of the plane, she spotted Kat waiting at the gate. Warren walked beside her carrying her luggage.

Before she reached the gate, Kat rushed out to greet her. They shared a long hug before Kat turned and greeted Warren with, "Thanks for returning her safely."

"He's a wonderful pilot." Serena said as they started to walk toward the terminal.

"Bye, Serena," Warren said almost sadly as he turned to leave. "Yer a real special lady. I enjoyed havin' ya aboard. Any time ya need a ride, this old sky jockey'll be glad to take ya."

Serena gave him a big hug and replied, "I'd fly with you anywhere. It was a real pleasure. I can see why Angus spoke so highly of you."

They watched as Warren walked to the jet, stepped inside with a wave, closed the door and headed for the runway.

"He's an interesting character," Serena commented as they walked out of the terminal to Kat's car. "He's full of astounding stories about hauling all kinds of people to many different places."

"I'll bet, but let's save that for later. Right now, I've the most wonderful news. You'd never guess what," Kat said, beaming.

"Jessica's pregnant."

Kat was stunned into silence for a moment. She looked at Serena, a hint of a pout formed on her face. "How'd you know? Who could have told you?"

"You just did. It was the first thing that came to mind when you said wonderful news. You know we can read each other like a book. How many times have we done just that with each other?"

"You're right. I should have figured. Anyway, I found out just last Friday. Jessica called to tell me it had been confirmed. The baby's due in December. She hadn't wanted to say anything until they were sure, but she's been suspicious for some time. I've been dying to tell you. I was going to call, but since I knew you were heading for home, I decided to wait. I wanted to see the look on your face. It was priceless."

They continued talking enthusiastically about the new life to come and about Lani and Angus. Like two schoolgirls, they chattered all the way home. This trip was the exact opposite of the quiet trip they had shared to Watertown some weeks before.

*   *   *

The next few weeks saw a number of significant events and much planning. Angus and Lani decided Saturday, August 11 as the date for their wedding. This was announced to the surprise of very few. Subsequently, merciless kidding followed them through their workday for some time.

The first news release about the ghost drew almost no attention. Several astronomers called to ask Angus about it, but, obviously, this was not earth-shaking news. Angus was pleased.

About this same time, Pat Yamaguchi made his visit. Shortly after he arrived, they sat down in Angus' office. When Angus introduced Lani to Pat, he looked her over carefully head to toe, nodding slowly in understanding. "I assume you are the three hundred-pound hag my old buddy here told me about?"

Lani cast a sober glance at Angus. "My oh-so-complimentary boss frequently exaggerates."

Angus grinned. "I'll admit to stretching the truth a bit."

After some more good-natured kidding back and forth with both Angus and Lani, Pat started in on the project. "I was hoping to bring my confirmations when I came, but the Mt. Hopkins MMT is still busy. It's more than a year past first light, and they are still backlogged after the two-year hiatus to expand to the new bigger mirrors. I'm now scheduled for August 3 and 4. If luck is with us, we'll have clear skies and no more delays. We must do it before the sun cuts us off for a few months."

"You haven't had any problems downloading the data or understanding my notes have you? I know you didn't mention any problems in your e-mail."

"No problems so far. I've got everything ready to go, but normal confirmations don't have a high priority, and I don't have enough seniority to swing much weight. If I told them exactly what I was confirming, they'd make it top priority, but then the whole world would know."

"It's tough, I know. I just don't want to let anyone but a most trusted friend deal with this until we know when and how we're going to tell the world."

"Angus, you've thrown quite a load on a friend. I hope I don't let you down. This whole business scares the tar out of me. I haven't even told Beanie, and that's become a real problem. I told her I was working on something confidential with you, and she accepted that, probably because it's you. I hate not being able to talk with her about it."

"Hang on, old buddy. It's not easy here either. I've had problems you wouldn't believe." Angus was thinking of OSI, but wouldn't say anything about that. "It will only be a few months, at the outside. Our next few news releases are ready to go, but I still want your confirmation to be sure before releasing them."

"I almost didn't come, but I needed to get away for a couple of weeks. Soon as we finish, I'm heading for Honolulu to hang out with an old high school buddy who lives there. Beanie took a week off and will meet me there in a few days, so we can both loosen up."

"Good. That should help."

"Back to your ghost star. If your data is correct, you have discovered the most unbelievable object in the galaxy. How could an object as large as a star be accelerated to that fantastic speed?"

"We're still speculating on that and will be for a long time, I'm sure," Angus replied.

"You know there might be that temptation to publish before you and steal your discovery don't you? I wouldn't do that, but you had better be wary of anyone else you take into your confidence."

"Believe me, Pat, no other astronomers will be given the information you have until our data release scheduled for November. I'm giving you a leg up on all the rest. I know you will use that honorably," Angus stated firmly.

"Just to be the first one to confirm your findings will be quite an achievement. I appreciate your trust. You won't be disappointed."

Angus felt good about Pat. He was a truly reliable friend. They spent the rest of the day together comparing notes. Angus showed him around Gemini, took him to dinner with Lani and dropped him at his hotel. Next morning, Pat left for Honolulu.

*　　*　　*

The afternoon of July 10, John called Angus into his office. "I've just received a call from Charlie at Cal Tech, and it's not good news," John explained. "It seems no one has ever done any work on an object the size of a star moving so fast. Lack of data has hampered their efforts to set up a viable simulation. He says they can do the simulation, but it will take more time than he thought, and the results will be based on a number of unproven assumptions. He'll need at least another two weeks."

"Well, at least he didn't say they couldn't do it. We can handle another two or three weeks without messing up the schedule."

Angus was disappointed. His anxiety over the possible outcome would now extend another few weeks. When he shared the information with Lani, she asked, "Is that going to interfere with our wedding plans? We'd better change them now if it will."

"I see no reason it could," Angus replied. "You'll still be clipping my wings August 11."

"Wrong. I believe this will be an equal opportunity marriage. If you get clipped—I get clipped. You'll get no sympathy from me with those kinds of comments."

"Why is it every time I make a comment like that, you come right back to top it and put me in my place?"

"Just clever I guess. I suppose you'll keep on trying?"

"Have to. No choice. I must support my end in the battle of the sexes."

*   *   *

Plans for the wedding were set by late July. It would be at 2:00 on Saturday afternoon, August 11. The reception would be at the Namahoe home in the same setting as the New Year luau. The entire Namahoe clan would do the reception under the able guidance of Ali and Charlene. Angus called Warren to arrange a charter for Serena, Peter and Kat. When he heard Angus was getting married, Warren asked for his mother's phone number so he could confirm arrangements.

*   *   *

On Tuesday, July 31, John told Angus Charlie Botkin called to say he had some preliminary results of the simulation ready and wanted to deliver them personally. Charlie told him he needed to unwind for a few days and was taking him up on his earlier invitation. He would arrive in Hilo Wednesday afternoon and at Gemini by three. He declined to answer any questions about the simulation over the phone.

By three o'clock the next day Angus and John were in the lobby, nervously awaiting Charlie's arrival. He called to say his plane landed a bit early and he would take a cab there. As they watched, a cab drove up and disgorged a tall, thin man with a ponytail in tattered jeans and a garish Hawaiian shirt carrying an overstuffed bag. No one would ever expect this character to be a serious scientist.

As soon as John introduced Angus, Charlie commented, "You worked with Pat at Arizona, didn't you? I understand you found an unusual new star."

Surprised, Angus took a moment to answer, "Why . . . yes. I have, but how do you know my work . . . and Pat?"

Charlie laughed. "Pat worked with me at Cal Tech during our graduate studies before he moved to the University of Arizona. We still get together occasionally. I called him for some input on the problem you gave me. He was very helpful."

John and Angus glanced at each other in dismay, their minds racing. This was an unexpected development. "What did he have to say about the problem?" John asked, quickly regaining his composure.

"He said it was impossible. Nothing could cause a star to reach that speed," Charlie was very matter-of-fact when he answered, then asked. "Is that girl at the reception desk Jenny?"

"Yes, do you know her?" John answered.

"Not really, I asked her to marry me once, and now I'd like to meet her."

John and Angus looked at each other as John explained, "See now why they call him Crazy Charlie?"

Charlie sauntered over to the reception desk smiling brightly. "Are you Jenny?"

"Why yes. How can I help you?"

"I just wanted to repeat my proposal in person. Came all the way to Hawaii to see you."

Jenny looked askance at this strange man for a few seconds until the light of a memory glowed and she laughed. "You're that crazy from Cal Tech aren't you?"

"Guess I've been found out. I'm Charlie Botkin and I know you're Jenny. You're even cuter in person than on the phone. Are you sure you don't want to marry me?"

"You are crazy," Jenny answered with a laugh, her face bright as a new penny. "I'd accept, but I just couldn't leave my friends here in Hawaii."

"I'll move here."

"You're nuts," was all Jenny could say.

With that Charlie bowed, took her hand gently in his, kissed it, turned and walked away in an exaggerated, sadly hunched posture. Everyone watching laughed.

"Why is it nobody takes me seriously?" Charlie muttered sadly as the three of them headed toward John's office.

"You really don't want an answer, do you?" John commented, smiling. It was more a comment than a question.

After a few pleasantries they got down to business. When it came to science, Charlie was definitely not crazy. They spent more than an hour going over the results, Charlie explaining, Angus and John asking questions. Finally Angus asked, "The gist of it is, you really don't know what would happen, do you?"

"You know this guessing game we have to play," Charlie replied earnestly. "With so many variables and some important unknowns, it's guesses based upon guesses. We had to input certain things we can only guess into the simulations. We haven't a clue as to the accuracy of those guesses. That makes all of our answers problematic. It boils down to this: sim one was run using gravity and inertia alone to determine the results. That's the easiest, but it shows us just how tricky this question is. Change the timing by just a few weeks and the results are drastically different. In sim two we added the factors shown to compensate for the relativistic effects. We used several best guesses in the others and as you can see the results varied all over the map. It's a knotty question that has never been asked before. We're in totally uncharted waters here."

"You mean to tell me you are sure no one has ever considered such a situation?" Angus asked.

"Not that shows up in any publication. We did a thorough search with Cal Tech's computer and came up with zilch. Why would anyone pose an impossible question anyway? It is impossible, isn't it?" Charlie said slowly, paused, then with a surprised look he went on, "Wait a minute. This must be a real situation. You actually found a star going at that speed. You gave me an actual circumstance. Pat was wrong. It isn't impossible."

Shocked and a bit dismayed, Angus and John looked at each other then back at Charlie. It was one of those moments of startling realization when minds search desperately for words. The absence of words and the rapidly changing looks on their faces spoke volumes. After a silence that seemed to last forever, John said, "Angus, I think we have the twelfth member of our group."

"You're right, John," Angus replied. "I think he'll be OK."

"What's going on here? What group?" Charlie asked. "How close is that star going to pass and when?"

Charlie was completely puzzled and looked back and forth between the two men. Angus grabbed the phone to call Lani before starting his explanation. "Can you come join us in John's office? Dr. Botkin from Cal Tech is here."

"Be there in a sec," was Lani's cryptic reply.

"Tell her to bring some food. I'm starving!" Charlie commented. "How about a pizza?"

"Good idea! We can eat right here while we continue," John said as he reached for the phone to order a pizza from his favorite pizza place.

When Lani arrived and was introduced to Charlie, he took one look and commented to Angus. "What on earth did you do to get such a gorgeous assistant? All I ever get are pimply faced kids or wiseacre grad students."

Angus grinned and spoke up immediately. "I hadn't noticed. All I know is she's a topnotch astronomer and works quite well with me."

"You'll excuse me if I don't join this discussion," Lani commented. "I can hardly handle the compliments from such handsome, gracious gentlemen."

Charlie smiled at Lani. "I see you have a sense of humor as well. I'll bet you hold your own amongst these predatory males, maybe even run over them at times."

"I manage to keep them at bay."

John guided the three back to the problem. "Now that we've patted each other on the back sufficiently, let's get to work and tell Charlie about our group."

They took turns describing the discovery of the star, the formation of the group and what they planned to do. Finally, they asked Charlie about joining them.

Charlie had some definite opinions. "Look guys, you seem to be doing all the right things. Your concerns are genuine and your plans are about all you can do. Because I already have too many commitments, I'll have to decline your invitation to become a member of the group, except as a consultant. My grad students will help me with refining the simulations as new data becomes available. I will also search for anything I can find on relativistic effects that might help. Oh yes, have no fears. I'll definitely keep your secret."

Angus nodded his head in acknowledgment. "Great. We understand your decision and appreciate your help. I'll see to it you have all new data as we get it. Is there anything more you need right at the moment?"

"I'll need the exact speed and spatial coordinates of your star updated whenever you have new data. The mean determination and the probability ranges of those numbers is a better way to put it. I understand parallax has limits and that the apparent position of the star is very near those limits. Isn't there a new, far more accurate parallax process being perfected? I seem to remember reading of accuracy ten to a hundred times better than current techniques."

Angus donned his lecturer hat. "The Hipparcos satellite, launched into orbit in nineteen eighty-nine, measured the distance to many stars out to about three hundred light years from the earth, but the accuracy is only to within about 10 percent. Before Hipparcos, accuracy of parallax was within 10 percent out to only thirty light years. That's probably the origin of your information. We use the same process and I know of no newer, more accurate methods. I'll do a through search ASAP and if I find there is a better one, I most certainly will use it."

"That's probably what I remember," Charlie said, as he placed a thin bundle of papers in front of Angus. "These papers outline what I need from you to run a simulation. Let's go through them piece by piece to make sure we are all on the same wavelength."

It was after eleven when they finally wound down. Charlie looked haggard as they broke up. "Angus, I'll take you up on that invitation to stay the night with you. I don't relish the cab ride back to my hotel at the airport. If you'll let me sleep in, that is. I'm several hours ahead of you and need a night to recover from jet lag."

"John, can you drop us there on your way home?"

"Certainly."

* * *

Thursday, just before noon, Charlie drove up in a newly rented car and walked into the lobby of the Op Center. He was dressed neatly in slacks and a conservative shirt, obviously new. He stopped at the desk and spoke to Jenny in his most proper fashion. "I've kidded you a bit before, but I'd like to ask a serious question. Do you have a steady boyfriend?"

Jenny, who had broken off several months ago with the man she had been dating, was wary, "Aren't you being a bit nosey?"

"I was going to ask if you could possibly show me around after you finish work. That would not be appropriate if you had a steady boyfriend."

"I don't have a boyfriend, but still, I don't know you at all. I'd be a bit nervous going out with you." Jenny still didn't quite know whether or not he was serious.

"I'll provide references. How about Angus and John, maybe even Lani? You know them. I even bought this outfit this morning so you would know I don't always dress so casually."

"I don't usually date men I meet here at Gemini. I don't think it is a good idea."

"This is my first time here and will most likely be my last. I don't really have business here. I'm just an old friend of John's who came for a visit. I promise you fun, companionship and no wrestling matches. I'd like to see this place with someone younger than my parents and you're the only one I know. Please," Charlie responded, looking almost like a little boy using all his considerable charm.

Jenny smiled, a look of hesitation froze her face. "I suppose it will be OK," she finally replied.

"Then how's six o'clock? You pick the place to eat. I'll rely entirely on your judgement, but remember, I like expensive food."

Jenny pulled a Hilo map from her desk and placed it on the counter and marked a spot on the map. "Right here's where I live. I'll write the address and phone number on the map. Think you can find your way?"

"No problem." Charlie said with a smile.

It was Sunday afternoon before Charlie left for California. Jenny took him to the airport.

*   *   *

Angus was terribly disappointed at the information from the simulations. He realized how long it might be before they had any accurate knowledge about what would happen in thirty years. Lack of certain knowledge about that event was frustrating even though it held out the possibility nothing bad would happen. Angus disliked indefinite answers, especially those with definition so far in the future. He wondered how the rest of humanity would react to not knowing. Thirty years of waiting for the answer to such a possible catastrophe would certainly place a terrible strain on each and every person who understood. The future looked difficult even if the ghost passed without physical effect.

*   *   *

It was Friday, August 10, and the wedding was just a day away. Angus and Lani had taken the day off and spent the morning moving most of Lani's things from her old apartment to their new, larger place. They left the bed, couch and some basic necessities to be used by wedding guests. Angus already moved out of his old digs and was firmly ensconced in the new. Before noon, they headed south to help with preparations for the wedding reception. They were inside, having a light lunch, when the phone rang. It was Serena.

After speaking to her for a few moments, Charlene lowered the phone and said, "Serena has a surprise for us. She wants us all to step outside and look up. Right away."

They all went outside dutifully and looked up. As they watched, a small jet came into view and began circling. Charlene, phone still held to her ear, relayed a message, "She says 'Hi.' She's up there in that jet. Says she's here with the whole tribe and will see us all in about a half hour."

Angus could see the unmistakable markings on the plane. It was a twelve-place jet from Warren's stable. It had large auxiliary tanks on the wingtips used for long distance flights. *What was he doing all the way out here and with that plane?* Angus wondered. He had only asked Warren to fly the three from Watertown to Cincinnati as before.

In about forty minutes he received his answer when a large-windowed van with Serena at the wheel pulled into the Namahoe's parking lot. They stared in amazement when Kat, Peter, Michael, Jessica, Jim, Chelton, Ginger and Warren tumbled out of the van. Angus was beside himself, laughing and crying at the same time, seeing his entire family and hugging each one in turn.

After some time spent with introductions and greetings and still stumbling in surprise, Angus asked, "How'd all this happen?"

Warren spread a huge grin across his narrow, craggy face. "Yer mom and I cooked this up. She called me and asked if there was a chance I could take the whole bunch to Cincinnati to meet Chelton for a flight to Hawaii. I thought about it and decided I might's well gas up ol' forty-four, wing-tanks an' all, an' bring 'em the whole way. We stopped in Seattle fer a fill-up an' headed out over the ocean. Since they gotta head back on Monday, we thought mebe you'd like to ride along, seein' as yer goin' that way too. Besides I'd like to stay and see ol' thirty-five git hog tied anyways."

Serena put her arm around Warren. "When I asked about the cost, he said no more than for the first trip, said to consider it a wedding present from an old friend. I think it was incredible. He even stopped by New York City to pick up Chelton. He's going to stay for the wedding and then take us all back. There's plenty of room for Lani and you, unless you want to be alone," she added with a sly grin.

"We picked up another'n at the airport," Warren said as they all walked toward the house. "I understand she'll be along fer the ride back too."

Hanging on Chelton's arm, Ginger bubbled with excitement. "I'm taking a vacation and going to New York with Chelton. We will be at the wedding in St. Regis and then stay for a visit, so I can get to know this family I've just met. Then we'll head for New York City, Port Washington actually, where my mom lives. While there, Chelton wants to take me to see the United Nations."

Before long, Pilau, Leimai and the rest of the Namahoe clan interrupted their party preparations to meet the newcomers in a lively display of hugs, laughter and friendly conversations.

Suddenly Ginger began laughing, held up her hands and said, "Hold it. Do you notice that in this whole mob, I'm the only haole? I'm totally outnumbered by Hawaiians and Mohawks."

As soon as she said it, Pilau's eight-year-old daughter ran over to Ginger and said, "That's all right. There's a haole boy in my class and I like him . . . a lot."

The entire group howled with laughter. This was a happy bunch in the beginnings of a fantastic celebration. The rest of the day would be spent in laughter and good-natured kidding as the newcomers dove in to help with the reception preparations. With so many helping hands, the preparations were soon complete and by early evening they all settled down for refreshments and conversations.

"Where ya goin' fer the honeymoon?" Warren asked Angus and Lani.

"Niagara Falls, of course," Lani replied without hesitation. "What did you expect?"

"We thought you'd pick some exotic place like Hawaii," Pilau commented, smiling.

This brought a roar from the crowd after which Jim said, "This is the first time we've ever been to Hawaii, and we're only able to stay for two days. I can guarantee you that we'll be back."

"Young man, Kat and I have been around much longer than you, and this is the first time we've been here," Peter replied. "I think we're all lucky we could come and thankful to Warren for bringing us safely here for this splendid occasion."

They all agreed and thanked Warren who then stood up and said, "You folks are terrific families. I never had much family life m'self. I jest growed up, a scratchin' an' a fightin' till I left home at sixteen, an' that was to fight in a war. I never found the right gal to marry, so I got no kids. The Navy was my family fer twenty years an then, when I started flyin' football players around, they was kinda like my kids. That's when I met ol' thirty-five here. He became one of my special kids. He an' thet ornery one, what's his name, Angus? Oh, I remember, Cy Dooley. He became a minister didn't he?"

Angus shook his head in confirmation.

"What I'm tryin' to say is thet I'm havin' fun with the bunch of ya. Yer wonderful folks. I should be a thankin' ya all fer lettin' me join in the fun an' treatin' me jest like the rest of yer family. It means a whole lot ta this ol' jet jockey."

"Wait till tomorrow evening when we get you up on the dance floor with all the hula girls," Pilau shouted, laughing.

"I'm lookin' forard to it," Warren replied, grinning.

Chelton then stood up and said, "Angus. I think you are having a sensational bachelor party. Look at all the beautiful girls, and you surely couldn't find a nicer bunch of buddies. Lani, you, too, have had a great bachelorette party complete with handsome gentlemen and good friends. I say we give a big cheer for the soon-to-be-weds."

With that they all broke into a thundering cheer that faded into laughter. When the laughter died down, Ali suggested, "We all have a big day tomorrow, and as much as I hate to break up such a fine gathering, we all could use a good night's rest. You travelers have some unpacking to do, I'm sure. We've asked Kat and Peter to stay with us since we've plenty of room and we'd like to get to know them better. We have a couple more beds available here if you need them."

Serena the organizer spoke up, "Jim, why don't you and Jessica stay here with your folks. I can stay with Lani at her place and Michael and Chelton can stay with Angus. Oops. I didn't mean to forget you, Warren."

Chelton interrupted with, "I have a room reserved and paid for at the Mokuloa. Why don't Michael and I stay there? Warren can have Angus' spare bedroom."

"Don't you fuss none fer me," Warren said. "I kin git a room."

"Nonsense," Angus interjected. "You'll stay with me. We've got some catching up to do anyway." Then turning toward his cousins he added, "I'll bet you two haven't roomed together since Michael went off to college."

"You're right there, Angus," Michael answered. "It's been a long time since little brother and I spent time with each other. We'll bunk together."

Sleeping arrangements completed, the luggage for the ones staying was removed from the van. Michael and Chelton would drop Ginger off at her apartment on the way. It would be a peaceful night of
rest for some. The excitement of the coming day would bring fitful
sleep to others.

*   *   *

It was a spectacularly beautiful day for the wedding. A mare's tail
swath of white clouds floated high overhead as the guests began arriving at the little church. With Lani's large family and many friends,
some members of the church, several people from Gemini and a few
from the university, it would be an overflow crowd. Ruth had them
roll back the sliding wall between the sanctuary and assembly room
to provide more seating.

The ceremony was a mixture of a traditional church service, a Hawaiian ceremony and Lani's own ideas. An entourage of little Namahoes,
Ali and Charlene's grandchildren, walked down the aisle strewing flowers. Leimai, Leinaala, Jessica and Ginger were the bridesmaids, beautiful in their colorful native Hawaiian dresses. Pilau, Ron, Jim and Michael
were handsome in their ushers' outfits. Chelton served as best man.
They had each written their own vows and would repeat them without
Ruth's assistance. When Lani went first, she flabbergasted Angus by
singing the Hawaiian Wedding Song while looking straight into his
eyes. Tears streaming down his face, he took several moments to com-
pose himself enough to say his own vows. Before the close of the service, there were many tissues stemming the flow of joyful tears from
all. It was an emotional ceremony that Ruth concluded with wet eyes.
As they made the traditional church door exit, they received many leis
and a huge round of applause.

The reception was almost a rerun of the New Year's luau, but with
a wedding cake and a lot more people. Lani and the girls danced the
Hula and even got Warren on the dance floor with them as promised.
It was a glorious celebration indeed with many joyful stories and
anecdotes about the newlyweds being shared between the two families and their friends. Most of these were followed by bursts of laughter at the expense of one or both of the new couple. When Pilau
asked Angus if he was going to do his dance, Angus laughed and said
he would have to come to St. Regis to see that.

By the time the bride and groom changed and were ready to leave, the party was beginning to wind down. With a chorus of cheery good-byes, they hopped into Lani's car and headed away on their own. A new chapter was started in their lives. They would head over the top of the island to Kailua where Angus had reserved a special room for their wedding night. Angus drove with Lani snuggled tightly against him.

Angus glanced quickly at his bride nestled beside him. "Do you know what your new name is?"

"Mihalani Thomas."

"Wrong! You are now Mrs. Sitting Duck!"

They both had a good laugh and then began recalling moments from the wedding and party. It had been a gloriously exciting day. They were both highly stimulated by the day's happenings and the promise of the night to come.

They were a handsome pair as they entered the hotel and headed for the elevator to their room. A number of pairs of eyes followed these two people so obviously in love. A few people guessed correctly their newly married status, it being so obvious.

Naturally, Angus carried her over the threshold into the room, plac-ing her carefully on the huge bed. Their two small suitcases were wait-ing on the low table at the side of the room as Angus had arranged. He had not wanted to be disturbed by a bellhop handling luggage. Look-ing about, Lani noticed the large hot tub in a tiled area of the room. Not far from the hot tub was a large pink shower with clear glass doors. There were several other interesting features to the room.

Reaching up, Lani pulled Angus down on the bed beside her. Their faces were only inches apart, eyes reaching for each other's. "I love you," she whispered softly.

He drew in a breath filled with the sweet, warm smell of her. "I love you."

*   *   *

Sunday had been a day of packing for nearly everyone. Warren had moved from Angus' apartment to the daybed in Charlene's study, so that Angus and Lani could have their new apartment to them-selves. Earlier, the bride and groom had packed for the trip, and their luggage was in the apartment all ready to go. Ginger had been packing for several days, trying to keep her luggage down to one suitcase and a carry-on bag.

Late Sunday afternoon, the newlyweds showed up at the Namahoes. After some good-natured kidding, they all settled down in the family room to work out the revised details for the flight back to New York. When she started counting heads and thinking about the twelve-place jet, Serena said there appeared to be a problem.

"Adding five to the eight who flew out totals thirteen. I assume that's one more than the plane's capacity," she warned them.

Warren immediately solved the problem. "Ol' forty-four is a twelve-passenger ship. That's twelve passengers plus the pilot and copilot seats. We got plenty of room."

Serena was overjoyed. "Splendid! Then we can take everybody. I was about to suggest we draw straws to see who flew commercially. See what I get for assuming? What about weight? Could that be a problem?"

"I hauled as many as twelve football players with all their gear in this ol' crate. I reckon this bunch is lots lighter than that load."

They all had a good laugh at Serena's expense. She finally commented, "It surely doesn't pay to make a mistake or demonstrate ignorance around this bunch." Of course, she could dish it out as well as take it.

At quarter to six, Ali and Charlene left for the newlywed's apartment where they would park their car and transfer to the rented van. With Angus at the wheel of the van, they stopped to pick up the rest of the group, arriving at the airport a full fifteen minutes ahead of schedule. Warren had already been there for more than an hour, seeing to it his jet was ready for the flight. Besides the usual pre-flight check, he supervised the loading of the breakfasts he had ordered for the jet's small galley. This would be a first-class flight.

By seven, the van had been returned, all luggage had been stowed and seats had been selected. They were ready to go. As soon as he taxied to the end of the runway and received the OK from the tower, Warren released the brakes and opened the throttles. A loud cheer went up as the jet rotated and leaped off the runway into the sky. They climbed steeply to thirty thousand feet where Warren leveled off and set the autopilot.

He slid back the door to the pilot's cabin. "Our flight plan has changed a bit. The weather in Seattle don't look so good. We're now aimin' fer San Jose instead. That means we'll be gittin' to Watertown jest a bit later. Now, I need a couple o' volunteer stews. Can't call 'em waitresses up here, but somebody needs to serve them breakfasts from the galley. Better have four. Two to take 'em outa the racks an' two to pass 'em out. We got fourteen special Hawaiian breakfasts. That's in case one gits dropped. That's why I tol' ya not to eat this mornin'. Serena can show ya how to set up those tray tables."

Kat and Serena removed the trays while Lani and Ginger served. It was a breakfast of fine food and fellowship, high above the Pacific. When they finished eating Warren turned and said, "This is an equal opportunity jet. You men git ta clean up the trays and put 'em away." After a high-pitched roar and laughter from the women, he added, "Serena can show ya where and how."

The stop in San Jose was uneventful. They all disembarked during the refueling and walked around the terminal to loosen up after sitting for several hours. They could walk around in the jet, but it was a little tight to get any more than a stretch. Soon, they were winging over the Sierras as they flew steadily eastward. Warren pointed out Salt Lake City, Cheyenne, Sioux City and Waterloo, Iowa. He had a funny story about each town he pointed to. At Warren's suggestion, they made a stop at Madison, Wisconsin where Warren took them to one of his favorite restaurants. It had been seven hours since breakfast and the local time was past seven in the evening. Light snacks from the plane were all they had to eat, and it would be two more hours to Watertown where the time would be eleven.

"It ain't fancy, but the food's great," Warren promised as they entered the cabs for the short ride. The noisy restaurant quieted noticeably as the group of obviously different people were seated at a large round table right in the center. The Hawaiian clothes the women wore and their striking appearance drew a great deal of attention from the locals, including a few low, breathy whistles of amazement.

Warren stood up and announced, "This here's a wedding party from Hawaii. Them two jist got hitched in Hilo an' I'm takin' the whole danged bunch to Niagara Falls fer their honeymoon."

This was more than many of the patrons could take. One shouted, "You're crazy, old man. What are they really, a group of Hawaiian dancers or singers? That blonde don't look like no Hawaiian to me."

Suddenly one man stood up and pointed at Angus, saying, "I know who that one is, and he's no Hawaiian singer. That's Angus Thomas, one of the greatest running backs ever. What the devil kinda group is that, Angus?"

With a huge smile, Angus stood up and said, "Believe it or not, this *is* a wedding party, and this lovely wahine is my new bride, Lani. We did just get married yesterday in Hilo, Hawaii, and we are on our way to New York. This wonderful old man stretched it a whole lot with the part about them all going with us on our honeymoon. We've several more hours of flying ahead of us, so we would appreciate your letting us eat as peacefully as possible."

"OK, folks," the man who recognized Angus announced. "We know who they are and what they're about. Let's let them have their meal in peace."

After a few shouts of congratulations and friendly comments about the bride's beauty, the restaurant quieted down and they were able to place their orders and have their meal in relative peace. As they were getting up to leave, a boy of about twelve walked shyly up to Angus with a menu and pencil in his hand. He hesitated and then asked, "Mr. Thomas, My dad would like your autograph if you don't mind. He's the one who recognized you."

"Certainly," Angus replied with a big grin. "I'll even have Lani sign it as well." Handing it back, Angus added, "You tell your dad he has a fine, courteous son." The boy ran quickly back to his dad pointing to the signature as the restaurant exploded in applause. The group filed out of the restaurant to a number of congratulations and good luck wishes from the patrons.

As they walked to the waiting cabs, Lani said, "There are a lot of truly nice people in this world, no matter where you are." She saddened a bit as she realized the boy would be in his early forties when the ghost arrived. It was the first time she had thought of the ghost in several days.

The rest of the trip was in the dark. In the crystal clear night, lights of the cities below sparkled with unbelievable brilliance as they passed by. They could see the lights of many cities far from their flight path. It was a flight-weary group that finally touched down in Watertown. The Mohawk Inn van was right where they left it a few days previous. After Warren secured the jet for the night, they boarded the van for the trip to St. Regis and the inn where all but the Chums would stay for the night.

As they arrived, Serena put her hand on Angus' arm. "Sorry I don't have a honeymoon suite for you two."

"I think wherever we stay will be the honeymoon suite," Lani replied looking warmly at Angus.

It wasn't long before they were all settled for the night.

MOHAWK COUNTRY

After a short night, Serena and Kat were up at their usual time attending to the business of the inn. Elton Walker, the young assistant manager who had the whole responsibility for the first time, had done an excellent job. This was the first time Serena, Kat and Peter had been away from the inn together for more than a few hours, and they had all been a little uneasy. They brought him into the office and told him how pleased they were with how he had handled things. His grateful reply was, "That's because I had such good teachers."

Serena thought to herself that not only did Elton do a good job, but he was a diplomat as well. It was good to know.

Another early riser, Warren, had a quick breakfast and left to return his plane into service. "I would love ta stay here fer the festivities, but ol' forty-four doesn't make much money sittin' on the ground. Give the rest my regards an tell 'em bye fer me, God willin', I'll see 'em later." He stopped before getting into the car for the trip to Watertown. "Ya got a mighty fine son there an a doll baby fer a daughter-in-law. An that whole ornery bunch, why I'd be proud ta call any of 'em friend. An' you, yer about the nicest lady I ever met, so you take keer. Ya hear?"

"You are just too much. It was wonderful having you with us. Come back soon. You're one of the family now, you know." With a tear in her eye, she watched as the car circled the drive and headed down the road. Warren reminded her a little of her own father, a gruff, salty exterior protecting the soft, vulnerable heart inside. Like some others she knew, they were warm, wonderful men, a bit scarred by a tough and painful early life.

*   *   *

The Mohawk Inn was situated on a low hill about a hundred feet above water level at the mouth of a stream that emptied into the St.

Lawrence. The windows of the dining room faced about fifteen degrees north of due west and provided an excellent view looking up the big river. A wide expanse of grass covered the slope all the way down to the water. A wooded area started at the left or south end of the inn and meandered down toward the stream edging the lawn. There were no trees on the hill from these woods around the grassy shoreline as far as the eye could see through the windows from inside. To the right, the shoreline of the St. Lawrence stretched eastward. About fifty feet north of where the woods approached the shore began a row of short piers jutting out into the little cove that was the mouth of the stream. The row of piers and the small fishing boats moored to them followed the shoreline out of sight behind the woods. Several boats were upside down on the shore appearing like beached aluminum whales on the grass. From time to time fishermen and their guides would come and go in the small boats. The busiest times were in the morning and at dusk.

The activities at the piers could be seen clearly from the dining room and from the porch running the entire length of that side of the inn: The coming and going of the fishermen, the loading and unloading of equipment and catch, the viewing of the catch and the associated photo taking, even the cleaning and packing of the fish into ice chests at the long table, were all easily viewed from the inn. Occasionally, a freighter would pass on the seaway, heading to or from the many Great Lakes ports far to the west.

At a little after nine, the wedding party began gathering at a table by the windows. Fishermen who eat early and head for the boats had long since deserted the dining room. By ten they were all at the table except for Angus and Lani. Charlene's "I wonder why they're so late?" was greeted by a round of laughter.

Michael's comment, "We'll be lucky if they show up by dinner time," drew another round of laughter.

"What's this about dinner time?" Angus asked as he and Lani walked in. "It surely got a big laugh."

After a few more laugh lines loosened the group, Serena interrupted their humor at Angus and Lani's expense by telling them, "We'd better get to the final arrangements for tomorrow night. I think we can excuse the newlyweds and the other moonstruck pair. Ali, you and Charlene earned a little vacation as well. Why don't you all relax and just do whatever? The rest of you have finished breakfast and had best get to work. Michael is in charge of the seating arrangements and Jessica the decorating. Because of her condition, I don't want her doing any lifting or climbing. You just tell the others what to do, Jess."

As the designated workers left the table, Lani pulled Angus over to the window and gazed at the panorama of the river and woods. "It's absolutely breathtaking," she exclaimed. "Much greener than I imagined and so different, so beautifully different."

"Yes, it is, but you should see it in January. Everything covered with a dazzling white blanket—the trees dark and naked—the river choked with ice from shore to shore and the silence. The silence is overpowering. All you can hear is the wind in the trees and the rumble of the ice on the river. It's a stark, bitter cold beauty, but it is just as beautiful to me."

"I can't imagine. The green leaves gone from the trees and the river frozen; it seems impossible now as I look out on this scene. And snow falling. I've been in the snow atop Mauna Kea, but I've never seen it falling. I want to see your home in January. I want to experience all you've known. I want you to take me to a football game in the fall with all the beautiful colors. I want to see Niagara Falls, frozen," Lani said, eyes sparkling in excitement.

Angus laughed at her child-like enthusiasm. "You will, hon. Just slow down a bit, be patient. We'll do all those things in time. Now, how'd you like to go for a boat ride?"

"Of course! But can we have breakfast first? I'm famished."

They returned to join the remaining four late risers for a leisurely meal. As they were relaxing Lani said to Ginger, "Angus asked me to go for a boat ride. Would you and Chelton like to join us?"

"Wouldn't you rather be alone? You're on your honeymoon, you know."

"Of course not. Honeymoons should be for all kinds of enjoyment, not just being alone. We'd love to have you along if you want," Angus suggested.

Chelton joined in. "Let's go with them. It's been years since I've been on the river. With my short, infrequent visits, I never have time to."

Ginger looked at Angus and Lani. "Fine by me, if you two are absolutely sure."

"How about you, Ali, and Charlene?" Angus asked.

"I think we'll just walk around the grounds. It's so beautifully different. Outside of a couple of trips to California, we've not been anywhere on the mainland. This is our first trip to any place like this. Besides, I don't think those little boats could carry six."

"Oh, we won't be using a fishing boat. We've a twenty-foot deck-boat at the far end of the docks. There's plenty of room on that," Angus answered.

"Maybe later. Right now, I'd just like to take a walk. Is that OK with you, Ali?"

"Sure, Char, let the young ones go off on their adventure. I'd rather go for a walk too."

Angus retrieved a serving tray from the kitchen and started clearing the table. "I can see you've been here before," Ali commented as he rose to help.

"Since the regular help won't be back till lunch time I thought we could clean up. It'll only take a few minutes to clear this away and set up for lunch," Angus suggested.

"Seeing we're sort of freeloaders, I think we should help out as much as we can," Ginger added.

Soon Ali and Charlene were off on their walk around the inn and the two couples headed out for the river on the boat. They spent the next few hours riding several miles up and down the St. Lawrence, dodging the occasional freighter that passed by. Chelton and Angus pointed out place after place where they had experienced adventures in years past. The two men took turns telling stories of these happenings in their past. As they shared, laughed and cried, bonds of friendship and kinship grew stronger and stronger. They would all need those bonds in the years to come.

*   *   *

Serena asked the local tribal elders if they would do a traditional Mohawk marriage ceremony in full dress. The answer, a resounding yes, was followed by, "How could we refuse one of the most important members of our tribe—and for our most famous living member." Serena held considerable influence in the Mohawk community.

With the preparations for a huge bonfire on the beach in front of the inn, everything was in order. Wednesday evening brought a new dimension into the lives of the Hawaiians. Each was furnished several articles of Mohawk adornment to wear at the ceremony. Lani and Angus were spectacular in their full Mohawk wedding regalia. The entire ceremony was spoken in both Mohawk and English for the benefit of the Hawaiians. Starting at sunset, the ceremony was illuminated entirely by the bonfire, punctuated by flashes from Michael's camera as he recorded the proceedings. It was another magical moment for people so different and yet so much alike. Ali and Charlene marveled at the sinuous dances and how different they were from their own. Yet at the same time, the message spoken in dance was similar.

When the ceremony was finished and the bonfire began to die, they headed for the inn. Hordes of biting insects, held at bay temporarily by the huge bonfire and by some repellant chemicals sprinkled in the grass, were beginning to descend on them, and the inn offered protection.

"That's one problem we don't have in Hawaii," Lani commented as Angus swatted a mosquito on her arm.

While the food was being served, Lani and Charlene entertained them with a hula. Lani brought tears to many eyes as, again, she sang the beautiful Hawaiian Wedding Song to Angus. The many local friends marveled at this beautiful young woman who so touched their hearts with her song. They commented how different yet strangely familiar she looked with her dark hair and eyes so similar to their own.

During the evening, the many friends, cousins and other relatives stopped to chat with Lani and her parents. Fascinated by the Hawaiians, they asked many questions while sharing much of their own culture in return. Like Angus and Serena before them, they were amazed at the many similarities they found between their own culture and one separated by thousands of miles and tens of thousands of years.

It was well after midnight when the last guests walked out the doors. It had been a marvelous evening of sharing as two peoples bridged the gap of cultural differences.

*   *   *

The next day, Angus and Lani headed for Niagara Falls. Where to after that, they would not say. Chelton and Ginger lingered a few more days to visit with Jim, Jessica, Peter and Kat. Ginger spent the time getting to know her new man's family and home. Charlene and Ali decided to remain for at least a week. They were fascinated by St. Regis, the people and the river. Serena promised to take them to visit the many interesting sights nearby in northern New York and across the river in Canada. Ali said he might even like to try a little fishing.

Angus rented a car for a leisurely drive to Niagara Falls, and then, who knew. He could drop the car anywhere in the country and catch a plane back to Hawaii when they wished. When pressed by Serena for where they were going, he replied, "It's no secret, Mom. We really don't know. We'll decide that after we get to the Falls."

Serena watched until the car went out of sight. She was proud of Angus and rightly so. She knew Lani was a kind, caring wife and had grown to love her dearly. As she turned to go inside, she uttered softly. "Godspeed, loved ones. May God watch over you." Her most valued purpose in life was riding in that car.

*   *   *

The week passed quickly. After much discussion, Ginger, Chelton, Jim and Jessica rented a car and left for a leisurely trip home. Even after several days together, they had much to talk about. Ginger and Jessica hit it off well. Jess could see the depth in her brother's choice and hoped they would stay together. It was a wonderful trip with all of them sharing and teasing the whole way.

Ali and Charlene stayed for two weeks since the construction business was a bit slow, and Pilau was taking care of things. Serena thoroughly enjoyed being able to return the hospitality they had so graciously extended her in Hawaii. During one of their conversations at breakfast Charlene asked Serena, "Tell me about Kat's Michael. He seems almost lost, so quiet and apart from the rest."

Serena responded with a pained expression. "It's a sad story. After college he went to law school where he met a lovely girl named Soleil. I think it's French and means sunshine or something like that. Michael called her Sunny. After he graduated and passed the bar they were married and moved to Syracuse where he joined a law practice. They were doing well. She finished law school and joined a family law practice there in Syracuse. They were married only four years when a drunk driver, trying to elude the police, hit her car head on. She was killed instantly. The drunk was seriously injured but survived. I believe he is still in prison. It was his second drunk driving accident in just two months. He had no license but was driving in spite of that."

Charlene looked sadly at Serena. "What a terribly sad story. No wonder he seemed in pain. He is, terribly."

"Yes, we're all quite concerned about him. Shortly after it happened, he quit the law office and disappeared for more than six months. We were worried sick. One day he showed up at the inn, completely surprising and delighting us, like the prodigal son, you know. He was in a rather poor mental state but wanting to recover. He just wanted the pain to go away. Of course, it never will, and I doubt we'll get the old Michael back until he admits that to himself and deals with it. We are afraid he has a sort of death wish. You know, Indians are famous for working high steel. As ironworkers, they make excellent pay but at a high risk. Michael enrolled as an apprentice ironworker and was living right here on the reservation with some friends, almost in hiding. He said he finally gained the strength to see his family, and that's when he showed up. He has become a journeyman ironworker and constantly volunteers for the most dangerous jobs. It truly distresses us all. We've tried reasoning with him, but he's a stubborn Mohawk, and we can't seem to make any headway. Fortunately, he's never even been injured on the job, but that's all he does, work. He doesn't even take time to fish in the spring when the smallmouth are running, and that's the highlight of the year for many Mohawk men. I have no idea what he does with his money, but he must be earning a lot. Still he lives a frugal lifestyle here when he's not away working."

"I feel so bad," Charlene said. "I was wondering why he seemed so distant from the rest. I thought for a while it was his picture taking, but when he finished that he just disappeared. I'm almost surprised he came to the wedding in Hawaii."

"He idolizes Angus. Always has. Kat even enlisted Angus' help in trying to talk to him, but even he couldn't get through. We keep hoping he'll snap out of it. Several times he seemed to be coming around, then suddenly he'd draw back into his shell. I thought the wedding might do the trick. He seemed almost his old self there. Even cracked a few jokes. During the trip back, I could see him regressing. We've decided to just love him and pray for his deliverance. Surely someday he'll snap back. I pray for that day frequently. It's definitely between him and God now." Changing the subject, Serena said to Ali, "Why don't I ask Peter to take you fishing? We could use a few Walleye for dinner, and I'd like to take Charlene to Watertown. I'm sure you'd rather go fishing than spend a day with two women shopping."

Ali brightened at the prospect of getting out. "That's a definite yes. Can he get away?"

"He just happens to have a day open on his schedule. You must know, he's the best guide in this whole area and that's no stretch. I'll bet when he saw that open day I marked on his schedule, he figured I had some major job for him to do. He'll be tickled when he finds that job is to take you fishing."

*   *   *

On Friday, August 24, they finally heard from the newlyweds. They called from the inn on the rim of the Grand Canyon. "How on earth did you end up there?" Charlene asked, motioning Ali to get on another phone.

"I told Angus I wanted to see the whole country up close, and we've done a lot since leaving Niagara Falls. We went to a play on Broadway, walked through Central Park and then flew to San Francisco. After a couple of days seeing the city we rented a car and drove up to Yosemite and then to Sequoia National Park and the huge redwoods. We went to L.A. and saw Hollywood. I was not impressed. Then Angus took me to a little church in South L.A. where I met this huge black minister, Cy Dooley, an incredible man who seems to be working wonders with the seriously troubled youths in the area. Next we hopped another plane from L.A. to Tucson where we saw some of his old friends and visited where he used to work. We rented another car and drove through the little town of Sedona in a beautiful red canyon and finally ended up right here at the Grand Canyon."

"My goodness, Lani. You are so excited. You're talking faster than I've heard you talk since you were a teen. It sounds wonderful. We'll have to sit down and hear the whole story when we all get home. Incidentally, your father's on the other line. We've been having a marvelous time here but will be leaving tomorrow. When are you planning to come home? Do you know?"

"Hi, Daddy! You should see this spectacular place. I don't know if I ever want to go home. I love you. Here's Angus."

"You'll have to excuse my bride. She is so excited she can hardly speak coherently. I wonder if this trip hasn't overloaded her input devices. She never wants to sleep. She sleeps only on planes or when we're driving after dark. I bought her a digital camera with a whole lot of flash memory cards to store images. She must have taken several hundred pictures by now, maybe a thousand. She is so wound up!"

Ali chimed in, "You sound a bit wound up yourself. Don't go without sleeping until you collapse. You will have to come back to earth someday, you know. Here's your mother."

Serena took the phone. "Hi, Son. Did I hear correctly that you are in Arizona?"

Angus confirmed their location and gave a similar, but somewhat less excited, rundown on their trip. "This is our second day at the canyon and tomorrow we'll head for Las Vegas with a stop at Hoover Dam en route. We'll fly directly home from Vegas on Sunday. We will be home late Sunday afternoon, not too long after Lani's folks. I'll call again when we get home. Right now my little wahine wants to go walk on the rim of the canyon."

The three parents stood almost stunned, then burst out in laughter. "Can you believe those crazy kids?" Ali commented shaking his head. They sat talking about those crazy kids for quite some time.

19

God laughs when men make plans.

*A*ngus and Lani arrived at their new apartment late Sunday evening. They had just finished unpacking and decided to retire early to try to catch up on some much needed sleep. Before they could get to bed, the phone rang and Lani answered. It was Ginger sounding ominous.

"Get yourself and your new hubby down to Gemini just as fast as you can. I've something extremely frightening to show you. Call your parents and Ruth and ask them to come too. Quickly. I already called John and he's on his way. I'll call Francis and Oona as soon as I hang up. Please hurry."

Lani understood, hung up and dialed her folks while relaying the message to Angus. They said they would call Ruth and pick her up on the way to Gemini. Without changing clothes, Lani and Angus hurried down to the parking lot and headed for the Op Center in Lani's car. John was just going in the door when they arrived.

"What's this all about, John?" Angus asked as they entered the building.

"All I know is that Ginger picked up a news story from London with her machine and wants us to see it firsthand immediately. She's bringing it with her. It must be serious. That one's not the least bit flighty about the news, so it must be something big. She said she was calling the entire group in Hawaii."

401

Soon Francis and Oona drove up with Ginger just a short distance behind, driving fast. She jumped out of her car and ran to the door ahead of Francis and Oona. She held some loose sheets of paper in her hand. They all headed for the first open room where Ginger spread her papers out on the table.

"Read that. I believe we do have a major crisis," she spat out as she flattened the papers on the table.

Reuters News: London, August 26, 2001, 9:00 A.M. GMT
Dr. Richard Rumley, an English astronomer of some note, dropped a bombshell early this morning at his hearing for some alleged spying activity at the Gemini telescope installation in Hawaii. Dr. Rumley claims he is completely innocent of all charges and that, in fact, Dr. Angus Thomas was the real criminal and that he, Rumley was the actual victim. He claims to have absolute proof Dr. Thomas stole his research into the so-called newly found star Dr. Thomas described in a recent news release. He claims to have data about this star, soon to be released, that proves him to be at least a year or more ahead of Dr. Thomas. Since Dr. Thomas is an American, this has become an international issue bearing on the very core of the international cooperative effort at the Gemini Project. Dr. Rumley's attorney explained that all proper authorities in the U.K. and the U.S.A. were being made aware of the charges presented by Dr. Rumley. Both he and Dr. Rumley refused to talk to reporters. The foreign office would not comment as yet, and it is too early for the Americans to know of the charges. Further bulletins will be posted as soon as they are received.

As they were reading, Ali, Charlene and Ruth arrived. The entire group was grim and silent. Thoughts raced frantically through each mind. Angus finally broke the silence. "There is some good news. Outside of Rumley's lies, there is nothing of importance in the release, certainly nothing about our star that we have not already released. In addition and thanks to the vigilance of our news expert here, we learned of this long before anyone will expect us to. Let's develop an active response as soon as we can do so thoughtfully. Ginger, what's your slant on this? You are certainly the best qualified to let us know what can happen."

"I knew I would be asked that, so I am prepared. Please read this revised news release which, with your permission, I will insert into yesterday's wire schedule. It will appear to predate this Reuters report because news releases from Hawaii are notoriously tardy due to the time differences and since we are close to the International Date Line."

News Release: Gemini Observatory, Hilo, Hawaii
(Saturday, August 25, 2001, 7:00 P.M. local time)
Dr. Angus Thomas reported today new measurements of his recently discovered Ghost star indicate it is traveling at a phenomenal rate of speed. It appears to be the fastest moving object ever discovered within our galaxy. The exact speed has not yet been determined accurately, but it is definitely faster than any other known object in the Milky Way galaxy. Dr. Thomas reports that once his newly acquired test data is finally analyzed carefully, an announcement of the estimated speed will be made. Dr. Thomas' records indicate he started working on the Ghost while at Kitt Peak in Arizona about sixteen months ago. He moved to the Gemini project because it offered better data-gathering power for this kind of object.

"What do you think? If we decide it's a go, I'll call my office and have Mili place it in the queue for transmittal. The sooner the better. Incidentally, we all owe Mili. She's the one who actually found this. She had forgotten something she wanted and had gone to the office to get it. Out of habit she turned on the computer to see what had happened since Friday and picked this out as she glanced through a whole bunch of news reports. She called me immediately and read it to me over the phone. I went there as soon as possible, read the print-out Mili made and called you. Thinking about possible fast action, I came up with the revised news release. I asked Mili to get it ready for the queue and wait for my instructions. Your OK and it will be in the mix in about one minute."

"How long can we wait and still get it in?" John asked.

"We're pushing the envelope already," Ginger replied. "Don't take any more time than absolutely necessary."

"I say go for it," Angus replied.

John carefully read through each of the papers several times as the others watched over his shoulder. "Call Mili," He said when they all shook their heads and spoke in agreement.

"And pray," Ruth added as Ginger dialed.

"By now the fat's in the fire for sure," Angus commented. "I'd like to be a little mouse and see Rumley's face when he reads that release. I hope you're right about the sloppy dating."

"There's a small chance the wrong date will be discovered and corrected by the wire services. They're normally not very careful about boring scientific releases," Ginger reported. "After that Reuters dispatch gets distributed and hits the New York News, any report from Dr. Thomas will be front page. I'm counting on that fact to push our release right there beside the Rumley story on the front page. My guess is they will be printed side by side with the emphasis on the dates. If that happens, we'll have a great advantage. In America, they'll pick up on your sports hero status and that gives us another big advantage. That won't carry as much weight in the U.K."

"Now let's go through all the information we have carefully and determine our next steps. With our release schedule completely out of whack and that Rumley thing, we're going to have to almost start over," John stated.

"I'd like to know something," Ali started. "What is the worst thing that could happen if we shared all we know with the public right now? Sooner or later they're going to know anyway. Is there any big advantage to postponing the inevitable? Humans are a rugged species. I've always thought they were at their best in a crisis. They will still look to us for information about the future of the star. I don't think this Rumley thing will come to much. My guess is he'll end up with egg and a few other things all over his face. I say, release the data to astronomers and get confirmation as soon as practical. Release the information we can put in laymen's terms to the public and see what happens. Feedback from that will direct our next steps."

Oona stepped back from the table. "Frankly, I like it. Put like that, it makes lots of sense to me. Incidentally, why not work up a worse case scenario right here and now. We're missing two, but we can talk to them on the phone tomorrow to get their input."

"Let's try to determine if there is any real value in waiting," Francis commented. "I, too, would like a picture of the worst that could happen."

Angus, visibly shaken by the Rumley news release, was regaining his confidence. "If we release before we get the next readings, our results are within about four percent. That gives a window of passage nearly eight light years across. Our next readings should reduce the error by about a third to about five light years. I had hoped to have that information before releasing any hint of real danger. Actually, it will provide us with a more defined guess as to the path. We will not have enough information for an accurate simulation since the arrival time is also in the same variable range. During that time, all the planets will move a distance that will greatly change the gravitational effect as the ghost speeds by. It will still be a crapshoot until at least ten years from now and perhaps a lot longer. Maybe Ali's right. We can release what information we now have any time we decide. Just remember, once it's out there it's show time. There's no turning back. The genie will be out of the bottle. To paraphrase an old Mohawk saying in English, you can't undead a dead man."

John was also relaxing some after the initial shock. "I think we should do the following: First, let's give it at least a day, maybe several. By then we should have the results on our news release. Next, let's all think hard about releasing our six-light-year guess soon rather than our four-light-year guess four or five months from now. What will the differences be? Early tomorrow we can inform the other two and get their input. They'll probably call us first if those releases show up where and when you think they will. Last, consider our course of action in the remote possibility that Rumley actually has any viable data. Personally, I'll bet it's all a con game. He has to know the overwhelming evidence the police and his own government have on his illegal activities. He's just throwing up a smoke screen to create doubts in the minds of the public. The media feeds on that kind of conflict."

Charlene finally spoke up, "Let's not let that lowlife panic us. Should we decide to release in the near future, we must plan both the wording and the timing carefully. We quickly responded by releasing what we did. I think that was a wise move, helped by unbelievable luck. Let us not be rushed into action with inadequate preparation. That's all I ask."

"In other words, make haste slowly. Is that what you're saying?" Lani asked her mom.

With that comment they had their first laugh of the evening.

"Very well put," John said.

As Ginger picked up her papers and they all started to leave, she said, "I think we should all try to get a good night's sleep. I can guarantee those phones will be ringing early in the morning."

*   *   *

At 1:30 in the morning, Ginger's phone woke her, just as she predicted the night before. It was Chelton, and he was greatly disturbed.

"Do you have any idea what I found on the front page of the paper this morning? Why wasn't I informed?"

"Wait and listen carefully," She said firmly, resisting the instinct to bite back at his angry words. She proceeded to tell him the entire story without permitting interruption. She finished by asking him to read her the date of their release.

"You're lucky. Just as you expected, it's dated a day before the Rumley story."

"Praise be to a friendly God!" Ginger exclaimed emphatically.

She went through their reasoning behind the decision to act so quickly without calling the two missing members. Chelton understood and agreed. He still asked, "Couldn't you have called me after and let me know?"

"That was after one your time. Would you have slept any after you found out? We'd have only given you five or six hours of sleepless anxiety. You could have done nothing."

"You are right. Were our situations in reverse, I probably would have done the same thing. I'll call Serena right away. She may not have received the news as yet. If we're lucky, I'll save her the shock that blew my mind."

Ginger was grateful for his sympathetic response. "Thanks, lover, for understanding. I was sure you would once you heard the whole story. I'll try never to do such a thing again, unless I have to."

"I'd like to talk, but I'd better call Serena right away. Please keep me posted on this. I don't want any more surprises."

"I'll definitely keep in touch. Incidentally, why don't you call me when I get to the office at about seven? I'd like to hear Serena's response, and we can talk about our next steps."

After they hung up, Ginger lay awake, thinking. Momentarily wounded by Chelton's anger before she had a chance to explain, she realized what pain anger from a loved one can bring. She was grateful she had been able to resist that primal instinct to fight back. She relived the entire episode several times, admitting she would have been at least as angry were the situations reversed. As her tension slowly released, she finally gave in to sleep.

*   *   *

Chelton was in touch with Serena in a matter of minutes after his call to Ginger. No, she hadn't seen any news yet; she was too busy with chores at the inn. When he was finished with the details, Serena agreed they had probably done the best thing.

"What a gut-wrenching experience that must have been," Serena commented. "They had to make instantaneous decisions that could have worldwide consequences. I'm sure, had we been there, every-thing would have been concluded just as it was. I'm proud of them."

"You're right on."

"Thank you for calling me before I saw it in the media. You know I would have been as shocked as you and maybe a little angrier."

"You, Sunflower, angry? That's hard for me to believe."

"You're joking of course. I know you've seen me angry."

"Very few times that I can recall. Very few indeed."

"Well anyhow, I'll certainly watch the TV news to see what slant they place on this. I'll say one thing, that little gal of yours sure trumped old Rumley's card. That was a clever little trick she was able to pull off."

"Yup. She did good. They all did good."

"Sometimes the good guys have to be a little trickier than the bad. It will be interesting to see how this plays out. I suppose we'll be on the phone a lot over this in the next few days."

"Maybe we can set up conferencing over the internet. You do have access there, don't you?"

"Of course. Angus suggested that before we left Hawaii, remember? Peter set it up and showed me how to do conferencing. You won't catch this Mohawk unprepared."

"It had completely slipped my mind. So we're all set to have a conference over the Internet. That's great. I'll send Angus an e-mail immediately to tell him of our conversation. We can plan our confer-ences that way."

"Sounds like a plan to me. I've got to get back to work now. I'll be watching the TV news while I'm working."

After hanging up, both went to watch for the story on the TV.

*　　*　　*

At six, Angus sat bolt upright in bed, waking Lani who asked sleepily, "What's going on? You scared me half to death jumping up like that."

"I woke up startled because it's getting light and no one has called. That's strange. I was sure we'd hear from one of them long before now. Maybe nothing's hit the news." As he spoke, Angus reached over and turned on the radio and began searching for a news broad-cast. There it was, on the Hilo station.

"Hilo has hit the world news with two conflicting stories about one of its resident celebrities, the famous all-pro running back, Angus Thomas, who is now an astronomer at the Gemini Project. Saturday, Dr. Thomas released startling news about a new star he has been studying for two years. It is the fastest known object ever found in our galaxy. That news would not be so startling if it weren't for charges made earlier today by a former colleague of Dr. Thomas, a Dr. Richard Rumley. Dr. Rumley claims that Dr. Thomas stole from him the information on the star. A former Gemini astronomer, Dr. Rumley claims charges filed against him by the Hilo police are bogus and that Thomas is the real criminal. This reporter talked to Lieutenant Peter Hiakawa of the Hilo police just a few moments ago who reports Rumley's charge to be absolute nonsense. Hiakawa says that since the case is pending, he can provide few details, but he did say they have conclusive evidence as to Rumley's guilt in the spying affair. In addition, Rumley has been charged with attempted vehicle homicide after allegedly running down Dr. Thomas and nearly killing him. He also explained that Rumley had been turned over to the British government to face similar spying charges in Britain. When the British case is concluded, Rumley is to be returned to Hilo to face the criminal charges here. It appears Rumley's startling charges are merely a ploy to distract the public and create doubt. Listen for more information on our next news broadcast when we hope to be able to talk to Dr. Thomas and see what he has to say."

Angus immediately grabbed his phone and dialed John who had already heard the same news broadcast. "I'm surprised neither of us has received a call," John said. "They're probably trying to reach us as we speak. Other than Hiakawa, they know of no one but the two of us to call. I'll bet the local reporters will be all over Gemini when we get there. The first plane in from Honolulu will bring the big guns. I hope we're prepared for a busy day of being harassed."

"Why don't you call Gemini and warn the desk what's coming?" Angus suggested. "I'll call Ginger, who probably knows all about this. Maybe she can help keep us out of trouble."

"I'll call and then forward my phone to Gemini. That will give me a chance to get dressed and down there. Maybe you should leave your phone off the hook after you call Ginger."

"We'll keep the phone busy calling the rest of the group after I talk to Ginger. I won't get off it until they're all in the know. Then I'll definitely leave it off the hook."

"Good luck. I'll see you at the madhouse," John said as he hung up.

Angus clicked the phone several times until he received a dial tone then called Ginger. The phone had barely started to ring when Ginger answered, "Whoever it is, shoot. I'm in a big hurry."

"It's Angus. You've heard the news," he replied quickly.

"Yes, and so have Chelton and Serena. I've talked to Chelton and he called Serena. Here's what's going to happen. Listen carefully because I'm out the door when I finish. You are going to be deluged with reporters at Gemini. I'll be one of them. Treat me just like the rest. Be courteous, but don't tell them anything more than what's in the release. If anyone tries to talk to you before you get to the Op Center, tell them you will only talk to reporters there. Be firm. Stay in control. If you can, get the Op Center to lock the doors immediately. Suggest to John that you both talk outside the front entrance. Don't let any of the reporters inside, and try to keep them away from any of the other people there. Tell them the Op Center is a very important scientific institution and that those people inside must not have their work interrupted. John, as the head of the center, and you, as the person in the news, will answer their questions. As soon as I have asked you a few questions, I will leave hurriedly, jump in my car and speed away. After going 'round the block, I'll drive in the rear entrance to the employee parking and come to the employees' door. Have Lani or Jenny open the door for me. I need to talk to you, Lani and John together or separately as early as we can manage it. If whatever you have to say can wait till then, say 'Bye.'"

Angus thought for a moment and then said, "Bye," instantly followed by a click as Ginger hung up the phone. He remembered the front doors remained locked until eight each morning. Since he didn't have to call about that, he merely lay the phone on the table and hurried to get dressed. Lani was ready and waiting as he finished putting on his shoes. Just then the front door buzzer sounded.

"They're here," he almost shouted to Lani. "Let's head out the back door for your car."

Luckily there was no one at the back door. Approaching the Op Center, they could see five or six people standing at the front doors peering in. There was no TV camera truck or crew, and he realized he didn't know if there was one on the island. They parked the car and headed for the employee entrance where Kerry Anaaka stood protecting the door, arms crossed and looking official in his security guard uniform.

"John posted me at the door to keep the animals at bay. You folks have business here?" he asked with a big grin as he unlocked the door, adding, "I'll bet John will be happy to see you."

Angus answered with a slap on the back and a big "Thank you!" as they stepped inside. Remembering Ginger's instructions, he turned back to Kerry. "A cute blonde parking a yellow convertible will show up before long. Her name is Ginger Cari and she should be let in to join us."

John was waiting as they walked into his open office. "I don't think I'm ready for this. How about you? You dealt with reporters a lot in your football career. Any suggestions?"

"Just stay in control. Stay in control," Angus said emphatically. "If you want, I can handle the first barrage of questions. Ginger gave me some ideas, and my past experiences will help. The main thing is to say no more than what's in our news release and what we know from this morning's news." He then relayed what Ginger had said in their rapid-fire phone exchange of a few minutes ago. Angus was shocked when he saw from the clock that it was just six-forty.

"When do we face the mob?" John asked.

"Why not now?" Angus said. "Let's get it over with, so they can make the seven o'clock news."

They headed for the front door while Lani headed for the back to meet Ginger when she came in.

By the time they reached the full-length glass doors, there were eleven people standing waiting. Several had microphones, and there were two men with miniature TV cameras aimed at the door. Angus had forgotten that technology had substantially reduced the size of TV equipment. What used to require a truck could now be easily carried and used by even a small woman. He held up his hand to indicate the doors would be open shortly. He wanted to wait for a certain blonde reporter before opening the doors. Almost immediately, he saw Ginger's convertible coming down the street and double parking at the exit to the Op Center driveway. As she hurried up the walk, John unlocked the door, and they stepped out into bedlam. Angus immediately raised his hand and requested silence. When the sound lowered enough so he could be heard, he said loudly, "I have a statement to make. When it is quiet enough for all to hear, I will begin." He waited until all the voices were stilled.

"We will only answer questions from one person at a time, and we will select a new person for each new question. Anyone who interrupts will be moved to last on our selection list. You may direct your questions to me or Director John Carroll. That way, we will all get through this quickly and productively."

Pointing to a tall man in the front Angus said, "Shoot."

"Dr. Rumley stated the charges you made against him were bogus and that you were, in fact, guilty of stealing from him. What is your response to his charges?"

"First of all, I made no charges against Dr. Rumley. The city of Hilo, the state of Hawaii and the British government have made the charges. As far as proof is concerned, Lieutenant Hiakawa has already answered that question, having much more knowledge as to what proof they have than anyone here at Gemini. Next question," he said, pointing to a woman off to the side.

"The lieutenant said it was an attempted murder. Did it actually happen that way? Couldn't it have been an accident or possibly another person that ran you down?"

"I believe the lieutenant's words and my sworn deposition on the matter have already answered that question. Next."

After several more questions about Rumley were answered in a similar fashion, Angus selected Ginger.

Seeking to change the direction of the questioning, she asked, "Would you tell us, please, what exactly is this new star you have discovered, and is it any more than an interesting object for astronomers to study and write papers about? Usually those things are boring to the public."

"If the result of my work of the last few years is accurate and my calculations flawless, this is the fastest moving thing, by far, ever found within our own galaxy. It is a small star, a type called a red dwarf because much of its light comes at the red end of the spectrum. Our sun is a red dwarf star. The new star is probably much like our sun, but is only about half its mass. I came here to study it because of the power of the new Gemini telescope. I found the new star while studying a nearby star named Barnard's star. My work was being done at Kitt Peak in Arizona. A great deal more viewing power is needed to research this new star than was available at Kitt Peak. For this reason, my work was moved to Hilo and the marvelous new Gemini project. I believe the public may be more interested in these sorts of objects than you might think. General public interest in astronomical objects, particularly new ones, has grown sharply in recent years. I don't think the public finds them boring."

The next question came from a large man on the left. "Just how fast is this star moving, and how far away is it?"

"We recently concluded a long series of observations of this star, which my colleagues at Kitt Peak called the ghost. Until the latest data has been studied thoroughly and the calculations checked and rechecked, we can only say its light comes to us from about three hundred light years away and that it is moving much faster than any known nearby object. Its unusual speed makes it so interesting. Otherwise there are many other similar stars which are much closer, including Barnard's star which is only six light years away and about a third the size of the ghost. This new star's exact speed and distance will remain a mystery for many years or until we develop far more accurate instrumentation or new methods of measuring. We will be releasing the results of our latest measurements, including our best estimate of its speed, within several weeks. At that time, we will have confirmed our observations and have a more accurate answer. I must add that precise measurements of the object may not be available for many years."

After this answer Ginger turned suddenly, ran to her car and sped away. Sensing a good time to end the questioning, John announced, "That's all the questions we have time for right now. You all have deadlines, and we must get to work."

Amidst cries of objections from some of the reporters, including the two TV cameramen, they entered the Op Center, locking the doors behind them. When they were well away from the door, John said with a smile, "I think that went fairly well. You did an excellent job. I'm impressed."

"Thank you, John. I guess my previous experiences with press interviews helped. Now I'd like to hear what Ginger has to say."

"How'd we do?" John asked Ginger as she and Lani walked into his office where he and Angus waited.

"Perfect," she replied with a big smile. "You came across much more focused on the scientific aspects than on Rumley. That's why I switched subjects. Fortunately, the rest followed my lead. What happened after I left?"

"We closed the questioning, came inside and locked the door," Angus replied.

"You didn't just leave them hanging?"

"Of course not. John told them they had deadlines and we had work to do. There were a few complaints when we stepped inside, but we definitely had control. Just like you said."

"Very good. Is there a TV or radio in the center? We should watch the seven o'clock news. It'll be on in just a few minutes," Ginger suggested.

"There's a TV in the lunch room. Let's hurry," Lani answered as she stood up and headed for the door. They turned on the TV just as the news began. Nothing from the Gemini press meeting had yet reached the national news. The local news was another story. The meeting appeared in its entirety including John's closing statement. Ginger was pleased.

"Let's see what comments those two make. That's what I want to hear," Ginger said. "That may give us a read on how the rest of the U.S. will react."

The two news people, a man and a woman, talked about the Gemini project at length. They also mentioned Angus' football career in a glowing manner. Until this news report, they had not known he was in Hawaii or that he had become an astronomer. They expressed some interest in the new star, mentioning how big the astronomy business was for Hilo and the island of Hawaii. They treated the Rumley news almost as a joke, down-playing it as the concoction of a desperate man, deep in trouble. So far Ginger's little trick had worked well.

"Don't you have a story to file?" Lani asked Ginger.

"I filed it before leaving home," Ginger replied. "I knew just about everything that would come out in the questioning. Angus, you just about threw me for a loop when you went into such detail about the star. Then I realized it was all well known information or contained in the releases, so it worked out OK. Now we had better prepare the new releases and a few statements for the media."

"Shouldn't we get Frank Ito on this Rumley thing right away?" Angus asked.

"Already done," John replied. "We'd better contact the rest of the group to let them know what's going on."

Lani answered, "I took care of that while you two were talking to the reporters. I'm sure they all watched the news too. Angus, as usual, I checked your e-mail and noticed one from Chelton. He wants to do a conference over the Internet as soon as you can set it up. He says he and Serena are all ready. Just e-mail them the time for the conference."

They decided to try for the conference at nine, a little more than an hour away.

Internet Conference and Showtime

Everyone in the Gemini Community Action Committee waited in place for more information. At nine, three in the afternoon in New York, they started connecting for the conference and by nine-fifteen everyone had signed in. Fortunately, they were all set up for voice communication. It took them several minutes to become accustomed to waiting silently as each one spoke in turn. Serena quickly regained her leadership status and ran the conference, calling on each person to speak in turn. By the end of an hour, they were doing well adapting to this new and different method of communicating as a group while being in so many different places so far apart. The eight o'clock news in Hilo brought no new developments and the news channels in New York were rerunning their previous clips on the incident. As yet, nothing had come into the national news from the interview at Gemini.

They decided to take three specific actions: First, they would revise the news releases and their schedule to fit the new situation. The media and public reactions, including any new information, would be used to determine if any change of the exact dates and times became necessary. They decided the final release would be delayed no more than ten days, making the latest date September 6. Second, Angus would release all his data to OSI on Tuesday, two days before the same data would be released for confirmation by other astronomers and as he had promised. Third, they would maintain their group of eleven intact and in secret in order to be prepared for any more unexpected developments. This would turn out to be an extremely wise decision.

They discussed many aspects of each of the three actions. Ginger would develop the revised news releases with input from the group. All releases would be sent to each member via e-mail for corrections and approval before being given to the press. At 11:30 Hawaiian time, they closed the conference and went on their separate ways. Angus and Lani went to catch up on work that built up during their honeymoon. Ginger left to revise the news releases, and John had to get back to the business of the Op Center.

At 12:30, Angus received a phone call from Chelton.

"Angus, your little meeting with the media has hit the world news big time. You're a big hit in the U.S., not so big in the U.K. or the rest of the world. All the U.S. media are focusing in a positive way on you and your new discovery while nearly ignoring the Rumley news. Unfortunately, my British friends at the UN seem a lot more interested in what Rumley has to say, so we're not out of the woods on this one yet. So far, there is no word from Rumley. Apparently, he still refuses to talk to reporters. Luckily, none of the people here at the UN know we're related, so I am viewed as an impartial source of information. It provides me with an opportunity to hear many viewpoints I would lose if our relationship were known. I'll keep my ear to the ground for any trend that might spell trouble for us."

"That's mostly good news."

"I want to congratulate you on that TV news bit at the door. You came off positive, straightforward and knowledgeable. Ginger's question changed the focus and turned things our way. I got a big kick seeing her on national TV. My bet is some network people noticed her as well. She was very professional and looked fantastic. I'll bet she gets several job offers from that one little bit."

"You think so?"

"You bet. The cameraman focused close up on her for some time after she finished her question. Even in the shortened reports they show her complete clip. They like attractive women in their shots and she looked good on camera. So good I might even ask her for a date," he said, finishing with a laugh.

They talked for several minutes, feeling somewhat encouraged about the current turn of events. Before hanging up, they both agreed to remain vigilant for other possible surprises.

*   *   *

The group held another Internet conference Tuesday morning in Hilo. They approved the scheduled distribution of the full data Angus and Lani had compiled. It included his latest conclusions about the possible damaging path of the ghost. It also included the best information from Charlie Botkin's simulations. This shirt-box sized package of data would be sent overnight to Pat Yamaguchi and Charlie Botkin. They would be notified by phone the information was coming. One copy would be hand delivered to the federal offices in Hilo for delivery to Jan Lux of OSI. His work in Hilo completed, Jan had returned to his office in Honolulu. The three packages of data should arrive at their destinations at about the same time on Wednesday.

Thursday, the data would be released through normal channels for any astronomer who wanted to confirm the work. Angus and Lani planned to drive up to Waimea to personally deliver a copy of the data to Dr. Schuman of the Keck observatories. Angus called Dr. Schuman, who was thrilled that he was being given special treatment. When this was done, it would only be a matter of a few days before the final bombshell announcement would be made. If all went as scheduled, Monday, September 3, at ten in the evening, the third news release would announce the projected path and timetable of the ghost. The ominous possibility of the effect the star's passing might have on the earth would be included. That time was chosen so most of the world would get the news early Tuesday morning. If all went as planned, the whole world would know the terrible possibility by the time the sun came up in Hawaii on Tuesday.

It was a solemn group of eleven, separated by distance and time, that finally made the decision to proceed as scheduled. Even with the distortion of the internet, they could not hide the trembling hints of apprehension in their voices. The steps they were about to take could have world-changing consequences. They all prayed together for their own sound judgement and God's help in this fateful undertaking.

Humanity was about to slip into a morass of frightful speculation. Would the inner strength that has held people together through wars, famine, plagues and the atomic sword of Damocles prevail? What would the startup of a thirty-year clock of possible doom mean to the only species that knew the cataclysmic risk of the future? Thirty years of decreasing uncertainty, waiting for an end that might not come is a poor promise for stability. Time alone would define the answers. No human had ever before faced the fearsome knowledge soon to confront the entire human race. What would the countless faces of mankind show once they knew?

A somber Angus handed the two data packages to the express pickup early that Tuesday afternoon. In each package was a copy of the release scheduled for the following Monday, along with a request to keep the information confidential until the release came out. There were also instructions to place the release in the hands of a news service if it didn't appear by Tuesday morning September 4. He then headed for the federal offices with the remaining package. It did not contain the release or other instructions sent with the first two. The wheels that would roll for thirty years were now in motion.

Early Thursday morning, Lani and Angus drove to Waimea for a visit with Dr. Schuman and to deliver the package of data. Angus wanted to tell him about his discovery in person and thank him for how he handled the OSI incident.

"Welcome. Come on in," Dr. Schuman said with a big smile when the two were ushered into his office. "I am pleased you have taken time to deliver this information in person. I consider it an honor, especially since this has become a major news story. Sit down, please."

As they shook hands and sat down, Angus replied, "Sadly so, I'm afraid. Actually, that's nothing compared with what's to come."

"That sounds ominous," Schuman answered, losing his broad smile in an instant.

Angus began sharing an overall picture of the results of his research on the ghost to a startled Dr. Schuman. Shortly after he began, Dr. Schuman interrupted. "With your permission, I'd like for Dr. Oscar Dickson to join us. He's an associate as well as a good friend and will be working with me on confirmation of your work."

"By all means," Angus responded.

Angus and Lani, together with Schuman and Dickson, spent the next two hours going over the data and conclusions spread out on the desk in front of them. Because of the dreadful urgency, they promised to change the schedule of the Keck telescopes and have a preliminary confirmation of Angus' work within a week. The data Angus had provided would enable them to find the ghost easily and run spectral measurements to confirm the data rather quickly.

As they concluded their meeting, Dr. Dickson, who registered shock at the news, continued to display a constant look of amazement tempered with fear. He had the look of a man attacked by a wild animal that hadn't hurt him, yet lurked hidden, waiting to attack again. "I don't know how you have managed to maintain sanity. It must have been a terrible strain, holding this information while trying to find the least traumatic way to make it public. I think your efforts remarkable."

"To me, the most troubling aspect of this whole thing is just how little we actually know of what will happen when that star arrives. Unfortunately, it will be years before we have data accurate enough to determine the path, so viable simulations of the possible results can be generated. Even then, we may not know for sure until the time actually comes," Angus replied.

"We are actually much more fearful of what the people will do, how they will react to the news," Lani commented. "The wrong wording of a headline or a sensationalist comment from the media might trigger panic in many places."

Dr. Schuman leaned forward, his heavily lined face intent. "One thing is for certain, those tabloids will have a field day. I can see the headlines now, 'Ghost star spells doom for earth,' or 'Psychic sees face of God in doom star.' I can't imagine what all the crazies in the world will do. I pray for sanity and calm consideration but fear the opposite."

Angus nodded in agreement. "We should know in just a few days. I think there will be some initial excitement, but maybe thoughtful and reasonable minds will prevail. You know how a crisis can bring people together."

When they stood up to end the discussion, Dr. Dickson, still deeply troubled, turned a haggard face to Angus. "I certainly hope you are right."

On the way back to Hilo and the Op Center, they stopped for lunch, where they recounted their morning meeting and commented on how quickly the media had relegated their story to the back pages. They knew the short flurry just past would pale in comparison to what was to happen when the coming bombshell was dropped. Before they left the restaurant and headed for the Op Center, Lani leaned her head on Angus' shoulder for a moment. They were two people deliriously in love, completely unprepared for what was waiting for them at their destination.

20

As she started to turn the last corner, Lani quickly straightened her car and then turned to the left instead of the right for the last few blocks toward the Op Center. From three blocks away, she noticed several military vehicles parked in the access drive and quickly decided to head in the opposite direction. Looking out the rear window as Lani drove slowly away, Angus counted at least a dozen Marines with weapons standing in a semicircle around the entrance.

"What the devil is going on?" Angus exclaimed.

"I'm glad I saw that before heading down the street," Lani replied. "How can we find out what's happening? I certainly don't want to go there until we know for sure."

"I'll bet that's OSI's reaction to the data we gave them. Let's get across town and find a pay phone. I don't want to use my cell phone. I'll bet we're back to the old guessing game."

They drove downtown and then north on Highway 19 all the way to Wainaku, about five miles from the Op Center. They found a drive-up pay phone in a filling station where Angus called the Op Center.

A strange male voice answered, "Gemini Operations, this is Sergeant Raines. Please state your business."

Startled, but thinking quickly, Angus asked, "This is Dr. Dickson of the Keck Observatory. Where's Jenny?"

"She's not available. Is there anyone else you could speak to?" The sergeant asked gruffly.

"Yes, I'd like to speak to Dr. John Carroll please," Angus replied, trying not to sound alarmed.

After several moments of unintelligible muffled male voices the sergeant returned and said, "He'll be with you in just a moment."

Angus hoped John would recognize his voice and not give him away. He was now certain that until he knew what was going on, he did not want to fall into the hands of the military. Finally he heard, "This is John Carroll."

Very deliberately and hoping John would catch on, Angus said, "This is Dr. Oscar Dickson from the Keck Observatory. I'm returning your call from yesterday about possible cooperation on that solar flare project. Would it be possible to see you this afternoon?"

It took John just an instant to realize it was Angus and that he knew something was wrong. "No! It would not be a good time," John answered emphatically. "The military is here looking for two of our people, and I'll be tied up all day helping them." After a long pause he added, "Why don't we plan to meet at our favorite bar for lunch tomorrow, say twelve o'clock, as before? I will have some time then."

Good thinking, John, I get the message, Angus thought to himself, then replied, "That will be fine. I hope we will be able to cooperate on this. See you tomorrow noon."

Angus hung up the phone and said to Lani, "Here we go again."

"What was all that about lunch tomorrow?"

"That John is one quick thinker. Unless I'm mistaken, he plans on meeting me at midnight tonight at the bar we used before for a secret meeting. He definitely warned us not to come to the Op Center. We'd best not go home either. What can we do till midnight?"

"Let's call Ginger. My OSI-induced paranoia about tapped phones has returned, so I'll pretend to be a friend. I know she'll recognize my voice. Maybe she can tell us something."

Angus handed her the phone. "Do it!"

When Mili answered, Lani said, "Is Ginger there?"

"Who's calling please?"

"This is Lulu, a friend of Ginger's"

"Lulu?" Ginger questioned when she picked up the phone.

"Yes, Lulu from the big party. You remember."

"Oh . . . Lulu . . . of course. How are you?" Ginger caught on as she recognized Lani's voice. "I'm busy right now, but I would love to see you. Try me tomorrow. By the way, how about another interview? You know, like the one I did with your hubby?"

Lani understood clearly what Ginger meant and was quick to reply. "Good idea. I'll see about arranging one soon. I'll call again tomorrow."

"OK. What was that all about? I only heard one side of a strange conversation you know."

"We're to meet Ginger at the restaurant at the top of the Mokuloa. You know, where she interviewed you."

"How'd you figure that one out?"

By the time Lani had related what Ginger said, they were headed for the Mokuloa. Fearing Lani's little red car might give them away, they stopped and rented a windowless van, leaving her car in the rental company's lot. When they arrived at the hotel, Ginger's car was parked on the street somewhat away from the hotel entrance. Angus parked at the curb in front of Ginger's car, and they headed for the door. They reached the restaurant and walked to the far side of the bar to join Ginger, who was sitting at a table that could not be seen from the entrance.

"I'm glad you got my message," Ginger said as they sat down. "I'm sure my phone is not tapped, but I didn't want to take a chance. Lulu, that was clever. How'd you know what happened, and why didn't they grab you? When I heard about it, I was sure you two would be the first ones they'd be after."

Angus explained what happened. "We were in Waimea all morning at Keck headquarters talking to Dr. Schuman and delivering the data to him. We saw the military long before we reached the Op Center, so Lani turned away and we headed north out of town. I called John pretending to be someone else, about the same way Lani called you. I'm supposed to meet him at midnight in a little bar around the corner from my apartment. He gave me a clue just as you did Lani. Now, can you tell me what's going on?"

"The Navy has closed down the entire island. Nothing gets off; nothing comes in and no communications either. Try calling off the island and you get a canned message that says all communications are down temporarily. And get this, my news wire service and all

Internet access have been shut down as well. I can't get a word off the island and as far as I know, no word can get in. Local phone service seems OK, but I'll bet there are all kinds of monitoring going on. When the news wire and the Internet were shut down, I tried calling our office in Honolulu. That's when I was told all lines of communication were down. When I walked outside the office, several jeeps and a command car drove down the street. It was like an invasion. It was scary. I got in my car and drove over to the airport to see about going to work in our Honolulu office. There were several huge military planes there disgorging men and equipment and the airport was shut down. I asked a woman walking from the terminal if she knew what was going on. She told me it started about nine this morning when four military aircraft landed and started unloading men and equipment. They wouldn't let her leave her closed shop until just a few minutes ago when they told all the vendors and their employees to go home. They said it was some kind of a security emergency of a technical nature and there was no danger at all for anyone to fear."

Angus pursed his lips. "Well, Lux and his gang have brought out the big guns. I'm sure the data packages got away. They should have been off the island on Tuesday before I dropped off the data for OSI. That data I gave OSI triggered this, I'm sure."

Lani turned to Ginger. "What about our news release for next Tuesday? How will we get that out?"

Ginger laughed. "When we were putting the polishing touches on the news release, Francis asked me to find a way to make sure it reached the media no matter what. He thought something like this might happen as soon as OSI received their data. We know there are copies in the data packages you sent to the mainland. I made four more copies along with detailed instructions as to what to do with them. I expressed them out at about the same time you sent the data packages. They went to Chelton, Serena, my mom and Warren Tusla. I've talked to Chelton and he received his copy. He plans to read it to the UN General Assembly on Tuesday morning when they will be in open session. In the remote possibility of OSI detaining him, he will make two copies which he will arrange for two of his closest friends at the UN to present if he is not there. As we speak, the copies should be in the hands of a secure diplomatic courier for delivery to his friends at the assembly on Tuesday morning."

"Sounds like you've covered all the bases," Angus commented. "If this wasn't such a serious matter, it would be a fun game. What about the others—your mom and Warren?"

"The actual release is in a separate sealed envelope with specific instructions attached to the outside as to whom to contact and how to give them the information. That is to be done Tuesday morning by ten unless one of us calls to cancel. There's more."

"OK, what else?" he asked.

"There's an outfit in New York called Mail From Anywhere. They mail cards and letters from anyplace in the world and at any time you specify. They are used mostly by people who want to send a special personal greeting card from a special place to arrive on a special day for all kinds of reasons. I shipped them a package of ten envelopes containing copies of the release. Four are addressed to major news services. Four are addressed to the heads of state of Japan, South Africa, Germany and Saudi Arabia. One is addressed to the Vatican and the last to your friend Cy Dooley in L.A. Each of these will be mailed from their destination cities on Tuesday."

"I hope no one sneaks a peek inside those envelopes."

Ginger continued, "I used greeting card envelopes and hand written addresses. Each one was addressed to a person at a street address. No official titles, business names or government locations were shown. The one to the Vatican was the only one that might seem strange. I included a letter explaining our reasoning and that we were afraid certain individuals in the U.S. government would try to prevent the information from reaching the public. There's a saying, Extraordinary effort in extraordinary circumstances, which I think applies. This certainly is an extraordinary circumstance. Had I thought of more things to try, I would have done so as well. A little overkill can't hurt."

Lani nodded in agreement. "I'd say massive overkill and that ten too many are infinitely better than one too few. That is clever. Let's see if OSI can stop that."

They sat quietly for a moment staring, each deep in furious thought. Finally, Angus broke the silence. "I wonder what we should do now? I don't want to face OSI. We can't go to either of our apartments and we can't go to Lani's folks'. They'll probably cover all the hotels sooner or later. Do you suppose it would be safe at Francis and Oona's?"

"I don't know. OSI was there once. They might come back," Lani replied.

"Let's think for a while," Ginger suggested. "If we cross off all members of our group, Lani's family and close friends, it doesn't leave us with many safe havens."

After another period of silence, Lani suddenly brightened up and said, "I know. The Millers. We'd be safe there. I know they'd help us, and OSI surely doesn't know about them."

"Not a bad idea," Angus said. "You could call them from here. I'm sure the hotel phones are safe. Before you do, let's try to map out a strategy for the next few days."

They ordered a plate of appetizers and soft drinks to be less conspicuous in the almost empty restaurant. They spent the next hour reviewing their resources and searching for viable choices. Lani reminded them that her laptop, complete with SSR card, was in the trunk of her car. Angus' laptop was at the Lanes' house with his other possessions he had yet to retrieve. Maybe Ginger could find a way to get it. That would provide secure communications, albeit over short distances. They guessed that Ginger and Ruth would be the least suspect of the group and that Ginger would try contacting Ruth later in the afternoon. Angus and Lani would leave as soon as they could to get the laptop from her car and then head for the Millers' home.

When they finished, Lani called and spoke with Maria Miller, who said they would gladly help out. As they were leaving, Ginger asked Lani, "What was your cousin's name—the computer genius who set up your laptop? I'll need his number too if you have it."

"Sandy, Sandy Namahoe. I think I have his number right here," Lani answered, searching through her purse. "You're going to see if you can get one of those SSR transmitters for your computer, right?"

"You guessed it. That should give us a bit more secure communications capability," Ginger replied as Lani handed her Sandy's phone number.

"Great idea," Angus said, "Then we wouldn't have to try to retrieve my laptop. We might even get Francis to use it. I showed him how while I was there."

Armed with the Miller's address and phone number, Ginger headed for her car. A little cautious, Angus and Lani would wait inside the hotel until Ginger drove away before venturing out. Angus heaved a sigh of relief as they finally drove off in the van without incident. Retrieval of the laptop from Lani's car and the drive to the Miller's proved equally uneventful.

*   *   *

It was a bit past three when they walked up the steps to the Miller's neat little home. Maria gave them each a hug and then asked, "Do you know what's going on? Dan just called from the docks. Said the Navy won't let any boats go out. There's Marines all over the harbor and a small Navy warship out patrolling in the bay. He's on his way home by now."

"We have an idea what it's about," Lani answered. "Can we sit? It may take some time to explain."

"Of course. Let's sit at the kitchen table. I was about to have a cup of coffee. Would you like some?" she asked as she led them into the kitchen.

As they sat and talked, Angus told them as much of the situation as he could without divulging the news to come the next Tuesday. He explained, "There are some things we just can't tell you until the news is released to the whole world. I hope you understand. It's not just you we can't tell. It's everyone."

"It's a difficult situation," Lani explained. "I . . . we want so much to tell you, but it would not change a thing. Only a few more than a dozen people in the entire world know, and they are under the same self-imposed restraint as the two of us. I can't even tell members of my own family."

"If you say so, Lani. I've known you since you were quite small and know what a good person you are. We'll just wait till Tuesday. It's so hard to imagine that something about you and your new star could bring on all this. It's not an alien invasion is it?" Maria asked with a sudden look of fear in her eyes.

"Absolutely not!" Angus replied emphatically and with a little grin. "Nothing like that at all. It's something that might happen a long time in the future. Please don't ask any more questions. We've already said a bit more than we should have."

"All right. I won't, but when Dan gets here, you'll have to go through the whole thing again with him. He may not give up so easily."

"Then you'll just have to convince him it's OK," Lani replied.

A half hour later, when Dan did arrive, they discovered Maria was right. After much persuasion from Maria, Dan gave up and agreed to wait for Tuesday. Being there with only the clothes on their backs and not knowing how long they would stay, Angus and Lani went to a nearby shopping center to pick up what they might need. Maria went along to show them where to go and to pick up some groceries to feed their guests.

At five, the phone rang. It was Ruth asking for Lani. Ginger had driven to Ruth's to let her know what was going on since she was afraid to use the phone.

"I'm calling from the church. I seriously doubt they have this phone bugged," Ruth said. "Ginger has reached Sandy. He is going to pick up that SSR card to install on her computer by the time she gets home. He said there was no point in putting one in my computer as the local SSR network had been shut down just like the Internet services. He said you should be close enough to Ginger for a direct link. I'm way too far away."

"That's good news. Did she say when she would try to contact us?"

"She said once she's in business, she'll try every half hour starting on the hour. She just left, so my guess is it will be at least 6:00 or 6:30 before she's ready. Incidentally, she drove by your folks' on the way here. Noticing a military vehicle in the driveway, she kept on going. I hope your folks aren't too worried. I'll head over there in a little while. If the military doesn't interfere with a little female pastor on a pastoral call, I may be able to tell them you're OK."

"That would be splendid. They must be worried. It would be a great comfort for them to know where we are and that we're OK."

"I'm going to try. Meanwhile, I'm going to pray a lot. With help from the good Lord, I'm sure it will all work out."

When her call was completed, Lani relayed Ruth's message. Angus would be at the computer by six to see if Ginger was able to make contact.

It was 6:30 when the words, "Thirty-five, are you out there?" scrolled across his screen. Angus yelled as he realized they had secure communications to at least one point. A few notes back and forth and they learned that neither had any new information. They decided to check with each other at 8:30 and 11:00. Ginger would monitor the network from 1:30 on to find out what Angus learned from John.

*   *   *

At 11:30, Angus left alone for his rendezvous with John. There was no point in them both taking the risk. When he walked into the bar, John was in the last booth dressed in black sweats with a hooded top.

"What's with the outfit?" Angus asked with a grin when he sat down.

"It's not funny," John replied sharply. "There's a Marine Jeep with two guys in it parked in front of my house. They followed me home and have been out there ever since. I had to dress completely in black, then climb out a side window and crawl through my neighbor's yard to keep from being seen. I had no idea where those two were, but they were out there and maybe with a few buddies. Do you know how far it is from my house here? My guess is five miles at least. Now, I'll have to climb back in that window without being seen. I hope this meeting is worth it. I'm sorry. I'm not upset with you. I'm just ticked at this whole stupid situation. Our government is doing exactly what we thought they might do. At least OSI is. They want to quash the scary part of our information. They want to keep it from the public. Who knows what they might do to achieve their ends or how long they would keep it secret if they succeed."

"Relax a minute, John. You're jumping all over the place, and that's not like you. Why don't you start at the beginning and explain to me all that happened?"

"OK, Angus. I'm sorry to be so flustered. Let me get my thoughts together." After a short silence and a deep breath, John began. "Shortly after nine, I happened to be up front when several military vehicles drove up and a bunch of Marines jumped out to cover both entrances. A Marine captain walked in the door and asked Jenny for me. She looked my way with that what-do-I-do-now look, so I walked over and told him who I was and asked what this was all about. He handed me a document which he explained gave the military virtual control over the island and over the Gemini Operations Center, in particular. In effect, it was martial law. He was polite, but firm. I will say all the Marines were courteous and polite, real professionals in their dealings with our people. He immediately replaced Jenny with a Marine sergeant to man the phones. The sergeant asked Jenny to help him become used to the phone system. He was courteous and quite considerate. As soon as the phone was secured, the sergeant used the PA system to announce their presence and their authority. He urged everyone to continue working as before and they would do their best not to interfere. Then he asked for you. When I explained you were away he dispatched two Marines to your office. Finding it locked, he asked me for the keys. They opened the door, went inside and closed the door. At this point he asked to speak to me in private, so I took him to my office. This is what he told me:

"At four this morning, he was called for a briefing on this mission by his superior officers. He was to assemble his entire company for a detailed briefing at five. It was emphasized this was a peaceful mission and that all weapons were to remain unloaded during the entire mission. All people encountered were to be considered friendly and were to be treated with courtesy and respect. His company was a group of communications specialists who were to secure all methods of communication on the island. Communication to and from the island would be completely cut off, including arrival and departures by boat and plane. Local communications were to be left in service. The Gemini Operations Center, specifically, was to be isolated from the rest of the island, and all in and out voice or data transmission would move only with their permission. There were several people who were to be found and detained. These included only you, Lani, Lani's parents and me. I have no idea why they ignored the rest of our group. At eight they began boarding the transport planes for the short trip from Oahu. By nine they were landing at Hilo Airport, which had been closed earlier. One transport was to land at Kailua to secure the airport there. Several small ships had been ordered to cover the ports and were close enough to secure the harbors before the transports landed. He said he had no idea why this was being done, only that the island was to be completely secured as quickly as possible. By the time the two of us sat down in my office, the one thing they hadn't completed was finding you and Lani. Should you contact me, I was to urge you to come in for questioning. All of us were to be interrogated by someone coming at two. We both are quite certain who that is going to be. He assured me you would not be held after the questioning."

"Very interesting. At least they treated you well."

"In fact, they were almost apologetic. Even our friend, Lux, was polite when he arrived around two. He was courteous, not friendly, just stiffly polite. In fact, he actually complimented you on keeping your word and on the detailed conclusions included with your data. He said that as soon as his superiors received the information, events were completely out of his hands. He seemed almost relieved. The orders that brought the Marines had come directly from Washington. The mission was actually well underway when he was called to conduct the first questioning. Apparently, a number of higher officials are on their way here right now. My guess is they will arrive sometime tomorrow."

"Did he say why they acted as they did?" Angus asked.

"Just what we supposed, of course. I thought you assumed that. They don't want the public to know. Protect them from themselves. You know the mentality. They are going to do everything in their considerable power to prevent that next release from appearing. Rest assured, if, by some miracle it does get out, they are prepared to brand it sensational nonsense completely unfounded in fact. You, my friend, will be thoroughly discredited and branded a fake. Those are my words, of course, not his. Remember the old Roswell story? I have no idea as to its validity, but this could be in for the same treatment."

"I don't think so," Angus countered firmly. "We have provable facts and countless astronomers from other countries who will confirm my work and conclusions. I don't see how it could possibly be denied. Certainly by thirty years from now everyone will know. They can't hold back the truth that long."

"That's true, but don't ever accuse those government-control types of thinking more than five or six years into the future. You, also, must know some of them believe they are responsible for thinking for the ignorant public. These clowns are convinced they must protect the common people from the terrible possibility of knowing the truth and firmly believe they, alone, are capable of making decisions in such circumstances."

Angus looked incensed. "That's hogwash!"

"You know it . . . I know it . . . even the people know it. But those misguided idiots who think they know what's best for everyone believe it's gospel. I'll bet those men who pledged their lives, property and sacred honor to create this country knew that as well. That's the reason they fought the Revolutionary War against oppressive government. I think it's called liberty."

"My goodness, John, you mounted a soap box. Bravo! And I say that seriously. We may need a lot of that in the days to come. Awhile back, I was beginning to think maybe we were guilty of the same kind of thing—keeping the information from the people—protecting them, so to speak. Ali's speech about how people could handle it brought me out of that. We've merely been struggling to find the best way to share news of a frightening menace, not keep the news from them."

"I guess I can get worked up over stupidity and those self-righteous, self-serving, self-centered egotistical know-it-alls who think they know better what's good for us than we do ourselves. Maybe this terrible possibility will shock people into assuming responsibility for their own actions and relying less on others telling them what to do. Like Ali said, a challenge like this will definitely make people stop and think."

"That's for certain. Now, I have some news for you," Angus explained. "Ginger has constructed what I think is a foolproof method for our release to hit the news at the time planned. I know you don't know about this, so listen to some good news for our side."

By the time Angus had finished, there was a big smile on John's face as he said, "If Chelton reads that message before the UN, we will have achieved our goal. I can't see even a remote possibility of them intercepting all the news releases we've managed to plant. Surely some will get out. I wonder if our guards will anticipate our providing backup news releases?"

"I doubt they know anything about our planned news release," Angus replied. "They don't seem to suspect Ginger, and she's got sense enough to destroy or hide any copies of that release or of our schedule. No one else even has a copy. We took care of that after our last Internet conference. Remember? We even destroyed all the papers generated in the development of the schedule to make certain no one accidentally found them. I think we're in good shape on that score."

"Since we're cut off from the rest of the world, there is no way we'll know what happens unless our military friends tell us," John said. "We may be in for a long information drought. Longer than the five days before we hope the news will get out. I wonder what they will do when and if Chelton reads that release at the UN."

Feeling powerless to change the current situation, Angus was completely subdued. "It is going to be a long five days. I don't relish the wait."

John's thin, turned-down mouth showed his frustration as well. "There is not much else we can do *but* wait. Tomorrow, I'm going to wish you were with me. I am not looking forward to the inquisition that will fall on me when that Washington crew shows up. Frankly,

I'm glad I'm not the primary astronomer. I can claim ignorance of much information you would have to know and answer. They're not going to like hearing we don't have precise knowledge about the ghost's path and won't for years. They're probably not going to like anything I tell them. You know the type. I'll bet during your football days, you ran into some coaches who couldn't take an answer for an answer."

"One or two," Angus agreed, then looked about. "We'd better head out. It looks like they are closing soon, and I'd feel better if we walked out with a group. I'll run you back near your house, so you don't have to walk so far."

As they drove toward John's house, they tried to figure how they would be able to communicate. Finally Angus exclaimed, "I have it! Can you get to my computer? Would they let you in my office alone?"

"As far as I know they spent most of the day in there. I have no idea what they were doing because the door was kept shut. Why?"

"There is an SSR network transmitter in my computer. If you could get hold of that and install it in yours, we'd have a secure method of communicating, only when you were alone, of course."

"I would be surprised if I could get away with that. I wouldn't know how. The inside of a computer is Greek to me. I just use them," John said, then paused and remarked, "Hold on. I could have Jack Mercer do it. He's always fussing with one or more of the computers. I'll try and think of a way he could do it without raising suspicions."

"That's a great idea. He installed the SSR card in my PC and set it up for me. He could do it in a flash if lady luck smiles on us again and they let him in."

"How do I use the darned thing?"

"After you boot the system and open the SSR communication program, anything you type will appear on the screens of all computers logged on. Ginger, Francis, you and I will all be seeing the same screen and can all type as well. Just in case someone discovers you or you can't write freely, hold the 'Z' key down to print a bunch of Zs. We'll know your end is not secure, and we won't write anything. I can even cut you off the network from Lani's laptop, so nothing the rest of us types will appear on your screen."

"How will I know when to try?"

"I generally check my screen each hour on the hour, sometimes more often. Don't worry. If you try and get nothing, try again later. If you leave the message up and the network on, your message will be on my computer the next time I look. If you turn off your monitor no one will see anything until you turn it back on. Just don't let those people know what you're doing."

When Angus finished explaining the SSR radio network, he turned down the street next to John's and asked him to say when to stop. Slowing, but not quite stopping, he let John get out. He then picked up speed and headed for the Millers' house. John had some difficulty climbing back inside through the window without making a sound but finally made it on his fourth try. As far as he could tell, the Marines never knew he had been gone.

As Angus drove along, he wondered if he and Lani should turn themselves in. This was still America, and they certainly wouldn't be subjected to truth serums or torture. All they would face would be questions and brow beatings. By the time he had arrived, his decision was made; he would not turn himself in, at least for the present.

*   *   *

Friday was a long day. Dan grumbled because they couldn't go fishing. Lani and Ginger had several SSR communications without any new information. Around two in the afternoon, Ruth showed up. Her pastoral visit to Lani's folks had been a success. The two Marines there stayed outside and didn't bother Ali and Charlene. When she explained the purpose of her visit, they apologized for having to stop her. They were very official, but courteous. Lani's folks were glad to know she and Angus were OK and where they were staying. Ruth got the Millers' address from Charlene so she could visit in person, thinking it less risky than a phone call.

They visited for about an hour, sharing all they knew about the situation. As Ruth was leaving, Lani and Angus walked with her to her car and relayed the information they couldn't speak about with the Millers present.

At six, Angus received his first communication from John. Jack had successfully transferred the SSR equipment from Angus' computer. He had explained to the Marines that it was part of his normal maintenance schedule. They watched, but didn't interfere. John reported he had been questioned at length by three men and a woman from Washington. One of the men was an astronomer who frequently explained to the others what John was talking about. It hadn't been as bad as he had imagined. They would tell him nothing about how long the shutdown would last or what else they might do. They wanted desperately to get hold of Angus for questioning. Most of their questions had been about his possible actions and whereabouts. John's last remarks were, "They're widening their search net. They'll probably find you eventually, but stay out as long as you can. I'll try to keep you posted on anything new. Good luck."

Angus cleared the screen and typed a message to Ginger. There was no answer. Apparently, she was not home, so he would try again at seven. Same thing at seven—nothing. Angus began to worry. When Ginger didn't answer at eight, he knew something was not right but had no idea how to find out what. He and Lani discussed possible methods of checking on Ginger, finally deciding to stay put and check the computer every hour. They would have a long wait.

21

A bit after eight, Angus watched a message came across his screen from John. "I'm leaving to go home and will not be back at Gemini until Monday. Everyone, except the operating crew, maintenance staff and other personnel required to run the telescope, was ordered to leave by nine. There was much grumbling from those who had scheduled time on the telescope, but there was no arguing with the captain's orders. The astronomer who came with the group from the mainland, Dr. Arden Sokol, is scheduled to use the telescope Friday, Saturday and Sunday nights to try to confirm Angus' work. The group from Washington was quite upset that you and Lani have not been found to help them in this effort."

Angus immediately typed back, "That's interesting. I'm quite concerned about Ginger. Haven't heard a word from her."

"I hope nothing's happened to her. Since I won't have access to my computer until Monday, this will be my last message until then. Good luck and good-bye."

"I hope things go well. Have a nice weekend."

*   *   *

By Saturday evening, Angus was getting frustrated. By late Sunday afternoon, he was going stir-crazy. With no information coming in and no safe place to go, he was beginning to act like a caged

435

animal. Lani was doing her best to counter his growing agitation, but the information vacuum was wearing on her as well.

Finally, Angus could take it no longer. He quit pacing and looked at Lani almost wild eyed. "By now, OSI surely knows we have that van from our use of a credit card. I'm going to drive to the south side of Hilo and leave it in a parking lot. I can walk to Francis and Oona's from there to see if they can be contacted. Then, I'll walk back here to the Millers'."

Lani grabbed his arm; her face looked almost as fierce as his. "I am going with you."

"Absolutely not!"

Lani looked back at him with fire in her eyes. "You'll take me with you, or I'll turn myself in. I'm as frustrated by this isolation as you are."

After an emotionally charged discussion, Angus realized he was getting nowhere, so he caved. "All right, you win. We'll do this together."

"Now you're being sensible," Lani said as the discussion ended.

They told the Millers what they were going to do. Just in case Ginger might finally use the SSR network, Angus showed Maria how it worked. She had used a computer before and caught on quickly. Dan didn't want to have anything to do with "those danged electronic gadgets."

"If we don't return before morning, you'll know we either found another safe haven or the Marines have us," Lani told them as they left at about 6:30.

They drove south through Hilo, finally pulling into a shopping center where they planned to leave the van. Remembering John's all black outfit, Angus suggested they stop and get some black sweats to wear for their walk. Angus parked the van as far from lights as he could.

Lani stepped quickly out of the van. "You stay here. I'll be a lot less conspicuous shopping by myself."

Angus didn't like it, but agreed she was probably right. Noticing her conspicuous white shoes he said, "Better get us both some black running shoes without reflective material and some socks too. Those white shoes would stand out like a neon sign."

After checking with Angus for his sizes, Lani headed for the store. She would pay cash so as not to leave a credit card trail. Angus waited nervously in the van for what seemed like forever.

He heaved a huge sigh of relief when she finally walked out the doors with two plastic bags in her hands. He acted as lookout while she stepped into the back of the van and changed into her new black outfit. She did the same as he changed. They placed their discarded clothing and shoes in the two plastic bags. He threw the keys into the glove compartment and grabbed the bags of clothes as they left. They did not lock the van.

It was around nine when they finally walked down the street to the Lanes' home. They avoided busy, brightly lit areas, sticking to side streets as much as possible. There were no vehicles on the street as they approached the house. They walked up the driveway. When they reached the garage entrance, they noticed two vehicles parked outside. Since no outside lights were on they could just barely determine that one was a dark sedan with white lettering on the back, a military vehicle. The other one was unmistakable even in the near dark. It was Ginger's yellow convertible.

They stopped at the bottom of the steps for a whispered discussion of their findings, what it meant and what they should do.

Lani placed her lips against Angus' ear to whisper. "It looks like we found Ginger and maybe a bunch of Marines as well. Let's not rush into anything. The place may be swarming with them."

"My guess is just two and they're both inside. I don't think they would expect us to be here, not now anyway. I'm going to creep up the steps as quietly as possible. You wait here."

"Not in this lifetime. I'll be right behind you."

"OK, but walk carefully. There could be a guard posted outside that doorway."

They walked cautiously up the back steps to the entrance Angus used when he stayed there before. Angus still had his key. Though no street light shone on the yard, there was enough scattered light from the glow of the city, they could make out the walk and the door with eyes that had become accustomed to the dark. There was no person visible to their limited sight. Angus carefully tried the door and found it locked. He found the key, silently slid it into the lock and slowly opened the door. They crept silently inside, closing the door carefully behind them. They walked slowly down the hallway to the top of the wide center stairway. Light from the kitchen lit the bottom of the stairway, casting a glow all the way up the three levels of the house to where they stood. They could hear voices from the kitchen, catching a few words, but missing most of what was being said. As they waited, they recognized the voices of Francis, Oona and Ginger. There were at least two others, probably Marines.

Angus carefully opened the door to his former hideaway on the right and pulled Lani inside so they could not be seen from below. They had another whispered conference in the dim light at the top of the stairs. Angus explained his plans. "I'll sneak down the first flight of stairs and step into the bedroom hallway on the right. It's out of sight from the kitchen door. I'll try to hear what's being said. That will help us decide what to do next."

"We'll sneak down." Lani corrected. "You're going nowhere without your shadow."

Angus gave up. He closed the door silently and they both crept down the stairs and into the hallway above and across the stairway from the kitchen doorway. They could now hear clearly what was being said.

Francis was talking and sounding quite frustrated. "I keep telling you, *we have no idea where they are.* We have worked with them on the Gemini Community Action Committee for only a few months. We know a few members of their family but none of their friends outside the committee. How could we possibly know where they might be hiding?"

Angus recognized the voice of the next man who spoke. It was Jan Lux. "We know there is more to this committee than meets the eye. We are going to hold you here until we get some answers. You know that under military orders, we can do this legally. I don't like it any more than you do. There are a great many better things for me to be doing on a weekend than sitting here interrogating three uncooperative citizens. Why don't you tell us what we want to know, and we'll be on our way?"

Oona nearly exploded in anger. "Listen, Mr. OSI, these two Marines drag this young woman out of her office, bring her here and then hold us all prisoners in our own home for two days with all our communications cut off. Yesterday afternoon you arrive and for four hours repeatedly ask us the same questions, the answers to which you will not accept. Then this afternoon you come back and ask the same questions. I don't care what authority you have or what methods you use, we can't tell you anything we don't know. You say you must rely on our cooperation and have been told not to use force. We have cooperated to the best of our ability, and it doesn't satisfy you. I've had it. I am now going to walk out that door, walk through this neighborhood of influential people and tell anyone I find what's been going on. Should you try to stop me, you will have to use a great deal of force. I will hit, kick, bite, scratch and otherwise physically attack anyone who interferes. I hope my husband and Miss Cari will do likewise."

Angus heard the sounds of chairs being hurriedly moved back from the table and then a loud, "Hold on!" shouted by Lux. "You won't have to do that. I'll call it off for now. It's been a long day for us all. If you do know anything, we are certainly not going to find out with any more questioning. We'll leave you alone, but please remain available as . . . "

He was interrupted by the obvious sound of a two-way radio call. They could make out only parts of what the Marine was saying. "You found the van they rented? Where? That's just a couple of miles from here. Watch for them to come back to the van. They may be inside shopping." By this time, the Marine had walked to the far end of the kitchen, and they could not understand anything he was saying. Angus and Lani retreated down the hall as the Marines, Lux and the rest walked out of the kitchen and toward the entrance.

"If you hear from them, please tell them we need their help with the telescope. It's very important. After helping us for a few days, they will be free to go. That's all," they heard Lux saying before he left with the Marines. Soon the sound of a car starting and then going down the driveway told them their tormentors had gone.

As they retraced their steps to the kitchen, Oona asked. "I wonder where they could be?"

"I haven't the slightest idea," Ginger said loudly, following with a warning voice so quiet Angus could barely hear, "The walls may have ears."

"Why don't we take a walk upstairs and out in the backyard?" Francis said, obviously seeking a place unlikely to be bugged.

Lani and Angus stood still as the three passed the hallway on their way to the backyard. They didn't know how to make their presence known without startling the others. After the three had gone outside, Lani and Angus crept up the stairs and out the door. They could just make out the three of them looking up and away from the door as they shut it silently behind them. Angus snapped his fingers loudly, hoping to get their attention without scaring them.

"What was that?" Ginger asked as she heard the loud snap.

"Just us chickens," Lani answered in a low voice.

Still a bit startled, eyes not yet accustomed to the dark, Francis asked, "Who is that?"

"Lani and Angus," Angus replied. "We're right here by the door."

Looking intently in the direction of the voices, they could not see a thing. In their totally black outfits they were practically invisible to each other, let alone those who had just come from a brightly lit room.

"Is that really you, Angus?" Ginger asked hesitantly. "I can't see you at all."

Lani found Ginger and gave her a big hug. "We were so worried about you when you didn't answer us on the network. I'm glad you're OK."

"It is you!" Ginger exclaimed, still unable to see her. "How did you get here? Why? I thought you had a secure place to stay?"

All five stood in the backyard sharing with each other the many happenings of the last few days. After much discussion, they decided it unlikely the Marines had planted any bugs or surveillance devices, or if they had, it would not have been in Angus' hideaway, so they headed there where they could see each other. After an hour of fruitless effort to derive a workable plan, Francis finally called a halt.

"Let's get a night's rest and see if we can come up with something in the morning. We'll all be fresher then. You can stay here, but I know Ginger wants to head home."

When Ginger left, it was nearly eleven. Angus retrieved his own laptop from the dresser drawer where he placed it nearly two months ago. He set it up and typed a greeting and OK message for the Millers. He left it turned on, just in case Maria saw the message. About ten minutes later, as they were about to go to bed, they were delighted to see a message from Maria pop up on the screen. "Ginger, Where are you? Please answer."

Angus immediately went over and typed, "It's Angus and Lani. We're safe and sound in a great place. Found Ginger too, and she's OK. Have a good night's sleep. We'll keep in touch this way. Try on the hour if you want to get us. We'll be on at seven in the morning."

"Thank goodness," rolled across his screen followed by, "Glad you're OK. It's nice to hear from you. Keep up the good work. I'll try at seven in the morning."

Having recovered from their frustration of the last few days, Angus and Lani slept soundly.

*   *   *

Monday passed without incident. Angus and Lani stayed put and communicated with Ginger, John and Maria via the SSR network. For all intents and purposes, it was a normal workday in Hawaii except for the island being shut off from the outside world. Angus had a hard time sleeping. Several times during the night he awoke and turned on the radio to see if there was any news. Lani woke up each time and joined him. It was hard for either to sleep. When there was no news at all at six o'clock, Angus feared all of their plans had failed. Either that or the incoming news blackout was still keeping them ignorant of what was happening in the rest of the world. Ginger sent him a quick message on the SSR, "No news is bad news." To which he replied, "We're going absolutely nuts."

Hearing Oona's call, they headed down to the kitchen. After staying cooped up in the guest room all the previous day, they decided to venture downstairs this morning. They were greeted by two long faces. "We've been watching the news since five. There hasn't been a whisper of our release. Do you suppose they found and stopped them all?"

"We won't know that for sure until this afternoon," Angus commented.

"You don't suppose they would keep us isolated after the news was out, do you?" Francis asked.

"I doubt that," Lani answered. "I can't imagine that not one of those messages went through. Maybe we'll hear something later."

Just after 9:30, a ring of the doorbell sent Angus and Lani scurrying up the stairs to be out of sight. Before they closed the door, they heard Francis downstairs say loudly, "I see you Marines came back."

Angus grabbed the laptop and quickly slid it under the bed, just in case. Then they stood against the wall next to the door, trying to hear what else was being said. After about five minutes there was a loud knock on the door. They knew it was not Francis or Oona. After a second knock and a short wait the door opened and Lux walked in followed by two Marines.

Seeing Angus, Lux grinned and said, "Gotcha!" After a short staring contest. Lux said, "Why don't we all go downstairs and have a little talk," then turned, walked out of the room and down the stairs. Angus and Lani followed as one Marine stood on either side of the exit door in the hallway. They walked downstairs quietly. At least the hiding was over. Now, maybe they could get some answers for themselves.

"I suppose you'd like to know how we knew you were here?" Lux asked as he reached under the kitchen table and retrieved a tiny transmitter no larger than a dime. "This little baby sent us your voice earlier today, so we decided to pay you a visit."

"So what now?" Angus asked.

"Before we head for Gemini, where I hope you will help our people confirm your findings, there are a few things I'd like to tell you. Please sit down. We really do want to work with you and mean no one any harm."

"You've a strange way of showing that," Angus commented as he sat at the table with Lani.

Lux continued, a smug look of satisfaction on his face, "After receiving your package of data, I immediately contacted Washington, where it was decided your conclusions could not be allowed to be published at this time. We stopped your news releases by isolating the entire island of Hawaii. Our people on the mainland tracked down many of your contacts by searching through recent mail or shipments of any kind. After finding a copy of your news release in papers sent to your friend Pat Yamaguchi, we knew what we were dealing with. When we found that he had been in contact with a Dr. Botkin, we met with him and retrieved that release as well. We found the releases your mother and cousin were to use. We retrieved an unopened copy from a lady on Long Island named Cari. She seems to be the mother of the young lady who was here last night. Our next step was to warn all news services and foreign governments about an elaborate and dangerous hoax being perpetrated by unknown persons, using your good name. They were told not to use the releases and to report to the U.S. government if they received a copy. In the meantime, all people who know of the release are being held incommunicado and will be so held until we can get the matter under control. Since you and possibly a few others on the island are the only ones with the credentials to confirm the release, you will not be available for any interview until your government permits. You may have severely tested our ability to handle such news, but it appears we passed the test. At ten this morning, Hawaiian time, news of the hoax will be aired by all the media at a special press briefing by a high government official in Washington. Mainland TV feed will be opened at that time. You might want to watch the briefing on your TV."

Noting some significant absences from Lux's list of recipients of the releases, Angus decided it wasn't over yet. He still had hope, so he commented, "This game will not be over until the clock runs out folks. There are still about thirty years on that clock, and I doubt you and your anal-retentive friends in Washington have that kind of staying power. You won't be able to hide the truth forever."

They all walked into the recreation room to watch the big screen TV. It was a silent group who watched as the TV came on. At a few minutes after ten, the special news briefing was announced. It took a few minutes for the spokesman to come out. It was Dan Burman, head of the OSI. He first read a brief statement.

"I am taking this unusual step of coming before the media to tell of a diabolical hoax that was attempted and that could have caused unbelievable fear and misery for billions of people around the world. When I tell you about the hoax, you will realize why we have taken such unusual steps to protect everyone. The hoax centers on a star discovered recently by one of our most famous astronomers, Dr. Angus Thomas. Yes, this is the same man who thrilled many with his tremendous talent on the gridiron before becoming an astronomer. This hoax was in the form of a news release purported to have originated from Dr. Thomas and that says this star will destroy the earth and all life on it. This is absolutely untrue, and we are currently talking with Dr. Thomas, who will help us find and punish those responsible. A former colleague now under criminal investigation is a possible suspect in the case. It may prove that the hoax was being used to discredit Dr. Thomas. Since this is being thoroughly investigated as we speak, I can divulge no names or information about possible suspects. I will now take a few questions."

"When can we see a copy of the release you describe?" was the first question.

"After we have analyzed it thoroughly, we will release it to the press."

The questions and answers went on for at least fifteen minutes. Dan Burman declared the session was over and before walking away from the microphones, he stated that further information would be provided when it became available.

Angus was looking somewhat defeated. Lux was beaming.

For the next ten minutes, several commentators discussed what had been said. All wanted to see a copy of the release and wondered why it wasn't provided. Before closing the news, they promised to investigate and provide more information on a later newscast. It was four in the afternoon in Washington and all would be scurrying for more information for the six o'clock news.

"How do you expect me to agree this was a hoax?" Angus asked Lux.

"Because that's what it is," Lux answered. "We all know that."

"You know that's a story concocted to hide the real truth from the people. You think the people are stupid enough to fall for it, don't you?" Oona spat out.

"Just how long do you think you can isolate the entire island of Hawaii?" Francis asked.

"Just as long as it's necessary," Lux replied.

"Thirty years?" asked Lani. "You'll isolate this island for thirty years just to hide a truth that someone else will discover before long anyway? You're out of your mind."

"It won't take that long," Lux said. "It'll be over long before that."

"What do you plan to do if we don't accept your brainwashing? Maybe douse the whole island with poison gas? Or Anthrax? Or use it for a target for hydrogen bombs? That's one way to shut us up and hide the truth," Angus said angrily.

"What about the ones like these two young Marines?" Oona asked. "They're not blind and stupid. They can see the truth of it. How are you going to silence them? You'll have to, you know."

Irritated by Oona's words and the obvious tension in the faces of the Marines, Lux said, "They won't question. They're Marines. They'll do as they're told. Won't you boys?"

Before they could answer, Oona looked straight at them and said. "I always thought the Marines held honor at a high value. Does that mean you would lie to protect some bureaucrat's job, some desk jockey who would send you to your death at a moment's notice to satisfy his craving for power? Is that what the Marines call honor?"

"No, ma'am, it's not like that. Not like that at all," the corporal replied.

"No? Then tell me what it is like. Here you are with four good, honest, respected citizens of these United States—citizens who have never been in trouble with any kind of law—educated, even famous people, known for their honesty—citizens who, after much soul searching, decided the world had a right to know the possible danger to the entire earth. Then there's this Washington-bought gunslinger using you to hide the truth from the American public about something that has absolutely nothing to do with national security. He and his cohorts in Washington are using all the power of the U.S., including you Marines, to browbeat these good citizens into lying about something he and his buddies have little knowledge about. Is that what Marines are all about?"

"No, ma'am, this isn't wartime, and we're supposed to be polite and not hurt anyone unless trouble starts. My orders come from my lieutenant, not this civilian."

"Why don't you call your lieutenant and ask him to tell you the truth about this mission? Tell him the Marine's honor doesn't call for forcing honest citizens to lie to satisfy some civilian jerk's idea of how to protect the people from the truth. I'd like to hear his answer to that," Oona finished with a hard stare at Lux.

"You'll do nothing of the kind," Lux ordered, visibly shaken. "You are to obey my orders just as if I were your superior officer."

"You be sure you do that," Lani chimed in. "That will demonstrate what kind of guts you Marines have."

For just an instant Lux appeared as if he was thinking of striking Lani. Seeing this, Angus sprang to his feet only to see two Marines instantly place themselves between Lani and Lux with their batons held ready across their chests.

"Mr. Lux. Please step back," The corporal said. "Our orders were to see to it that no one got hurt. If that means protecting people from you, that is what we will do."

"They are real Marines after all," Oona commented.

"Why don't we try to relax," Francis suggested. "We have enough problems as it is. As long as we're here together, we should try to get along. The New York evening news will be coming on shortly. If our captors open the network feeds, we'll be able to watch it on cable. I'd like to know what's going on in the outside world."

"It is my understanding that incoming TV signals will be left open after the press conference," Lux admitted. "I, too, would like to see the news."

The New York evening news aired at noon in Hawaii. The first part of the program showed the press briefing seen earlier and there was not much else. Several times the commentator mentioned that despite repeated attempts, they had been unable to reach Dr. Thomas to ask him about the hoax. They thought it unusual that all channels of communication with the Big Island were down and had been for several days. They seemed disturbed that the news service in Hilo had been off line since Thursday.

When the world news was over, the sports reporters came on. After the scores they announced they were bringing a special live report on a late breaking story from Los Angeles. When they cut to the L.A. studio, Angus almost fell off his chair. There in the guest chair next to the L.A. sports reporter sat his old friend Cy Dooley. *What on earth was he doing there?* he thought.

The interviewer started, "Surely you folks remember Cy Dooley, the bad boy of the NFL for so many years. You'll remember Cy experienced a drastic reversal of form after several years of building a bad reputation both on and off the field. After the change, he remained a greatly feared offensive lineman until he retired but off the field? Well, Cy turned into a good citizen and role model. Cy, it's been a long time since you were on our program. Tell us what you've been doing."

Cy explained how he had become a minister and was working with troubled youths in south L.A. He told how it was Angus Thomas who had been so instrumental in his change and just how much he cared for and admired Angus.

"That's the same Angus Thomas you heard about earlier in this program," Cy continued. "I talked with him early last week just after that hokey business about that guy in England. He told me some things that would curl your hair. He said I would receive the full information about this new star of his today in the news. Well, all I heard in the news was that bunch of lies you heard earlier from Washington. I have a copy of a news release he was afraid might be stopped by Washington, and I'm going to read it to you."

Cy read the entire release to the dismay of Lux and the hopeful joy of the rest. Passing copies of the release to the host and several others on the set, he continued, "There's a little note in here that says the pope received this same information today. Since we're sort of in the same line of work, I hope the pope will confirm this message and read it to his people. I personally guarantee that this release confirms what my old friend told me over the phone. This is no hoax. I will personally go to Hawaii and get my friend with his latest data and bring them before the public, so the truth will be known. Let's see if those keep-it-from-us boys in Washington can stop this old lineman. Here's one for the people."

A stunned sports announcer looked at Cy incredulously and said, "This is for real, isn't it? I remember the great Angus Thomas, friends. He was as honest and straight as they come. I never knew he became an astronomer though. Thanks, Cy, for being here with us and sharing this startling news. I hardly know how to respond. We . . . we'll just have to wait for more news about this."

In the confusion, the announcer's open mike caught, "What a bombshell to drop on our sports program," before they cut back to the New York broadcast.

When they did cut back to New York, the reporter there was as unprepared as the one from L.A. After a longer than normal pause he said, "I hardly know what to say after that. I hope our news staff will get on top of this story right away. Those are serious charges leveled against the people who had the press briefing earlier. Now, a special message." As a series of ads ran, everyone looked at Lux who seemed to be shrinking into his chair.

Despite the seriousness of the moment Angus could not resist retaliation. He looked directly at Lux and said, "Gotcha!"

The Marines' radio crackled into life. They were being ordered to return for a briefing in one hour. Jan Lux looked almost like a beaten man as he stood up and headed for the door in silence. As they were starting to go, the younger Marine asked Angus, "Is that really you in that picture? It does look like you, but I was wondering."

"Yes, it was in the Pro Bowl about ten years back. You see this guy right here? That's Wen Laughten. About a second after that picture was taken, he smeared me for a loss. I felt that hit for days."

The young Marine smiled at Angus. "Thanks Dr. Thomas, I'm glad your friend, the big black man on TV, I'm glad he straightened everything out. What he said sounds scary, but I'd still rather know the truth. I hope you don't have any more trouble."

The Marine corporal echoed what the younger one said, "I'd rather have the truth as well. We are Marines, you know."

"I believe most people think as you do. Just remember, a lot can change in thirty years. It will be a long time before we know for sure just where and when that star will pass. I believe the chances are good there will be little or no effect on the earth. By the way, thanks for standing up for my wife. That act said a great deal about you."

When the Marines had gone, the remaining four looked at each other, hardly knowing what to say. "I'm going to call Mom," Lani said suddenly. "I wonder if she watched the news?"

No, she hadn't. They had been surprised when suddenly the two Marines drove off in their Jeep without a word. Lani told them the entire story since they hadn't seen any TV for days after the mainland feed was shut off. They would watch now to see what would happen next. Next, she called Ginger at the office. Mili said Ginger left as soon as the news was over, saying she wouldn't be back until tomorrow. She then asked if they had seen the news. "Isn't it great? That friend of Angus, that Cy Dooley fella? He sure told 'em didn't he? Ginger stood up and cheered when he finished, said that was the best news for months. She didn't say, but I'll bet she's headed for you guys, if she knows where you are."

"She does," Lani answered. "You're a good friend, Mili. If ever you can use our help, please call us."

After thanks and good-byes, Lani called the Millers to tell them and found out they had seen the whole thing. "Now we understand why you had to keep your secret," Maria said.

Lani answered. "I promise we'll stop by and tell you the whole story soon."

As soon as she hung up, the phone and doorbell rang at the same time. Oona let Ginger in and Francis picked up the phone. It was John reporting the Marines left about 12:30 and things were returning to normal at Gemini. Then he asked for Angus.

"I just received a call from Schuman at Keck," he told Angus. "Apparently the Marines arrived there shortly after you left. They never asked for a thing, just stayed and watched who came and went, probably watching for you. They left a little before one. Schuman reports their confirmation of your star is mostly complete and, so far, everything checks with your data. He'd like you and Lani to come up as soon as he has finished. I think he wants to take you for a tour. He might even try to steal you away from us, so be careful. We don't want to lose you. I'll bet that within a few weeks, you will be the most celebrated astronomer in the world."

"Come on, John."

"Absolutely. You are about to become one of the world's biggest celebrities. Unfortunately, there will be some that will hate you. You'd better think about bodyguards."

"John, don't be ridiculous. Bodyguards? What for?"

"You have just condemned a great many people to a life without hope for the future. They will not see the possibility of the destruction of the earth. In their minds, it will be a certainty. You are responsible for them learning of this, so a few of them may strike out at you in anger. It will take a while, and you'll probably see some hints of this growing hatred in the media. Just watch for it so you can be prepared when it comes. Remember the story of killing the messenger? Well, you're the messenger, so be careful."

"That doesn't sound too promising for the future."

"When you talk to the press, be positive. Don't put down those prophets of doom. Be genuinely interested in their concerns but emphasize the infinitely small chance of, say, the star striking the earth. If you can get them to concentrate on that, it would minimize their thinking about the range of damaging possibilities that do exist, and that would be so difficult to explain to them. As long as you are the first to describe the possibilities, those after you will probably follow your lead."

"You've given this quite a bit of thought, haven't you?"

"Ask your wife and her parents about the doomsayers that appeared as the lava crept toward Kalapana. They've had firsthand experience with those kinds of minds and could be a great help to you."

"Great idea, John. Incidentally, we'll be here for a while, and then I think we'll head out to return the rental van and get Lani's car. We should end up at our place about nine. I assume we'll be at the Op Center in the morning. I wonder how long it will be before the island rejoins the world?"

22

On their arrival at their apartment, Angus and Lani were greeted at the entrance by two Roman Catholic priests who recognized them immediately. "You are Dr. and Mrs. Thomas, are you not?"

They were quite puzzled. "Yes, we are."

"We have a most urgent message for you. May we come in and speak with you?"

"Of course," Lani answered.

Angus opened the door and guided them to their apartment. Once inside, they introduced themselves, "I am Father Dumas and this is Father Chapin. We received an urgent request directly from the pope to contact you as soon as possible for confirmation of the news release. Apparently, this message was among the first to get through once communications were restored. We rushed here immediately."

Angus indicated the living room. "Please sit down and tell us how we can help you."

"Thank you. Now tell us, is this terrible thing true? Does the earth really face possible destruction by this new star you found? Is it a certainty?" Father Dumas asked.

"Possible? Yes. Probable? Maybe. Certain? Absolutely not. I believe that is the most complete answer I can provide at the present. It will take years for us to learn for certain just what might happen about thirty years from now. As far as we know at this moment, it is likely we won't be sure of the event until it actually happens."

With an obvious sense of urgency Father Dumas asked, "Then you are confirming the accuracy of the news release they have at the Vatican?"

"Yes. It is absolutely true. I have been following this star since first discovering it in June of last year. We have completed two high-grade observations since the discovery, each one six months after the previous. All are consistent, providing the conclusions outlined in the news release. Several days ago, we furnished data to Dr. Schuman of the Keck Observatory right here on Hawaii. His preliminary findings agree with ours. He called to say his confirmation would be complete by the end of the week. Incidentally, I am not the one who sent the release to the Vatican. That was the work of a young lady who would prefer not to be named. She is also the one who sent the release to Cy Dooley."

"Such being the case, we must call the Vatican immediately. May we use your phone?"

"Certainly," Angus replied.

Within about ten minutes the pope's office was on the line. After several involved conversations with waits in between, Father Dumas offered the phone to Angus saying, "His Holiness would like to speak to you."

The ensuing conversation was somewhat unnerving for Angus. He could hardly imagine actually speaking to the pope.

"This is Angus Thomas, your . . . Holiness."

"Father Dumas tells me you have verified the press release sent to me. Is that correct?"

"Absolutely."

"I have another man of the cloth to thank for calling this to my attention, a friend of yours, the Reverend Cy Dooley of Los Angeles. When I heard about his broadcast, I arranged to view a taping of it made by the staff here. When you see him, thank him for asking me for help. I trust he will like my response."

"I'm sure of it."

"I will soon make a public announcement of your release since I, too, think the people have a right to know. I believe with God's help, they will be able to handle it."

"Our feelings exactly!" Angus replied, reassured by the pope's easy, friendly manner.

"Please repeat to me the first phrase you used to tell Father Dumas about the news. I want to have it correct since I may quote you."

Angus thought for a moment, then repeated, "Possible? Yes. Probable? Maybe. Certain? Absolutely not. I think that says it all."

"An excellent and concise statement. May I quote you in my talk?"

"Certainly. I will feel greatly honored."

"I understand from an American here that you are a famous athlete in your country. You are soon to be a world famous scientist. I will pray for your ability to handle this awesome fame your discovery has cast upon you."

"I know exactly what you mean. Our director at Gemini warned me of the same thing. I genuinely appreciate your prayers."

"From what I've learned of you in the last few hours, I feel certain you will handle it quite well. Now, I would have a few more words with Father Dumas. Would you give him the phone, please?"

Angus handed the phone to Father Dumas and stood there, still awestruck. He turned to Lani and said, "Can you believe that? I was actually talking to the pope, just like to an old friend."

Lani beamed, then, showing her knack of bringing Angus back to reality, replied, "Yes. That's my man. Just don't let it go to your head. We'd like you to stay here amongst us mere mortals."

When Father Dumas finally got off the phone, he told Angus, "His Holiness is impressed by your honesty and the consideration you have given to the release of such possibly damaging information. He would like to meet you in person in the future. It may not be soon, but he asked me to take care of the arrangements after things settle down. It will probably be after several months that we will be contacting you to find a time and place suitable for both of your busy schedules."

"I am overwhelmed," Angus admitted. "I'm not a Roman Catholic, but I consider it a great honor to be asked to meet with the pope."

"You are most gracious," Father Dumas replied. "With good fortune, his talk will be broadcast in an hour or so. It is now Wednesday morning at the Vatican. The sudden announcement that the pope will make an important speech to the people has already alerted the media. They are informing the public as we speak. I will call to let you know the exact time and channel where it can be seen as soon as we find out."

"Thank you. We'd appreciate that," Lani said as they started for the door.

Father Dumas turned and faced them, a broad smile on his face. "I understand you two are recently wed. May the grace of God and good fortune bless your marriage."

"Thanks again, Father. Considering what's in store for us, we are most grateful for your blessings," Angus said as they left.

Later Father Dumas called to say the broadcast would be aired at 10:30 on their local TV channel. There were a flurry of calls to all members of the group, both families and numerous friends with requests to pass the information on. When Ginger finished her reports, she called Lani and asked if she could come over and watch with them. She said Mili wanted her out of the office and that she didn't want to go home and watch the talk alone.

When she arrived, Ginger almost bounced into the apartment. "May I touch the man who spoke to the pope?"

Angus opened his arms toward her. "Will a hug do?"

"Even better," Ginger replied, smiling.

The three friends sat and watched the talk, which was certainly momentous. After explaining that he had personally talked with Dr. Thomas and had been assured the news release was completely factual, the pope read the release slowly and completely. He followed the release by repeating the quote he had obtained from Angus. After the quote, he went into great detail about the meanings of possible, probable and certain. He left no doubt that it would be a long time before the outcome would be determined. Finally, he thanked those responsible for providing him with the information with the following words:

"I thank the Reverend Cy Dooley of Los Angeles for having the courage to make the earlier announcement and for asking me to talk about it. I thank Dr. Thomas and his dedicated group for the way they handled this potentially damaging information. I thank a young lady who prefers to remain nameless for the clever courage to get the message to Reverend Dooley and the Vatican. I think this is all a demonstration of the power of God to direct us to the best conclusions. Consider what has happened. A minister of a small church in America makes the first announcements of one of the most momentous things to face the human race and while on a sports program no less. The second announcement, the one just made, came from another servant of God here in the Vatican. With God's grace, this terrible menace will pass without harm to our precious earth."

When it was over, they sat almost transfixed listening to the commentator reviewing the pope's speech.

Suddenly Lani turned to Ginger and asked, "Don't you have a story to write or send? Isn't this fantastic news? Won't you miss out?"

"Not to worry. Momma Cari's little girl has everything under control. At this moment a complete story is being filed in Honolulu and New York with my byline. I wrote a report of a series of exclusive interviews with Dr. Angus Thomas, including the last one, just five minutes after the pope's talk. I hit hard on what happened here with the military and OSI. My hope is the media will use that report right away, since it is the only current information they will have from here. Mili is taking care of everything. She even rushed me over here out of her way so she could work in peace."

"What about the talk by the pope?" Angus asked. "You couldn't have included that."

"Why not? I had a good idea what he was going to say. I wrote most of the report and told Mili to pick out any important lines and finish the story for me. She's quite good at it."

"What if something unexpected had come up?" Lani asked.

"Then I would have called Mili and told her what I wanted to say. She knew where I was. If she ran into a problem, she would have called before now. Incidentally, Angus, why isn't your phone ringing? There must be literally hundreds, if not thousands, of reporters calling you by now from all over the world."

Angus laughed, turned and pointed to a black box with flashing lights directly under and about the same size as his desk phone. "That's your answer. I picked it up from the phone company just before we were married. It only lets calls through from numbers entered into the caller ID memory section. All others get routed to an automated answering service at the phone company without ringing here at all."

Ginger asked, "Suppose I try to call you from a phone not on your list. I won't be able to get through."

"Of course you will. After dialing my phone you will hear two short beeps. As soon as you hear those beeps, dial the last four digits of your home number and it will go through."

"Very clever," Ginger said. "What do those numbers on the front mean?"

"That's the number of calls it has taken since it was last reset," Angus answered without looking at the phone.

"You mean you have received a hundred and seventy-nine calls since you last checked?" Ginger asked.

Turning instantly and seeing the number on his new toy, Angus exclaimed, "Dang. There were only seven when we walked in with those two priests. How am I going to retrieve all those calls?"

"I hope you two are ready for what is about to happen," Ginger cautioned. "Remember my warning after we slipped that second release into the news? That's nothing compared with what you will see in the next few days. This island is going to crawl with reporters and cameramen from all over the world. Forget about the limitations of commercial airlines. They will charter big jets to bring them here hundreds at a time. There won't be a hotel room left on the island and you won't be able to find a single place to hide. You may have to turn the Gemini Op Center into a fortress to hold off the mob. It is going to be chaos of the highest order."

"Why don't you handle the press for me? You know how to do that."

"Not on your life," Ginger replied emphatically. "You'll need at least two dozen Cy Dooley's to stem this tide."

Lani took Ginger's hands, pleading, "Come on, Ginger. We need your help. You can't just warn us and then stand back to watch the carnage."

Ginger smiled at Lani. "Of course, I was just kidding. I'll gladly help. You've actually taken several good steps already. That phone box is a great first step. If you want, I can be your press secretary. It would be a real feather in my cap, and Pete Radcliff would gladly let me do it. He'd ask for something special in return, like first shot at new information. He'll work with us. Since we are going to need more help, I could probably steal Mili away too. With her experience, she would be invaluable."

The three sat down to plan their first steps. Ginger made several suggestions for actions to be taken to accommodate the press and try to retain some privacy. She and Mili would begin by taking care of the calls from Angus' phone service. They continued planning until well after midnight.

*   *   *

The pope's address sealed the doom of the effort to brand the news release a hoax. Soon after it was over, the media fell all over themselves in attempting to make up for being beaten to the truth by the L.A. sports program and the pope. Ginger was right. Her report was used extensively in all media programs. She was named as an outstanding reporter, a coming star in the world news. The clip showing her asking the question of Angus was run in the background during many commentaries on her report. All programs stated they were trying to contact Angus and Ginger for further information. Ginger, too, was destined for fame and would be forever linked to the "ghost story," as the media had it labeled.

Within a short time, a number of follow-up stories appeared in the media. OSI claimed to have been tricked into believing the news release was a hoax. They quietly apologized for the error and promised to find and punish those responsible. No one at OSI would permit an interview. Politicians all over the world fell over themselves trying to get media time to talk about the ghost. A number of U.S. congressmen declared their intention to "mount an investigation to get to the bottom of the government's role in the attempted hoax."

*   *   *

Cy's revelation and the pope's address were aired while the UN was in open session. Rumors about both reports passed around the chamber by voice and the growing disturbance finally was near pandemonium. As the chairman struggled to regain control, two men kept shouting for the opportunity to speak. Finally, one of them walked up and handed the chairman a note. When the chairman confirmed the rumors about the speech by the pope were accurate and then announced there was a copy of the news release in the hall, things quieted down in anticipation. Chelton's two friends stood together at a podium and told how Chelton Chum had sent them copies of the release to be read the previous day if he were not there. They explained they honored the request from the U.S. government to hold the release since they believed it to be a hoax.

After a short conference between the two, one of the men took the mike and announced, "We would have liked to have Chelton Chum read this release to you. For some reason, he has been absent from the seat he usually holds next to ours. This is most unusual. He always lets us know if and when he will not be present. In his absence and at his request, I will read what he sent us."

He read the release and continued to hold their attention as he read several paragraphs of reassuring words Chelton had planned to say. When he finished, the chairman announced he had been told there were several TV reports that were so important, they would be shown on the monitors there in the chamber within just a few minutes. After a short delay, the cut from the L.A. sports program was shown, including Cy's request of the pope. This was followed by the pope's entire address. During the pope's address, Chelton walked into the room to the applause of several who were near his seat. He sat down just in time to see and hear the commentator reading from Ginger's report, with her clip being shown in the background.

When the TV went blank, the chairman rose and addressed the body, expressing his concern about what the news might cause in the many unstable populations around the world. He had noticed Chelton come in and take his seat, so when he was finished, he asked Chelton if he would like to comment.

Chelton stood at his place, took the microphone from his desk and began. "Dr. Angus Thomas is my cousin and a very dear friend. When he discovered this strange new star and the menace it promised, he knew the news would be difficult to handle. Wanting to inform the public in the most reassuring, considerate and accurate way possible, he formed a group of people so dedicated. This was a daunting task. Once formed, the group was greatly hindered by the actions of agents of our own government. These agents, while well-meaning and acting strictly to protect our citizens, could not know the reality. Fortunately, the perseverance of Dr. Thomas and his group of concerned citizens prevailed in the end. The struggle to get the information released in a timely and humane manner has been accomplished. I commend my two friends here at the UN who withheld the information they believed to be a hoax and then came forward as soon as they found it to be true. I now return the floor to the chairman. I will gladly answer questions, if the chairman sees fit to permit it."

After several minutes of applause, the chairman conducted an orderly question period that lasted nearly two hours before he brought it to an end. Many people were moving about in the hall during the questioning. Most were trying to contact others in their governments to relay what was happening and get instructions as to what to do.

There was a great deal of activity from reporters and cameramen for the entire session. When it finally closed, every media person in the place was trying to corner Chelton. It was total bedlam.

*   *   *

Instantly the ghost became the center of most conversations, both public and private. The news clip of Ginger's question and Angus' answer was shown so many times most people could recite it verbatim. Angus' terse phrase, Possible? Yes. Probable? Maybe. Certain? Absolutely not, became the defacto answer to any question about the threat of the ghost. The island of Hawaii was overrun with media people as Ginger predicted. Ginger proved to be an excellent press secretary for Angus and Gemini. Orderly, well-run TV and general press meetings became the rule. The media people did not like the term "probability" used by all scientists when there is a range of possible answers to a question. They wanted it in black or white, not shades of gray. Angus often explained absolute answers might have to wait till the star actually arrived. Until then, all answers needed to be intelligent guesses with a range of possibilities. It soon became apparent that the news from Hawaii was not going to change until December when the next half-year measurements were taken. Almost as suddenly as they appeared, many of the media people vanished. Those who were working on in-depth coverage remained to attend the less-frequent and smaller press briefings.

Aftermath

The media spotlight slowly shifted from Angus and Gemini to the reactions of various governments and to many strange predictions made by different religious groups around the world. Three Middle Eastern dictators announced the whole thing was a plot by Western nations to gain control of the world and that there was no ghost star. Several cults, centered on the ghost, sprang up in California, preaching the certain end of the earth in the year 2030. The ghost story was the subject of discussion for practically every talk show on radio and TV, from the intellectual to the completely brainless. There were a few riots in the overcrowded slums of various cities around the world, but for the most part, there was much less disruption than Angus and the group anticipated. Soon nearly everyone held the belief that, somehow, the star would pass with little or no effect on the earth.

Tuesday, September 11, terrorists attacked New York and Washington with hijacked commercial aircraft, killing thousands, and creating another immediate crisis. At first a few thought this was prompted by the announcement about the Ghost star, but it was soon realized it must have been planned for years. With an angry and determined US girding for a war against terrorism, and most of the rest of the world closing ranks to join in the fight, the menacing star was almost forgotten.

By December, when the next measurements were due to be taken, the world was totally absorbed in the war against terrorism. Even so, Angus turned down numerous requests to make guest appearances on popular national TV shows. He fulfilled nearly all requests for appearances that could be done in Hilo. He didn't want to take time away from his work until after the December measurements were taken and the path of the ghost was recalculated. Both Pat Yamaguchi and Dr. Schuman would confirm his work as before. Angus and Dr. Hans Schuman became good friends, sharing information freely. They clearly liked and respected each other.

One strange thing happened just before the end of the year. Noting Ginger and Angus together so often during press briefings, one reporter linked them romantically. It was probably just to spice up his story. At the next briefing where he was to release the results of the new measurements, Angus was asked if it were true. He immediately called Ginger over, put his arm around her and asked, "Who is your very dearest friend, Gin?"

After a slight pause, Ginger looked in Angus eyes and asked, "Do you really want to know?"

"Of course," Angus answered.

With that Ginger turned, walked away from the podium and came back with Lani, stopping to say, "This is my best friend, Lani Thomas." The entire group of reporters roared with laughter and then burst into applause. They enjoyed the little joke. Up to this point, Lani had been able to remain obscure and out of the limelight. With the two striking women standing side by side, one fair, the other dark, the cameramen had a field day. Lani would no longer remain out of the picture.

Angus then introduced Lani saying, "Not only is this lovely lady my wife but my research assistant and an important working member of the team here at Gemini. Within the next few years she will earn her doctorate in Astronomy and, if I am fortunate, will continue working with me."

More cheers and applause came from the group, who had grown to like this friendly man and his easy way with the press. During the briefing, Angus reported the latest data sharpened their predictions about the probable path of the ghost. He reminded them several more years of observations would be necessary before data would be available accurate enough to attempt to predict the eventual results. He cautioned that even then, the little-known relativistic effects could cause a very different series of events.

During the preceding months, Ginger received and studied many offers before selecting the one she thought gave her the best opportunity. December 20 was Ginger's last day as Angus' press secretary. Within the week, she was leaving to take an anchor position as Lois Cari on a major TV news program in New York City. The program's manager thought her actual name, Lois, more appropriate for a news celebrity than her nickname. The fact that she could be near Chelton in New York City certainly helped her make that decision.

A teary Mili said good-bye, along with the entire group from Hilo, as Ginger walked to the plane. She would be missed. At Ginger's recommendation, Mili took over her job as Angus' press secretary. Lani, too, was damp eyed as she hugged Ginger and they said their good-byes. They had become close friends and would miss their lunches. For Ginger, one adventure was coming to a close, another was just about to open.

On the last day of December, Dr. Richard Rumley was found dead in his English prison cell. He had hanged himself.

Early in March 2002, Father Dumas called and asked if Angus and Lani could come to the Vatican for a visit with the pope after the next series of readings were complete. They made arrangements for an early July visit. The observations in June of 2002 merely confirmed the previous measurements and only slightly improved the accuracy of the data.

When their current work was wrapped up, they flew to Rome for their visit with the pope. After their meeting with the pontiff, they visited Rome for a few days as tourists. From Rome they went to Paris, then London and then New York for a visit with Chelton and Ginger, as well as with Jim, Jesse and their new little girl, Hannah.

They spent three days there, visiting and recounting their whirlwind European trip.

*   *   *

During 2002, the populace of the planet concentrated on news of the expanding war against terrorism. News of the menacing star could not hold a candle to the more immediate reality of the war. Birthrates in most of the developed countries were creeping up to pre-announcement levels after dropping drastically right after the news of the ghost was made public. People everywhere were turning to religion to help them deal with the future. The growth of attendance to religious services more than doubled by June of 2002. In America, religious leaders were delighted as churches, synagogues and mosques suddenly overflowed with people eager to renew their faith. While numerous new cults appeared and some flourished for a short time, the long-term growth was almost all in traditional organized religions.

A number of wild, charismatic leaders appeared suddenly. Some used TV to garner members. One was soon in trouble with the law when his lavish and lascivious life using the members' donations was discovered and made known. Another, a woman named Christy Wexter who seemed almost on the brink of insanity at times, finally bowed out when she appeared suddenly at the top of El Capitan in Yosemite, screamed unintelligible epithets at all those around her for nearly an hour and then flung herself off to be obliterated on the rocks at the foot of the monstrous cliff. Most of these "quackers," as they came to be called in derision, soon faded from view, but a few continued to gain members into what came to be called "doom cults."

The next observations in December of 2002 resulted in only slight changes in the reports. Observations and conclusions of numerous other astronomers agreed well with Angus' work. The most likely path had actually moved outside the orbit of Jupiter to nearly intersect the orbit of Neptune. This offered a small bit of encouragement, which the media focused on heavily during the Christmas season following the latest observations.

Christmas was coming in just two weeks when Angus and Lani completed their preliminary work on the latest measurements. They were soon to leave Hawaii for a Christmas visit with his family. Lani was excited at the prospect of experiencing Christmas in the snow and cold for the first time. Her eyes sparkled as they nestled into their seats on the plane after saying good-bye to her family and friends. They would stay overnight Tuesday in Chicago, where, in the late morning, Warren would pick them up and whisk them to Watertown.

*   *   *

It was a brilliantly clear winter morning as they left Chicago in Warren's jet. Lani was disappointed seeing there was no snow on the ground when the plane climbed over Indiana. By the time they reached Canada, glistening patches of white began to appear. From that moment on, Lani bounced from one side of the small jet to the other looking for snow.

"Ya never been in snow before?" Warren asked.

"A few times we drove to the top of Mauna Kea to see the snow, but there never was much when I was there. The wind blowing up the mountain peppered it with brown volcanic dust. It wasn't pretty like the pictures I'd seen of snow on the mainland. I've never seen it falling. I hope we get snowbound while I'm here."

"You don't want to wish for that," Angus said. "I can guarantee you'll see plenty of snow."

"If ya never been in the snow, I bet ya never made snow angels when ya was a kid, did ya?" Warren asked with a smile.

"What's a snow angel? Is it like a snow man?"

"Nothin' like that. Ya jest lay down flat on yer back in the snow and move yer arms as high over yer head as ya can and then down to yer sides. Sorta wave them in the snow. Ya do the same thin' with yer legs from side to side. If ya git up careful like, ya leave an impression in the snow that looks jest like an angel," Warren explained. "I haven't made one since'd I was a little kid."

"We used to make them when I was little," Angus commented. "We always had lots of snow."

"Yeh, yer headed fer snow country fer sure. Watertown's not always open this time of year. Snowstorms, even little snow squalls can make it impossible ta land. I couldn't a brought ya here yesterday. Too snowy. Today's supposed to be clear with scattered snow squalls. Let's hope none a them squalls are there to keep us from landin'," Warren said hopefully.

Before they landed, Lani enjoyed viewing the wide panoramas of white. There were lines that were roads crisscrossing past grey

stands of naked trees, barns and houses. She squealed with excitement as the jet closed on the ground then landed on the cleared
runway in the brilliant sunshine. It was a crisp, bright, clink of an
icicle kind of day in Watertown as they bid Warren good-bye and
greeted Peter, who came to pick them up.

Riding along the snow-covered road toward the Mohawk Inn,
Lani's excitement kept her bouncing around in her seat as she turned
to view every field, woods and structure they passed. "It is so spectacular," she exclaimed over and over as the many scenes of the snow-
covered countryside greeted her eyes. When they drove through the
first snow squall and she saw falling snowflakes for the first time, she
was almost speechless. All she could say was, "Look! Look!" as the
woods and fields nearly disappeared in swirls of white.

When, finally, they reached the inn and were driving up the drive,
Lani shouted, "Stop! Right here." Startled, Peter stopped the car in the
middle of the drive. Bundled in her new, warm winter clothes, Lani
immediately jumped out and flopped down on her back in the freshly
fallen snow beside the drive and began waving her arms and legs.

Angus also jumped out of the car after her. "What on earth are
you doing? Are you crazy?"

Lani lay flat on her back in the snow; bright eyes and a huge
smile faced Angus from the ground. "I think I just made my first
snow angel. How did I do?" she asked, then blew repeatedly to watch
her white breath in the cold air.

Angus reached down for her hand to pull her up. "You're one
wild Hawaiian. Let's get inside. It must be below zero. You're going to
freeze."

At her insistence, they walked the few hundred feet to the inn
entrance, struggling through the deep snow. Peter drove on and was
removing their luggage by the time they reached the parked car.

"Hawaiian squaw heap looney," Peter joked as he helped them
shake the snow off their clothes.

Angus pointed his finger at his head and circled his hand in the
universal sign of insanity. "You can say that again."

From the warmth inside the entrance, Serena and Kat shook their
heads as they watched the scene unfold. As the two men gathered the
luggage, Lani took off running back into the deep snow once more.

Falling in a heap after a few steps, she rolled over on her back and made another angel. Everyone watching shook their heads in wonder.

"Has that wife of yours gone loco?" Kat asked as Angus and Peter brought the luggage inside. "Shouldn't you go get her? She'll freeze. It's eight below out there."

Angus laughed as he watched her through the window. "Let her have her fun. She's never seen snow like this before in her life. She's a little kid again. It won't hurt. If she doesn't come inside within a reasonable time, then I'll go get her."

They watched as Lani walked about, making snow angels every few feet. About the time Angus thought about going out to get her, Lani headed for the door. She stopped outside and shook off most of the snow, laughing with joy all the while. She was breathless with laughter as she walked into the warmth. Her first words, uttered through a huge grin, were, "When can we go skiing?"

Lani struggled out of her heavy coat and rushed over to give Serena and Kat each a big hug and kiss. There was much discussion and several admonitions about the extreme cold as they all greeted each other and removed their outer clothing and boots.

Angus helped her out of her boots. "It will be dark soon. We can think about some skiing tomorrow."

Lani looked shocked. "It's just after four. It can't be getting dark yet."

Kat picked up one of Lani's errant mittens and handed it to her. "You forget. You are in the north country now, just a few days before the shortest day of the year. It starts to get dark a little after four. Before five, it will be pitch black outside."

"I never realized. That will take some getting used to."

Serena, the constant mother, warned Lani, "You'll have to get used to the extreme cold as well. Angus, you had better teach your wife a bit about the cold. She's not accustomed to it like us. She could be frostbitten without realizing it."

*   *   *

The next few days were full of wonder for Lani as she took in the new and drastically different sights and sounds of northern New York in winter. While the Christmas tree in the inn was up and decorated when they arrived, Lani was delighted to learn they were to have a tree trimming party at Kat and Peter's house. Friday, Chelton, Ginger, Jim, Jessica and their daughter, Hannah would fly to Buffalo and rent a van for the trip to St. Regis. Saturday would be Hannah's first birthday, and a party was planned.

Friday evening, the gang arrived safe and sound. As they were unloading the van, Serena noticed there was one more in the party than had been expected. Once inside, amidst confusion of dropping luggage, the hugs and greetings, the squeals of a happy one-year-old and the removal of heavy coats and boots, Serena found herself face to face with Terry Murdoch. Her heart nearly stopped.

"It's been a long time," Terry said as he took Serena's hand. "Jim and Jesse asked me to come along for the holiday. I happily accepted their invitation. I hope you don't mind an extra person."

Caught off guard for an instant, Serena quickly regained her composure, replying, "Of course not. I . . . we're all glad you could be with us. We're all family."

As Serena's eyes left Terry's, she looked directly into the Cheshire cat grin of Kat.

Later, she stopped Kat. "I see the hand of mischief at work here."

Kat knew exactly what she meant. "Believe it or not, I had nothing to do with it. I was almost as surprised as you when Terry appeared. I asked Jim and Jesse. They invited him so he wouldn't be alone during the holidays. I thought that was quite nice of them."

Serena was pleased there had been no plot. "I'll buy that. I'm sure you understand my first impression."

Saturday evening, they had a fabulous tree trimming party at the Chums', spiced by a wide-eyed one-year-old constantly wanting to get into all the pretty things. Jesse finally gave up and decided it was time to whisk Hannah off to bed. After the party broke up, Angus, Lani, Serena and Terry walked back to the inn for the night. As they walked along, Terry told Serena he would like to talk with her when they were in out of the cold. He wanted to explain what happened at the wedding, why he left so suddenly.

Lani and Angus stayed outside on the porch. Lani wanted to view the snow in the moonlight. Serena and Terry entered the inn and sat down on chairs in the foyer.

Terry leaned forward and looked earnestly at Serena. "I'll get right to the point. After Jim and Jess's wedding, I left a warm, friendly group of people because I was scared. Frankly, you scared me because I was so drawn to you, and I rather believe you felt the same. Please hear me out before you say anything, it will only take a few minutes. Anyway, when I got home, I was really torn. I probably started to call you a dozen times or more. As time went on and I didn't call, it got progressively harder for me to even think about it, and, finally, I gave up. I buried myself in my work, which finally took over my entire life except for Jim, Jesse and Hannah. Your son's discovery of the ghost star with the terrifying possibility caused me to rethink about life and about you. I tried but couldn't find a right way or a good time to talk to you until Jim and Jesse asked me to join them here for Christmas. I have no idea where I stand or if you have any interest at all, but I would like to start seeing you . . . trying to find out if there might be something there. You don't need to answer until you think about it. I certainly understand if you say you are not interested. Please think about it."

Serena looked thoughtful, first at Terry, then out the nearby window and then back at him. She finally interrupted the silence. "I believe I can answer you now. I, too, was surprised and a bit frightened at what I felt when we met. I was hurt when you disappeared. Obviously, it was not the time for us. That may have been for the better as a great deal has changed in the eight years since then. I put the incident completely out of my mind until Angus told me about the terrifying possibility of the ghost star. Strange as it seems, you popped into my mind for the first time in years. When you walked in yesterday, it startled me. I was immediately reminded of the dance we had the last time I saw you. We should now be eight years the wiser. I would like very much to see you and do some of the things I haven't done for so long."

They sat there for a long time, looking at each other. Finally, Terry reached out and took Serena's hand. "It's a beginning."

Outside on the porch, Lani leaned her head on Angus' shoulder, looked out across the snow sparkling in the moonlight and said, "You know what we've been suspicious of, don't you? Well, today I took that test we picked up. I'm pregnant!"

Glossary and
Aids to Understanding

This Glossary has translations and definitions of the Mohawk and Hawaiian words used as well as definitions of many scientific terms. The letter in italics placed after the definition is an identifier indicating the type of word:

> *h* = Hawaiian,   *m* = Mohawk,   *e*=explanation or definition

absorption lines—See *Frauenhofer* lines.

ala moana—Seaway. *h*

ala—Way, path. *h*

ali'i—Chief. *h*

ali'i niu—Big chief, number one. *h*

aloha—Hawaiian greeting: good bye, welcome, hello. *h*

Anias—Angus in English. *m*

Atonwa—Thomas in English. *m*

Barnard's Star—Named for the man who discovered it in 1916, it is the second closest star to the earth after the triple star Alpha

Centauri, and at just less than six light years from earth, Barnard's Star has the fastest apparent motion of any star. It is also rapidly approaching earth at nearly ninety miles per second and will pass within four light years of the solar system in about eight thousand years. A red dwarf, about one-sixth the mass of our sun, it emits less than 5/100 of a percent of the energy of the sun and is not visible to the naked eye.

blue shift—Shift of spectral absorption and/or *emission* lines toward the blue end of the spectrum. It indicates an approaching object.

diffraction grating—A device which splits or *diffracts* white light into the colors of the spectrum.

emission lines—Lines in a spectrum that are brighter than the nearby background. They represent light emitted in a narrow band by atoms at high temperature as electrons drop to lower energy states. *See also absorption lines.*

ecliptic—The plane of the earth's orbit around the sun. All planets except Pluto orbit quite close to this plane.

Frauenhofer lines—(absorption lines) Lines in a spectrum that are darker than the nearby background. They represent light absorbed in a narrow frequency band by atoms or molecules of cooler gases. It occurs when light passes through a gas and electrons in the components of the gas are raised to higher energy states, thus removing energy from the light. Named for their discoverer. See also "emission lines."

galaxy—Large grouping of stars. The Milky Way is our galaxy and is a spiral. Other galaxy types are elliptical, barred spiral and irregular.

Gemini—See "The Gemini Project" immediately following the glossary.

globular cluster—Dense grouping of stars bound by gravity in a roughly spherical shape, much smaller than a galaxy. There are a number of these clusters within the gravitational control of our galaxy.

haole—White or non-native person. *h*

kai—Sea (also moana). *h*

kalua pig—Pork baked in an earthen pit or oven. *h*

kane—Man, male. *h*

Kateri—Catherine in English. *m*

Keck Telescope—See the Keck Twin Telescopes section of the description of Mauna Kea following the glossary.

kaukau—Eat, food. *h*

Koloa ho'omoe—sitting duck. *h*

lei—Garland, usually flowers, often given in greeting. *h*

mahalo—Thank you. *h*

Mauna Loa—Long Mountain. *h*

Mauna Kea—White Mountain *h*, a long dormant volcano. The top, at 13,800 feet, is home to a dozen world-class telescopes. See the description following the glossary.

mauna—Mountain. *h*

moana—Sea (also kai). *h*

morph, morphing—To change smoothly from on form to another.

muumuu—(*mu'u-mu'u*) Hawaiian dress. *h*

nene—Hawaiian goose. *h*

nui—Large. *h*

okaara—(*oka-ra'*) Eyes. *m*

otsista—(*otsis-ta'*) Star. *m*

otsitsakowa—(*otsi'-tsa'-ko-wa*) Sunflower. *m*

parallax—A process used to determine the distance to relatively nearby stars. It works for stars up to thirty light years for instruments with 0.1 arc second resolving power or up to three hundred light years for instruments with 0.01 arc second resolving power. It is accomplished by measuring the angle of a line of sight to a star from points at opposite sides of the earth's orbit using two readings taken half a year apart. This provided a base distance for triangulation of about 192 million miles, the diameter of the earth's orbit. Having one side and two angles of a triangle, another side (the distance to the star) can be calculated.

Pele—Hawaiian goddess of the volcano's fire. *h*

plot—In this case, a graphic representation of a spectrum with light intensity on the vertical scale plotted against light frequency on the horizontal.

pupu—Appetizers, hors d'oeuvres. *h*

red shift—Shift of spectral absorption and/or emission lines indicating a receding object.

red dwarf—Common type of star; our sun is a red dwarf.

spectra—Plural of spectrum, see below.

spectral lines—Dark (Frauenhofer) lines in a spectrum caused by absorption or bright (emission) lines caused by emission of specific wave lengths of light by various ions, elements and compounds.

spectrum—Colors produced when white light is split by a prism or diffraction grating—a rainbow is a commonly seen spectrum.

SWAG—Acronym for sophisticated wild assumed guess.

WAG—Acronym for wild assumed guess.

wahine—Woman, female. *h*

The Gemini Twin Telescopes

Man has been wondering about and reaching for the stars for thousands of years. For this continuing quest we demand bigger telescopes, faster computers and more commitment.

Conceived and started more than a decade before the end of the millennium, the Gemini project is an ambitious undertaking of a group of nations including Argentina, Australia, Brazil, Canada, Chile, the U.K. and the U.S. Twin eight-meter telescopes of a radical new design are nearly complete: Gemini North on Mauna Kea on the Big Island of Hawaii and Gemini South at Cerro Pachon in Chile. When completed, they will be available to any astronomer from any of these countries with an acceptable proposal. While not the largest of the current generation of star gazers and with finances limiting the array of optical and infrared cameras and spectrographs, Gemini shines brightest in collecting images and spectra in the infrared section of the electromagnetic spectrum. In the infrared, Gemini is able to look through much of the obscuring dust that blocks visible light and into star-forming regions. It can also look far back through the river of time searching out the earliest images of the farthest galaxies with their visible light shifted into the red as they move away from us at mind-boggling speed. Nearby cool stars including red and brown dwarfs are also accessible to these twin eyes on the heavens. They are viewed with the hope of finding planets in existence or forming in our corner of the Milky Way galaxy.

The milepost in any observatory project when the first image is collected that represents accurately the final product of the project is called "first light." For Gemini North it was achieved early in 1999, several months after its original schedule. Release of the telescope to general use by the astronomers occurred in June of 2000. Just before the end of the millennium, the Multi-object Spectrograph was installed. Once final assembly and positioning of the mirrors and instruments are completed, more than a year of effort by the Gemini staff will be needed to tweak the equipment to as close to perfection as possible. The final stage will be the installation of the Natural Guide Star Adaptive Optics System to compensate for atmospheric disturbances that would otherwise degrade the images. Gemini will use as much cutting edge technology as practical to make it the premier instrument in the world in the near infrared.

During this shakedown effort, many of the engineers picked up their tools and expertise and moved to the southern twin of Gemini North, under construction on a mountaintop in northern Chile. Gemini South, about a year behind Gemini North, will provide the same viewing potential of the southern skies as Gemini North does of the northern. Fiberoptic connections will eventually permit simultaneous viewing of the overlapping fields of view with both Geminis. This provides, in effect, a single, huge telescope for far more accurate research.

Except in older observatories, astronomers no longer look through telescopes directly. Electronic telecommunications from all instruments to viewers using computers in remote and more comfortable locations is now the norm. Using fiberoptic cable connections from the observatory, scientists do not have to brave the cold, thin air of the mountaintop or make the two-hour trip from Hilo to do their work. Accordingly, an operations center was constructed in the University of Hawaii's University Park in Hilo. Personnel moved from temporary quarters into the new facility late in 1999. By late in the year 2000 the Gemini operations center was running smoothly thanks to a dedicated core group of scientists, engineers and administrators.

Mauna Kea Science Reserve

Mauna Kea is a long-dormant volcano and is higher than Everest if measured from the sea-floor from which it rises. Sitting atop the 13,800 foot summit is a dedicated science preserve managed by the University of Hawaii's Institute for Astronomy. By the year 2001, a dozen major research telescopes were in operation there, representing a capital investment of more then $500 million and employment for hundreds of Big Island residents.

Surrounded by thousands of miles of thermally-stable ocean, the summit has no nearby mountain ranges disturbing the upper atmosphere or filling it with light-reflecting dust. There is relatively little city light pollution, and the air above the summit stays clear, dry and calm most of the time. It is an ideal location for earth-bound telescopes.

The giant eyes on the skies include the previously described Gemini North telescope used in the story and eleven others. In addition to Gemini, this outstanding gathering of world-class telescopes consists of the ten-meter W.M. Keck twins, the eight-meter Subaru Japanese national, the NASA infrared (IRTF), the Canada-France-Hawaii, the University of Hawaii 2.2-meter, the 3.8-meter United Kingdom infrared, the Smithsonian-Taiwan sub millimeter array, the James Clerk Maxwell fifteen-meter sub millimeter, and the Cal Tech ten-meter sub millimeter.

Unique in the group, the twin W.M. Keck telescopes are the world's largest optical and infrared telescopes. Each weighs three hundred tons and stands eight stories high yet operates with nanometer precision. Each twin uses a revolutionary ten-meter primary mirror composed of thirty-six hexagonal segments working in concert as a single reflector.

Financed through grants totaling more than $140 million from the W.M. Keck Foundation, the Keck telescopes are operated jointly by the California Institute of Technology, the University of California and NASA, the last to join the partnership in 1969. Fully operational since October, 1996, the powerful instrument has four times the light gathering power of the famous Hale telescope on mount Palomar, and seventeen times that of the Hubble space telescope. The Hubble can see more clearly, but the Kecks can see farther and gather information from far beyond the reach of any other telescope.

Among other research projects, Keck astronomers are discovering new galactic clusters, exploring gravitational-lens systems, detecting primordial deuterium at multi-billion light-year distances, helping solve the riddle of gamma-ray bursters, and undertaking detailed spectral analysis of individual stars—brown dwarfs—previously beyond reach.

Typical of the cooperative nature of contemporary astronomy, teams use the Keck telescopes for detailed exploration of deep space images taken by the Hubble space telescope. While the Hubble can pinpoint distant objects sharply, only the massive power of the Kecks can unlock some of the secrets of these ultra-deep explorations.

Ghost Passage Scenarios

There are several possible scenarios for the Ghost passing in decreasing distances from the sun and earth:

Four light years from the sun: This is the current distance to the nearest star and passage at this distance would have almost no effect on the entire solar system.

Two light years from the sun: At this distance, gravity would probably disrupt the objects in the Oort cloud beyond the orbit of Pluto, sending many new comets falling toward the sun and through the orbits of the planets. The chances of a collision with the earth would be greatly increased. The closer it comes to the sun, the more objects could be sent through the solar system with the possibility of one striking the earth with cataclysmic results. The period of time with the increased possibility of an impact would be many years, or even millennia. We just witnessed comet Shoemaker-Levy striking Jupiter with cataclysmic results. The possibility of just such an impact with earth would be greatly increased. The likelihood this would happen would increase the closer the object passed to the sun.

Within the orbits of the planets: There are three scenarios, all bad, that could describe the direct effects on the planets of a near pass. With all planets, the star could pass inside their orbit, but on the opposite side of the sun in which case not one of the following scenarios would happen. Using the earth for a typical example, the most distant effect would be orbital disruption. This could result in drastic climate changes if the disruption were large enough. The earth could be kicked into an orbit farther out, resulting in a massive ice age, or farther in, resulting in drastic global warming, or much more elliptical where it would switch between too hot and too cold each year. It would depend on the shape of the orbit, just how hot and then cold it would become.

Should it come even closer, its gravity would distort the earth, first creating giant ocean tides and finally cracking the crust apart with the resultant outflows of magma as the mantle flowed through the broken sea floor and continental crust. The oceans would boil and violent storms would scour the broken surface. No creature could survive.

Its closest approach could be nearer than the sun. This would suddenly increase the earth's heat energy. The closer it passed, the greater the heat. Since it would take at most just eighteen minutes for the star to pass by closer than the sun, it would have to pass quite close to create serious damage. The tidal and/or orbital changes would probably destroy all life before the heat could do any damage.

The possible errors in all scenarios because of the high speed and possible relativistic effects: It will only take about 10 hours for the Ghost to pass completely through the solar system from and to as far from the sun as Pluto's orbit. Since any tidal effect will be virtually negligible at more than one astronomical unit from any planet, serious damage from tidal forces are very unlikely. (An astronomical unit is the earth to sun distance of 93,000,000 miles.) Orbital change is another matter and the most likely possibility for cataclysmic change. Even here, the transient effect of the rapidly moving star may need a fairly close approach to any planet to cause a significant change in its orbit. Also, since the inertial energy of the star is about 81% of its rest mass, its gravitational mass is only 19% which considerably lowers the aforementioned effects. It would, therefore, have to come within about 18 million miles of any major part of the solar system to do any damage. At that distance, the radiant heat becomes a problem for only about four minutes at most. Only an extremely close approach to any planet poses a real danger. Under the circumstances, that will not be known until its visual distance becomes less than ten light years. At that point in time, it will already be entering the Oort cloud and its closest approach will be but a single year away.

To order additional copies of

BLUE
SHIFT

Have your credit card ready and call

Toll free: (877) 421-READ (7323)

or send $24.95** each plus $5.95 S&H* to

WinePress Publishing
PO Box 428
Enumclaw, WA 98022

www.winepresspub.com

**WA residents, add 8.4% sales tax

*add $1.00 S&H for each additional book ordered